Nick moved until his body brushed Cynda's from shoulder to thigh as his expression grew more serious.

"You need to let people care about you, firebird."

Cynda's insides flipped at the sound of that nickname. "Don't call me that."

His eyes were so dark and bright, and his lips so near hers. Scents of male and stormy seas and arousal washed over her.

Nick stared straight into the center of her being and whispered, "Let *me* care about you."

"No," Cynda said, loud, harsh, panicked that he said those words out loud. Even as she spoke, she was melting into him. When his lips touched hers, Cynda thought the universe might catch fire. A hint of wintergreen and liquid fire tingled across her tongue as their mouths joined completely.

Cynda shivered and burned everywhere. Nick tasted perfect. He felt beyond perfect. So, so good.

And that was bad.

Also by Anna Windsor

Bound by Shadow

BOUND
BY FLAME

A NOVEL OF THE DARK CRESCENT SISTERHOOD

ANNA WINDSOR

BALLANTINE BOOKS · NEW YORK

A Ballantine Books Mass Market Original

Copyright © 2008 by Anna Windsor

Published in the United States by Ballantine Books, an imprint of The Random House Publishing Group, a division of Random House, Inc., New York.

BALLANTINE and colophon are registered trademarks of Random House, Inc.

ISBN 978-0-345-49854-0

Printed in the United States of America

www.ballantinebooks.com

OPM 9 8 7 6 5 4 3 2 1

For my family,
because they have
to go insane with me every time

(prologue)

Moonlight flickered across the dark bog-waters of Connemara as Cynda Flynn bounced against her father's shoulder. Warm breezes brushed her freckled cheeks, and the Irish night smelled of grass and mud and flowers as *a Dhaid* carried her like she was still a baby.

Cynda frowned and shifted in her father's arms. She was almost six years old. She could have walked, but *a Dhaid* kept her pinned tight, with a damp blanket pulled around her.

"Are you still angry about the roof and the trees?" she whispered as she squeezed his neck. "I wouldn't have done it if—"

"Hush," *a Dhaid* told her, fast and sharp, his voice flat in the summer air. Then he muttered, "*Síofra*."

Shee-fra. Cynda repeated the syllables slowly to herself. A funny word, like the old people used. She had heard that word more than once, and never in a good way. It meant *changeling*, a fae baby swapped for a human baby. Children who got called shee-fra weren't very nice.

Cynda squirmed inside the wet blanket.

She knew her father was unhappy with her because she couldn't stop playing with sparks and smoke and flames. They had walked so far, so long—what was he planning to do?

He would never hurt her. Not *a Dhaid*. But they had no relatives who lived so far from the village. She had only come this distance a few times, with her mother, taking clothes to the nuns who lived in the big place.

Why wouldn't *a Dhaid* tell her where they were going?

When moonlight reflected off his round face, Cynda saw that his eyes looked wide and half-wild. Wet trails wound down his cheeks, and now and then she caught a whiff of old smoke from his clothes. Smoke from the roof she had burned. Smoke from the trees she had destroyed. *A Dhaid*'s heart beat so hard she could feel it as she lay against him, holding tighter and tighter as he picked up his pace.

Cynda sensed more than saw the mountains looming in the distance.

They *had* to be near the big nun place.

Kylemore Abbey.

She stiffened.

Was her father planning to leave her with the nuns to teach her a lesson? Surely not. That school was for very wealthy girls who had presidents and kings and ambassadors for fathers. Not Cynda. *A Dhaid* tended sheep, and her mother made shirts. Her brothers and sisters helped at one task or the other, and nobody from her village went to fancy schools like the one at Kylemore Abbey.

But her father did take her to the old abbey, straight to an arched door Cynda knew from those previous trips with her mother. The door where service people came and went. Her father's big fist hammered on that door until lights blazed and the door came open to reveal two nuns.

Cynda squinted in the sudden brightness. The nuns in the arched doorway wore black-and-white nundresses, and Cynda wondered if the women slept in those uncomfortable-looking robes and hats.

In a mix of English and Irish, her father introduced himself and said, "Our priest told me to ask for Sister Alastrine."

The nuns gasped. They glanced from *a Dhaid* to Cynda.

"We haven't heard that name in many years," the smaller, meaner-looking nun said, speaking too clearly, as if Cynda and her father might be slow of thought. "Are you certain your priest gave you that name?"

Cynda fidgeted inside her wet blanket and thought about making fire to light the women's behinds. She could see sparks in the air. She could always see sparks, and she loved to touch them, call to them, and turn them into bright, pretty flames.

Maybe fire would wipe away the short nun's fierce frown. She didn't like the short nun, and she didn't like frowns.

"I must see Sister Alastrine." Her father's words sounded tight, like he might be afraid. That made Cynda afraid and she grabbed some of the sparks, just a few to hold, to make herself feel better.

The blanket around her made a sizzling, hissing sound, and a tiny jet of smoke drifted from Cynda, straight into the two nunfaces in the doorway.

Without another comment, the taller nun nodded and held open the door. Then she crossed herself and hurried away. Cynda figured she had gone to get Sister Alastrine, whoever that was.

Will Sister Alastrine cane me? Or wear out my palms with a switch? A Dhaid *said nuns once did that to him.*

Cynda picked at her blanket as her father took her through the arched door into Kylemore Abbey. Smells changed from fresh-outside to cleanser, bleach, and something like pine. Polish, maybe. For floors or wood. The air inside felt cooler and more still. All the clean, shiny things made Cynda nervous. Too nice. Too much. Not like home at all. She would have asked *a Dhaid* why he had brought her here, why he didn't just punish her himself, but he was praying. So was the nun who had stayed behind in the room with them.

Instead of interrupting her father's conversation with God, Cynda amused herself by making flames dance over the short nun's head.

The nun never looked up, and she never stopped praying. For a long, long time. Her delicate face reminded Cynda of one of those expensive glass dolls she saw once while traveling with her mother—beautiful, but stiff and pale and fragile, white as snow with roses blooming on the cheeks. When the nun's eyes flicked open to study Cynda, Cynda noted they were brown like her mother's eyes, only these brown eyes seemed cold like the rest of the nun. Cynda couldn't see the woman's hair, but she was sure it would be so brown and stiff it didn't look real, like that doll's hair.

Nuns and dolls, dolls and nuns.

Cynda yawned.

This was boring. And stupid.

She needed to change things before she fell asleep and woke up at home, with *a Dhaid* all the more angry because she hadn't paid attention to her punishment.

Before Cynda could decide what to set ablaze so the glass-doll nun would stop muttering to herself, the tall nun returned, leading a woman in green robes, with long red hair streaked silver-white. She was so little, not much taller than some of the girls Cynda played with, but her eyes . . .

The sight of those blazing green orbs made Cynda turn loose her fire. Embers rained into the room as the woman in the green robes let go of the nun who escorted her. Both nuns watched the bits of fire fall, but said nothing. The taller one seemed at peace, but the mean nun glared, like she wished she could slap the little woman in the green robes, just for being in the abbey.

The little woman ignored both nuns and walked

straight toward Cynda, seeming stronger and younger and taller all at once.

Those are evil eyes, Cynda told herself. *Maybe she's blind. Maybe she can't see me.*

Yet she already knew the woman could see everything, right down to the bruise on Cynda's left third toenail.

Cynda shivered inside the blanket. She tried to press back against her father, but he thrust her out, out, over the marble floor, almost throwing her, blanket and all, into the old woman's arms.

Panic welled in Cynda's belly.

The woman reached for her, but before those knobby fingers so much as touched the blanket's worn fringe, Cynda called to her fire. She didn't want to hurt the woman. She just wanted her to stop, to go away and leave Cynda safe with her *a Dhaid*. He'd finish his business. They'd go home. Cynda knew she could do better and try not to burn anything ever again. Ever, never. No. She wouldn't. Except this one more time.

The woman's green robes burst into flames.

Cynda waited for the screaming, the cursing, the horror that always came when she used her fire—but the woman laughed instead.

She waved a gnarled hand in the air, and the flames on her robes snuffed to trails of smoke, barely leaving a singe mark.

Cynda gaped.

The nuns crossed themselves. The glass-doll nun murmured, "Devil."

The woman's green eyes flared, and she treated both nuns to a ferocious glare.

"She is no devil, Sister Julia," she said in a voice so powerful the words bounced off the walls and floor and Cynda's ears all at once. "That child is a warrior of the old blood, and she'll be bearin' the mark of the Dark Goddess."

The woman extended her thin arm as Sister Julia and the other nun cowered. She let her robe sleeve slide down to reveal a tattoo that seemed to pulse and glow in the low lighting. Cynda could make out drawings of a dark broom, mortar, and pestle etched in a triangle around a crescent moon.

"She is a Sibyl, as am I. If you can't understand that, you can't remain in this abbey. Our arrangement is older than your ancestors—almost as old as time itself." The woman turned back to Cynda, only now she was smiling, and fire blazed like a halo around her red and silver hair. "If you remain here, Sister Julia, you'll be givin' us *both* our due respect."

Perfect, smooth, controlled fire extended slowly down the old woman's shoulders and arms, until yellowish orange energy played off her fingertips, too.

Cynda marveled at the sight. She wanted to reach for the fire, but she didn't dare. She didn't twitch or breathe, or anything else. This time, when the woman moved to take her from her father's arms, Cynda made no attempt to fight her, even though her heart and mind screamed that she would never again see her father or mother or her sisters and brothers.

She knew better than to battle the woman now. She knew what the woman was capable of, if she could make such perfect fire, whenever and however she wanted.

I burn down houses and trees. This woman could burn down the world.

"I'm Mother Keara, child." The woman grasped Cynda firmly, pulled her from her father, threw down the wet blanket, and set Cynda's bare feet on the cool stone floor. "Daughter of Mara and granddaughter of Alastrine." The whole time she spoke, fire danced around Mother Keara, but all Cynda felt was pleasant, loving heat.

When Cynda gazed up at her, Mother Keara let the

flames ringing her head grow even taller and more frightening to everyone but Cynda. "I'll be takin' you for my own, to join the sisters of Motherhouse Ireland, and teach you the ways of fire and war. Would you like that?"

Cynda shook as she gazed at Mother Keara's fire, but her pride and pain wouldn't let her turn around and run to her father. The terrified nuns hovered on the edges of her awareness, and she pushed them from her mind, too.

Cowards.

What did they matter?

Cynda's lips trembled.

What did her *a Dhaid* matter, or her mother, or her brothers and sisters, if they would give her away so easily? Because that's what they were doing, she had no question. Abandoning her—only, not to Sister Julia and the nun school.

To Mother Keara, who knew how to make fire better than Cynda.

"Where is Motherhouse Ireland?" Cynda asked without letting her voice tremble.

Mother Keara looked pleased, as very few people had ever been pleased with Cynda. "Through a secret passage and down a tunnel, in a valley not far from here. There, you'll learn to stand in the fire and speak when no one wants to hear your words. You'll learn to let the flames burn as you speak when cowards would choose silence." At that, Mother Keara glared at Sister Julia, the tall nun, and Cynda's father. When she looked back to Cynda, her expression immediately softened. She held out her lumpy, aged hand. "You'll learn to speak until no smoke obscures the truth, that I promise. If you come with me, I'll show you where your *real* sisters live."

Cynda bit her lip, but still didn't look at her father or at the nuns. They could all go away. They could fly straight to whatever hell held the devils they talked about, or the changelings, or everything else she had been called since the day she first touched sparks and made fire.

Smoke flowed over her skin, but she managed not to burn anything. After a few deep breaths, she took the old woman's hand.

"Sibyl," Mother Keara whispered as she squeezed Cynda's fingers, those green eyes blazing with what looked like joy. "There are fire Sibyls, earth Sibyls, and air Sibyls. Once, long ago, there were even water Sibyls, before a great tragedy took them all. S-i-b-y-l. Say the word, child."

"Sibyl," Cynda shouted, trying to be big, hoping her words would bounce off the walls and floors and everybody's ears, too.

Her skin tingled.

Heat pulsed from Mother Keara into Cynda's palm, up her arm, and straight down to her aching heart, soothing her as only fire could.

Drawing strength from the fire inside, she said to Mother Keara, "Show me where the Sibyls live."

The old woman smiled again.

Walls of flame surrounded them now, burning bright and strong, yet setting nothing on fire but the air, and, seemingly, everything Cynda had ever known.

Somehow she managed not to glance back at her father as the old woman led her into the beautiful fire, then through it, and away down a long, long hallway.

(1)

Cynda knelt behind a dumpster in an alley near Sixty-fifth and Lexington. Her teeth chattered. Smoke rose from her shoulders as she shivered and bumped her sheathed Celtic broadsword against the hulking cop crouched beside her.

Nick didn't react.

Sleet clattered against dumpsters and fire escapes, pelting the top of Cynda's tightly zipped leather face mask. Her toes ached like she had a good case of frostbite, never mind her leather boots, gloves, and bodysuit.

March in New York City *so* sucked.

First chance she got, she would kill Riana and Merilee for having "previous commitments," best friends and sister-Sibyls or not. How could they strand her in a friggin' sleet storm?

The smoke around her face got thicker.

Nick, who in his heart-stopping human hunk form, was a cop, had dragged her into the frigid night to meet with his prize informant. Cynda adjusted the strap of her special glasses and peered through the overlarge lenses. Stupid things reminded her of motorcycle racing goggles, in fetching shades of black rubber and yellow polycarbonate. Highly attractive.

Not.

Probably had icicles hanging from both sides to add to the effect.

But the treated lenses detected sulfur dioxide left behind by demons sent to do the bidding of their Legion masters. So the lenses had become standard issue for Sibyls on patrol all over the world.

Of course, most Sibyls didn't have far-too-sexy cops to babysit. Teaming up with law enforcement was a pain in the ass, even when law enforcement meant the OCU— New York City's low-profile Occult Crimes Unit.

Cynda pulled at her ugly demon-hunting goggles again and wished she could see the sulfur traces without them, the way Nick could.

"Be still and quit smoking," he rumbled. "If he sees you, he'll bolt."

A thousand retorts flashed across Cynda's mind, but she clamped her mouth shut. More heat rushed through her body. It took every bit of willpower she possessed not to set Nick on fire, and her leather bodysuit in the bargain. She'd freeze to death if she burned holes in her clothes—and he'd laugh his ass off, too. At least the sleet was slowing some, and ah, there, yes. Finally stopping.

"Maybe your informant was shining you on," she muttered.

"He's reliable. If Max says he knows something about Legion activity, then he does."

Cynda cut Nick a sideways look, then had to turn her whole head to see him through the goggles.

"The Legion's been quiet for too long." Nick's expression stayed distant, but tension bunched at his eyes. "They haven't left New York like everyone thinks. That's bullshit. I've been on the inside, Cynda. I *know*. We have to find out what the cult's planning before it's too late."

She wanted to argue with Nick just to keep warm, but part of her knew he was right. In the four months she had worked with him, they had busted a slew of Legion houses before cult activity fell off the radar.

Nick knew his stuff.

He had good instincts, almost as good as her own,

and the stirrings in her gut agreed with him. The Legion *wasn't* gone. No way. The zealous freaks were cooking up something extra nasty to gain the upper hand with their ancient enemies, the Sibyls—but what would it be?

Cynda had no idea.

Flames broke out along her gloved fingertips.

She *hated* not knowing. She usually had inklings, at least a hunch about actions to take to protect the Sibyl family she loved more than anything on Earth, but this time, nothing.

Nick had infiltrated the Legion, lived with the murdering maniacs for almost five years, and paid a major price for that, and he had no guesses, either.

Cynda glanced at him again, gradually pulling her fire energy back inside her chilled body. Even in the middle of an ice storm, she could smell his unusual scent of ocean and musk. His chiseled face looked almost exotic in the low light, with his black hair pulled into a ponytail at the nape of his neck. A gold chain, the talisman that controlled his *other,* hung inside the open collar of his black shirt.

The way the chain lay against his skin tempted her to kiss it—or grab it and twist. Hard.

Making Nick's eyes bug out might give her a little satisfaction.

Kissing him—now, that would be satisfaction, too, but if she ever let herself kiss him once, she'd want to do it again. Maybe a lot.

Smoke poured out of her boots.

Not going there. Gotta stop.

Even if Nick did feel some attraction to her—which he had never indicated—Cynda didn't do attachments other than her bond with her Sibyl sisters. She'd learned when she was just a little girl—nobody else was reliable, or worth that risk.

But did Nick's jeans *ever* fit him like a faded blue glove. No jackets, hats, mittens, or anything to guard against the cold. *It's a discipline,* he had told Cynda more than once. *Mind over matter. A mental thing.*

Yeah.

Most mental things involved straitjackets and locked hospital units, but insane or not, the man was one tasty package. He kept his powerful body in a ready stance, with one big hand on the ground like a football player ready to charge forward. The most striking feature, though, was the way her goggles made his muscular silhouette glow dark red about the edges.

Because he's not completely human.

That little reminder sobered Cynda, but didn't curb her tongue. "Couldn't you at least get an informant who shows up on time?"

"Max does his best." Nick didn't twitch or shift. Totally still. Totally calm. "He's Irish like you, so he follows his own rules."

She let out a cloud of smoke and popped his hip with the flat tip of her broadsword. "What's that supposed to mean?"

Nick didn't answer. His dark eyes stayed focused on the alley's icy darkness with characteristic intensity and single-minded concentration.

"Why would anybody tell you anything?" she mumbled, more to herself than to the big jerk beside her.

"Most people find me charming. Don't know what's the matter with you."

Cynda flicked her fingers and showered his hair with sparks.

Nick rubbed his hand over the dark strands and snuffed the flames without so much as looking at her. He could deflect her elemental powers better than anyone she had ever known, save for Mother Keara.

"You—" she started, but Nick shook his head and cut her off before she could say anything else.

His body tightened.

Cynda swiveled back toward the alley, smoking from more places than she could count.

A tall, thin man made his way slowly through the darkness, fingers trailing along one grimy, icy brick wall. Obviously, he couldn't see in the low light as well as Cynda or Nick, or at least he wanted them to think he couldn't.

Cynda squinted at the man. Blond. About six feet tall, underfed, pock-faced—just the way Nick had described him, except his face seemed badly bruised.

Max Moses, the informant.

Waves of heat rose from his body. Traces of red hung about his tattered overcoat, and his gait hitched and sputtered as he blundered down the alley. Cynda squinted at the red flecks clustered around Max's shoulders and neck. Not enough sulfur traces to equal a demon, no, but weird. And wrong.

"Something's off about him." Cynda's words came out soft against the curtain of smoke shrouding her head.

Nick hushed her with a sharp gesture. "Max drinks. He's a sensitive. Has to block things out."

Then Nick stood and strode away from Cynda's hiding place.

She swore to herself and barely held back a jet of fire. Her hand tightened on the hilt of her sword. Those red streaks almost had a pattern. If they'd been on Max's skin instead of his clothes, they might have been bruises, as if someone—or something—had grabbed Max from behind.

And tried to choke him.

Nick reached Max at the same moment Cynda caught

a darker flash of red to her left, farther away, near the mouth of the alley. Her heart rate kicked up and she barely kept back her fire. She blinked, tried to fix on the signal, but couldn't.

What was it?

A spell?

But spells were intricate procedures, requiring tools and setup and patterns, all kinds of props. "Magic" was more elemental science than anything, and elements had to be handled carefully, bound and controlled, or "locked" to channel their power—like the fire, air, water, and earth power locked along the double-edged blade of Cynda's sheathed sword.

She didn't know any paranormal group that could cast random spells in a dark alley.

And now, she didn't see a thing.

Back to dark.

But it still didn't feel right.

She reached out with her pyrosentience—her fire sense—but got nothing back. Her eyes darted to the numerous dumpsters and fire escapes. All dark and quiet and still. All empty.

Screw this.

Cynda rose to her feet and drew her sword, making no sound. Whatever was out there, it could eat steel and explain itself later.

Max remained deep in conversation with Nick, not paying attention, but the red demon residue on his clothing blared at Cynda like a bullhorn.

Didn't Nick feel something off in this situation?

She sensed it, stronger and stronger. Wrongness. Like darkness creeping through the alley, spreading into the city.

The taste in her mouth turned acrid, the way it always did when she was nervous—and she hated being nervous almost as much as she hated being cold. Her eyes strained inside the goggles, searching up, down, left, right.

Where was that streak of red residue?

There.

No wait, there!

On the fire escape nearest Nick, the one just above his left shoulder. A flicker of red. Just a hint, and then it was gone.

Cynda ground her teeth. Her leathers gave at the ankles, and she knew she had burned holes in her fighting suit. Her Sibyl instincts told her this was a creature, some type of being her Sibyl triad hadn't encountered before.

As if in response to her thoughts, malice radiated across the alley. It struck Cynda, pummeled against her like the cold. Now her instincts *shouted* wrongness, and not just in the alley.

Everywhere.

Her pyrosentience swept in all directions. Touching— yet not touching. What the hell was out there?

Her muscles tightened. Her belly burned. Flames surged along her arms, gathered at her hands, but she couldn't throw fire at the thing, whatever it was. It might deflect the heat and fry Nick and Max, if it had the ability to fight elements.

A centering breath . . .

The weight of her sword . . .

Yes.

"Nick!" she shouted. "Heads up!"

His attention snapped to her at the same time she gave a battle cry and launched herself from behind the dumpster. Jerking warmth from the air, building sparks, breathing flames, Cynda ignited her sword. The fierce blaze flared orange, lighting up the end of the alley.

Heart pounding, body seething with heat, she leaped past Nick and his informant. With her free hand, she grabbed the bottom rung of the fire escape. The metal was ice-cold and rough through her glove as she hoisted herself to hang off the edge.

Whatever was there, she'd take it down at the ankles.

She sucked in a breath of cold air as she swept her blazing sword low across the first platform.

Cynda's blade connected with something solid.

Something with powerful protections.

Her swing stopped mid-arc, thrumming, vibrating. Like banging the blade into a stack of cement bricks. Pain ricocheted up her hand, wrist, and arm. Her teeth slammed together.

The force of the blow ripped her sword from her hand. It clattered against metal as it fell to the fire escape platform, just out of her reach.

Shit!

Red flickered in the air above her head. Just as Cynda lost her grip on the platform, she saw a distinct man-shape wink into reality, and she heard its angry, danger-ous howl.

She let out a shriek as she fell backward, fast and hard. Bolts of agony shot through her back and limbs as she slammed ass-first into the ice-crusted pavement. Breath left her in a harsh rush.

Nick shouted as the informant bolted down the alley-way, his footsteps pounding the asphalt as he ran. "Stay down," Nick ordered Cynda as he drew his weapon.

"Bullshit." Heat from her face clouded her goggle-vision as she caught her breath and scrambled to her feet, fire blazing along her shoulders.

Where the hell was the thing she'd just hit?

Let's see if it can eat fire.

She paused as her gaze followed the direction Nick had his weapon pointed.

Aimed at . . . nothing?

Wait. He was training his gun on—

On a bucket of paint?

Thick, white fluid slopped over the side of the bucket that hovered in midair, right in front of Nick.

Cynda blinked. Smoke rose off her cheeks and chin.

The bucket *floated* in the alley. Red flecks covered the handle and bottom in a pattern just like hands. Nick kept his Glock trained on the paint, clearly intending to pump elementally locked bullets into whatever was holding the can.

The paint can didn't stick around to be shot.

It flew upward, above Cynda's head, to the fire escape platform.

She was letting her power build up inside her, trying to get ready for whatever came next, but this was way past wrong.

"Shoot it," she shouted.

"No." Nick held fast. "We don't know what it is."

"Shoot it anyway!" she screeched over the pounding of her heart. Gouts of flame roared from her fingertips. "We'll identify it later!"

Nick snarled something unintelligible, and Cynda hated, hated, hated his years of cop training in the judicious use of deadly force. If he had been a Sibyl, that paint can would have been *so* full of holes already.

When she caught sight of Nick's face, his devastated expression struck her like a blow to her belly.

Nick *never* looked like that.

His hesitation was more than habit. Something was tearing at him, way down deep, and the sight of his pain rattled Cynda completely.

Nick didn't want to shoot the creature.

The paint can jerked sideways. It soared upward, then turned itself upside down. White paint rained from the fire escape.

Cynda lunged sideways to avoid the bath, but paint splattered her leathers, and she barely kept to her feet. Her mind was still spinning from the look on Nick's face. Holes opened in her bodysuit as fire spit forward, lashing out at nothing and everything.

Above her, the spilled paint coalesced on a man-shape frozen in defensive posture—and the man had wings. Two sets of them.

Big wings.

Cynda's mask burned straight off her face. Before she could finish processing what she was seeing, the empty can clattered to the fire escape, as if an invisible creature had dropped it from above the being now coated in paint.

We're fighting invisible shit now?

A distinct sound, like wings pumping, came from above paint-thing. Cold swirled down, blasting her face. Whatever had dumped the paint was leaving. She knew it in her gut.

Nick spoke to the winged paint-thing in firm cop-tones. "Come down slowly. My bullets are elementally locked, and I *will* shoot."

The thing on the fire escape laughed.

A horrible, wicked, grating sound.

Cynda's skin crawled. She drew a rush of fire energy to her, and flames flared in her palms.

"Come down." Nick's words carried a grim finality. "Last warning."

Paint-thing turned its blank face toward Cynda, and it grinned like a horror-movie skeleton.

"Fire bitch." It raised one hand and pointed at her. Like a prayer, it murmured, *"Maroídh muidh thú."*

Her heart jerked. *We will kill,* it had said—in Irish.

She needed her sword and she needed it *now*. But the blade lay on the fire escape platform at the thing's feet.

At the corner of her vision, she saw a new flash of red, this time right beside Nick.

"Nick! Next to you! Shoot!" She leaped toward him, pointing at the flash. "Shoot now!"

Nick squeezed the trigger and she heard something hit the ground not five feet from them.

The flare of red Nick had just shot at became visible, crouched in front of her, obviously injured. Man-shaped. Winged. Like paint-thing.

It stared at her. Not a random glance. A deep, soul-snatching study, as if it had been sent to this alley for Cynda and Cynda alone.

Cynda called a huge ball of fire to defend herself, but the creature blazed a brilliant red, burst into smoke and flames, and rained dirt in the spot where it had been. Wind danced around the smoldering pile, stirring bits of ash into the air. It stank like sulfur, only a hundred times worse.

Up on the fire escape, metal rattled as paint-thing clambered up the stairs instead of descending. When the creature had enough room to spread its wings, it jumped and sailed above their heads like a big malicious crow.

Cynda fired flames at it once, twice. Missed!

That massive sense of wrongness focused in her chest, squeezing, squeezing, until she wanted to shriek from dread. Her fire sputtered. She raised her arms to knock paint-thing out of the air, but her energy was spread in too many directions. All she did was singe the being's feet.

More flashes of red entered the alley on either side.

"Ambush!" Desperation surged in Cynda's blood, driving back every bit of pain she'd been feeling. She threw fire, but she didn't know if she was hitting anything.

Nick turned his sharp eyes on the flashes and started shooting, dropping red streaks wherever he spotted them.

They swarmed forward, blazing in the dark, frigid night.

Cynda's ears rang and ached as the creatures erupted into spews of dark earth and wind and flames with each of Nick's well-aimed bullets. She coughed from the stench.

Fear heightened to a whole new level, sending hot prickles over her skin as more and more flashes of red came toward them.

She released a rush of fire energy in all directions, powerful communication, a cry for help swirling toward short-distance communication aids. Wind chimes in Sibyl dwellings nearby, maybe in Riana's brownstone or the townhouse on the Upper East Side above the Reservoir, where Cynda lived.

Then Cynda gathered her heat. Filled herself with it until her blood, her skin, her mind roared with the force of it. Flames rolled up and down her arms as she raised her hands toward the red streaks, held it, held it—and let it fly.

Fire blasted toward a group of the streaks coming for her. Hit them.

And did nothing.

Nothing!

Shit, shit, shit!

Paint-thing flew over their heads again, and Nick took it down with his next shot. Cynda saw the white-coated creature crash to the ground and explode into earth, wind, and flames.

More flashes of red, and more.

More! Five, maybe six?

She and Nick were friggin' dead.

Her fire blazed everywhere, hot and wild and absolutely useless. Her clothes burned. Her skin burned.

Nick rammed his empty Glock into its holster and started throwing punches, connecting here and there with the invisible enemies. He lunged forward, then dropped to his knees and choked something Cynda couldn't see.

If my fire won't work and I can't reach my sword—fuck.

Strong fingers closed around her neck as something grabbed her from behind. Squeezed so hard she gasped for air.

She drew her arms upward and swung them back. Her elbows buried themselves in what felt like flesh—yet not—as she socked whatever it was in the gut with all her strength.

The fingers went lax as the thing fell, but it yanked her back with it. Cynda cried out, grabbing for air as she fell. She hit the ground just as something whistled over her head.

Long and wooden, with a sharp point.

The tip's brutal, unnatural gleam as it flew overhead told Cynda it was elementally locked. Way past lethal for her, and for Nick.

"Spear!" she managed to yell as she separated herself from the wheezing thing behind her.

Nick rolled off the being he'd been pounding and he crouched, looking left and right.

Another spear sang through the alley. Cynda blasted it with a jet of fire and slammed it against the alley wall. The damned elemental locking kept it from burning. She ran for it, grabbed it from the asphalt, spun and rammed it toward the place where Nick had been straddling and beating on the invisible thing.

Pay dirt.

Flesh gave. Bone snapped.

The thing on the ground flashed into view before it caught fire and turned to dirt and ash and air currents.

She yanked the spear free and spun toward another set of red flashes. A spear screeched toward her, just a few feet away.

She tried to swing her stick toward it, but Nick jumped between her and the missile.

The spear caught him in the chest, just below his right arm.

He sailed backward like something was shoving him across the alley, propelled by the force of the blow. His head struck a dumpster and his body slumped to the ground. He lay still.

"No!" Smoke rippled from Cynda's bare elbows and knees, where she'd burned away her leathers. She struck out with the tip again and again, behind her, above her, turning red flashes into heaps of flaming earth. She kicked what she couldn't stab, over and over, trying to work her way toward Nick.

Sweat coated her skin. Her chest hurt from breathing so hard. Her arms and legs ached from every movement.

More red flashes came toward her. Too many!

Spear slashes burned into her calf, her arm. Something grazed her side. Yanked her hair. Her muscles sizzled and throbbed from fighting, but the invisible demons kept coming.

A foot closer to Nick. Another few feet. How long had Nick been out? Was he bleeding too much? She was bleeding. Fire crackled from every inch of her body now.

Almost there.

She'd help Nick. Push the spear out of him, use her fire to seal the wound. If she could wake him, he could change to his *other* and heal himself. She had to get there. Had to!

Something brushed past her. She snarled, whirled to stab it, in time to see Nick's gold chain lift off his neck—then snap. Torn from his throat.

Cynda grabbed for the floating chain.

Nick's talisman. Without it—

Whatever had hold of the chain didn't try to dodge her. It let her snatch the thick strand of gold.

Then the being tackled her.

As the thing took her down, she caught the scent of something like a spicy breeze blowing through a Caribbean town. A bizarre flash of thought in a split second.

Cynda hit the alley pavement again. Crushed into it by the thing that had taken the chain. Her head and shoulder slammed against asphalt. Cold agony shot through her joints, her muscles. Her thoughts got fuzzy, but fire blazed along her back.

Whatever creature had knocked her down was already gone and out of reach of her flames.

She gasped for breath.

Through the smoke in the air and the haze in her mind, she saw Nick rising from the ground.

Only he wasn't Nick anymore.

He was the *other*.

A huge golden god of a Curson demon that would kill and grind and eat and stomp with absolutely no regard to who was friend and who was foe.

Without his chain talisman around his neck—

Red streaks scattered in every direction, running from Nick.

No . . . not Nick.

They were getting away from the *other*.

Breathe. Cynda gripped her sides. Blood coated both of her hands.

Nick-*other* started pummeling red streak after red streak before stopping and roaring so loud it echoed down the alley.

Cynda sucked in her breath.

No red streaks left.

All gone. Or dead.

Like she was about to be.

The hulking, golden Nick-*other* started toward her. In his *other* form he wouldn't recognize her.

Crap!

She held up the chain out of reflex and commanded the Curson demon. "Don't move."

Nick-*other* came to a halt. And stared at her. Huge and fierce and angry at being controlled. Energy rippled off the being, pushing at her, shoving at her, challenging her. Daring her to let it take another step.

Through the smeared lenses of Cynda's goggles, Nick's golden glow fractured like sun through a piece of crystal. She snatched off the goggles with her free hand and flung them to the ground. Muscles screaming with pain, Cynda kept her eyes focused on the Curson demon and pushed herself to her feet.

"Don't . . . move," she commanded again as she slowly edged toward it.

The *other*'s shoulders heaved up and down with every deep breath it took. The eight-foot golden being's muscles bulged and she could tell it was fighting against her control.

She eased forward. "Nick, I'm going to put your chain back around your neck."

More deep breathing from the *other*. A rumble rose up in its chest and her heart skipped at the sound. She was half-afraid her control wouldn't be enough, and she'd be so much Silly Putty in its big golden fists.

"Nick . . ." She reached him and raised the gold chain. "Kneel and bow your head."

The *other* growled, louder this time, and Cynda almost jumped back.

Seconds passed, each one longer than the last.

With a furious snarl, Nick-*other* knelt on the asphalt, still glaring directly at Cynda.

Finally, it bowed its head.

Letting out a painful breath, she draped the chain around his neck. Shaking with a little fear and a lot of adrenaline and exhaustion, she took the broken ends, centered a burst of heat, and melded the ends together.

Instantly, the transformation began, and she stepped back.

Cynda forced her bruised, bleeding body to remain still as she watched Nick's golden sinew fade into bone, then muscle, then flesh, and finally, back into the human Nick. On his knees on the frozen alley stones, naked.

Cynda sank down in front of him as he stared at her, unmoving.

Every part of her body throbbed, but her focus quickly shifted to Nick, who looked miserable all over again. No, it was past miserable. The man seemed half-destroyed. She knew it was because he had to kill some of the creatures attacking them—yet, it was more, too.

What?

The sight of Nick, the most arrogant bastard in the universe, so torn up made Cynda's heart do funny things. She wanted to reach out to him, comfort him, but for once in her life, she had no idea what to say.

"Sorry," he murmured, his voice hollow against the stones. "Let you . . . down."

Cynda's pain faded into the distance.

Did he really just say that?

Nick's expression changed, and for one pulse-thumping moment, Cynda thought he might lean forward and pull her to him. Not just hug her, but hold her. Maybe even kiss her.

Her mind cartwheeled across the image, how hot it would feel to touch his bare skin, scrub her fingers across those hard muscles as his heat flowed into her and chased away the cold.

Her breath got shallow, and warm tingles traveled all over her skin.

Nick didn't move, and his expression didn't change.

He is attracted to me?

Shit!

Shouts came from the end of the alleyway where Nick-*other* had taken out the host of red flashes.

Nick kept staring at her another second, two, three— then turned his head away, and something inside Cynda snapped. She wanted to lunge forward, take his face in her hands, and make him look at her like that again.

The cold got colder.

Cynda realized she was shaking all over. Muddle-headed. Disappointed, yet too exhausted to be anything but glad to hear reinforcements approaching.

"About damned time you got here," she managed as Riana, the earth Sibyl of her triad, rushed to her. Riana's husband, Creed, Nick's twin, hurried to Cynda's side next, followed by Merilee, the triad's air Sibyl. Merilee had her bow ready, an arrow already nocked.

"What happened?" Riana asked as she knelt next to Cynda and Nick. She was wearing a red evening gown, but she had daggers in both hands.

"Fuck." Nick shook his head as if to clear it.

"We got jumped by invisible demons." Cynda rubbed her chest and shoulders, sending healing energy through her skin, into the gashes and cuts and punctures, wishing it would work right that second. As for Nick, Cynda knew his wounds had healed spontaneously the moment he shifted into his Curson form.

"Invisible . . . demons." Merilee lowered her bow and retrieved her arrow, sounding like she didn't believe a word of what Cynda just said. Wind danced around her face, stirring her blond hair.

"Yeah. As in, assholes we couldn't see." Cynda picked up her demon-hunting goggles from the ground and shook them in front of her triad sisters. "And—and I think they were here for me. As in me specifically."

"She isn't kidding," Nick said as he rubbed the bridge of his nose with his thumb and forefinger. "Invisible, and after her. Creed, get her sword. It's up there on the fire escape."

Creed jogged away, following his twin's instruction.

Nick glanced at Cynda, and she saw the worry etched across his face. Worry for her.

Damn, but she totally didn't know what to do with that.

"Why is Nick naked?" Merilee asked as if just noticing the fact that the gorgeous hunk of a man had nothing on. In an ice storm.

Cynda ignored her like she was trying to ignore Nick. "The beings showed up only like red traces in these stupid lenses," she explained. "And I had this sense I was the target." She shook her head, then groaned from the pain in her neck. "Sorry. I'm a little fuzzy." She met each woman's eyes as she raised her head. "When we killed the things, they broke down into air, fire, and wind."

"Invisible demons made out of three elements," Merilee said again, more serious now, actually sounding worried. "Targeting Sibyls specifically?"

"No." Cynda rubbed her hands together, then rubbed her throbbing arms. "*Me*. Cynda Flynn. I sensed that they wanted me."

Riana frowned and released a tiny burst of earth energy. The ground beneath them groaned once, and a few pebbles shook loose from the alley walls. "You're bleeding all over the place. Let's get you back to the brownstone." She looked at naked Nick and the alley gave another quick shake. "I think we have other business to take care of, too. Like, pants."

All of a sudden, the night seemed even colder and darker to Cynda. "It's frigid out here." *Anywhere but the brownstone. Please.* "My ass hurts. My friggin' hair hurts. I want to go home."

"No." Riana got to her feet and slipped her daggers

into thigh-sheaths. "The brownstone. Now. Before we run into more trouble."

The leader of her triad had spoken, but Cynda didn't want to obey. "Come on, Riana, I'd rather go to my place."

Nick was getting to his feet, still shaking his head—and staying out of the argument.

"You need to rest and heal, and you need your family around you." Riana looked around the alley with a worried expression. "If you're a target, we're staying together tonight."

Cynda's chest ached, inside and out.

Not fair, playing the family card.

But it worked, just like Riana knew it would.

It *always* worked.

"Need some goddamned clothes," Nick growled at his brother as Creed returned with Cynda's sword.

With a sigh, Cynda sheathed her blade.

Then she let Riana and Merilee lead her out of the icy, dirt-littered alley, toward the one place—other than *hell*—she really didn't want to go.

(2)

Nick fought to stay on his feet as a wall of water slammed into the building.

Tons of liquid beat the air out of his lungs. His pulse drummed in his ears. His chest burned from the need to breathe.

Nick grabbed a concrete pillar and held tight as the water flowed around him and rose above his head.

This is it. I'm over.

He opened his mouth to shout. Water rushed into his throat, his nose, and he couldn't stop himself from sucking it down. He waited for pain to crush his lungs, for darkness to take him.

Only, the water didn't kill him. He could breathe it, taste it, feel its cool flow rushing through his blood and body like life itself.

This must have been how the water Sibyls felt, before that tidal wave wiped them out centuries ago.

Not bad. He supposed he could get used it.

Then the dead people started floating by.

First came two little boys.

No. Damn! They're so young. Nick could barely make out their faces, but the kids could have been doubles for Creed and him when they were toddlers, right down to the mirror-image scars along their upper arms.

Before he could register any more details, the boys drifted off, replaced by a pretty brown-haired woman Nick didn't recognize. He didn't even have time to give her his full attention before the current swept her away, too.

After that, his grandmother flowed into view.

What . . . the . . . hell?

His grandmother had been dead since he was a boy.

But there she was, right in front of him, seeming more asleep than dead, like the morning he found her cold in her bed.

Nick's gut tightened.

Even drowned, the old woman's face looked so damned sweet it made his heart ache. She died because of him—well, him and his twin. Having two half-demon teenagers had been too much for her heart.

It would have been too much for anyone.

As his grandmother drifted off in the flowing currents, he almost reached out for her limp body—but another corpse floated in front of him with unnatural speed.

This one he really didn't want to see.

The woman's ash blond hair swirled over her head like a mermaid's crown, and her opaque blue eyes opened to stare at him.

To accuse him.

His biological mother. His true parent. Not the surrogate who died giving birth to Nick and Creed. This was the woman he had been forced to kill four months ago.

"Go," he tried to tell her, but his words got lost in the steady flow of water.

His mother's pale claw of a hand moved to her throat, to point out the blue bruise, the impossible angle of her neck.

Nick's insides burned. He clenched his fists, wishing he could shove away the sight, the thought, the memory.

He looked away.

Anxious, loud voices broke into his consciousness. The water he was breathing turned to fire. Nick grabbed his throat as he gulped molten flames and coughed—and opened his eyes.

Twisting pains in his ribs and shoulders cleared his senses.

He was flat on his back, lying on something soft. No water. No fire. No dead mothers.

He was dry.

Wearing a T-shirt and jogging shorts that weren't his.

He blinked and saw nothing but sunlight and wavy lines.

"Not her," someone moaned as Nick rubbed the bridge of his nose and shook off the dream or hallucination or whatever the hell it was. He thought the woman talking was his brother's wife, Riana, the earth Sibyl who didn't like him very much. "Nori trained with Cynda, for the sake of the Goddess. Bela Argos will be devastated—and now we're short in the South Bronx. Our whole north flank is weak."

"I couldn't make out everything that came through. Communications aren't my specialty." That breezy voice belonged to the air Sibyl, Merilee. She sounded five miles past stressed. "But I understood the attacks happened up and down the East Coast, and over in Ireland. All very specific."

"How stupid can those idiots get?" Sarcastic. Total bite. Had to be his brother's OCU partner, Andy Myles. "Jesus, I so need a vacation. I can't understand why the Legion would target fire Sibyls. That's like yanking a tiger's tail."

"Watch out for the teeth," Nick mumbled. He tried to sit up, but sagged back against the overstuffed sofa that supported him.

Somebody grabbed his arm and steadied his weight.

Nick forced himself upright, pushed his twin brother Creed's fingers off his shoulder, and shook his head to clear his senses. When he sucked in a breath, the scents of sage, jasmine, vanilla, and fruit washed over him, and he remembered where he was—in the brownstone in upper Manhattan, where Cynda and Merilee used to live before Creed got it on with their Sibyl triad leader Riana, and actually got himself married. Though he obviously hadn't managed to defeminize the place any.

Creed sat down beside Nick, obvious relief on his familiar features. "About time you rejoined the living, bro. What was that about teeth?"

"An old saying." Nick's head throbbed as he spoke. "If you yank a tiger's tail, you'd better have a plan for the teeth. Tom Clancy wrote a book about that."

His jaw hurt, and his chest, and his right shoulder ached along the scar that ran from his shoulder to his elbow. Underneath that flannel shirt, Nick's twin had an identical scar, only on his left shoulder. The mark of a Curson birth. Cursons were half-human and half-Asmodai-demon, always twinned, always joined. And always fatal to the surrogate, the "donor womb" as those poor women were called by the Legion.

We're death walking—or at least I am. Images of his dead grandmother and staring, floating mother flipped through Nick's consciousness. *Death follows me everywhere.*

That thought brought reality blasting through his every fiber.

"Cynda?" He searched the room with his eyes, even though it made his head swim. "Is she all right?"

"*She* is," Riana Dumain Lowell, Nick's new sister-in-law, said in a sharp, pained tone. "But we lost one of Bela Argos's triad in the South Bronx."

Nick winced. His chest tightened. "Did I hear you say last night's attack was widespread—against the fire Sibyls?"

When he looked up, the wavy lines parted enough for him to see Riana nod. She was sitting on a giant oak table the size of a small dance floor. The Sibyls used it as a worktable and a communications platform. Above her, on the walls of the alcove at the back of the living room, hung runes and mirrors that Nick had seen come to life when a fire Sibyl—when *Cynda*—danced on that oak platform.

His brother Creed occupied the other end of the couch. The blond air Sibyl Merilee sat in a chair opposite Riana, holding a notebook. Creed's partner Andy sat beside Merilee in another chair, also with a notebook.

Dark circles ringed Andy's eyes, and her freckled skin was a shade past pale. She looked seriously pissed. "Yank a tiger's tail, have a plan for the teeth." Andy gripped her notebook so tightly it curled in her hands, as if the pages were damp and limp. "No doubt the Legion does have a plan. What the fuck are they up to now?"

"We have to find out." Riana's ink-black hair fell loose about her tanned face, and her cool green eyes gazed at Nick without blinking, like he was somehow responsible for what happened tonight, like he might have an answer to Andy's question.

Nick returned her gaze and did his best to keep his temper, for his brother's sake, and for Cynda's. Going at it with Riana might relieve tension, but it wouldn't solve anything. Gideon—his *other*—rumbled inside him, like distant thunder rattling against his skull. Nick took a breath and ran through a set of calming, meditative statements he used to settle his demon-half, all the while keeping his expression passive.

Cynda has green eyes like you, he thought, studying Riana. *Only hers are brighter.*

Images of Cynda helped him relax another fraction.

After a few more breaths, he let his attention shift around the room. Cynda had red hair, like Andy, but Cynda's looked like dark flames around her face, shorter and a bit curly, giving her an impish appearance he enjoyed.

So delicate, yet so deadly.

Where was she?

"Cynda's resting downstairs," Riana said, as if reading his mind. They all did that, the Sibyls, answered questions before he asked them. Irritating, but he guessed it was part of the package. These women had fighting skills and powerful abilities still beyond his full understanding. That didn't bother Nick. It intrigued him, and yes, raked his nerves, but it didn't put him off.

His hand moved reflexively to his neck. The talisman chain was there, of course, right where it belonged. Yet he did remember changing into his *other,* as Creed and the Sibyls called his and his twin's demon forms. It was after he took a hit with a spear. Nick rubbed his aching shoulder.

"Elementally locked spear tip," he said to his silent audience. "We were meeting with my informant when something attacked us. Some *things*. Couldn't even see the bastards."

Riana nodded slowly. "Reports from Ireland, Philadelphia, Boston, Baltimore, and D.C. all say the same thing. Did you take off your talisman as a last resort?"

"I didn't—" Nick began, then bit off his own sentence. He didn't take off that talisman and change into his *other,* his demon form, on purpose. He would never risk something that dangerous without someone to hand the talisman to, someone trustworthy who knew how to use it. And Cynda had been too engaged in the battle to be ready for the handoff.

Problem was, Nick had a good idea who did take off his talisman, and he didn't want to share that information. Not yet. Not until he knew for sure, figured out what it meant, and decided what to do about it.

"Yeah," he finished simply, holding Riana's gaze.

After years undercover in the psychotic Legion cult,

Nick could lie without blinking an eye, if the stakes were high enough. He massaged his cramping shoulder and shot his twin a look.

Creed seemed ultrafocused and calm, a new thing, since the whole marrying-the-woman-of-his-dreams gig. That and Creed had subjected himself to some god-awful procedure performed by the crones at Riana's Sibyl Motherhouse in Russia. Those old bitches had done something that melded Creed's talisman, a gold ring, into the skin of his chest. Creed could now control his *other* almost as well as Nick had learned to control his through meditation and the mental disciplines of martial arts.

"Good thing Cynda got your chain back on." Creed held up his hand, let it shift into the glowing, golden ham-fist of his *other*, then back to fully human again, without singeing his shirt at all. "I'd hate to have to punch your lights out."

"In your dreams." Seeing Creed do a part-shift made Nick feel a little strange. Before those Russian biddies "transformed" Creed, Nick was the only one who could do tricks like that. Hell, he only burned off his clothes when he changed completely.

"Okay, let's review," said Merilee, the air Sibyl, staring at her notebook. Nick had learned that Sibyls preferred paper-and-pencil recording, since it wasn't prone to electronic malfunction—a common event around those with elemental powers. "From what you've said so far, what we've been able to get from the communication chimes without Cynda to interpret, and what she told us before she went to rest, the two of you met Max Moses, an informant, in the alley, to gain new information about the Legion's next move."

She turned a page. "Cynda observed traces of sulfur dioxide on the clothing of Max Moses, but not the shade typically produced by the single-element, man-made

Asmodai demons we're used to fighting. Then you were attacked by elemental creatures, probably some other type of demon, composed of all the elements, invisible to the naked eye."

Nick waited for Merilee to mention the floating paint can, and the way something invisible had snatched off his talisman. He dreaded it, but the punch never came.

She didn't say anything about that.

Was she waiting for him to bring it up? Testing him?

"That's the size of it," he said. "Best I remember."

Merilee looked up. Her blue eyes seemed troubled, but open, not like she was holding something back, or getting ready to pounce. "Meanwhile, similar battles took place up and down the East Coast, and in Ireland. Any fire Sibyl separated from her triad was attacked. Some were even assaulted with their triads present. We lost one Sibyl in New York, nine in the U.S. total, and the Ireland count's not in yet."

Nine women like Cynda. And God knows how many in Ireland. Rage boiled inside Nick, and this time, he growled inside along with Gideon. He'd give anything to be back in that alley.

He should have fired sooner.

He would have fired sooner, if he'd had any idea what was going down.

"What did you find out from your source?" Andy asked. She took notes with paper and pen, too, but not because equipment malfunctioned around her. Because she was cop-trained, through and through, like Nick and Creed. Take notes about everything, thorough notes, and worry about typing it on a computer later.

Nick said, "Max thinks he found a Legion house in the Bronx, toward the north."

Merilee and Riana visibly flinched at the mention of the area of New York hardest hit by Legion attacks last fall. Asmodai had killed one Sibyl, gotten another put in prison—where she died—and sent the third member of the North Bronx triad back to Motherhouse Ireland, probably forever. A ranger group was currently patrolling the area, but they didn't know it as well as the shattered triad, or even Riana, Cynda, and Merilee's group. Now, by the sound of it, the South Bronx triad was broken, too. Not good.

"The place is near Van Cortlandt Park, which fits with the demon activity in that area a few months back." Nick gestured toward the north section of the city. "I'd have found out more, but my snitch split when the demon action started."

"You got the address?" Andy yawned but kept scribbling. Tough broad. Nick liked her. He gave her the address.

"I'll get in touch with Captain Freeman and put eyes on the house," she said, staring at her notes. "We'll get intel and specs, then plan a raid for this time next week."

Riana shook her head. "What if that place is full of these new invisible demons?" She paused, then said the one thing Nick had been hoping she wouldn't say. "They sound like Astaroths, and we don't even know what Astaroths can do."

Creed went rigid on the couch.

Nick felt himself go just as stiff. "There's no evidence that the invisible things are Astaroth demons," he countered as calmly as he could.

Liar. Nick, buddy, sometimes you suck.

Creed's fists doubled, and Nick caught a glimmer of gold around the edges of his brother's skin as his twin's control slipped a fraction. "As far as we know, there's only one Astaroth in New York City," Creed said. "In the whole world, for that matter."

Nick nodded, still thinking about how much he

sucked. Was he really willing to hold back on these women to protect a brother—a demon—he barely knew? A confused creature, a being Nick didn't even know how to read or judge or interpret?

But he's my brother. He glanced at Creed. *Our brother. He didn't ask for what happened to him.*

This time last year, Jacob had been a little boy. A terrible blood ritual had aged him mentally, physically, and emotionally to adulthood, and turned him into a supernatural creature with unknown abilities. Only, Nick knew something about the Astaroths. In his time undercover, he had read Legion communiqués on them, and shared what he felt was prudent with the Sibyls.

I have to find Jake, find out if it was him in the alley. Maybe he dumped that paint to help us. Nick closed his eyes. Opened them. Found himself staring at his twin. *I have to give him a chance. I'd do the same for you, wouldn't I?*

"There's no real indication that we have more Astaroths on the loose," Nick said. "This is probably some Legion revision in the creation of Asmodai. But to be safe, let's get the intel before we move on the Bronx house."

And give me some time to figure out what the hell I'm going to do.

Before anyone else could speak, Nick stood. For a few seconds, he wondered if he might fall, but he managed to shake off the dizziness.

"Here on out, Cynda doesn't stay alone." He glanced around the room, searching for any sign of disagreement, and found none.

Riana, however, looked more uncomfortable than usual. She shifted on the edge of the big table, seemed to argue with herself for a second, then come to a decision. "I know this is a lot to ask, Nick, but when Merilee and I aren't with Cynda, will you see to her safety?"

At the stunned looks from Andy, Merilee, and Creed, Riana added, "He *was* one of them for a time. He knows how the Legion thinks, how it operates better than any of us. Plus, he's Curson—and stronger for it." She clasped her hands in her lap. "Cynda would scorch anybody else who tried to protect her."

"Consider it done," Nick said without hesitation. "You didn't even have to ask."

Riana gave him a grateful look, which impressed Nick, since the two of them definitely hadn't hit it off. Riana had wanted him to submit to experiments into the nature of Curson demons, but Nick had told her— politely at first, then not so politely when she persisted— where to put *that* idea. Since then, there had been a major chill between them. The fact that Riana would stuff her pride and ask him to protect one of the women closest to her heart said a lot. More than anything, it proved Riana would do whatever she had to do to take care of her own.

In that, we find common ground, Nick thought. Out loud, he said, "I want to see Cynda now."

"We, uh—we haven't told her about Nori, the Sibyl who died." Merilee sounded more than a little worried. "After debriefing, Cynda meditated to heal herself, and she's been sleeping it off ever since. We were planning to give her the bad news when she woke."

"I'll take care of it." Nick glanced toward the kitchen door. "And the bodyguard thing, too. I've got at least a fifty-fifty shot of not spending the next six months in a burn unit."

This made Merilee laugh. Creed smiled. Andy just shook her head.

Riana got up without speaking and started for the kitchen.

Nick followed her, aware of Merilee, Andy, and Creed trailing after him. He walked behind Riana as quietly as she walked, across the tile floor of the kitchen, through another door, and down a set of stairs to the bedroom Riana usually shared with his twin. New smells reached him as he approached the bottom of the steps. Lavender, like Riana. And, to his surprise, some sweat and leather and woodsy guy odor, too.

Way to go, bro. Invade her domain. Throw your gym shorts in every corner. Conquer the place by inches if you have to, but get the job done.

When Riana opened the bedroom door and moved out of his way, all of Nick's inner sarcasm vanished. His chest tightened, and he stepped inside the quiet, cavelike space alone. Everyone else stayed in the hall, and he pulled the door closed behind him.

Candles lit the room, reflecting from mirrors on the dressers and walls. In the soft yellow light, he could see Cynda's long-legged form lying still in the bed, beneath cream-colored satin sheets that were pulled up under her arms, just above her breasts. The sheets outlined her perfect curves, not to mention the swell of those full breasts. Her red hair curled in wisps around her beautiful, sharply defined face and athletic shoulders, and her bright green eyes remained closed. Freckles were scattered across her nose and cheeks and her bare shoulders, too.

The satin covers rose and fell with each steady breath.

Nick realized he wasn't breathing himself, and instructed his lungs to work. Slowly, steadily, he matched her breathing, relieved to be sharing air with her.

She's okay.

He heard low conversations begin out in the hall, and felt more private now that the others were distracted. Nick let himself relax, really relax for the first time since he woke in the brownstone. Cynda's fresh-washed scent of vanilla mixed with cinnamon filled his senses, and he wanted to kiss her. He had wanted to kiss her since the day he met her, but she wasn't interested in him.

At least, he had assumed she wasn't, until that moment in the alley.

The way she had looked at him . . .

Nick ground his teeth and reined in his primal instincts. That was the heat of battle.

He didn't know how she really felt, did he?

And he wasn't the kind of man to force himself on any woman, especially a willful powerhouse like this one. If she wanted him, she'd have to come to him in her own time, her own way.

He could be patient.

Even if his body ached for action right now. Part desire. Part relief at seeing her well and whole and healing.

How could I have let her get hurt?

He couldn't take his eyes off her, didn't want to give up the sight of her.

Cynda's eyelids fluttered, and suddenly she was looking at him. Her face and neck were bruised, but already, the dark colors were fading. Sibyls healed so fast.

Damn, he wanted to kiss her worse. He knew, staring at her so fragile and vulnerable and naked under those satin sheets, that he couldn't wait much longer. Nick felt his skin catch fire when their eyes connected as if Cynda had thrown a wall of elemental power straight at him. Only, she hadn't. He wasn't actually burning—for once. It was just how she made him feel.

Those bright green eyes. Alive. Real.

For a moment, he didn't react. He knew his face was too serious, but he couldn't change it.

"We kicked some ass," she mumbled, barely coherent.

The sound of Cynda's lilting voice jarred Nick out of stasis. "You betcha, baby. Us, ten or twelve. Demons zip."

She gave him a weak thumbs-up, and a flame danced at the end of her thumbnail. Nick couldn't help shaking his head at her.

"Those were Astaroths, weren't they?"

Nick shrugged. He thought about repeating his we-have-no-proof lie, but he couldn't. Not to Cynda. Instead, he told the truth. "I'm not sure."

Cynda hesitated, cut her eyes to the door, then looked back at him and said, oh-so-quietly, "I didn't mention anything about the floating paint can. Yet."

A connection formed between them in the air, tangible and electric, as Nick tried to manage his shock.

She had kept a secret for him—from her triad sisters. Unthinkable. Unbelievable. But she did it.

She saw how I felt about hurting the Astaroths. Or she guessed something when I didn't want to shoot them in the alley.

More than that, it mattered to her. How he felt. What he wanted.

Cynda took a deep breath and let it out, making the cream-colored sheets shiver. "I was thinking the one with the paint might have been—"

Nick cut her off by putting his finger to his lips. "We'll talk about that later, okay?"

Cynda's mouth tightened. "My silence does have an expiration date."

"Understood. And thank you."

"Family's . . . important." She gave a little shrug, and the sheet slipped down her bare skin, to the top of her breasts.

Nick's cock throbbed, stiff and miserable in his jeans, and he had to force himself to pay attention to Cynda's next words.

"Family is family, I guess," she said. "Even if they aren't what you want them to be."

"Or who you expect them to be." He centered himself as best he could, regained control of his body with a few mantras, then crossed to the bed and eased himself onto the mattress beside Cynda.

The urge to touch her nearly overwhelmed him, but he kept himself under the tightest control, even when she looked up at him, green eyes almost expectant, like she was hoping for something good.

Heat flowed between them.

He wasn't imagining that. Nick was sure of it. His muscles tightened. His cock got hard all over again, this time a pulsing misery.

What he had seen in the alley, Cynda's emotions, her interest, it wasn't just wishful thinking.

I could kiss her.

I could kiss her right now.

As if she could hear his thoughts, Cynda's body tensed in anticipation, and it was all Nick could do not to bend down and ease that satin cover down across her nipples, her belly, her legs, slowly, letting the silky fabric brush her skin until he bared her completely. Left her lying before him, exposed and waiting for his lips.

But that wasn't an option.

Damnit.

Once more, Nick used a few mantras to calm his body and restore his focus. "Speaking of family, firebird, there were more attacks against fire Sibyls last night." He tried to keep his tone calm. "You'll be needing some extra protection."

"I wondered." Her pretty mouth tugged into a frown. "It felt—well, personal, in the alley. Like I was the target. Because I'm a fire Sibyl."

Nick felt some relief that she had missed the whole protection comment for the moment. They could come back to that when she got stronger.

As for the rest, he hated what he had to tell her, hated that the news would wound her, but she had to know. And he intended to be right here for her, every second, while she dealt with it. Whatever she said or did, he was man enough to take it.

"You *were* the target." He reached to touch her cheek, but put his hand back on his knee. "And other fire Sibyls, too. Not everyone came through as well as we did."

"Oh, Goddess." Cynda turned on her side to face him, grabbed his wrist and squeezed, her green eyes boring into his. "Who? Where?"

Steeling himself for a possible outburst of emotion, flames, or both, he said, "The fire Sibyl from the South Bronx triad got killed."

"Nori," Cynda whispered, and let him go.

She rolled to her back and stared at the ceiling, tears flowing down her freckled cheeks.

Nick put his hand on her shoulder.

She didn't burn him or jerk away, which surprised and pleased him.

"I'm sorry, Cynda."

Cynda swallowed and nodded. Then she put her hand over his and kept crying, staring at the ceiling and yet obviously at nothing at all.

Nick let her cry. He knew she needed to do it, had to do it.

The way Sibyls interacted, they were like sisters and cousins. Each triad was family to the next. He respected that, even if he had never known a bond like that with anyone save for his long-dead grandmother and his twin, Creed.

Second by second, minute by minute, he sat beside her without interrupting the flow of her emotions—and he was watching when dark anger began to edge out the grief on Cynda's face.

Nick understood that, too, and he welcomed the sight of it. That was the fight in Cynda. The warrior.

Next would come—

Fire exploded in a ring around Riana's bedroom walls.

"Suck it up," Nick said sharply, to get her attention. "Haul it back, firebird. *Now.*"

Cynda glared at him, but he felt the rush of air as she brought the fire under control, doused it, and absorbed the heat energy back into her body. Black streaks marked all four walls, and melted candles now dripped quietly down plaster and wood, spilling onto the floor.

Nick's eyes watered from the tang of ash and flame, but he didn't dare blink.

Cynda tried to sit up, but he was ready for that, too. He let Gideon join him, shielding him from serious burns as he eased Cynda back down to the mattress and held her there, all too aware of every inch of her body.

She threw fire at him, thrashed against him, but Nick wouldn't relent, or let himself go past protecting Cynda from herself.

"Not yet," he said, almost nose to nose with her, with Gideon's echo in his words. "Rest until you're healed. Then we'll find the bastards behind this and roast them— together."

Cynda's warm breath spread across his face.

She was half snarling, half growling with the force of her rage and determination. Her eyes blazed as she said, "Swear?"

Nick heard the feral rumble in his own voice as he said, "On my family's lives."

(3)

"I don't need a bodyguard." Cynda stormed away from Nick and out of Riana's kitchen, trailing fire through the air behind her. "Riana! Where are you? We need to talk."

She stopped beside the communications platform and glared into the projective mirrors Sibyls used to transmit messages across long distances. Chimes clattered all over the brownstone, answering the hot whirlwind of Cynda's energy.

The kitchen door swung softly on its hinges.

Cynda didn't have to look to know Nick had followed her into the living room. He was shadowing her. Sticking to her like demon-man glue because Riana had *asked* him to.

I'll kill her.

Riana knew Cynda didn't need a complication—a distraction—like Nick Lowell beside her, twenty-four/seven.

Cynda wanted to scream.

Physical attractions aside, relationships never worked out in her life, and she sure didn't need to start one now, even if it was just sex.

"Nobody's here but us," Nick said in tones so calm Cynda ached to roast him—tight low-riders, muscle-hugging T-shirt, black boots, and all. "Riana and Creed went for a run to the townhouse. It's time for you and me to hunt down Max Moses before morning report."

Cynda didn't turn around. Her shoulders sagged as she absorbed the fire energy she'd been gathering. She felt unnaturally tired for so early on a Monday morning, and a little sore from the ordeal in the alley last Friday night. Most of her cuts and bruises had healed, but she still wished she could buy a new ass.

Sunlight streamed through the front door and windows of the Upper East Side brownstone, into the home that was no longer hers, but she barely had the will to deal with that thought. She pressed her hands against her flannel-lined jeans and heavy white tunic, trying to keep a grip on her emotions, just as she had been forced to do so many years ago at Kylemore Abbey, when her father gave her away.

Nick said nothing, and didn't try to approach her.

A little coolness washed across the heat of Cynda's anger. The man knew how to give space at the right moments, which was wonderful and horrible at the same time. One less thing to hold against him, one less excuse to ignore the wild sensations he stirred in her body.

Her fingers twitched.

She wanted to reach into all the sparkles of sunlight, touch the pulsing bits of spark and flame, and find some fire. She could taste its sweet sulfur tang each time she opened her mouth, smell its hypnotic, acrid scent wherever she went, whatever she was doing. Fire burned everywhere, inside everything. On good days, she took what she needed from the world's ample, hidden flames, and that burning heat cradled her like a gentle, insistent lover.

On bad days . . .

Cynda closed her eyes.

On bad days like this, she blew shit up.

Visions danced behind her eyelids, images of fried clothes, smoking walls, singed hair.

She opened her eyes fast.

To center herself, she pushed up the sleeve of her tunic and focused on the tattoo on the inside of her right forearm—mortar, pestle, and broom, in triangular points around a dark crescent moon.

The mark of a Sibyl.

She was a warrior now, the pestle of her triad, not some shaking six-year-old abandoned because her fire making scared her family half to death. At Motherhouse Ireland, Cynda had learned the ways of the Dark Goddess, and fought for control over her own elemental power. The mark on her arm, the mortar, pestle, and broom, signified that Cynda had won that battle—mostly—then sworn an oath to use her weapons, advanced fighting skills, and command of fire to save the untrained, weak, and innocent from the supernaturally strong.

Not to blow shit up.

Especially her former home.

Cynda's throat tightened.

Familiar scents of sage and apples, and even a hint of lavender made her want to cry. Her home. This had been *her home*. Now that Riana had married Creed, everything had changed. This little stay back at the brownstone just ground that point deeper into her heart, and made Cynda grieve the loss of her home, the previous simplicity of their triad and living together as a group, all over again.

She moved her gaze from her wrist to her palms.

Life's no fairy tale and I'm no princess. Time to grow up.

Though sometimes, she really wanted to be the happy, blessed girl in the bedtime tales, the girl who got everything she ever dreamed of having, everything she ever wanted or needed. That girl never had to worry about being homeless or friendless or without a loving family. That girl never had to find the strength to start over.

Or blow shit up.

"You . . . okay?"

The low, rumbling question startled Cynda. Every

muscle in her body tightened at the sound of Nick's voice, but she still didn't turn around.

She didn't want to deal with him right now. She just couldn't. Yet thanks to Riana's overcautious worrying, she *had* to.

Instinct told Cynda that Nick was the type of man who would want pieces of her she hadn't given to anyone since the night her father left her at Kylemore Abbey. And she never would, not again. That lesson had been learned. She needed to resist Nick's charms, which shouldn't be hard, given his stubborn arrogance and his tendency toward an absurd level of protectiveness. Like in the alley, for instance, when he had tried to keep her down while he did all the fighting.

Why didn't I tell Riana and Merilee about that paint can? Cynda tried her best to ignore an image of Nick, naked on his knees, looking at her like his soul had been torn in half. Then like he wanted to kiss her. She shook her head. *Why didn't I insist we were fighting Astaroths, especially when they were targeting me?*

The image of Nick on his knees wouldn't go away.

And she would *never* forget the look on Nick's face in that alley, when he hadn't wanted to fire on the unknown demon. Nick had already sacrificed so much in the battle against the Legion, and now he might have to sacrifice his brother, too.

A change in the air currents, an increase in heat and ambient bits of fire told Cynda that Nick had moved nearer.

She imagined she could feel the warmth of his breath playing against her neck, and she definitely caught a whiff of his unusual scent. That mixture of ocean and musk. Everything dangerous and intriguing, yet too vast to be conquered.

She moved toward the communications table.

Nick followed.

"I asked if you were okay," he said. His voice reminded her of distant thunder, barely contained. Always so serious, and so brief.

With a deep breath and a mental push to repel any fire energy she might have gathered on reflex, Cynda turned to face him.

Nick stood only inches away. He gazed at her with his inscrutable black-diamond eyes, clearly waiting for—no, no—*demanding* an answer.

Heat skittered along Cynda's skin, but she fought to control it.

No good.

A tiny hole opened in Cynda's sleeve before she could pull back her flames.

The rest of her started to smoke.

Nick started to smile.

Damn him!

Cynda thought about setting his shirt or hair on fire. How funny would *that* be? But of course, the jerk wasn't backing down. He was just standing there, wanting to know if she was okay, and he wouldn't quit.

It was answer him or humiliate herself, so she said, "I was just—" Her voice broke.

Damn him twice.

"Never mind," she covered quickly. "Let's just go. I'm fine."

Nick held his ground.

Those black eyes flashed, *Liar.*

Cynda clamped her jaw harder and shoved away heat energy. Hard. A burst of fire struck the nearest wall and exploded with a *whump*.

Nick didn't turn his head. The meaning was clear.

I'm not afraid of you. Burn the whole place down if you want to, and I'm not moving.

Cynda's eyes flicked toward the waning bit of flame she had thrown. The wall didn't catch on fire.

When she turned her eyes back to Nick, her heart snapped and bumped like Pop Rocks pitched into a campfire.

Nick gave her a look somewhere between amusement and concern, and that only made her twice as mad. Her heart beat faster. She wanted to punch him. Grab him. Kiss him. Slide her heated fingers into his jeans and see what she found—and how he liked her then.

Get a grip. You don't *need this. You don't!*

But what would it feel like to make love to such a dark, intense, powerful man? What kind of a total rush, total release . . . ? Nick could best her in a fair fight, and hold his own against her elemental powers. Nick Lowell was a man Cynda knew she couldn't dominate.

Scary as hell. A total first.

I don't need this.

A new sliver of smoke rose from Cynda's left foot, but she mentally caught it and dispersed it, along with the rest of the heat energy shimmering around her like a living halo. "Back off, Nick. I don't want you at my elbow all the time. First thing at the townhouse, we're talking to Riana and Merilee, and we're working this out. I don't need so much protection."

Nick's dark eyes remained calm, though his words had a sharp edge. "A bunch of dead fire Sibyls say otherwise."

"Screw you!" More flames blasted from Cynda's body, ringing the room, but burning out before they did serious damage. Cynda turned her face away from Nick and seethed. The loss of so many of her friends and fellow warriors across the globe chewed at her, and he knew it. Worse, the sensation of Nick so determined to protect her, oblivious to her temper and fire, made her dizzy.

Did he know that, too?

Nick moved until his body brushed hers from shoulder to thigh. Streaks of fire raced through her chest. She heard herself gasp, hated that she did it. Retreated a step. Her calves brushed the communications platform.

Nick once more moved toward her, against her, without grabbing her or trapping her, but she didn't step away this time. Couldn't.

Chest to breast. Hip to hip.

She was touching him. He was touching her, and looking at her like *that*, like he had in the alley.

Cynda trembled at the rough, delicious sensation of Nick's steel-hard thigh pressed into hers, his carved chest teasing her nipples.

His eyes were so dark. His face was so close to hers.

Her entire body quivered as she imagined burning away their clothes. His kiss would be fierce and consuming. She could almost taste his tongue in her mouth, feel her fingers wrapped around his cock.

Goddess, but he felt good.

His simmering gaze dared her to make it more.

Cynda's vision prismed.

The world cracked and shattered to nothing, leaving just her, just Nick, standing in the center of a bright orange firelight.

She wanted to make it more, right here, right now.

But . . .

"Back . . . off," she said through her teeth.

Nick's smile was so sensual it sent ripples of liquid desire through her entire body. "If that's what you really want," he murmured in that unbelievably sexy bass, "make me."

Cynda raised her hands, inches from Nick's face.

She should let loose with a fireball he would never forget.

But she didn't. She just glared at him. Wanted him to move. Wanted him to stay and push her another inch, so she could fight him outright, or kiss him until she lost her mind completely.

His expression grew more serious. "You need to let people care about you, firebird."

Her insides flipped at the sound of that nickname. Smoke rose off her skin. "Don't call me that."

On the last word, she faltered, because his eyes were so dark and bright, and his lips so near hers. Scents of male and stormy seas and arousal washed over her. She raised her hands another fraction, intending to blast Nick a good one, but he grabbed her arms and stroked them. Up and down, up and down, gentle, but also a little rough.

Cynda sucked in another breath. Her mind emptied. Even the firelight she had imagined winked out of existence. Now the only thing in the universe was her body and his, and all the places they were touching, the way his hands moved over the fabric of her tunic, coursing across her steaming skin.

Nick seemed heedless of the smoke swirling through the air, so thick it almost made a curtain between their faces. He also ignored the flickers of fire at her elbows and wrists.

Everywhere he touched her, more flames erupted, singeing holes in her tunic and his T-shirt, too. His low rumble of pleasure vibrated against her, and her jumbled brain fixed on the iron muscle of his chest pressed to hers.

Nick stared straight into the center of her being and whispered, "Let *me* care about you."

"No," Cynda said, loud, harsh, panicked that he said those words out loud. Even as she spoke, she was melting into him, catching fire up and down her back and chest.

Nick's skin took on the golden glow of his *other*. His powerful arms wrapped around her, and he held her tight against his hot body. Cynda expected to feel trapped and forced, but instead she felt shielded, from everything, anything in the universe that might wound her.

Her inner fire burned and burned, leaping out, blasting against Nick, but his *other*'s glow absorbed every flame she threw. She couldn't burn this man no matter how much her skin sizzled.

Cynda's head really spun then.

With Nick, she could lose control, surrender completely—and she couldn't hurt him.

He'll keep us both safe.

When his lips touched hers, Cynda thought the universe might catch fire.

Molten heat flowed over her mouth.

She smacked Nick's chest with both hands, but didn't pull away. Didn't want to, even though her better sense demanded it. Instead, she wrapped her fingers in his T-shirt and held on for the ride.

A hint of wintergreen and liquid fire tingled across her tongue as their mouths joined completely.

Cynda shivered and burned everywhere. So good. He tasted perfect. He felt beyond perfect. So, so good.

And that was bad.

Wasn't it?

Her brain tried to intrude, but she shut out reality and lost herself to the wet heat of the kiss. His lips, his mouth, his tongue, she wanted them everywhere. She wanted Nick to taste every inch of her. Cynda wished he would pick her up and carry her straight back to Riana's basement, and take her now, now, even if that wasn't her bed, even if this wasn't her house. She didn't care. She had never cared less about anything in her life.

Nick held her close, closer, refusing to give an inch as flames raced along her chest and arms—*their* chest and arms. Cynda's belly blazed from the sensation of heat joining heat, the snap of her fire joining with the golden force of his inner demon. Untamed energy. Raw power.

Chimes rang throughout the brownstone. No incoming message. Just Cynda and Nick, Nick and Cynda, casting off heat like a star going nova.

His hands moved to massage her back, her waist, then her ass.

Cynda moaned and pressed harder against him. Her breasts ached as she crushed herself into his chest, falling farther into his endless kiss. The heat on her skin moved lower, inside her trembling body, to that place at her center that throbbed with longing and need.

Nick moved his head just enough to take his lips from hers.

Hissing with frustration, Cynda cupped his cheeks in her hands, turned his face back to her own, and kissed him, longer, forever. He bit at her bottom lip and tugged it into his mouth, driving her wild with delicious shock. Even with the power of fire at her fingertips, she was helpless against this, against him.

At that second, she didn't give a flaming damn.

With mild surprise, Cynda realized she wasn't giving off flames or smoke anymore. The heat was still there, flowing through her veins, cradling every muscle in her body, but she wasn't destroying anything at all. Nick's glow had faded. He was fully human now, stroking her, holding her, kissing her possessively, fiercely, one hundred percent human male.

When Nick broke away again, he moved his lips to her ear. "I *will* be guarding you when your triad's not around. Deal with it."

"Yeah, whatever," Cynda shot back, then groaned as Nick nipped at that spot below her ear, and lower, almost to her shoulder. She pressed her hands against the muscle of his chest and dug her fingers into the taut flesh.

This time it was Nick who groaned.

He kissed Cynda, slower, deeper, drawing out the

connection until she thought she'd burn to death on the spot.

Had anything in her life ever felt this hot?

When he finished, he pressed his cheek to her forehead and held her for a long while, letting her sag into him, use his strength to stand and just . . . be. She realized she was gasping instead of breathing, that her whole body was shaking, shaking in his embrace.

"We have scum-hunting to do." He kissed the top of her head and squeezed both of her arms, causing a rush of shivers and new waves of desire. "Time to go."

Cynda sighed, wishing Nick didn't have to be such a dedicated cop—but also not wanting to deal with the endless amount of crap she'd get from Riana and Merilee if they showed up late and all ruffled for morning report. Reality crept back in a few steps, yanking her from her dreamy distance, reminding her of Legion attacks and dead fire Sibyls, and everything they had to accomplish before more warriors died.

Nick *had* promised they would hunt down the bastards responsible—together—and he was ready to make good on that deal. For now, they needed to hit the streets and find that worm of an informant Max Moses, and shake out whatever he knew.

Smoke rose from her shoulders again. She didn't want to let Nick go.

Knew this would happen. He's a distraction. This absolutely does not need to happen.

She and Nick would have to talk about this later. Like the bodyguard crap.

Truth be told, Cynda also didn't want to give up her last few moments in the brownstone, feeling like this—so calm and relaxed and at home, like she used to before everything shifted. Nick's touch had stirred her up in so many ways, but settled her down, too, helped her think, helped her realize she needed to say goodbye to the place, her way, in her own time.

She pulled back from him and gazed into his black eyes. "Go pull the Jeep around. I'll be right behind you."

Nick's eyebrow twitched, communicating his mistrust faster than any frown. "About to bail out the back door on me?"

"I'm not splitting, Sibyl's honor." She lifted her hand to her nose and made a V over the top of it with her index finger and middle finger, parodying an old television show about witches. "I'm still pissed about the whole bodyguard thing, but I'm not stupid." She lowered her hand. "I just need a minute to myself. In here, alone, I mean."

Nick's expression darkened a fraction, but he didn't argue with her. He gave her another quick kiss on the forehead, a long stare that said *Don't you dare double-cross me,* and headed out of the brownstone. The man was so tall he almost bashed his head against the wind chimes hanging by the front door. His black ponytail bounced between his broad shoulders as he ducked under the metal pipes and slipped out the door.

Cynda could only stare at him, and then at the spot where he had been. Her body still felt hot and tingly from touching him so intimately—and they both had holes in their clothes. Oh, yeah, they'd get some crap over *that* one, even if they did make it to report on time.

And she still didn't want to leave.

She knew it was time to go. They did have work to do. But leaving the brownstone dragged at her. She felt rooted to the place where she stood. Stuck.

It's time to go.

Her hands and fingers caught fire. She raised them and stared at the flames, pulling the fire energy back inside her one inch at a time until the outbreak waned.

The brownstone, like that long-ago Irish village and her blood family, like that judgmental mean-ass nun—what was her name? Sister Julia—was her past now.

Cynda knew she needed to surrender this home, let it fade from her heart, even though she had spent a few blissful days here, recovering from her battle wounds. Even though she'd just had the best kisses of her life in the living room.

No problem. I can do this.

No flames. No sparks. Not even a teensy bit of smoke. *I can handle this.*

But she had trouble giving the brownstone one last look.

A lump rose in her throat, and she didn't bother trying to make it go away.

"It's only change," she said out loud, to whatever powers and forces in the universe might be listening. "I didn't have to leave this home because I did something wrong. Nothing's ended, nothing's lost. This is a new chapter in the life of Cynda Flynn."

Part of her right tunic sleeve smoldered and started to melt. She swore and tore it off, then stamped it out beside the table.

It would leave a black mark on Riana's new carpet, to go with the black marks all across Riana's bedroom wall downstairs.

Those black marks would say, *Cynda was here.*

Cynda whispered, "And don't you forget it."

Then, before she could cry or set fire to anything else, Cynda collected her Celtic broadsword from the stairwell closet and made her exit from the brownstone.

(4)

Nick stared at the road as he guided the Jeep down the FDR Drive toward East Thirteenth, in Manhattan's East Village. It was hard, keeping his mind where it needed to be, with Cynda in the vehicle.

With Cynda anywhere near him.

Had been since the day he met her, but now it was worse.

An announcer on the radio talked about the record amount of precipitation New York City was experiencing. Nick edged through the light snow and stop-and-go early-morning traffic, and squinted into the gray winter daylight. Cynda's soft smell of vanilla and cinnamon kept distracting him from his view of the East River, but he didn't mind.

Sonofabitch.

Was *that* why Creed hadn't worked to change the brownstone into more of a guy space? Did his twin actually enjoy the feel and smell of his new wife lingering around every corner?

Wife. Shit.

Like I'd ever let a woman risk being that close to me.

His gaze drifted from cabs to buses and back to Cynda.

She was so beautiful with her wild red hair and burned-up tunic and jeans. She didn't give a damn about all the burn holes. Just took them in stride. Being a fire Sibyl probably made her accept more than a lot of people.

Like me?

Crazy-assed thought.

He needed to take her to bed. Yesterday. But screwing was screwing. Sex didn't have to mean relationships and futures and weddings. Besides, women who stayed too close to him for too long tended to end up dead. He didn't need that kind of entanglement, and he didn't think Cynda wanted it, either.

Except, he *did* want to kiss her again. Now. He wanted to pull the Jeep over, grab her, and look into those green eyes. He'd had his share of women, but no question Cynda put them all to shame.

All that spark. All that *fire*.

"Max Moses lives here?" Cynda asked as Nick pulled into a parking space near the Jacob Riis Houses and flipped his police placard onto the dashboard. "They've been fixing these places up, haven't they?"

"Much as they can. Max's mother lives in that building." He pointed.

Cynda shot Nick an uncomfortable frown. "We're leaning on the guy's mother? That's pretty low."

"You haven't met Delilah." Nick turned off the Jeep. "Leave your sword in the car."

He pocketed the keys and got out as she glared at him, but she unbelted the sword and placed it on the floorboard. As she opened her door and let in a spit of white flakes, Nick kept a sharp eye on her. She'd kept her word about not running out the back of the brownstone, but the whole bodyguard issue pissed her off. Sooner or later, she'd do *something* stupid. He was sure of it.

As soon as Cynda was clear of the Jeep, Nick flanked her, keeping his body between her and the street. Trouble could hit from any side, but he figured the tenement's grounds were a safer bet than the road.

He and Cynda didn't speak as he guided her toward one of the thirteen multiangled brick high-rises that made up the main section of the Jacob Riis Houses. The building he needed had about twelve floors, dingy brown brick but washed and clean, and with a rehabilitated children's park directly in front. The reds and yellows of the park rides and toys stood in contrast to the older, tired building behind it.

"Sixth floor," he told Cynda as they walked inside.

The elevators, of course, were out of order, so they took the six flights of stairs. Even with all the polishing, painting, and fixing up, graffiti made a comeback here in a hurry. So did the stink of bleach and piss.

Nick glanced at Cynda. She didn't so much as wrinkle her pretty nose. Most people would have been gagging, unless they wore a badge. As they left the stairwell, she seemed almost relaxed, laid-back, or disinterested. A casual observer would take her for an easy mark.

Big mistake.

Cynda noticed everything.

Nick watched as she scanned in front of her, beside her, behind her, like the most seasoned cop, aware of every little piece and part of the environment. No doubt she'd remember facial details of the few people they had passed on the grounds, in the entry, and the one or two who brushed by in the stairwells.

Impressive.

Once they reached the door to Delilah Moses's apartment, Nick gestured for Cynda to stand to one side, and he did the same. Better safe than sorry with this pistol of a woman.

He knocked. "Delilah?" He waited a few seconds, knocked again. "It's Nick Lowell."

From inside the apartment came a distinctive, predictable grunt, followed by, "What's the useless streak of piss done *now*, cop?"

"She's Irish," Cynda muttered. "Old school."

Nick put his finger to his lips, then said, "Just need to find him. Give us a hand?"

The sound of locks and chains being removed echoed in the otherwise quiet hallway, along with some swearing, and, "May the devil take that boy sideways, all the trouble he brings to my door."

Cynda's brows came together. She relaxed her arms at her sides, keeping both hands free, loose and ready to fight off a potential threat.

Again, Nick was impressed. Cynda would have made a good cop.

The door opened with a squeak and a scrape.

Delilah looked a lot older than the last time Nick saw her, what, two or three months ago? Stark white hair now, trapped in a frizzy bun. She'd lost weight and added wrinkles, too.

Why the big change?

Her cloudy brown eyes cut toward Cynda.

"She's with me." Nick said. "Name's Cynda."

"Her shirt's got holes in it," Delilah grumbled as she admitted them to her small one-bedroom unit. "Pants, too."

Nick automatically catalogued his surroundings. Like everything else at the Jacob Riis Houses, her unit had a newish coat of off-white paint, already dingy from city air. Her small living area boasted only a three-seater sofa, a chair, a television, and a couple of end tables. Off the living area on one side was a kitchen, and on the opposite side were the closed doors to the bedroom and bathroom, which Nick had searched several times before. His enhanced senses told him nobody lurked behind those doors. It was just him and Cynda and Delilah.

His eyes watered at the stink clinging to everything. Mild skunk with a lot of garlic, coupled with spicy meat and yeast. He coughed even though he was trying not to.

Cynda took a deep breath, like the stench was heaven

itself. "Corned beef and cabbage. Brown bread." She smiled. "Those were my favorites growing up. That and Dublin coddle."

"I go a little heavy on the parsley, and my bacon's smoked when I make coddle," Delilah said as she seated herself in the single chair, sounding like a happy girl instead of the mean viper Nick knew her to be. Ignoring him, she asked Cynda, "*Fíor-Ghaeltacht?*"

Cynda nodded. "I was raised in a valley near Connemara." She settled on the end of the couch nearest Delilah, where the woman had beckoned for her to sit.

Delilah glanced from Cynda's red hair to her burned shirt and jeans. "Connemara, you say. Well." She sucked in air, let it out, then gazed into Cynda's eyes. "I think I understand."

Nick sat on the other end of the couch and watched as the two women seemed to speak a language all their own. He felt a step behind, and definitely to the side. Left out completely.

"Do you, now?" Cynda asked in a gentle yet challenging voice. "Do you really understand?"

Nick winced. He tensed and waited for one of Delilah's tirades, but the old woman just averted her gaze from Cynda's.

Modest, almost, studying her knees.

Nick leaned back on the couch, too surprised to say a word.

Delilah Moses raised her eyes to his and said, "Hear me, cop. Take your lady far away. Things aren't safe for her kind here."

Nick's mouth came open, but he clamped it shut.

Cynda's expression never changed. She looked unnaturally calm and peaceful. If it weren't for the holes in her tunic and jeans, she might as well have been one of those beatific statues in a church.

This is totally fucked up. Nick managed to yank out

his notebook and pen. "Why should I take her away, Delilah?"

"Rats eat yer meat, man." The old woman's expression turned sour, more normal. "Just do as I say."

Nick held back a grin. Now *this* was Delilah. "What's Max gotten himself into?"

Delilah waved a thickly veined hand. "Like I know. The cocknose ratbark." She made a noise as if she was thinking about spitting, but didn't. "If it's not one set of hoodlums, it's another. God gives the boy a gift, a prescience, and he pisses it away on Guinness and the ponies. This time, though . . ." She touched her head, chest, and both shoulders, crossing herself as if to ward off evil. "This time it's him who'll answer to Saint Peter, not me. I taught him right and true, you understand?"

This last question was directed at Cynda, who granted Delilah a dignified nod, which seemed to make the old woman feel better.

What am I missing? Nick didn't like being out of the know, but in his gut, he trusted Cynda. Any idiot could see her presence had mellowed Delilah, and they'd already gotten more out of the old crone than Nick expected.

Once more, Delilah looked at Nick, and jerked a thumb toward Cynda. "Take her away from here. Tonight. Don't wait."

"What's the threat?" Nick asked.

Delilah shook her head. "Wish I knew. I'd be spillin' it in a second—for her." She smiled at Cynda in a way that made Nick wonder what the old woman was seeing.

"Is Max part of the threat?" Nick kept his pen ready.

"That piss artist is mixed up with everything shady, may the cat eat him." Delilah settled against her chair arm, easing closer to Cynda as she spoke. "Especially this bunch of beggars callin' themselves the Legion."

Cynda's spine straightened. She leaned forward and

gave Delilah an earnest, searching look. "Do you know the name of the person he's working for in the Legion?"

Nick took a breath and held it.

Delilah crossed herself again, and Cynda didn't push her.

Well, if she couldn't—or wouldn't—he would. "How about the man's name?"

Delilah looked at Cynda and sighed. "Men. Always assumin' they're in power, yes?"

Cynda smiled, but her green eyes gave a wicked flash as she glanced at Nick and said, "Absolutely."

Delilah glared at Nick. "It's no man, ya whiskey-dick. It takes a woman to get this devious. This . . . evil." She crossed herself twice this time.

Nick cleared his throat. "Give me *her* name?"

Delilah's eyes grew hard and flinty. Like Cynda right before a fire explosion. Nick half expected the couch beneath him to start crackling and smoking.

"And if I hang myself out to dry for you, cop . . ." She pointed a crooked finger right at Nick's nose. "Will you be mindin' what I said and takin' your lady out of this city?"

Nick stole a glance at Cynda, who nodded imperceptibly. She was sitting so still, so careful and regal, she could have passed for royalty.

"Yes," he said, wondering if he was lying. and why it mattered.

"You're lyin' to an old woman, but I'll tell ya anyway. I got part of the name. Initials, mostly." Delilah gestured to Nick's pad. "Write this down. J. C. Downy. That's who signed Max's checks, like it's all up-and-up and legitimate, though God knows, it's not." She rolled her eyes. "Good sums. Trying to make him dress nicer, too, and stay off the weed and drink some." She shrugged. "It may work a while, but if you go puttin' silk on a goat, it's still a goat. He'll be back to his old ways in no time."

"Thank you," Cynda said before Nick could respond. "What can I give you in return for taking this risk with your life and Max's on my behalf?"

"Wait a minute," Nick began, but Cynda cut him off with a glare that would have melted Queen Elizabeth's ass to her throne.

"Two things," Delilah said, clearly ignoring Nick, and clearly expecting and waiting for the offer Cynda made. "The first is my boy, Max. He's a whiskey-dick like this'un here, for sure. This cop won't be takin' you away, and you'll pay for that, mark my words. But Max's my blood. The boy's all I've got. If ever he comes into your sight, don't kill him unless you've no other choice—and make sure whatever's left of him gets back to me for fixin'."

Nick sat, disbelieving, as Cynda agreed. "I give you my word I'll do whatever I can."

Delilah's smile looked both shy and frightened. "And the second—that word of yours. Will you seal it in the old way?"

Cynda's eyebrows came together, but just as quickly, she relaxed.

Before Nick could tell her not to or ask what that was supposed to mean, Cynda offered Delilah her hand.

Delilah looked at Cynda's palm and waited.

Little flames broke out on Cynda's skin, small, tightly controlled.

A sound of wonderment escaped Delilah. "Knew I was right. Yes, I did."

Quickly, she took hold of Cynda's hand, and the two of them pressed out the flames with the force of their grips.

Nick knew Cynda had managed the fire so the old woman wouldn't receive any serious burns, but he still didn't have a clue why the handshake was happening.

Delilah Moses stared at the soft red streaks on her

hand like she had just been touched by an angel. She let out a long, satisfied sigh and said, "Max has been keepin' himself at East River Park, or up in Central Park—and sometimes over in Washington Heights. I don't think he's about today, though. I think he's gone to see *her*. The high-and-mighty Missus Downy. One of her places is somewhere north. The Bronx, maybe up by the Sound. I don't know the rest of 'em."

Nick scribbled that down. Surprise on top of surprise. The last time he'd had a chat with Delilah, the old woman had almost shot him in the foot to protect Max. Yet she just handed Cynda information for a bargain and a flaming handshake.

Delilah saw them to the door of her apartment like they were old friends, gabbling on to Cynda in her heavy brogue about something called treacle and the best brown bread she ever ate, and some abbey in Ireland, near where Cynda was raised. When they stepped out into the hall, though, the old woman didn't shut the door.

Instead, she stood looking expectantly at Cynda.

What now? Nick gripped his notebook, watching both women.

Cynda raised her right hand, thought for a moment, then said, "Walls for the wind, a roof for the rain, and drinks beside the fire." She moved her hand, and a tight ring of fire sprouted on the outside of the woman's door, etching a pattern that looked like three spirals contained in a larger circle, just above the little gold apartment numbers. "Laughter to cheer you, those you love near you, and all that your heart may desire."

Once more, Delilah reverted to a young child and actually clapped her hands. "Thank you, lady. I never thought to be blessed by one such as you. You've brightened an old woman's life."

Cynda's graceful tilt of her head was her only answer.

Delilah made a little curtsy, like European women gave royalty. To Nick, she said, "Long travels to ya, cop."

"Long travels," he repeated, then realized the old witch had insulted him by hoping he'd leave, that she wouldn't see him, for a long, long time. His face went hot.

Before he could take her to task, Delilah slipped back inside and shut the apartment door. The design in the wood over the apartment number still glowed a faint red.

It gradually stopped smoking.

Nick stared at Cynda.

"It's an Irish thing," she said in low tones. "Older people know about fire Sibyls, and they treat us like fae, or nuns—well, more like priests, really. Druid style. It gets all mixed up in pagan rituals, saints and Catholicism."

Nick had no idea what to say to that.

Cynda frowned and waved a hand. "Never mind. Look, she knew I was a Sibyl, and because of that, she put her life at risk to give us that information. That means I owe her certain things, like granting reasonable requests and offering protections. In turn, she'll do whatever she can to help me in the future. That's the way our world works, Nick. Rules. Just like cop-rules—only, lots older. You never know when old-school bargains might come in handy."

Nick gestured to the still-glowing design on the door. "And that?"

"A Celtic symbol for birth, death, and infinity." Cynda admired her handiwork. "It should keep away most minor demons and spells, but Captain Freeman should send a car over here. Downy might find out Delilah opened up to us, and I want her to have protection, at least for a while."

Nick glared for a second, then realized she was right and he swore. The whole time he was making the call to

HQ on his cell, he had to say inner mantras to calm himself and back down a notch before his skin glowed any brighter.

The amused look on Cynda's face didn't help one damned bit.

As they headed back for the stairwell, Nick asked, "What you promised Delilah about Max—could you clue me in?"

Cynda shrugged. "If Max needs to be shot, you'll have to pull the trigger, not me. That's all."

Nick stopped at the stairwell door, blood pounding in his temples. "That's *all*? You're making ancient blood oaths or fire oaths or whatever the hell that was—about which perps you'll defend yourself against and which ones you won't—and that's *all*?"

"Look, you're the one who wanted to be my shadow," Cynda snapped, shoulders smoking. "I only came because you made me. But—what? I was supposed to be demure and quiet while you played big bad cop? Sorry, I don't work that way."

She started down the steps.

Nick caught a whiff of smoke and glanced down at his boots.

The laces glowed red and dropped to the stairwell in little burning bits. He stamped out the embers and glared at the retreating fire Sibyl.

Swear to God, if I didn't have to guard her, I'd handcuff her and lock her in a basement.

Instead, he hurried after her, shadowed her down the steps and out of the Jacob Riis Houses, and did his best to shield her on the way through the slush and snow, back to the Jeep. At least he got her inside it before more old Irish women tracked her down and asked for promises, incantations, or flame-coated handshakes.

No sooner did they get their belts fastened than his cell phone rang.

He checked the ID.

It was Creed.

"Hey, bro," Nick said when he answered. "We found—"

"We've got another dead fire Sibyl," Creed said through the speakerphone, loud enough for Cynda to hear.

She jerked her head up and gazed at Nick, horror and shock etched across her beautiful face.

Creed's voice sounded furious, but oddly flat. "Her triad found her in a dumpster near the brownstone. OCU's already on-scene."

He gave the nearest cross streets.

Nick punched off the phone, cranked Riana's Jeep, and rammed it into gear.

He didn't have to look at Cynda to know what she felt.

The entire Jeep gave off sparks.

Flames belched off the windshield as he squealed tires getting back on the FDR.

A mile or so later, when he took Cynda's hand, she was shaking.

Cynda didn't say anything, but she didn't let him go, and she didn't blow up the Jeep, either.

(5)

Cynda felt completely numb except for the spot where her hand touched Nick's. The world around her didn't seem real at all.

Another dead Sibyl?

Another dead sister?

How could this be happening?

She tried to swallow, but her closed, tight throat wouldn't cooperate.

As Manhattan raced by outside the Jeep's windows, she couldn't process anything past the unnaturally bright sunlight.

Who had died?

And how?

She had a brief mental image of finding one of *her* triad dead, and felt it like a gut-punch. Her hand drifted to her belly. That would tear out her soul. How could anyone survive such a loss?

Cynda glanced at Nick, suddenly more grateful than she ever thought she could be for his offer of protection. She was so damned stubborn. If it had been anybody but Riana, Merilee, and Nick trying to keep her under wraps—she could have been the fire Sibyl dead in that dumpster.

I'm an idiot. About that. And everything else.

"What if your brother Jake wasn't trying to help us in that alley, Nick?" She squeezed his fingers, breathing in his ocean-musk scent to keep her mind clear. "What if he's involved in these terrible things? We should tell Riana and Merilee what we saw."

The pressure on her hand didn't change, but Nick's expression grew impossibly dark. "Whatever you think you have to do."

"Don't shut down on me." She jerked her hand away from his. "I don't want to see Jake hurt—or you. Talk to me."

She got a look from him that said *Thanks, but I'd rather die.*

Aloud, Nick said, "Some things don't require discussion."

Cynda yanked back her fire before it melted the rearview mirror. "What, like your parents' deaths?"

Nick gripped the wheel so hard his knuckles went white. "They weren't my parents."

"Davin and Raven Latch created your biological material." Cynda wished she hadn't let go of his hand. The physical connection might have helped her get through to him. "You saw your father dead, and you killed your mother to save us all. That was only four months ago. It's still fresh."

Nick's voice plunged so low it sounded like a growl. "Drop it, Cynda."

"You have to face it. Clearing the air makes people sharper, Nick." Heat moved around the Jeep, responding to the surge in Cynda's energy. "You can't separate Jake from what happened to your parents. The Latches made his genetic material, too. Do you think you owe Jake something because of how they died?"

"Off . . . limits." Nick was talking through his teeth now.

The windshield cracked down the middle, black lines on either side of the split. Heat. Pure heat. Cynda barely kept herself from setting the seats on fire as she faced Nick. "Why is it off-limits?"

Nick glared straight ahead as they shot toward Central Park. His skin glowed a faint gold from head to toe, and when he spoke, his words echoed with the force of his very, very near *other*. "Not a damned thing I can do to change it, is there?" He gave Cynda a quick glance, and she didn't miss the blaze of gold demon shining through his black eyes. "I'd kill the bitch again if I had to. What do you want from me?"

Cynda went still. Her heart slammed against her ribs, and she sucked in hot breaths of air and smoke, of flames and the tangy, alien energy of Nick's *other*.

She bit her lip to keep her mouth shut as Nick turned his attention back to the road. As the blocks and minutes passed, his unnatural glow subsided. The miserable, thunderous look on his face did not.

Cynda felt as if a steel curtain had slammed down between them—or more specifically, wrapped itself around Nick. The sudden separation and distance hurt so badly it sat like a ton weight in her belly.

Nick had sealed himself behind a wall of pain, unreachable. Unapproachable. Every instinct, all her training, told Cynda to storm that wall, burn it down, blow it apart. That's what fire Sibyls did. They communicated. They forced other Sibyls to communicate, even when they didn't want to, even when it hurt.

She eyed Nick, imagining she could see the golden shape and form of the demon-half who shared his skin.

Yeah. I make other Sibyls communicate. Not other . . . others.

But what was she going to do about Jake, and about talking to her triad?

It was clear Nick didn't think his demon-brother was involved. That Nick wanted—*needed*—more time to find Jake, talk to him, try to understand where he stood in this battle between the Legion and the Sibyls.

Could she give him that?

What would it do to her triad, to her Sibyls, if she chose to let Nick have that time?

What would it do to Nick if she didn't?

She lurched in her seat as Nick hit the brakes at the end of an alley behind a building on Sixty-fourth, a few yards back from a collection of flashing lights, marked and unmarked vehicles, and police personnel. He parked the Jeep at a curb, repositioned the police placard, got out, and slammed the door.

Cynda expected him to go striding toward the crime scene, which was ribboned with police tape, but he waited, tapping his hand on the Jeep's hood as she unfastened her seat belt, opened her door, and forced herself into the cold winter morning.

When she joined him in front of the vehicle, his stone face softened a fraction. He didn't touch her, but he looked like he wanted to, at least a little bit, and that meant everything.

"I don't want to fight with you, firebird," he said.

Cynda held his gaze. "I know."

"We're built different, you and me."

"I know that, too."

Nick nodded.

For now, Cynda figured that would have to be enough.

"You ready?" Nick asked, inclining his head toward the chaos of the murder scene.

Cynda clamped her teeth together and set her jaw. Nausea rolled through her, washing back and forth, back and forth in her tight stomach, and she was already starting to smoke at the neck and elbows. Still, she knew she had to do this. She wanted to see the dead Sibyl, wanted to find out everything she could. Understand. Evaluate. Then track down the killers and fry them in the hottest fire ever made.

Nick took Cynda's elbow. "Come on. I won't let you go."

He led her forward, and she didn't resist. She tried to

focus on his touch, on his towering presence beside her. Even when he was a total ass, he was supportive in his own way. No matter what, he was there. Right there.

Seconds later, he took her through a side barrier, after he flashed his shield and she showed her ancillary credentials, something the OCU had created just for the Sibyls, for situations where they might be needed ... like this.

Crime-scene workers clogged the mouth of the alley, dropping numbered markers, sketching, photographing, and making notes. Cynda noticed the telltale stench of burned human flesh, charred bone, and incinerated hair. Her eyes began to water, and her throat clamped shut. Nothing in the world smelled so distinctive, or so gut-wrenchingly horrible.

Burned? How? How did someone—or something—burn a fire Sibyl?

Her stomach rebelled, but she warmed herself with all the heat energy she could draw, pushing the sick sensation down until she could breathe without vomiting.

She and Nick moved forward, toward Creed and Andy, who were standing with the OCU captain Sal Freeman by a taped-off dumpster.

Andy looked uncharacteristically miserable, so pale Cynda was worried that she'd puke, or just fall down.

Then Cynda saw why.

Crime-scene workers swarmed the dumpster like worker bees, processing, shifting, sifting, carefully moving and replacing items near what had to be the body. A scorched nub of a human hand protruded above the dumpster's metal lip. Just a nub. All the fingers had been seared off.

And it's one of my friends. One of my family.

She stopped, yanking her elbow loose from Nick's grip.

He stopped beside her and didn't try to force her to

keep walking. He just scanned the area around them once, twice, and again.

Cynda saw him from the corner of her eye, but she couldn't rip her attention from the burned hand in the dumpster.

Dear, sweet Goddess.

Cynda felt the horrible reality in her mind, her heart, her bones.

She blinked back tears. Fire snapped and arced over her head as she battled rage and disbelief.

No being could kill a fire Sibyl with her own element unless she was unconscious, unrousable. She must have been taken by surprise, overwhelmed. More than one attacker—a lot more.

Like the ambush in the alley.

"Monsters," Cynda muttered.

Nick put his hand on her shoulder and glanced down at her, eyebrows raised.

Cynda shook her head. *Not yet.* She told him with her eyes. *I can't.*

He gave a single nod and went back to standing beside her, watching left, watching right. Guarding. Protecting.

Dimly, Cynda saw a car approaching, backing slowly toward the police barricades. That would be the coroner arriving. No one would move the deceased until he made his initial assessment and bagged everything to protect trace evidence.

When she turned her head toward the opposite end of the alley, she saw a contingent of Sibyls. Riana and Merilee held tight to Serlena and Tavis, the earth Sibyl and air Sibyl of the South Manhattan group. They were newer to New York City, having come from their Motherhouses a few months ago to replace members lost in the big Legion battle.

Poor Maura, the fire Sibyl in South Manhattan, had been left all alone, devastated by the loss of her triad sisters, and then she had to face the formidable task of accepting and training not one but two new and very green warriors.

Bit by bit, the meaning of the scene seeped into Cynda's awareness even as she tried to shove it back out.

"No," she said out loud, but the sound didn't change anything at all.

Her chest ached so hard she thought it might split from the weight of her own grief. In the dumpster.

The fragment of the burned hand protruding over the trash bin's metal edge—

That's Maura's hand.

It's Maura who died.

Flames roared from her hands even as she staggered from the realization.

Nick caught her and glowed, absorbing the heat. "Suck up that fire. You'll contaminate evidence."

Cynda wanted to beat the man to death. She wanted to beat something, and he was handy. If he kept his hands on her, she would have had an excuse—but he didn't.

The second her fire eased, he let her go and went right back to his silent watch.

Clouds swirled around Cynda, inside and out. She could barely think. Waves of heat rose from all of her limbs, and it was all she could do to keep new fire from breaking out everywhere, everywhere, and burning forever.

She had just seen Maura, what, a week ago?

Maura, who was just like her. Big mouth. Bigger temper. Hell with that big African *shotel* she carried—the blade curved so harsh and sicklelike it seemed to want blood.

Drawing air and shoving it out again, Cynda stared at the burned hand. Her vision wavered.

Who got you, honey?

Blasphemy.

A fire Sibyl burned to death.

Maura.

Cynda whipped toward the bereaved members of Maura's triad.

What did they do? What did they *not* do?

"Easy, firebird," Nick said in a low, private tone. "Don't say something you'll regret."

Nick's voice jarred Cynda. Flames spiked from her ears and hips.

But through her buzzing, buzzing mind, sounds slowly penetrated.

"We were trying to look after her, but she wouldn't stay, wouldn't listen," the little air Sibyl Tavis said to Merilee between rib-racking sobs.

"She went out by herself," Serlena, the young earth Sibyl, added, hanging on to Riana. "Said she needed to clear her head, think, see what connections she could make or find."

"We thought she might be heading to the brownstone to talk to you, or maybe the townhouse to find Cynda." Serlena pointed north, toward the Reservoir. "It was daytime. Morning. We didn't think—we followed, but not close enough. Not close enough! We didn't even see what got her."

Riana held the girl as she cried, stroking her dark hair.

Cynda's fingers curled. She wanted to comfort the young Sibyl—and screech at her until the girl spilled how the triad could have been so close, yet too far away to save Maura's life.

Does it matter? She's dead. She's gone forever.

Even though she didn't want to, Cynda gazed at Serlena and Tavis. Somewhere in her angry, aching heart, she knew they'd never get over this. They'd move on, fight in some other triad. But Maura's death would haunt them the way it would haunt Cynda. They would all carry an empty spot where Maura should have been, until they returned to Motherhouse Ireland for that final rest.

Captain Freeman gestured toward the Sibyls at the mouth of the alley. "Here comes the coroner and his people. Get the Sibyls out of here before the regulars and the press show up." The tall officer's handsome face tightened, and his voice dropped. "For now, this is just your garden-variety fucked-up slaughter. No supernatural elements. Got me?"

Assents from everyone, even Cynda.

Andy stayed next to Freeman, looking exhausted, but taking dictation as he barked other ideas and instructions. Creed headed for the Sibyls.

Cynda's instinct was to follow him, help with Serlena and Tavis, but Nick grabbed her arm before she took a step. "No way you're going anywhere without me. Especially not now."

Rage welled in Cynda, sending sparks into the dumpster, which made Nick squeeze her arm all the harder. "Stop. Now."

Hating him, despising his rationality, Cynda focused all her energy on yanking her fire power back inside her own skin.

Meanwhile, another group of Sibyls, dressed completely in black, emerged from the far end of the alley, walking slowly.

Cynda immediately recognized the earth Sibyl in the lead, with her exotic, slanted eyes and her dark hair pulled back in a severe bun, accentuating the aquiline nose and high cheekbones. Harder than steel, and just as deadly, Bela Argos made her approach to the bereaved triad, with her air Sibyl Devin close at her side.

Just the sight of Bela, the dignified Sibyl's grief over the loss of her own fire Sibyl Nori, took Cynda's breath. And all of her fight.

Bela looked so much like Riana. She *was* so much like the mortar of Cynda's triad, it was like looking into a mirror showing the future.

If I died, Riana would look just like that.

Riana's heart would be broken. All that made her proud and brilliant and so incredibly powerful would be diminished for a long, long time. And Devin, the air Sibyl, the way she was frowning, the way the light in her eyes had gone dark and the wind wouldn't even touch her hair—that would be Merilee.

The North Queens triad arrived, and North Brooklyn, plus the ranger group handling the north Bronx, too. Together with Bela Argos and Devin, they took Serlena and Tavis in hand. There were enough fire Sibyls to manage communications and transports, though it might be some time before Maura's body could be taken home to be laid to rest in Ireland.

"Get me her blade," Cynda said to Nick, who looked at her like she was a few cranks past overwound.

"It might have evidence—"

Flames hissed on Cynda's fingertips. "The Mother-houses are just as capable of evaluating trace evidence as the NYPD. More so, if it's blood evidence." She gestured to the departing Sibyls, strewing smoke and sparks. "They need something to grieve, to have, to hold, until they can take Maura home. The Mothers will analyze everything twice as fast and send the results back to us. Give me that *shotel*—unless you and Freeman want to try to explain what it is to the medical examiner and the reporters."

Nick gave her a long, frustrated look, but, keeping an eye on her with every step, he approached Sal Freeman, Creed, and Andy. For a few seconds, he spoke to them in a low voice.

Freeman glanced from Nick to Creed to Andy to

Cynda, then to the dumpster, which, oddly enough, suddenly seemed to have a sheen of water running down its gray metal sides.

A few seconds later, Freeman spoke to the OCU crime-scene technicians.

One of the worker bees immediately dipped into the dumpster and reemerged with a wet plastic evidence bag. Handling the package very carefully, the technician transferred it to Freeman, who stepped over the increasing slick of water and gave it to Nick.

"Did somebody bash a spigot?" Freeman bellowed. "Find that tap—shut it the hell off before we wash away something important!"

More technicians scattered in different directions, examining the wall and the dumpster for the source of the water flow.

Nick gestured for Cynda to follow, and the two of them headed down the alley toward the slowly progressing parade of Sibyls.

Riana must have sensed their approach, because she held up her hand for the women to stop.

As Nick and Cynda reached the group, Bela Argos stiffened visibly. She pulled Serlena against her and gave Nick the kind of mistrustful, angry look most Sibyls used to give Creed before he won his acceptance and his position as Riana's husband.

Cynda recognized that expression because she had worn it often enough herself, when Creed first came into their lives.

So now it was Nick, the odd man out, the one who had to prove himself?

After all he had done to save Sibyl lives?

Oh, no way. No way at all.

Cynda wound up to read Bela the riot act, but Nick stopped her with a single warning look.

Avoiding confrontation with Bela, he simply surrendered Maura's curved African blade to Riana, saying, "Cynda wanted them to have this."

Riana turned the evidence package over in her hands. "It needs to be analyzed."

"Motherhouse Russia can do that," Bela Argos said, her voice colder than the winter air. Her gaze raked across Nick, then Cynda. The hatred and suspicion wavered, shifting back to the flat, devastated sorrow that so wounded Cynda when she first saw it.

"Thank you," Bela added, as Serlena and Tavis cried and reached to take Maura's *shotel*.

At least the blade would be something.

For now, it would have to do.

Riana and Merilee stayed back as the group of Sibyls once more processed into the far reaches of the alley, moving until they turned the corner, and left Cynda's line of sight.

She realized Riana and Merilee had her arms, that they were holding on to her so very tightly, as if they were afraid it would soon be them cradling Cynda's Celtic broadsword as their last remnant of her.

"It won't happen," she assured them. "I've got you two. And I've got Nick." She looked at him, at his surprised expression. "I promise on my oath as a Sibyl I'll let you all watch my back. And I promise I'll be careful."

One at a time, Riana and Merilee hugged her, and thanked her, and made her feel like a total ass for ever resenting the protection they offered and arranged. It was for her, sure, of course—but more important, Cynda now realized, it was for them, too.

That's what families did, right?

Families looked after their own.

She'd do well to remember that, about herself, and about Nick and Creed and Jake.

Over the top of Merilee's blond head, as Cynda held

her triad sister, she locked eyes with Nick and tried to let her gaze tell him everything.

I understand now.

A little more time—just a little, get a move on—but yes, a little more time for you and Jake.

Aloud, she said, "Families take care of their own."

At that, a look of relief flickered across Nick's dark, handsome features. He nodded once, then immediately went back to scanning the alley, up and down, back and forth, taking care of Cynda.

(6)

Tuesday morning, a day after Maura's death, Nick stood in the corner of Cynda's room, arms folded, eyes alert, watching the fire Sybil communicate with the Motherhouses in Greece, Ireland, and Russia.

Cynda's dancing—the best part of the whole show, the part that blew open the ancient mystical channels linking the projective mirrors on her walls—was already over. Nick's blood still thrummed from watching her whirl and leap. Every move made his cock ache.

He studied her in her sexy green shirt and those ass-hugging jeans. She had an athlete's arms, delicate, yet solid, as she gestured and explained. Her red curls, wilder than ever, hung in ringlets against her pretty face and ears.

Beautiful.

Sexy.

And mine.

Soon.

Guarding her, watching her virtually every waking minute of every day—

Soon.

At least Cynda was seeing reason now, and not complaining about staying with him or with her triad at all times. He did not want to be digging her or any other fire Sybil out of a dumpster ever again. The thought of it felt like hot spikes in his gut.

Cynda spoke in Irish dialect to an ancient-looking woman in green robes, reporting that Maura, the dead

Sibyl, had apparently been staked through the heart, pitched into the dumpster, and set ablaze.

Staked. Old-martyr style.

That still bugged him.

Wasn't that what some countries did to witches early in the last millennium? Witches and vampires, or other evil creatures.

Nick glanced at the mirror.

Was that wrinkled crone behind the glass studying him?

Yeah.

Like scientists studied diseases under a microscope.

Was this witch one of the ancient Sibyl leaders he had heard so much about? If so, meeting the Mothers just moved to the top spot on Nick's I'll-take-a-pass list.

To keep his mind off the old woman's staring, Nick focused on Cynda and her room instead. He was glad that the fire-breathing redhead had chosen the L-shaped corner suite of the mansion-sized townhouse when she moved in, on the third floor overlooking the front entrance, near his own room.

Convenient.

In pretty good shape, too, if you didn't count the water stains at the ceiling corners, and on the wall by the door. Plumbing in the entire townhouse had fallen apart in the last few months. Nick was working on that, but progress was slow. Damned leaks seemed to play hide-and-seek.

Cynda had installed a new four-poster bed with gauzy white drapes on one end, next to the refurbished stone fireplace big enough for a witch's cauldron. The other side of the suite had been painted a light lavender, way too bright. That space was mostly consumed by the hanging mirrors anyway, and runes tacked to the walls, and in front of it all, that gigantic wooden table Cynda stood on to do her dance—similar to the table back at the brownstone the triad sisters had shared. The platform had big metal underpinnings, as well as a smooth, polished surface and a lead-lined trench carved around the edge. Stupid thing was big enough to hold half the Cirque du Soleil, if those freaks chose to show up and perform in a place now widely rumored to be haunted.

The OCU and the Sibyls had, of course, redecorated the place since they took possession of the dwelling owned by Nick and Creed on the Upper East Side near the Reservoir. The five-story Federal-style brick townhouse had, after all, belonged to their father and mother. The parents who died.

The mother I killed.

Nick tensed, remembering his earlier conversation with Cynda about Senator Davin Latch and his wife, Raven. Nick didn't want to give them the honor of calling them parents, even though a big part of him remembered them that way. Sick, twisted—but parents, who took some pride in what they had created, and the potential Nick and Creed showed.

Those maniacs were not *parents. More like donors. Yeah. Sperm and egg donors.*

He had no need to go there. The Latches and all their madness were over. He did what had to be done.

His gut ached like it always did when he thought about that bloody scene four months ago. Sweat coated his face and arms, even though he wasn't hot. Nick clenched his jaw and wished he could dig a knife in his chest and cut out those memories. He'd pitch 'em out the nearest window and never look back—but something Cynda said back in the Jeep kept bugging him.

"You can't separate Jake from what happened to your parents. . . . Do you think you owe Jake something because of how they died?"

Nick hadn't thought about it in just those words.

The heat on his face eased, and he forced his muscles to relax.

He didn't think he owed Jake anything, no. But . . . maybe Jake felt differently. Nick had an idea now about how to reach the Astaroth. Something he hadn't tried— at least not in the right way. He would, today, later.

His eyes moved on to Cynda's massive Celtic harp, dominating the corner of the room opposite that big table. Nick shook his head. Now *that* thing had been a pain to move. Two or three times, he had dented the floor with it, damaging their new HQ.

Well, HCQ.

Head Case Quarters, as every other precinct lovingly referred to the townhouse.

Plumbing issues aside, the place was pretty solid. At least they didn't have to deal with the press here. Besides, they couldn't have Sibyls and half demons whizzing in and out of the old Fourteenth Precinct, down on West Thirtieth. The police annex wasn't set up for that level of traffic, or for enough privacy to hide the real purpose of the OCU with so many new people involved. So, the OCU had moved operations to the townhouse. Here at HCQ, Sibyls and the OCU could interact freely, and without public scrutiny. Any public or media-related work would be conducted by the OCU alone, down at the little set of offices they maintained at the old Fourteenth.

A loud hiss from Cynda drew Nick's attention back to the redhead on the communications platform. Now Cynda seemed to be talking to women in blue and brown robes. At the other two Motherhouses, he presumed.

Whatever they were saying, it made Cynda frown.

At least the brown-robed crones and blue-robed harridans didn't seem interested in Nick like that one from Motherhouse Ireland.

The old woman in green was still glowering at him

through that other mirror, the one with the carved bog-oak frame that Cynda liked best. The crone's expression reminded Nick of how the Sibyls in the alley had regarded him, like he was a cross between cockroach and rat, though they hadn't said a word about why.

Nick felt Gideon rumble in the back of his mind, creeping forward, ready to help him face this threat, whatever it was.

He tried to brush Gideon backward, but the beast wouldn't go.

Clearly, the old woman in the green robes didn't have positive feelings toward Nick, if Gideon was so friggin' riled.

What, did she want his inner demon neutered the way Creed's had been?

Nick twitched at the thought. So did Gideon. Like a muscle spasm, only deep in Nick's brain. He rested his hand on the thick chain around his own neck. His talisman. The key to controlling the Gideon part of his essence.

We have different ways, Creed and I, he told that Gideon aspect of himself. *I would never let anyone melt you into me, or whatever those Russian Mothers did to Creed.*

Gideon responded with a peaceful, trusting silence, though Nick sensed his beast-half continued to keep a close watch on the crone in the green robes.

Abruptly, Cynda raised her hands.

The images in the mirror blurred and faded as the fire Sibyl danced quick circles on the table, arms up, fingers sweeping back and forth like she was literally clearing the air.

Nick kept his breathing even as he watched the magic unfold, from the way Cynda moved to the way the mirrors shuddered against the walls, changed in texture, seeming to grow two-dimensional again even as the energy in the room moved and shifted around Cynda.

She was the center of all things and reality in that moment, and then—then it was just over.

The pictures in the mirror, now flat and indistinct, slowly blinked into nothing, then into reflections of the bedroom. After a few more minutes of slower dancing, Cynda stopped, her chest rising and falling, rising and falling. She spoke some quiet words, then climbed off the table and walked toward Nick, frowning.

He didn't question her. In his months of knowing Cynda, he had learned that silence gave her more room to speak.

"That was harder than it should have been." She raised one hand and rubbed her eyes. "The Mothers are beside themselves, and the adepts, too. All of us, everywhere. It was so hard to concentrate. I kept screwing up the chants and dances like I was a novice—and I know they all noticed."

She hugged herself and looked absolutely fragile.

Nick ached to take her into his own arms and kiss away her stress and troubles, but he knew better. That would be like leaching a flame's oxygen until it snuffed into sparks and smoke. It was way too easy to smother Cynda. As much as it went against his instincts and tendencies, he did have to let her lead more often than he was accustomed to doing with anyone.

"Bela Argos made sure the Mothers got Maura's *shotel* right away." Cynda seemed to hug herself even tighter. "Won't take them long to get the results to us." She shivered as she continued. "They want us to stay together, the triads, in several large groups, scattered across the city. Three or six in any patrol or incident response."

Nick gave a nod of approval. "There *is* safety in numbers."

Cynda gazed up at him. "And safety in letting friends and family take care of you. Thank you for guarding me, Nick. I'm sorry I've been such a bitch about it."

The way her eyes flickered, the way she leaned toward him—it was too much to take.

Nick bit back a groan as he bent down and brushed her soft cheek with his lips. "I'll always keep you safe. I'll never let you get hurt again." He moved his mouth across her jaw, her chin.

Cynda responded, instant and certain, turning her mouth to his until they were kissing, deep and hard and full.

Nick pulled her closer, cupped her firm ass with both hands and squeezed until she moaned into his mouth. He could feel her nipples, hard and ready against his chest, and he wanted to take her right on her big table, pump himself into her this minute, this second.

She rolled her hips against his, grinding herself against his pulsing cock like she wanted the same thing, until he damned near lost control, until he almost picked her up and carried her to the huge slab of wood, tearing her clothes off with each step.

But she pulled back a second later and stopped him, palms against his chest, carefully pushing him away from her.

Body roaring in protest, Nick turned Cynda loose. She looked conflicted and uncomfortable, and her voice came out in a whisper as she said, "You've got another day to find Jake. That's all I can give you. I'm sorry."

Nick's chest tightened.

Don't push.

Fuck he wanted to. Push, grope, ignite, satisfy . . .

But she really was fragile right now. He could see it in those beautiful eyes, feel it in his blood, even though he wished he didn't. Her softness, the way she seemed like she might break from a single word, made him ache for her all the more.

He reached out and cupped her cheek, running his thumb along her jawline until he saw her shiver. She didn't ask him to stop, or turn her face away from his touch, so he stroked her jaw again. She seemed to loosen all over, as if she might want him to hold her after all.

"We'll talk about Jake later, firebird." Nick brushed her hair behind her ears, then risked a kiss to the top of her head, which she didn't resist. "And us."

"We say that a lot," she murmured, gazing up at him with those gorgeous green eyes. "Later for this, later for that. We're storing too many emotions and problems on back burners, don't you think?"

"Everything's staying warm." Nick lowered his head and moved his lips across her cheek, up, then down, toward her neck. At her ear, he said, "Some things might get hotter."

Cynda trembled outright, and moved into him, just a step, the slightest movement, but Nick savored the fresh brush of her body against his. When his fingers slid down to her neck, she caught them and, half-mad, half-playful, said, "Stop that."

He kept his eyes on hers and his hand wrapped in her fingers. "Do you really want me to stop?"

Cynda sucked in a breath. "No. Damn you."

She closed her eyes, then opened them and let go of his hand. "But we have to get back downstairs and deal with this J. C. Downy revelation."

Nick stroked her cheek once more, taking his time, reminding himself that he could be patient even if the top of his head blew off his body. Not to mention his cock. Waiting was what she needed right now, what she had to have.

He could give that to her.

Nick realized that if he could, he would give Cynda anything she wanted. Anything in the world.

When he nodded and took his hand from her face, Cynda's expression shifted between disappointment and relief—with a touch of the devil.

Be sure, firebird. Because I'm sure. And I'm not waiting much longer.

"Duty first," she said as she slipped around him and headed toward the door. "Pleasure later."

"I'll remember that," he muttered as she escaped the bedroom and started down the hall.

Nick made a quick check of his clothes and his already-laceless boots.

Nothing smoking or burning.

Miracle.

Less than fifteen minutes later, Nick sat next to his brother in the ballroom-turned–conference room, in a row of folding chairs, trying to pay attention to the daily briefing even though Creed was aggravating the living piss out of him.

"Her room's three doors from yours." Creed gave Nick's arm a punch. "Just knock and slip in one night, and give it to her fast and hard. She'll still respect you in the morning."

"If you weren't my brother, I'd let you go a round with my *other*," Nick said in a low, menacing tone.

Creed snorted. "I faced huge, snarling Russian wolves to get *my* woman. Surely you can handle a little fire."

"Don't start with the wolves again." Nick let Gideon's golden glow shine through his whole body. "I mean it."

Creed laughed some more, but shut up. Finally.

At the front of the room, Sal Freeman banged on a chalkboard and yammered at the group of twenty or so OCU officers. Cynda's triad, a ragtag group of ranger Sibyls, and triads from South Queens and North and South Brooklyn stood to the sides, listening.

The Sibyl numbers were dwindling fast.

Nick ground his teeth. Time to get a handle on this—now.

Freeman gave out the name of J. C. Downy, and set all the air Sibyls to researching it, as well as a few OCU officers with good electronic skills or archives connections. Everyone agreed the raid on the Bronx house should take a backseat to ferreting out Downy and bringing that witch in for questioning.

Cynda went next, relaying messages from the Mothers, along with the order to stay together at all costs.

As the meeting broke into smaller groups, Cynda faded off to talk more directly to the Sibyls. Creed gave Nick another two seconds of ribbing, then headed out of the conference room and down the long hall. Nick heard his brother's footsteps echo, then ascend the wood and marble staircase as he went to pick a room for himself and Riana, since the triad needed to stay under the same roof.

Because of Nick's symbiotic relationship with Gideon, his hearing remained unnaturally sharp, as did his eyesight. Near the conference room windows, he could see the gentle wisps of smoke rising from Cynda's clothes as she spoke in the hallway with Merilee and Riana. Andy stood off to the side wearing her sunglasses even though she was in the house, smoothing down her crazy auburn hair, and waving one hand to say, *Yeah, yeah, yeah. Hurry up.*

If Nick looked closer, really looked, using the full breadth and depth of the enhanced perception his partnership with Gideon allowed him to enjoy, he could see the ring of heat that clung to Cynda like a best friend, or a possessive, protective force. Merilee's ring of energy looked like a contained whirlwind, faint but definite, waxing and waning with her level of attention. Around Riana, the air didn't move at all, as if she centered it by her very presence. Andy . . . well, there was something around Andy, too, but the color and shape were ill defined. Bluish, chaotic, and a little thick, almost like a window Nick needed to polish with his elbow before he could see inside.

That Andy had a psychic residue didn't surprise Nick. In his experience, most officers in the OCU had some paranormal talent or other, whether they knew it or not. Probably why they were drawn to the service in the first place. He had often wondered if the same was true for similar police units worldwide, and figured that it was.

Yep. Here we are, all the freaks and geeks, NYPD and otherwise.

Welcome to Head Case Quarters.

Several hours later, as the arguing, planning, patrol assignments, and tactical diagrams reached their peak, Nick's mind wouldn't stay on the tasks at hand. He needed to find Jake, and with every passing second, that need increased.

Cynda was right. They couldn't keep the secret forever. He had to locate the boy—the man—the demon—whatever the hell he was.

Now.

Where to start was the only question, but after his conversation with Cynda in the Jeep, Nick kept coming up with the same answer.

Start where everything began—and where it all ended, too. He needed to seek Jake at the spot where they were most connected. If he were Jake, and they did share genetics, that's where he'd go to make sense out of things, find the answers he needed.

After making sure Cynda was with her triad, Nick excused himself from the strategy meetings, showered, and dressed in his single-weave tunic and pants. He didn't bother belting. He had long ago surpassed any belt a martial-arts training program could offer him, and he preferred the looser fit when he worked out.

Walking quietly to avoid attention from Sibyls and cops alike, he made his way down to the ground floor, then to the door that opened onto the steps leading down to the basement. The door was new, a replacement for the one that had been destroyed in the battle with the Latches last fall. This door had a lighter, safer feel to it, like it wasn't made to keep out enemies, or hold in horrors.

Yet another improvement. A door. Just a simple door.

Lights flooded the stairwell, too. Another plus, like the OCU photos tacked to the paneled walls, mixed with plaques that bore mottoes like *Fidelis ad mortem,* the NYPD pledge of "Faithful unto death," and the OCU slogan of *Consilio et animis,* "By wisdom and courage."

Nick descended the hardwood stairs, dodging stacks of books on war tactics, encyclopedias, and textbooks somebody had taken off the shelves of the townhouse's library, and found that some idiot had tacked up a small chalkboard near the bottom that read, *Credo Elvem ipsum etian vivere.*

Roughly translated, "Elvis lives."

That had to be Sal Freeman, just seeing if Nick was paying attention.

He wiped out the chalk and wrote, *Fac ut vivas.* "Get a life."

Then he opened the new lightweight wooden door at the bottom of the steps and walked into what was still his personal version of hell.

More a chamber than a basement, the huge, windowless stone room was at least brighter than it had been in the days of the Latches and the Legion. Lights blazed from everywhere, and the cold slab of the floor had rugs and exercise mats tossed in various positions. Straps, balls, and bars had been made available, too, for people who liked a more free-form workout that didn't involve treadmills or televisions. It smelled like leather and sweat, cleanser and air freshener down here now, instead of sandalwood, oil, and blood.

No more perverted rituals.

Just exercise.

And hopefully . . . a ghost. Of sorts.

Nick often put himself through his paces in this place, trying to get used to it, purge all the hated memories and images from his system.

Would Jake try for the same resolution?

If he's really on our side. If he's sane.

Sometimes Nick even sparred in the basement, if he could find Sal Freeman or talk somebody else into blocking his kicks and punches. Mostly, though, he forced himself to meditate in this room, this specific nightmare of a place. When he couldn't achieve that, he just sat and remembered—but not without purpose.

A few times, he could have sworn he wasn't in the basement alone.

At those moments, he had figured he was just on edge, but after everything with the paint can in the alley, and after what Cynda said in the Jeep—Nick was pretty sure he *hadn't* been alone.

Nick did a basic set of stretches near the spot where Riana had been forced to kill Davin Latch to save her own life.

That's where I saw my father. Already gone before I got here.

Nick didn't blame Riana for her actions. In fact, he thought she was a hero for giving the old bastard what he deserved.

If Cynda had been listening to his thoughts, Nick knew she would have tried to force him to say it wasn't easy, seeing his father dead on the townhouse's basement floor.

Okay, so it wasn't easy.

What difference did that make?

Nick stretched for another few minutes, then pushed himself through a few exercises. He paused near the next problem-spot and studied the floor.

Right about there, I killed . . . her.

If Nick hadn't changed into his demon form and snapped his mother's neck, she would have used her biosentient abilities to cover the stone walls with the blood of Sibyls and her own children—Nick, Creed, and Jake included.

But, no, that didn't make it easy.

Once more, Nick stretched, this time extending his left arm and leg. He took a slow breath and waited, waited, holding position—

And it happened.

That . . . tingle on the back of his neck.

The sense that someone—something—else had entered the chamber.

Nick kept his breathing easy, his motions careful.

Gideon joined more fully with him, and he was aware that his skin had taken on a golden glow. If he turned Gideon loose, he would change, grow taller, wider, even more muscular, into a being more light than substance. And he'd run off the "ghost" he had been busting his ass to locate.

All in all, he'd rather not.

Unless his demon-brother forced his hand.

"Jake?" Nick asked, careful to keep his voice quiet.

Nothing answered him, but that prickly sensation on his neck didn't go away.

The Astaroth was here. Nick knew it as surely as he knew his own heart rate. He did have some kind of connection to the creature. *Or maybe to the boy I didn't save.* Nick's chest tightened. *Whatever part of the real Jake still exists, age-accelerated, demonized, but maybe present in some form.*

"You come here to visit them." Nick sank slowly to the nearest mat, folding his legs into a sitting position. Nothing fast. Nothing threatening. He kept his back to where he thought Jake might be.

"I visit them, too." Nick closed his eyes and took a slow, meditative breath to help Gideon stay regulated and calm.

After a long few minutes of silence, Nick tried to make himself ask the question his conversation with Cynda had provoked, but it stuck in his throat. He squared his shoulders and raised his chin and ran through a few meditations. Breathed. Breathed more slowly. Formed the words.

"Are you pissed at me for killing our mother, Jake?"

The sentence seemed to fall into the air.

Nick centered himself and waited.

Tried to be calm.

A sound like a sigh echoed through the chamber.

Then a low, insistent, "No."

The response was barely audible, yet it sounded like a blast of thunder in Nick's mind. He turned slowly toward where he heard the voice.

The temperature in the room dropped a few degrees.

Nick saw his own breath in a frosty rush. The scents of cherry bark and mullein—like aged wine or some sweet spice—drifted through the gym. Between him and the door, on a blue exercise mat, a human figure began to coalesce. At first, as it shimmered into full sight, it was tall—as tall as Nick in his demon form.

It had golden eyes, see-through pearly skin, fangs, claws, and a double set of huge leathery wings. It reminded Nick of an eerie, haunting monster carved out of marble or alabaster, set atop some church to scare away evil spirits. The sight of the Astaroth made Nick's gut twist. He strained to see traces of the lost little boy, the original Jacob, in this being, but failed.

Seconds later, the creature pulled in its wings, and they vanished with a little swirl of dust. It closed its golden eyes, seemed to concentrate, and other changes happened. It got more . . . solid. The skin darkened. Muscles filled out, became more compact as it reduced its height to a little over six feet. By the time it finished shimmering, it—he—Jake—looked like a normal adult male, dressed in jeans and a loose white shirt, both streaked with dirt. Nick would put Jake's age somewhere in his late twenties. He had olive skin as if he might be Italian or Greek. Shoulder-length blond hair, blue eyes, and a build like he pumped iron five times a week, minimum. He was wearing a chain like Nick's around his neck, but the chain didn't have the signet ring on it that Nick remembered Jake having, from that months-ago battle down here in the basement chamber.

His talisman had two parts. Is he missing half if it? Do Astaroths even need talismans like Cursons?

Nick wanted to give the kid a thumbs-up, tell him he didn't look bad at all. But he didn't think moving was a good idea, or speaking. He didn't want to spook the kid—well, man.

Not a boy anymore, that's for sure.

Jake studied him with clear, discerning eyes that didn't look childlike or innocent at all. More sophisticated, educated, intellectual.

And damaged, in that way only cops and shrinks would notice.

Jake's gaze moved from Nick to the spot in the basement where their mother had died.

In that same toneless, quiet voice, Jake said, "Our mother was evil. I'm glad she's dead."

Nick's muscles went slack with relief. A jumble of unexpected emotions battered against that door inside, the one he kept so firmly closed. Aloud, he managed, "Okay. That's out of the way."

"I haven't learned to stay . . . solid very long, and talking gets hard." When Jake held up his hand, Nick saw rows of knotty scars running from wrist to elbow. Other scars, too, round ones, and crescent-shaped. He squinted at Jake. The man was scarred all over.

What in God's name?

Jake flickered, then grew solid again. "Please listen. There are many Cursons, many Astaroths. They could make an army under the right general. That general could set a formidable force against the fire Sibyls—and win."

Many Cursons?

Sonofabitch.

Nick had wondered, but he had never been able to get at those files during his time with the Legion. Up until now, he thought he and Creed might be the only surviving demons of their type.

Guess not.

Another flicker, but Jake got himself back pretty fast. This time, though, the scars looked worse. Nick wondered why Jake didn't heal the way Nick and Creed did, whenever they shifted in and out of Curson form.

Was Jake that different? Maybe too human to heal completely?

So many questions, but he had to ask cop questions first, before Jake winked out for good. "Is J. C. Downy the one who has been killing fire Sibyls?"

Jake shook his head. The movement looked painful. "A leader never soils her own hands. Leaders give orders, and demons do the killings."

Nick shifted on his mat, leaning toward his brother. "Why them? Why only—"

"The fire bitches?" Jake shrugged, again looking like the movement caused him pain. "That's what some people call them. I don't know why fire Sibyls are hated more than the rest."

Nick didn't want to, but he forced himself to ask what he had to know. "Have you killed any Sibyls, Jake?"

Flicker.

Long flicker.

Nick squinted at the spot where Jake had been standing. He was gone—but no. Wait. There. Back again, this time sitting, much like Nick was sitting, cross-legged on the blue mat nearest the door.

God, those scars—and now bruises and cuts, too. Looks like he's been attacked by a couple of heavyweight champs.

Jake gave Nick a deep, direct stare. "I have not killed. There are those of us, Curson and Astaroth, who don't agree with murder. We disobey."

Nick froze in place, fixed on the scars. The bruises. Those cuts that now oozed tiny trails of blood down Jake's hands and cheeks. Nick's chest went cold deep inside, and Gideon crept forward, growling low and steady in the back of Nick's mind.

"What happens to demons who disobey, Jake?"

Jake closed his blue eyes. Opened them slowly. Even that small action made him wince. When he looked at Nick, misery wrote itself across every tense line and angle of the man's broken body. He glanced down at his hands and nails, which appeared to be covered with a layer of dust or dirt.

"We suffer."

Gideon surged, pushing Nick to his feet. He knew he was glowing. Couldn't stop it. Couldn't begin to control himself any better than he was. "Stay here, Jake." Nick heard the *other*-echo in his words. "Stay right here in the townhouse. Don't return to her. We'll help you, Creed and I. The Sibyls."

Jake didn't react to Nick's outburst. After a few seconds, he flickered, seemed to short out completely. When he reappeared, he was only an outline—and the wings and fangs and claws were back.

The Astaroth gestured to the empty chain around his neck. "As long as someone else possesses a piece of me," he whispered, "I have no choice."

Nick clenched his fists. "Can she force you, Jake? Can she make you do evil like our mother tried to do?"

Jake shook his head, more angular now, less human, less distinct. "I will die first—but, dying isn't easy."

"Have you tried?" Nick fought an urge to grab hold of his brother, shake him, refuse to turn him loose, now, or ever again.

"Many times." Jake—now fully Astaroth—held out his demon arms, showing wicked, roped scars. "I heal," he said simply. Then he looked skyward, as if he was perceiving sound Nick couldn't hear.

Once more, Jake began to fade away.

Nick sensed this time that Jake wouldn't be back. He lunged forward, made a grab for the Astaroth, and caught only air.

A whisper, faint, but real. "City Island, brother. City Island—"

The voice faded to nothing.

Nick stood for a few long seconds, searching the room, hoping, but knowing—"No."

He bashed his hand against his palm. "God*damn*it!"

More than glowing, half-changed to Curson.

Someone—Downy—was hurting Jake, and he couldn't do a damned thing about it.

His brain hurt. His blood roared.

He was roaring, too. With Gideon. The sound echoed off the stone walls.

Growling, snarling, Nick spun around and started kicking every exercise ball in the room. One after the other, they slammed against the stone walls. Some deflated. Others burst.

If he hadn't left, I would have helped him!

Nick grabbed mats. Throwing and tearing. And the weights.

God it felt good to bash the heavy iron and steel into the floor.

"Nick? Stop it!" The sound of Cynda's voice barely penetrated Nick's rage. He was more Curson than man now. So much for the friggin' clothes.

"City Island!" he bellowed before he lost the ability to speak. "We're going to City Island *right fucking now*!"

Women were streaming into the basement, ringing him. Whenever he tried to move, they did something to stop him. Air, or earth, or fire.

Then another Curson got in his face.

"Hit him if you have to," somebody shouted.

Nick was vaguely aware of roaring at the Creed-demon—right before he took a punch from his twin, directly between his eyes.

7

Cynda's gut ached as she revved the Jeep through yet more friggin' snow, carrying Nick, Creed, Andy, and her triad across the Triborough Bridge onto the Bruckner Expressway. She headed east through the Bronx, then turned north toward Long Island Sound and the City Island Bridge, all the while keeping her mouth firmly closed.

Nick rode shotgun, and the man hadn't said a word since they left the townhouse.

Before that, after he woke from Creed's punch and got dressed, no one had been able to drag much out of him past the fact Jake was J. C. Downy's captive on City Island, and they had to get Jake back.

It had taken Merilee only half an hour to locate four potential addresses—title transfers in the last ten years, female owners. One house, a three-bedroom cottage on King Avenue, was registered to a Juliette Christine Sweetbriar.

Cynda squeezed the steering wheel.

In Ireland at least, *sweetbriar* was interchangeable with *downy* as a name for the wild rose. Seemed like a good bet to Cynda and everyone else.

I hope I'm right.

She tried to make herself breathe evenly, calmly, but it was hard.

They had no idea what they were charging into, past a rescue of Nick's demon-brother. Merilee had printed out satellite photos of the address off Google Earth before the computer reacted to the nervous Sibyl energy in the library and shut down, refusing all attempts to boot it back up. The Sweetbriar house looked normal enough, but with the Legion involved, who could tell?

Before they left, the Sibyls decked out in their leathers, strapped on their weapons, and waited for the OCU SWAT officers to suit up, wheedle a warrant or two out of their favorite judge, and make the appropriate courtesy calls to the precincts in the Bronx covering City Island. Nobody could reach Sal Freeman, who had left for the day, but everyone had been right on point, ready to go, expecting Legion bullshit. So on Nick's order, they went—but Cynda's strong instincts kept nudging her, poking her. Different sensations pinged through her chest, from worry to fear to apprehension and to a sense of *finally, finally, we'll get to the fighting.*

She glanced at Nick.

Motionless. Mouth set. Eyes straight ahead. He had on jeans and a blue T-shirt. No sleeves. No coat.

He's locked down tighter than a military base on high alert. What happened in the townhouse basement?

When she took a breath, the air in the Jeep smelled like leather, oil, cold air, and Nick.

She wished he would tell her what had happened. Why did everything have to be so hard with him? Trying to talk to the man really was about as easy as dental surgery. And sometimes just as pleasant.

Riana, Andy, and Merilee exchanged terse, anxious remarks in the Jeep's backseat, and Creed answered now and then from the jump seat in the rear. Of course, they weren't conversing much with Cynda, because they were all mad at her for omitting the whole Jake-in-the-alley issue from her battle report. They'd be talking about that "later," along with all the other "later" stuff Cynda had simmering. Assuming they didn't all get eaten by whatever waited at the King Avenue house.

Asmodai? Those we can handle. We did a fair job

against Astaroths, or whatever those invisi-demons were.

Let it be something we've seen before.

She glanced in her mirror to be sure she wasn't losing anybody. Two other SUVs followed them, and a van with fifteen members of OCU SWAT. The SUVs carried Sibyl triads from South Brooklyn and North Queens, and the ranger group out of New Jersey. Still trying to breathe normally, Cynda led the caravan onto City Island Avenue and started counting streets. New mouth-watering scents of garlic, butter, rich cheese, and everything fried or baked flooded the Jeep, spilling out from the island's overstock of fresh-seafood restaurants. Her stomach lurched. Past lunchtime. All she had managed was a protein bar before Nick had his gym meltdown—but if she tried to eat now, she'd heave right into the Long Island Sound.

"I'm hungry," Andy announced from the backseat.

Her voice made Cynda jump.

Cynda watched in the rearview mirror as Andy rubbed her puffy eyes and yawned. "Let's hope Jake wants to be found in a hurry."

When was the last time she got a good night's sleep— and how much weight has she lost?

Riana patted Andy's hand. "I'll grab you a pizza later."

Andy yawned again, rubbing a damp patch off her right cheek with her sleeve. "Promises, promises."

Nick let out a rumbling noise that only Cynda could hear. She knew he was frustrated by the chitchat, could read *that* in his thunderous expression plainly enough.

"Maybe we'd respect your feelings more if we *knew what happened*," she said to him, keeping her voice low.

Nick didn't even look at her.

If she hadn't been at the fourth street off the City Island Bridge and needing to turn, she would have scorched him. Instead, she hung a left on Ditmars. She had only been to City Island a few times, but it amazed her how the little island still looked like a rural New England fishing village. Victorian architecture, narrow streets, picket fences—even some unpaved, sand-strewn roads, in a place that was officially part of the Bronx.

As per their hastily mounted plan, Cynda pulled to the curb just after making the right onto King Avenue, near the historic Pelham Cemetery, and waited for the other OCU vehicles to line up behind her. In the cold, sunless afternoon, with light, wet flakes swirling around its century-old tombstones, Pelham looked forlorn and ominous. The chalk-white grave markers reminded Cynda of so many bones jutting up from the snow-dusted ground, reaching toward the gunmetal-gray waters of Pelham Bay.

Before she zipped her leather face mask and strapped on her demon-hunting goggles, she glanced at Nick one more time. No change, except his muscles looked tight and too still, like the body of a panther ready to spring.

What should I say to him?

Something . . . but what?

It wasn't like her to be at a loss for words.

Finally, she muttered, "Good hunting, you big, mute asshole."

Nick turned his face toward her.

His eyebrow twitched. So did his mouth.

Was that a smile? Alert the media.

As the fourth SUV in the caravan squealed to a stop in the line of vehicles, Creed said, "Lock and load."

Cynda sucked air, ordered her stomach to cooperate, zipped her mask, and buckled on her goggles. So did Riana and Merilee. Andy pulled on her goggles, then joined Creed and Nick in strapping on a body armor vest. They covered their vests with black NYPD raid jackets.

OCU SWAT spilled out of their van, dressed in combat boots, black fire-resistant coveralls, and body armor. They all wore black gloves, black face-guards, demon-hunting goggles, and black Kevlar helmets. Each SWAT member carried an assault rifle loaded with elementally locked bullets now routinely supplied to OCU by the Sibyls. Every officer also had a full complement of standard-issue equipment—flashbangs, Stingers, and tear-gas grenades—in case they encountered resistance of the nonsupernatural variety.

SWAT formed a protective ring, shielding the two SUVs of disembarking Sibyls from public view. Nick, Creed, and Andy bailed out of the Jeep and took point, while Cynda, Riana, and Merilee slipped into the center of the formation with the other Sibyls. To the untrained eye, the group would look like a fully equipped standard SWAT unit on the move.

And they did move. Fast. At a run, weapons ready, toward the address Merilee had provided.

Cynda's heart marched in time with their boot steps. Her blood pumped with each crunch of ice and rock and sand. She kept her eyes fixed on the back of Nick's head, on his ponytail, his tense shoulders. She had orders to stay within arm's length of him, except during the actual house approach, when she would stay with Riana.

At previously designated points—thanks to the satellite photos—air Sibyls and snipers peeled off from the main group and took up positions in trees. Earth Sibyls and fire Sibyls stationed themselves north, south, east, and west, with two officers each, to intercept anyone attempting to flee from the target house.

By the time they reached the front porch of the sprawling green Victorian home registered to Juliette Sweet-briar, only Nick, Creed, Cynda, and Riana remained, along with four SWAT officers, two lugging a battering ram for forced entry, if needed. Those two stayed in front, while the other two SWAT officers went around to the back of the house.

Nick, Creed, and Andy made the approach with the SWAT members while Cynda and Riana sought cover behind some leafless, icy trees a few yards away. As Nick pounded on the ivory-colored door and bellowed, "NYPD!" Cynda realized she was holding her breath.

She let it out in a frosty rush.

Riana did the same thing. They glanced at each other. Cynda read the worry in her triad sister's face and gave her hand a quick squeeze.

On the Sweetbriar house's porch, nothing happened. Nick thumped the door again. "NYPD. Open up."

Cynda counted *one, two, three, four, five, six* . . .

Still nothing.

Nick gestured to the SWAT officers. He and Creed and Andy moved to the side, careful to stay away from any windows. The SWAT officers trooped forward, swept the battering ram backward, then swung it full steam ahead.

The door exploded from the blow, raining bits of ivory wood in every direction

Just as fast, the officer on the left yelled, "Plug 'n' shut," and heaved a flashbang into the opening. He spun to the side, plugged his ears and shut his eyes. Cynda clamped her lids shut, too, and jammed her fingers into her ears. Those things were so bright and loud. She felt the stun grenade's explosion in her bones and joints, and its blue-white flash of light tattooed itself on her eyelids even with her eyes closed.

By the time she opened them, the two SWAT officers had leaped through the opening, weapons ready, shouting, "Police! Down on the floor!"

Answering shouts came from the back of the house as those officers deployed into the Victorian through another entrance.

As shouts of "Clear! Clear!" rang through the cold afternoon, Nick, Creed, and Andy headed inside behind SWAT. A minute or two later, at a gesture from Nick, Cynda and Riana ran across the snow-coated yard and jumped to the porch.

Cynda had her hand on her sword hilt. Riana had her daggers palmed and ready—but the calls of all clear, the body postures, and the sounds of the officers' voices eased her mind a little.

Riana went through the door first.

Cynda followed, but Nick caught her arm and kept her beside him.

Breathing hard from nerves more than anything, Cynda went still, staring at the immaculate space around her.

Except for door splinters and the spent flashbang canister, she didn't see a single bit of dust or debris anywhere. Also no pictures, no nail holes in the wall, no furniture, not a blemish or hint that humans—or anything—had set foot in this house, except that it was unnaturally clean.

The goggles revealed no trace of demon residue, either.

"Going with SWAT to the basement," Riana called, following Creed, Andy, and the officers toward what was probably the kitchen area.

Cynda sniffed and caught the telltale odor of cleanser—bleach and pine. The air in the house felt as cold as the air outside. For some reason, the overly polished floors and wood trim gave her a sick, nervous twitch in her gut.

It looked . . . no—maybe smelled? . . . familiar.

She loosened her goggles and let them fall around her neck, and unzipped her face mask. Frigid air bit into her cheeks, and the stink of cleanser seemed even stronger.

There's an energy here. It's subtle, but I know it. I've been around it before.

Where?

For the first time in over an hour, Nick spoke directly to Cynda. "What's on your mind?"

She turned her attention to him and saw rage and frustration flicker across his face. His skin took on a golden glow.

This too-clean house was definitely not what he expected.

Her either.

"I don't have a clue what this is about." She folded her arms and scanned the pristine, empty living room again.

Nick narrowed his black eyes and studied her. "Something's on your mind."

Cynda shrugged and kept looking around. "Okay, I know it sounds stupid, but this house reminds me of somewhere. I just can't place it."

Before Nick could respond, scrambling noises broke out under the boards beneath their feet.

"The basement," Cynda shouted, blood pounding up her neck, driving heat into her face.

Nick grabbed her and pulled her to him. Fast, authoritative, he hustled her away from the hot spot, up against the Victorian's far wall.

The earth under the house gave a single, violent shake.

Cynda and Nick staggered. The house creaked on its foundation, and plaster dust drifted downward from a few corners.

All the shouting and scrambling stopped.

Seconds later, the SWAT officers and Riana—mask and goggles off—returned with Creed and Andy, marching a bejeweled, cuffed man in front of them.

Cynda recognized the lanky, pock-faced bastard immediately, even though he had on a decent blue suit, several gold chains, a bunch of gold rope bracelets, and at least four rings. The stench of urine and skunkweed clung to his clothes and blond hair like a bad omen.

"Max Moses." Nick gave a low whistle and shook his head. "Who did you steal that jewelry from? Your mother will be seriously pissed."

Max's eyes, blue, a shade like cornflower, looked dull and angry. When he spoke, he directed his comments to Nick.

"She's got me mum, the crazy bitch." Max bared his brown teeth at Nick. "It's your fault, see, for goin' over there and puttin' your mark on her door. They took her out, Downy's demons, right under your cops' noses."

Nick straightened and tensed as he listened to the informant's nasal Irish brogue—which sounded more like a whine to Cynda than anything else. She was getting tense, too, over what Max was saying, but she couldn't quite believe she was hearing him right.

"What's he talking about?" Andy asked.

"I've got no choice, you understand," Max told Nick. "It's you or Delilah—and you didn't spit me out."

Nick raised one hand, keeping his Glock in the other. "Slow it down. One step at a time, Max."

"Don't have any time left. Sorry." Max closed his eyes. Sweat creased every line and crevice on his ugly face.

Riana and Cynda moved at the same time. Before they could reach Max, he shouted, "Kill them all. Burn the house when you're done."

His cornflower eyes snapped open as Cynda grabbed for the chains around his neck to yank him toward her—and she understood.

Talismans.

"His jewelry!" She yelled, going colder than all the ice and snow in New York City. "It's all talismans!"

"Trap," Nick thundered.

"Trap!" SWAT echoed into the radios on their shoulders. Creed and Andy swung left, then right, firearms aiming at nothing.

Riana raised her hands, gathering earth energy. Cynda zipped her mask, yanked her goggles into place, and drew her sword.

The air . . . changed.

Turned electric.

Turned *wrong*.

The wall behind Cynda bulged inward.

Nick held his Glock to the side and tackled Cynda—crushed her facedown, arms out, against the wood floors. Her sword clattered across the wooden boards.

Pain fired through her arms and legs as the wall caved in and the Victorian exploded in roaring golden *others*.

8

Nick covered Cynda with his body and held her to the floor as Curson demons stormed straight over the top of them, through the outer wall and into the Victorian's living room. Their heavy feet crushed into his spine and shoulders. Pain thumped across his whole body, but he held his spot, held on to Cynda, and kept them from smashing her.

Glowing monsters clogged the space, steaming in the rush of cold air, bashing barriers between rooms and turning the entire downstairs into a thousand-square-foot battlefield.

Killing ground.

Nick looked up as demon energy scorched into his back. The stench of burning ozone filled his nose. Blood pounded in his ears as he half shifted to fend off the heat and weight—and the things didn't seem to notice him. He realized he had probably shifted enough that they took him for one of their own.

Gideon roared in his mind, digging at his insides. Nick wanted to turn his *other* loose so badly he could taste the tang of fire in his mouth.

Can't.

If Creed and I shift, Sibyls and SWAT won't know who to kill.

"Hit 'em in the brains or hearts!" Andy hollered to SWAT, firing her SIG.

She winged her target. The wounded Curson roared and charged her, but she rolled out of the way. Other demons squared off with human targets and trapped Creed and Riana between them.

Cynda struggled against Nick, trying to get up.

Shit!

More gunshots blasted against his senses.

He couldn't protect Cynda and fight, too. He shifted back to full human. Smoke and gunpowder made his eyes water.

Demons bellowed, and the house seemed to rock.

It *was* rocking.

Riana, using earth energy.

Chunks of ceiling and broken wall and dirt pelted the floor in front of Nick's head. Demons crashed to the floor, caught by surprise and knocked off balance. Nick kept Cynda beneath him for another long moment, shielding her as best he could, even though he could feel her fire sizzling through his raid jacket.

"I'm a Sibyl," she yelled loud enough to be heard over the crashing and gunshots. "Let me up!"

It was the last thing he wanted to do.

But it was fight or die.

He rolled off Cynda, jumped toward her sword, and kicked it back to her. They'd do this together. He'd cover her as best he could.

Cynda snatched her sword by the hilt and leaped to her feet in a single motion, smoking all over. With her face mask and goggles in place, he couldn't see the rage on her face, but he knew she was pissed.

Her blade burst into flames.

"Behind you!" he yelled as a demon charged her.

Cynda spun to meet it, sword raised.

Nick aimed his Glock at the thing's face, but Cynda cut the demon's knees out from under it, literally, before Nick could fire. The eight-foot golden monster bellowed and smashed to the wood floor.

Roaring almost as loud as the demon, Cynda swung her broadsword in a powerful downward arc and lopped off its head.

The world stopped.

Light blazed.

Nick saw nothing at all but searing, painful gold brightness. Something like a crate of dynamite blasted him so hard he felt the noise like fists against his ears. His sense of up, down, right, and left deserted him.

He staggered in a circle, then hit his knees and almost heaved.

Did some jackass throw a flashbang at a bunch of demons?

Spinning . . .

Everything spinning . . .

He took slow breaths, inhaling a dizzy combination of ozone, sulfur fire, and dirt. He let his head loll, and centered himself like he had taken a kick to the head in a sparring match. Gideon surged up in his consciousness, lending him strength, feeding him focus and energy.

Bit by bit, the room came back into focus.

Everything still seemed gray and wavy, but Nick saw all four SWAT members in the center of the room, down on their knees, puking.

Riana and Andy were down, too, near the back of the room—no puking.

Creed was on his feet by Riana but half-changed, his head glowing, his pulsing, golden hands sticking out of his raid jacket.

Thank God the demons were stunned, too. Frozen like big golden monuments all around the room.

What the hell?

Nick got to his feet and managed to turn back toward the destroyed outer wall.

Cynda lay flat on her face by a piece of that wall, next to her sword. Smoke belched through a gaping hole in the floor beside her, big enough to show the concrete basement below.

Cold rage and panic charged through Nick. Growling along with Gideon, he ran toward her, almost fell, found his balance, and reached her side as she rolled over. Her goggles had shattered. He stripped them away and knocked them aside. Her face mask and leathers were scorched nearly off in the front, leaving only strands of black covering bits of her bra and panties. Her face itself was strawberry red, and she had a bruise under her left eye.

"Sonofabitch." Nick touched the bruise with his fingertip as her eyelids fluttered. Then he grabbed her shoulder and pulled her toward him, intending to pick her up and carry her straight out of that damned house.

Have to protect her this time. Have to get her out of here. And lead the demons to the air Sibyls and SWAT snipers.

"Curson energy," she muttered, pushing back, shoving him away. She scrambled to sit up, already groping for her sword. "Cursons don't break down into the elements when they die."

Nick grabbed for her again, but she smacked him in the arm until he stopped trying to get hold of her. Bare shoulders smoking, she grabbed his face and stared into his eyes. "Don't get killed. You'll blow up."

Nick slowly processed what she was saying. So did the *other* inside him.

All at once the frozen demons thawed, bellowing and moving again.

"Plug ears and cover eyes when you take one down!" Nick shouted over the chaos. "Bastards explode when you kill them. Let's get outside. Now!"

He finally succeeded in looping his arm around Cynda and lifting her to her feet. Demons seemed to be everywhere at once. As he and Cynda moved, one of the beasts

fixed on them and lumbered forward, golden arms outstretched.

"Down!" Riana yelled.

Nick ducked and forced Cynda to the floor with him
as the earth Sibyl hurled a dagger past Nick's ear.

At the same time, he felt earth energy drape him and
Cynda like a cold, dark blanket.

A flash of light made him blink, and he heard a muted
explosion.

Another hole opened in the floor, revealing more of
the concrete basement.

Another demon gone.

Riana's earth energy peeled away.

That left what, ten Cursons? Twelve? Frozen in place.

Two SWAT members were on their knees again heav-
ing, but Andy, Creed, Riana, Nick, and Cynda had been
protected by Riana's elemental power.

"I'm a warrior. How many times do I have to tell
you?" Cynda hit his shoulder with her free hand once,
twice, three times. When he looked at her expecting rage,
he saw only serious concentration and determination.
"Fight with me or get out of my way."

Cynda's words punched deep inside Nick's consciousness. He sucked in a breath and let her go.

"Everybody pick one," Andy called.

All the functioning members of the assault team took
position in front of a different immobilized demon.

Creatures like me, Nick thought as he raised his Glock
and sighted his target. *Men like me.*

These poor bastards probably didn't even know who
they were fighting, or why. They had been commanded
by the holder of their talisman—what choice did they
have?

But he had to kill them or die. Let Cynda die. And
Creed and Riana and Andy, and the SWAT members,
too.

"Three," Cynda called, holding her sword with a two-fisted grip. "Two, one!"

Nick shot the Curson in front of him right between its glowing eyes.

At the same instant, he saw Cynda ram her sword through her eight-foot demon at heart level. Riana used another dagger, also to the heart. Creed punched his glowing golden fist into a demon's head, and Andy shot one in the brain just as Nick had.

Simultaneously, another blanket of earth energy coated them all, protecting them from the fallout.

Nick watched, gut-sick, as the dead Cursons blasted out of existence.

Gaping holes formed in the wood floor where their bodies had fallen. The house started to shudder. Too much damage. The structure wasn't sound.

Riana's earth cloak peeled back.

Winter cold slapped Nick in the face. He coughed at the stench of gunpowder. It cleared his mind—so he had a perfect view of the volley of elementally locked arrows that came screaming through the Victorian's destroyed walls.

The other Sibyls and SWAT members had reached the house—but they didn't know what would happen when the demons died.

Riana raised her hands. Not in time to form a full shield.

Nick didn't even get to yell before the whole world detonated in one motherfucker of a flashbang.

Frigid water streamed across Nick's face. He choked and jerked himself upright, feeling cold, wet concrete beneath his palms.

"Somebody find that friggin' water main," a man yelled.

Creed?

Ice water kept blasting against his chest, seeping in through rents in his raid jacket.

Nick scooted himself sideways. Calling to Gideon, he shifted the few areas of his body that felt damaged to *other* form and back again—both eardrums, a leg, an arm, his neck—and struggled to his feet. Afternoon sunlight felt like Sibyl daggers in both eyes, but he shook that off and squinted around him.

He was in the basement.

The Victorian had come apart in boards and plaster and chunks. The copper tang of blood mixed with the acrid smell of vomit and fire. Little blazes flickered from wires and wood. Geysers of water shot from the walls and through cracks in the basement floor, like half of Pelham Bay was leaking into the pit where the house used to be. Air Sibyls blew aside debris with gusts of wind, then knelt to tend to wounded members of the SWAT team.

One of the SWAT members had a board sticking out of her leg.

Nick lurched a few steps forward as he battled a wave of queasy frustration.

His brain wound back to full awareness, and his next thought was, *Cynda?*

As he turned to search for her, Creed stepped in front of him and grabbed both of his upper arms. "You with me?"

"Yeah." Nick coughed. "I'm here."

Creed let him go. "We've got six SWAT down, the four from inside and two that got hit by debris outside. The Forty-fifth Precinct's setting up a perimeter, keeping back the public. Ambulances rolled up for the wounded about three minutes ago." He gestured to a prone form lying a few feet from Nick and raised his voice over a new hissing, spewing jet of water that shot up near them. "Grab Cynda. She's unconscious, but Riana says she's okay. We gotta roll."

Nick went straight to Cynda, chest tight, barely sucking in enough air to keep himself on his feet. He dropped to his knees beside her and checked her for himself. Pulse steady. Color good. Respiration regular. Leathers torn to hell. Lots of little cuts.

He breathed a little deeper.

She'll have a headache from those blasts and the fall.

But she was still alive, and in one piece. Nick wasn't sure if he had protected her, but he'd damn sure done his best. He pulled off his battered, burned, and wet raid jacket, slipped her arms into it, and zipped it to give her a little cover.

When he scooped her off the wet concrete floor, she groaned and turned into him, draping an arm around his neck.

Nick didn't waste time trying to wake her. Creed was right. They had to get the OCU and the Sibyls off-scene as fast as possible.

Keeping his head down and his face turned from King Avenue, where most of the crowd was gathering, Nick followed Riana, Merilee, and Creed, who was carrying a moaning Andy, up a rescue ramp. They headed out of the basement, through a line of local Bronx officers, away from the Victorian at an angle to a side street, so they would miss onrushing press vans and emergency vehicles.

A few seconds later, Cynda woke up.

"Put me down right now," she growled as Nick carried her along the far edge of Pelham Cemetery toward the Jeep.

"No" was his only response.

He ignored her struggling and kept her cradled against his chest. Couldn't help himself there. He was too glad she was in one piece. Did make walking difficult, though. She almost knocked them down three separate times. He briefly considered carrying her potato-sack style, but he'd be flashing her half-naked ass to all of City Island. As it was, his raid jacket didn't give her much cover, especially since she'd burned some pretty big holes in it when he was wearing it, trying to protect her during the fight.

She planted her elbow in his ribs, taking his breath, but he kept walking. "Put me down or I swear to the Goddess I'll roast you."

"We have to get out of here, firebird. Be quiet, and don't smoke or burn anything. Civilians might see us."

She went quiet, and she didn't hit him again. He could tell she was beginning to come around all the way, and realize what was happening.

His head hurt, and every few seconds, he still wanted to vomit his guts out. Whenever he blinked, he saw big golden spots. The flashing red and blue lights from marked cars, fire engines, and ambulances lining King Avenue weren't helping.

Everywhere his hands touched Cynda's bare skin, heat blistered him—but she didn't make any flames or smoke.

A few seconds later, she tensed. "Riana and Merilee?"

Nick shifted his grip and held her closer. "Already in the Jeep, waiting for us. If you'd be still, we'd get there faster."

Cynda's green eyes went from cloudy and distant to present and alert. She could probably walk now, but he didn't want to put her down.

"What about Andy?" she asked, gingerly touching the bruise under her eye.

"Puking by the rear bumper, from what I can see. Creed's pouring water on the back of her neck." He let out a breath. Fifty yards, and they were on the road, straight out of this mess.

Cynda's mouth twitched, then pulled into a frown. "Any Sibyls seriously injured?"

He hugged her a little tighter, and she let him. "No, but we're sending six of OCU SWAT to the ER with burns and broken bones—and one serious trauma."

Thirty yards. Twenty-five. Nick walked faster. The Forty-fifth was doing a grand job holding the line around the Sweetbriar house and King Avenue, but they could only keep the press and public back for so long.

"What will the Forty-fifth—"

"Gas main," he said, anticipating her question. "And water main. When we woke up, the whole place was flooding. No one will be able to tell the difference."

The sound of Andy's obnoxiously loud retching rose over the dull background roar of police radio chatter and increasing crowd noise.

"Gas and water mains." Cynda rolled her eyes as they reached the safety of the Jeep. "How creative."

Nick opened the Jeep's front passenger door, slipped Cynda into the seat, and fastened her belt.

In the backseat, Riana groaned, pinching the bridge of her nose. "Anybody who makes a loud noise dies."

"Captain called before you woke up, Nick," Creed said from the hatch. "He's six degrees hotter than red-ass mad. We need to get on the road."

Cynda glanced once more at Nick and let him go.

Nick felt a weight form in his belly as he closed her door and got in behind her. He glanced back toward the nearly leveled Sweetbriar house and cursed himself for putting so many people in danger on an impulse.

No, not an impulse. It was for Jake.

Where is he?

Was he part of that setup?

Half of Nick's mind knew his brother had to have been part of the bait, probably sent to the townhouse to fire Nick up and lead them all into an ambush. But the other half of Nick's mind wasn't so sure—or didn't want to be.

Delilah Moses. Was she really a captive, or was that bullshit, too? That would have to get sorted out. Nick had no idea.

As for Max Moses . . .

A couple of horn blasts let them know the other caravan vehicles were ready to go.

"Lock and load," Merilee said from the front seat.

Nick tensed.

Max Moses.

The next time Nick ended up face-to-face with that slimy little rat-bastard, Max wouldn't walk away whole.

9

The air in the townhouse conference room sizzled like fifty fire Sibyls were losing their tempers—but it was just one Curson.

Well, one half-demon cop.

Nick glowed like a radioactive warhead as he towered in front of the conference table and stared down Sal Freeman, Andy, and Creed.

Behind the conference table, the chalkboard and the paper-tacked bulletin board trembled from the energy of his rage.

Cynda stood at the back of the room with Merilee and Riana, separated from Nick by two dozen desks and chairs. She wanted to interfere, but she also wanted to stay out of the way.

Far, far out of the way.

She had meditated to heal on the drive back from City Island as best she could, and changed into comfortable jeans and a shirt when they got to the townhouse, but every muscle in her body still ached, and noise and light still grated on her. All the shouting hurt somewhere deep in her brain.

"Six of our people down?" Freeman clenched both fists, impressive biceps bunching. "What kind of fuckup was that operation? We *plan*. We recon. We don't just muster the troops and take off blind, Lowell."

Riana had hold of one of Cynda's hands. Merilee had the other. They both squeezed her fingers.

"Recon wouldn't have helped." Nick faced his captain with equal stubbornness. "They knew we were coming. We need to move on to the Bronx house Max Moses told us about tonight and see what's there."

Freeman started to sputter a response full of four-letter words, but Andy cut him off.

"You're too close to this, Nick." She sounded so weary Cynda felt a surge of worry for her friend's health. Dressed in Merilee's jeans and one of Riana's droopy-looking blue Oxford shirts, Andy didn't even look like her usual self—a loud, brash fashion-disaster poster.

The wiped-out cop ran a hand through her unruly auburn hair and moved a step closer to Creed as Nick wheeled on her. She didn't give up her point, though. Andy would never surrender in an argument unless she really *was* on her deathbed. "You can't recon the Bronx house, especially not tonight. You'll blow it."

"I'm going," Nick snarled.

Creed shook his head. "No. Let us do this part. To-morrow. Hell, first of next week. The unit and the Sibyls need to rest."

Nick's expression darkened. "I'm not hanging Jake out to dry."

Freeman put his muscled frame between the brothers and got right in Nick's face. The captain's biceps bulged against his white sleeves, his collar was open, and his tie was long gone. His thick black hair looked heavy with sweat, and his color rose as he yelled, "You *will* stay at this townhouse while the recon team does its work. You *will not* move without my okay, or you'll hand over that damned badge!"

Nick jammed his hand into his jeans and ripped his back pocket yanking out his wallet. He would have thrown the leather at Sal Freeman's face, shield and all, if Andy hadn't grabbed his arm and snatched the wallet out of his hand.

Creed got hold of Nick's other arm.

Cynda blew air through her teeth.

Enough of *this* shit.

She shook off Merilee and Riana and strode forward. Before Nick could damage himself or anyone else, Cynda bumped Sal Freeman out of the way with her hip, stood on her toes, snatched the collar of Nick's shirt in both hands, and stared directly into his wild, dark eyes. "You're done, big man."

Nick struggled with Creed and Andy, and tried to pull away from Cynda's grip, too.

"Stop!" Cynda pressed herself into Nick, more than aware of his fury, of the steel-taut muscles shoving against her—and the barely suppressed *other*'s heat challenging her own.

Whatever.

After everything they'd just been through at the Sweetbriar house, if Nick's inner demon was going to hurt her, then let it show up and swallow her whole. She hoped she gave the friggin' thing indigestion.

Glaring at Nick, she channeled her elemental talent and lit Nick's entire body on fire.

Andy let Nick go and staggered back from him and the conference table, clapping her hands to her shirt to crush little sparks and dancing flames.

Creed jumped aside, swearing.

Even Sal Freeman peeled away from Nick. Riana and Merilee lowered the blinds until all the windows in the conference room were shuttered.

Cynda pushed the burning Nick toward the desks, a few steps away from her, and snuffed the flames on her own clothing.

She was getting low on shirts, and this one was wasted now. Holes all across the chest—and both sleeves, too. So much for commercial fire retardant. Stupid stuff sucked.

Nick stood still for a few more seconds, ringed in Cynda's fire from head to toe.

He blinked at her. Looked shocked. Seemed to focus completely on her face. Then he shifted fully into his *other* form, smoldered quietly as an eight-foot golden god for a moment, and morphed back to human male.

Naked human male.

No more fire. No burns. A little smoke and ash. His ponytail holder had burned away, and his dark hair fell wild around his face and shoulders.

Cynda gave him a slow appraisal, from his steaming face and shoulders to his sharply defined pecs and abs, *outstanding* package, rock-hard quads—definitely no worse for the burning.

Just the sight of him made her entire body ache. The pain in his eyes, etched on his face, that made her heart ache.

At least she had his full attention now.

"Better," she said, her voice lower than she intended, as her eyes once more drifted up and down his perfect body. "Pretty great, in fact."

"Oh, Jesus," Andy muttered, shielding her eyes from a first-class view of Nick's naked ass. "Talk about a sharing violation. Here." She thrust Nick's wallet and shield over his shoulder. He took it and placed it on the nearest desk.

Andy was out the door before Nick could thank her. So was Creed. Riana and Merilee lingered for about one second, then they left, too. Captain Freeman went last. He paused at the door, glanced at Cynda, and pointed to Nick. "He doesn't leave this building until tomorrow, got me?"

"I got him," Cynda said, trying to keep her pulse from racing. "I mean, you. Whatever."

Freeman slammed the conference room door shut behind him.

Cynda was pretty sure he turned the lock, too.

Nick didn't say a word. He just stood like a well-carved statue, staring at her, his expression absolutely unreadable.

If she reached out, her palm would be on that sculpted chest.

Cynda's heart pounded as she slowly walked toward Nick. The world outside the conference room drew away until it felt like they were the only two people in the whole townhouse, in Manhattan, in all of New York City.

Maybe if she touched Nick, he'd come to life again, and speak, and make sense. Maybe if she kissed him, she could heal some of the anguish that drove him to shred the gym, speed off to City Island with the cavalry in tow, and now almost ram his shield up his captain's nose.

"You're a shithead," she whispered, unable to tear her eyes from his.

One of Nick's eyebrows twitched, like, *Oh yeah?*

"First, you wreck the gym and behave like a maniac in front of half the OCU—and a load of Sibyls who don't even know you." Her hands ached from wanting to touch him. "Second, you dump the Jacob information on my triad before I tell them."

Nick didn't move, not even an eyebrow this time.

Was there any man in the world she'd rather have naked in front of her? Cynda couldn't stop looking at him. Didn't even want to try.

"Third," she said, her voice growing hoarse from the heat crawling through her body, "you act all macho on City Island and treat me like I'm a weak little girl who can't hold her own in a battle. Fourth, you were a complete jackass to your captain, your brother, and Andy when you *know* they're right—and you *know* Andy hasn't been okay in weeks."

She temporarily ran out of words, captured by the growing fire in Nick's black eyes. Emotion finally crept across his handsome face.

Desperation. Frustration.

Desire.

"Finished?" he asked in a low, gravelly tone.

"No, I'm not." Cynda finally let herself touch Nick, but just to smack her hands against him and push him back another step. The heat in her fingers left red prints in the center of his bare chest. "You told me you had control of your *other*. That you meditate, have mantras. So what was that before the raid, that little fit in the gym—and just now, with all the glowing? Do you have control of your demon-half, or don't you?"

Nick's eyes flashed. "You don't know what I saw in the gym. What I heard."

She leaned toward him, shoulders smoking. "Maybe that's because you *never tell me anything*!"

Nick flinched like she had slapped him. "That's not true."

Cynda waved a hand, trailing fire in the air between them. "What really happened with Jake in the basement, Nick?"

He opened his mouth. Hesitated.

Jets of flame crackled across Cynda's back, wasting another section of her shirt—and getting Nick's attention again.

"Talk . . . to . . . me." She crossed her arms. "Whatever it is, we'll handle it together. I swear that on *my* family's lives."

Nick ground his teeth so forcefully Cynda winced. The look on his face—utter disgust and agony. She didn't know whether to hit him or shake him or take his head in her hands and kiss him until he found the right words.

Nick's muscles tensed until she thought he might snap a tendon. "I know Jake probably set us up."

"I don't care about that part right now. The basement, Nick." Cynda kept herself focused by digging her nails into her own skin. "I want to know what happened when you saw Jake."

Silence enveloped the conference room.

Cynda waited.

"Downy's torturing my brother," Nick said at last, sounding distant and dangerous. "She's got half his talisman. I think she's cutting him, beating him, and he can't get away. It's not just him, either. Other Astaroths, and Cursons, too. Like the ones we slaughtered."

He turned his face away, his jaw working.

Cynda's breath caught hard in her throat. Tears jumped to her eyes. She hadn't given much thought to killing the demons who attacked them on City Island, but the weight of it hit her now, and hard.

Cursons like Nick, like Creed.

He had to kill beings just like him—who probably couldn't even help what they were doing. And even if Jake did set us up—could he stop himself? If Downy has his talisman, he is *helpless.*

No wonder Nick lost it in the gym, and just now, with his captain.

Cynda wanted to burn down the townhouse just hearing about Jake's condition and situation, and she hadn't seen the wounds. It wasn't her brother caught in the trap, and she didn't have to spend the afternoon shooting demons—*oh, Goddess, people?*—just like herself.

She was amazed Nick hadn't blasted the roof off the whole place.

When he turned his dark, pained eyes back to her, Cynda wanted to tell him she got it now. She wanted to say something comforting, but ended up shaking her head and hoping the truth showed in her face, that she understood the horror, that she was sharing his pain.

Nick stepped forward and caught her by both arms. Rough. Almost fierce. His palms burned against her skin, and his fingers dug into her as he tried to talk.

No sound came out.

Cynda saw everything in his eyes—his grief, his apology, his desperation.

His need.

This was Nick talking.

This was Nick communicating, beyond anything she had expected, or even dreamed.

Her heart shouted in response, and heat surged between them, emotional and physical, golden, glowing, twining like living ropes of fire.

The day's aches and pains and fatigue vanished.

Cynda's clothes blazed. She let them burn, helped them burn until they fell completely away, leaving her naked for Nick's scrutiny.

His eyes raked her face, her neck, her breasts and belly, then traced the red patch of hair between her legs. The competing emotions on his face coalesced into appreciation, then hunger.

Cynda couldn't stop the smoke rising from every place Nick's eyes lingered. Dizzy from the fire growing inside her, she moved closer and wrapped her arms around his neck.

As she gazed at his face, she gave herself up to the exquisite sensation of touching him, finally touching him everywhere. Her tight nipples scrubbed against his bare chest. Heat flooded Cynda from face to toes, pooling in her belly and lower, releasing a molten rush of desire.

Nick captured her mouth with his, predatory, insistent, yet soft, so soft. That jolt of wintergreen and tangy liquid flame claimed Cynda's senses, and she moaned against his lips, welcoming the forceful caress of his tongue against hers. His hands, exploring her, stroking her arms, her sides, her hips, her ass, pulling her closer to him. Forcing her heat against his. Absorbing her fire and giving it right back, a thousand times over.

Cynda couldn't breathe. Her heart forgot how to beat.

Her thoughts turned off completely, leaving nothing but raw sensation. She had never experienced anything like this, like Nick. His touches. His kisses. From hard and fast to long and so slow and deep and wet.

Nick broke away from her mouth and stared at her with a wild intensity Cynda could barely withstand.

A question.

He was making sure *she* was sure.

"Yes," she murmured, feeling flutters all through her body. "I'm sure."

Her body shook as his expression turned feral. Her knees betrayed her, and Nick was catching her, sweeping her up, forcing her down, spreading her across the conference table that dominated the front of the room.

"You're mine now," he said in that low, stirring bass. "I'll make you scream."

"We'll see," she challenged, gratified when he started to glow.

The smooth, polished wood felt cold against Cynda's steaming ass as Nick spread her legs and pushed his thighs between hers. She felt deliciously pinned by his possessive, merciless stare, by his muscled body. When he bent down and crushed his mouth against hers, his nipples chafed hers, and she moaned from the sensation of his iron-hard cock pressed into her swollen folds.

Cynda ached for him. Something new, something she had never known. If he took her now, he could thrust into her and hammer until dawn, and she wouldn't stop him.

She ran her fingers through his hair, pressed his lips against hers, but he pulled back and murmured, "I *will* make you scream, firebird."

Shock-fast, before she could react, Nick lowered his head, clamped his teeth over one nipple, and sucked it hard into his hot mouth.

Cynda cried out. Her head banged against the wooden

table. Flames shot from her fingers, but Nick's golden glow absorbed everything she threw as he nipped and sucked, then rubbed her other nipple firmly between his fingers. Each time his teeth scraped the sensitive flesh, electric bolts surged through Cynda's entire body. When he groaned against her breast, she almost exploded on the spot.

"Nick." She gulped air. "Please. Nick!"

He answered by sliding his hand one way, his mouth the other. Cynda felt his breath sweep across her chest, then he was licking her other nipple, sucking it, and rubbing the one he abandoned with his rough, demanding fingers.

Cynda groaned. She throbbed all over, ached between her legs so fiercely she thought she'd die. Waves of heat crashed behind her closed eyes. So fast, hurtling toward the edge and almost there *already*.

Was the ceiling on fire?

The walls, burning . . .

Smoke swirled through the room. Behind Nick, something crackled and popped.

"I can't take much more," she whispered. Barely audible. Hardly able to talk at all.

"You can." Nick slid his free hand down and stroked her once between her legs, teasing, his fingers liquid fire on her swollen center. As Cynda bucked and moaned, he said, "You will."

His mouth felt like heaven and hell on her skin, and his gentle nibbles made her shiver with shock and delight.

Again and again he bit her, sucked her, teased her. Fire burned through Cynda, licked back at Nick. All around them, flames and sparks danced and shimmered.

"Stop," Cynda finally pleaded, head spinning from the heat and toe-curling pain and pleasure. "I can't." But even as she spoke, she thrust her breast farther into his mouth. Nick captured her nipple in his teeth and flicked the end harder, faster with his tongue.

Cynda groaned and arched forward, pressing the sensitive flesh deeper, ever deeper. She couldn't help herself. She couldn't stop even as she pounded her fists against Nick's shoulders. He gathered her other breast, pressed it into the first, and sucked both nipples at the same time.

"Goddess!" she screamed. The fire built fast and thick in her belly, threatening to burst outward and consume whatever stood in its way. "I'll burn you to death. I mean it!"

Abruptly, Nick released her breasts, and Cynda screamed all over again.

Flames shot along the conference table, circling her body, shooting higher, higher, and crashing back across her like a waterfall.

Ignoring the fire, Nick slid his lips down her belly, and lower, lower, into the pulsing heat between her legs.

Out of her mind, Cynda thrust her hands into Nick's hair, grabbed fistfuls, and braced both feet against his shoulders.

Nick parted her lower lips with one deft move of his tongue, circling but never touching that sweet spot. Gentle strokes. Around, around, around.

Any second, he'd give her relief. She just knew it.

But he didn't.

He held her with his big hands on her hips, her feet pressed into his shoulders, with her whimpering as he took his time, tasting, kissing, exploring every inch. The smell of scorched wood and blistered paint covered the room, and through it all, Cynda could smell her own arousal, and Nick's, like lava about to burst into blue-hot flames.

She strained to move his mouth where she wanted it. "Bastard. Bastard!"

Nick laughed.

The rumbling sensation between her legs nearly drove Cynda over the edge. She almost ripped Nick's hair out by the roots, cursing him, writhing against his grip— and at last, at last, he swiped his tongue across her pulsing center.

Her body took over, arching out and up, pressing her flesh into his face, his mouth, that unbelievable teasing tongue.

Nick pulled her forward, sucking her into his mouth, catching her in his lips. Then he used his tongue to stroke, stroke, stroke on the delicate nub. Cynda gulped air, desperate, moving herself against Nick's tender assault. In and out of his mouth. His tongue tortured her, slower, then faster, relentless, endless.

Perfect.

"Don't you dare stop." She tugged at his hair. "I *will* kill you if you stop."

Pieces of flaming ceiling peppered the conference table.

Nick didn't stop.

Cynda thought she would split down the middle with the force of her orgasm.

Fire blasted through her, into her, out of her in every direction. Her mind expanded and contracted, squeezing in on itself just like her body. Curtains of flames coursed up and down her skin, joining with Nick's golden glow— and still the man didn't stop. Cynda thrashed.

She screamed, and screamed some more as the sensations kept coming, kept flowing. So hot. So consuming. Nothing like this. Never before. Her body couldn't stop moving, trembling, jerking as every part of her spasmed from the pleasure, so much, almost too much.

Cynda forced herself upward, panting, still moaning, and yanked at Nick's hair until he stood. His hair fell loose around his shoulders. She could barely see his grin through the smoke as she slid her hands down his belly, into those thick, curly short hairs. Not wanting to wait another second, she wrapped her fingers around his cock.

Big. Ooooh, yes. Thick, hard, ready, and she wanted him inside her right now. Five minutes ago.

But he was pulling at her wrists, telling her no, stopping her—why?

Damnit, why?

"Not now, firebird."

His voice rasped with desire, but he peeled her fingers off his erection.

Just about then, Cynda realized part of the table was disappearing beneath her ass. Burning away to so much ash and nothing.

A smoke alarm blared.

How long had that been going off?

Shit.

She blinked. Noticed the room behind Nick's gorgeous, naked body.

SHIT!

He caught her and pulled her to her feet before her ass wedged itself into the burning table. Her legs wobbled, didn't want to support her, but Nick gently held her upright as she threw every bit of energy she still possessed into drawing all the stray fire back into her body.

It was work.

A *lot* of work.

Minutes later, Cynda stood beside Nick, flushed with a totally different kind of heat as she stared at the disaster. "Oooooooh, shit, shit, shit. This has *never* happened before."

He draped an arm around her waist and pulled her against him. "It's not so bad."

"The walls are scorched, Nick."

"It's washable paint." He kissed the side of her head.

She gave him a little head-butt. "The desks are burned."

"Yeah, but only that front one's destroyed. I'll bag the pieces and pitch it out. We've got extras in storage." He kissed her cheek this time.

"The ceiling . . ."

He kissed her ear, her neck, sending tingles all along her shoulders and back. "Take a work crew an hour to patch it, tops."

She pushed him away before she started smoking and burning down rooms again. "You'll call for one?"

"As soon as I throw out the desk." His smile made her happy in strange ways. More than anything, she was glad to see him looking relaxed and unburdened, even though the price was her humiliation for the rest of her natural existence.

"Stop laughing, Nick."

"You screamed."

She hit him in the chest with both fists. "Shut up. Do you know the level of crap I'll be taking from my triad?"

"Yeah, but you screamed." He ran a hand through her hair, still grinning. "We'll, uh, have to give this a little thought before we go another round. By tomorrow, maybe?"

Cynda pointed her finger at his nose. "You—you—you put some clothes on and take this messed-up conference table to Merilee's library and hide it. Swap it out for one without burn holes and scorch marks."

Meanwhile, I'm naked, and downstairs, and who knows how many people are in this house tonight . . .

"Nick Lowell, you stop laughing right now!"

❨ 10 ❩

Nick woke later than usual Thursday morning and lay in his king-sized bed for a few quiet minutes, still sore from the battle—and hauling desks, swapping tables, washing scorch marks off walls, and patching the conference room ceiling enough for it to hold until the work crew gave it a real fix.

Damn, that woman is hot.

Smart, sexy, strong, and more willful than anyone he'd ever known.

Worth all the cleanup, and then some. Too bad all the destruction freaked her out too much to spend the night with him last night. It wouldn't have been so bad if he had brought her here to his space. He didn't have much in his room save for the bed, a desk, and a couple of bookcases. If she had burned it all to bits, that would have been no big loss, as long as she didn't feel guilty about it.

Nick could tell Cynda had a big heart. Huge. A lot of love to give the right man, someone who could handle her, tame her just enough to survive kissing her good night. And she tasted like some sweet, exotic spice. The way she moved and moaned and burned when he touched her, he didn't know how he'd ever get enough of that.

One thing he did know for sure, though—he wanted more. All of her. Now. If he could just figure out how to make love to her without burning down the Upper East Side . . .

He threw the sheet off his legs and got up, still

pondering that little dilemma. A problem for later today. For now, he had to get his lazy ass downstairs and talk to Creed and Andy about getting intel on the Bronx house. After Cynda helped him . . . uh, spend his energy, he knew they were right about needing to take more time in the planning. But not too long. No way he could sit around with his thumb up his ass indefinitely, not knowing what was happening with Jake or the Legion.

Half an hour or so later, he found Creed and Riana already downstairs in the kitchen, dressed in their running clothes. They sat at the big round cannonball table that dominated the kitchen, cradling coffee mugs and talking to Merilee, who was bundled up in a red flannel gown and robe, wearing some kind of fuzzy pink slipper-boot things.

Merilee smiled at him, but put her hand over some diagrams on the table.

Nick could see enough of the papers to know they were probably schematics of the Bronx house. He shook his head. "Don't worry. I'm calmer this morning."

Creed shot him a grin. "Would that have anything to do with the soot I saw you scrubbing off the conference room walls?"

Riana flushed and stared down at her coffee mug. Merilee laughed. Nick gave his brother a grow-up look followed by a hell-yes wink, then headed for the coffeepot.

Cynda stumbled through the kitchen door dressed in lavender silk pajamas, her red hair a delicate mess around her beautiful face. She had her arms wrapped around herself, shivering. "Stupid chills," she grumbled. "Stupid old haunted house."

Nick stopped walking the second he saw her. Her presence jolted him wide awake. He felt her all over his body, remembered her taste, her smell, her screams. He wanted to touch her. Maybe carry her back to the conference room and see if they could finish burning the whole place to ashes. Who cared? The townhouse was half his anyway. He could afford to rebuild rooms they destroyed.

As she passed between Nick and the counter, he caught her fragrance of vanilla and cinnamon, and his already-stiff cock ached. He took in the soft, sleepy look in her green eyes, the way her pajama top gaped to show a tantalizing bit of cleavage, and the way her hips curved in the loose silk pants. Then she glanced back at him and gave him a sexy smile.

He almost groaned out loud.

Could desire kill a man?

Cynda grabbed a cup from the nearest cabinet, then reached down to turn on the water. The knob came off in her hand. Water plumed from the pipe and splattered against her face with so much force Nick actually heard her suck up a good noseful.

She coughed, dropped the cup and knob into the sink, and fell backward onto the kitchen floor before the glass finished shattering.

Nick stood frozen, too surprised to move.

Cynda swore loud enough to wake up all the dead in a two-mile radius.

Water splattered against the ceiling, then arced back down to the cabinets and floor like some possessed fountain. Wind chimes jangled all over the five-story townhouse. The kitchen tabletop caught fire.

Riana, Creed, and Merilee leaned back.

Cynda's pajama bottoms and part of a kitchen curtain blazed, too. Her shirt probably would have burned if it hadn't been completely soaked.

Before Nick could react, Cynda swore again, pulled her fire energy back as best she could, and directed the force of her elemental power to the spouting water. The heat began to contain the geyser. Water hissed and evaporated as she got back to her feet.

"A little help?" she said pointedly to Nick. "Hello, big man? Earth to Nick!"

The sound of her voice jarred him into action. He leaned forward, fumbled in the sink for the faucet's knob, found it, and forced it back where it belonged. As he screwed the metal piece down into place, water jetted and pulsed, drenching him across the face and shoulders, then abruptly stopped.

"Stupid piece of crap," Cynda grumbled as he twisted the knob as tight as it would go.

He glanced at her.

She glared first at the knob and then at Nick while water dripped from her face and hair all over her chest. One by one, droplets of water ran down the cleft between her breasts, and her tight nipples pressed against her wet shirt.

Now Nick *knew* desire could kill a man.

He needed life support.

If Cynda couldn't read the raw desire on his face, she could sure see the bulge in his jeans. The metal under his hand heated and slowly glowed orange, stinging his palm.

He let go of the knob in a hurry.

Thankfully, Cynda managed to breathe and calm down before the metal actually melted and flamed.

It could happen, if she got mad enough. Nick had no doubt. He wiped his face with his sleeve, and fought an urge to wipe Cynda's face, too. That would probably be fatal at this point.

I think I'll marry her.

The thought caught him off guard, almost worse than the water spout. He almost laughed out loud.

"Hope somebody made coffee," Andy mumbled as she staggered through the kitchen door, wearing shorts, a long-sleeved shirt, and ugly purple socks, and looking an even bigger mess than Cynda. Andy's eyes weren't even completely open. Cynda had to get out of her way, or get trampled.

When Andy got to the coffee and found the huge puddles of water, her eyebrows came together. "Who showered in the sink?"

"Cynda," Merilee said.

Her top diagram caught fire as Cynda sat beside her, but Merilee smacked out the little flame with her hand.

Nick waited until Andy poured herself a cup, spilled some, yanked off half the paper towel roll, mopped up the spill along with some of the water, and got out of his way. Then he got his coffee ration, took his cup to the table, and sat between Cynda and Andy.

Cynda's leg pressed against his almost immediately, and Nick had to work not to start glowing. The throbbing in his cock came back with a vengeance, and he wondered if the cannonball table would burn through as fast as the conference table had.

"Did you speak with the Mothers this morning?" Riana asked Cynda, easing her coffee mug back to the table.

Keeping her leg firmly against Nick's, Cynda said, "They didn't find anything useful on Maura's *shotel*. The blade was clean. But they're sending out temporary replacements to all the triads who lost a fire Sibyl, until things calm down and the triad leaders have a chance to spend time with the adepts and pick a best match." She shook her head. "Between this mess and all the warriors we lost in that battle a few months back, the numbers are low. There aren't that many adepts ready to take on full service."

Merilee toyed with her stack of schematics. "Motherhouse Greece is in similar shape—about half as many adepts as they usually have."

Nick gestured to the diagrams. "Is that the Bronx house?"

When everyone looked at him, he said, "I told you, I'm calmer." He made a V over his nose. "Demon's honor."

"Didn't Samantha used to do that on *Bewitched*?" Andy asked blearily. Then she glanced at Riana, Merilee, and Cynda. "You keep telling me none of you are witches. Don't fuck with my head this early in the morning."

Cynda snickered. Everyone else just kept looking at Nick with his fingers over his nose.

Merilee slid the diagrams to Cynda, who passed them on to Nick.

He picked up the papers and flipped through them. About twenty in all. Air Sibyls were nothing if not thorough, he was learning. More and more, Merilee reminded Nick of a mad librarian. Using a combination of hand-drawn pictures and notes plus architectural diagrams and plain paper photos printed off her moody computer, she had pretty well lined out their target. A two-story fieldstone house, 1700s vintage, that reminded him of the historic Valentine-Varian House over on Bainbridge.

Ten windows across the front, black shutters, and two chimneys, one on either end of the place.

"Does it have a basement?" he asked.

"No, thank the Goddess." Merilee made a motion for him to dig deeper, where he found documents describing modifications made to the house over the years, as per city permits. One of the renovations involved filling in the house's root cellar with concrete pillars to support an aging floor joist. The attic had been torn out, too, replaced with skylights and a loft bedroom.

Good. Fewer opportunities for surprise.

He would have gone on to the next page of information, but Cynda started rubbing his leg under the table. Her touch was soft, and her movements subtle. Nobody could tell what she was doing except him, and his thoughts jumbled, turning circles, then zeroing in on the exact movements of her hand.

Damn.

Nick raised his head and looked at her.

Her green eyes glinted with amusement. "Don't get too intense," she said, her voice sugar-sweet and innocent. "It's days before this is going down."

On her last two words, *going down,* her palm slid directly over his erection, and she stroked him through his jeans.

Hot damn.

Creed gulped the last of his coffee and let his mug clatter to the table. "So, bro, what's your plan for now? Tell us before report, and we'll do our best to get Freeman to agree."

Nick's cock bucked against the ever-tighter fabric as Cynda rubbed him again, a little harder. Sweat broke out along the back of his neck.

For a moment, he couldn't speak, and he sure as hell couldn't think of any plan beyond jerking Cynda out of that chair, hauling her upstairs, tearing off her wet silk pajamas, and turning his bedroom into a first-class barbecue pit.

Everyone was looking at him now, especially Cynda, with that grin of hers.

What would she do if he grabbed her and kissed her right here, in front of everyone?

He was getting close.

Mustering all the will he possessed, Nick strangled his coffee cup and forced his attention to his twin. "I'm hunting Max Moses and bringing the bastard in. The surveillance unit checked Delilah Moses's apartment last night, and she *is* gone. Place was torn to hell. We need to find out if Max was blowing smoke about her being Downy's captive."

"I'm starting to think Downy's a spook." Merilee leaned back in her chair. "The CIA kind, not the sheets and chain-rattling boo kind."

"Why?" Riana asked, taking Creed's hand in hers.

"I've been through every database I can access, and two I'm not even supposed to know exist, and none of her data traces back to anything solid." Merilee reached across Cynda and took back her papers from Nick. "Her Social belongs to a dead woman, her passport tracks to some kid from Jamaica—the island, not New York. I've got fixes on her in Boston and Philly and Washington, D.C., real estate transfers and purchases. But I can't prove she even exists."

"She exists," Cynda said, her palm going still on Nick's cock. "Gut instinct on that one."

He didn't know what was worse, the steady rub, or the pressure from her fingers—and the anticipation they might move again. When she eased her hand away, he almost reached under the table and snatched it back.

He glanced at Cynda's face, and his arousal faded a fraction. She looked serious and troubled. Morning sunlight illuminated green traces of the bruise under her eye, healing Sibyl-fast, but still obvious.

A new set of emotions pummeled Nick. Worry. Concern. A strong desire to cart her off, caveman style, to some safe place where no one could bother her or hurt her, or shoot at her, or send demons exploding through a wall behind her head.

Where would that *be?*

Cynda put both hands on top of the table, laced her fingers together, and stared at them.

Nick stared at them, too, and wished she were still touching him.

"What if J. C. Downy doesn't have anything to do with the Legion?" Cynda asked.

"She has to be Legion." Andy took a long sip of coffee. "She attacked us with fifteen Curson demons yesterday. Did you miss that?"

Cynda trained her gaze on the ceiling, like she was forcing her thoughts into words. "Downy didn't set the demons on us. Max Moses did, and he commanded them with their talismans." When she looked down again, it was at Riana. "Any one of us could have done the same thing. We *have* done it, at one time or another, since Creed and Nick showed up."

Riana let go of Creed, leaned forward, and propped her elbows on the table. "What are you getting at?"

"Just because the Legion made those demons doesn't mean they're in control of them, any more than they've got control of Nick and Creed." Cynda's eyes shifted from Riana to Creed, and then to Nick. "If they bolted from Legion control, why wouldn't other Cursons do the same thing?"

"Long-lasting, durable—but too costly . . . and too independent," Andy said.

A small shock coursed through Nick when he looked at Andy, because the woman's face had changed. She was totally awake now. Tense. Sitting straight in her chair, fingers tight around her mug, so tight her knuckles were turning white.

"Excuse me?"

Andy didn't speak. Almost seemed like she couldn't. She seemed to be growing more pale by the second.

Creed cleared his throat. "That's something our—our parents, said in front of Andy and me, Nick. When they had us prisoner upstairs in the library, they said the Legion abandoned the creation of Curson demons because we were failures for their purposes—because we're too independent."

Nick turned more completely toward Andy. He had known she went through some serious trauma at the hands of the Legion, but he hadn't realized the severity of the toll it had taken. Andy was still responding to that ordeal, all these months later, like cops who didn't get over making a kill, or taking a hit in the line of duty.

Battle fatigue. Post-traumatic stress.

He gently pried her coffee mug out of her fingers and set it on the table. "Take a breath, champ. Those assholes are dead. If they rise from the grave, Riana and I will kill them again."

Andy shot him a hateful, agitated look, but she took a breath. And another.

On her other side, Riana put her hand on Andy's arm.

Andy flinched at her touch, but quickly relaxed. "Sorry," she muttered, obviously embarrassed.

"No way." Merilee shook her head. "You've got nothing to apologize for."

"Why don't we take a walk?" Riana suggested. Her gaze swept around the table, landing first on Merilee, then on Cynda.

The Sibyls stood at the same time. Cynda's hand brushed against Nick's shoulder. She gave it a quick squeeze.

Andy didn't protest as Riana helped her out of her chair.

Less than a minute later, the women were gone, leaving Nick and Creed at the table alone. The room felt oddly empty and flat.

Nick stared at the kitchen door, still feeling traces of Cynda's presence, breathing in that last bit of vanilla and cinnamon scent she left behind. He had a stupid high school urge to follow her just so he could look at her, and he almost hit himself with his coffee mug to knock that thought out of his head.

For a time, it was quiet.

Then Creed said, "Bro, I think you're in trouble."

Nick didn't bother arguing.

Andy wasn't good.

Cynda knew that when she checked on her friend after an exhausting day of meetings, arguing about the best plan to safely target the Bronx house, and a brief triad mission. She, Riana, and Merilee had been called out to break up a catfight between two voodoo priestesses trying to sacrifice the same pig to feed the god Bosou Koblamin. Who, in Cynda's opinion, was one mean-ass bastard. Like they needed three-horned voodoo war Loas showing up in Manhattan right now anyway. She'd had to shower for an hour to scrub off the scent of pork and fresh blood.

When Cynda finally found Andy, she was sleeping like the dead in Merilee's extra bed in the far corner of the library, near the fireplace where Merilee kept a good, warm blaze.

"Captain Freeman said she's been up here since our walk this morning," Merilee whispered as they eased away from Andy so they wouldn't disturb her. They crossed the massive library, back toward Merilee's makeshift "room," which was located between two towering library bookcases. On the way, they passed the partially scorched conference table, which Nick had tucked against a wall and covered with a nice white tablecloth. He had even put a vase and flower on one corner and a book on the other. When Cynda squinted at the book, she saw its title.

Kama Sutra.

Cynda almost tripped. Her entire face flushed red. *I'll kill him.*

Merilee laughed outright when she saw Cynda looking at the table and the book. "That cloth doesn't hide everything. I checked. Looks like your ass burned straight through?"

"Shut up." Face actually smoking now, Cynda hurried past the table without looking at it again.

"You should definitely sleep with Nick at least ten or fifteen times and get it out of your system," Merilee said.

"Shut up!"

When they reached her bed, Merilee flopped onto her pillows. "There are ways to contain the damage, I'm sure." Her loose blue jogging suit sagged against her thin frame, and her short blond hair stuck up in all directions, still damp from her shower. "We can always build you two a fireproof chamber."

Cynda groaned as she took a seat in the leather wing chair near Merilee's bed. If she didn't stop thinking about how it felt to have Nick's arms around her, how delicious his naked, powerful body felt pressed against hers, she'd catch the drapes on fire. All of a sudden, her jeans seemed tight against her sensitive skin, and her cotton tunic brushed her arms and belly too softly.

Every inch of her responded to thinking about Nick in ways she couldn't predict, couldn't control, and that drove her nuts. Which was why she came to spend time with Merilee before she went to find Nick and see where all of this was leading—or whatever it was she planned to do with him.

Sometimes just being around her triad sisters helped her feel calm and connected to the universe, helped her think her way through knotty problems.

Merilee rolled onto her belly, propped herself on her elbows, and grinned at Cynda. "Maybe you should go ahead and set a wedding date."

Cynda gaped. "Thanks, but you can cram that idea sideways and rotate it."

"Oooh. Cramming and rotating. See?" Merilee's grin widened. "Your brain is stuck on sex. Do it often and well. You'll feel better."

Cynda would have popped her triad sister with a fire jet, but she didn't want to risk flames around so many books and papers. "But Nick's . . . complicated. And somber and moody and intense. I don't get a casual vibe from him at all, and I *don't* do relationships."

"Then we should get you out of this hole to socialize and play the field." Merilee waved her hand like her giant library was some tiny prison.

Cynda almost laughed.

The townhouse's library was easily half the length and width of the entire building. Merilee had cleared out some old encyclopedias and moved her archives into the big, high-ceilinged room. The balcony and window curtains were, of course, open. Merilee said closed curtains made her feel trapped.

Her mess, however, never seemed to faze her. Already most of the tables were filled with stacks of notebooks, papers to be filed, and piles of disorganized notes. Tacked up to the wall near the room's only desk was a detailed map of the city, a copy of the one in the conference room. Pins marked routes to the target houses they had cleared or were watching, and Post-its held vital info gleaned from police surveillance. The whole room smelled like old parchment, leather, markers, and tape. It might be a mess, but at least it was a mess with a purpose. Merilee could find information about anyone, anywhere, make a note about it, and never forget it.

Finding her toothbrush? Now, that was an entirely different matter.

"Socialize and play the field. Yeah." Cynda did her best to keep her expression light. "Sorry, honey. I'm not feeling social these days. Besides, I'm not allowed to go anywhere without an escort, remember? And that would be Nick."

"I'll escort you." Merilee paused, then wiggled her eyebrows. "Want to wake up Andy, go to the gym and pick up some hot boy toys? Have a nice no-angst, no-strings-attached workout?"

"Now that idea has merit." Cynda tried to smile, but the thought of gym guys turned her stomach more than usual. She had never been as free and relaxed as Merilee. It was hard to let her guard down, even for a few hours, with somebody she'd never have to see again—but now that Nick was in the picture, it felt . . . *wrong*.

Oh, not good.

Bad, in fact.

Horrible.

"Shit." She banged the back of her head against her chair.

"Mmm-hmmm." Merilee's expression turned serious, and the mischief left her blue eyes. "I thought so. You're already exclusive."

Cynda dismissed that little bit of madness with a flick of her wrist. "Nick and I haven't gotten anywhere near talking about that."

"Don't you get it?" Merilee touched her chest. "You're exclusive here, whether you've talked about it or not." Her finger stayed directly over her heart. "Now, I know you'll feel better if you admit *that*. At least to yourself and me, even if you don't tell anyone else."

Everything inside Cynda wanted to yell at Merilee that she was completely out of her mind. Her hands shook, then smoked, and she bit her lip to keep from letting out sparks.

Was she really this close to having a serious bond with somebody other than a Sibyl?

Can't do it. Won't do it.

Have I already *done it?*

It took a little work inside, but when she thought she could breathe without blowing flames like a psychotic dragon, she said, "Yeah. Okay. You might have a point about the exclusive thing."

"All right." Merilee stretched her arms over her head and bent her legs one on top of the other, assuming one of her yoga poses. "If that's how you feel, why are you up here hanging out with me and our favorite zombie cop? You should be with him."

"I'm supposed to take you seriously when you're imitating food?" Cynda leaned forward in her chair and clasped her hands together. "Stop that. You look like a long blond pretzel."

Merilee didn't stop. "If you did more yoga and meditation, you wouldn't be wound so tight."

Cynda's mouth came open. "I am *not* wound tightly."

"And I'm a brunette." Merilee un-pretzeled.

"Screw you."

"No thanks." Serious-Merilee face again. "That's what you need to do with Nick. Now. G'night!"

"Merilee." Cynda smacked her hands against the chair arms. "Sex does not solve all the problems in the universe."

"Prove it."

"You're hopeless."

"And you're horny." Merilee arched her back and stretched her arms toward the ceiling. "Please, go scratch the itch before you blow up something we can't fix. Sexual frustration is dangerous where you're concerned—at least at this level."

Cynda pushed herself to her feet, shaking her head.

What was she supposed to say to that?

Nothing.

There wasn't anything she could say.

Merilee studied her with those too-smart blue eyes. "It's never been like this before, has it." A statement, not a question. "All these years I've known you, I've never seen you almost burn down the house. Scorch a few sheets, freak out a few one-night stands, okay. But damn, woman. That table, that conference room—go talk to him, Cynda."

No sense arguing. Cynda took a slow, slow breath and let it out. She *did* come here to sort out her thoughts, didn't she?

Feeling drained, yet jumpy and excited, too, she headed away from Merilee's bed. Before she rounded the bookcases, she stopped and looked back. "Will you take care of Andy?"

Merilee reverted to pretzel-shape, this time with her long legs bent around her neck, her back stiff, and her arms flat on the bed. "Absolutely. Consider her my new project. I think I'll buy her a two-week vacation in Austin, Texas. Or maybe Houston."

Cynda tilted her head to see Merilee's face in that bizarre pose. "Why Texas?"

"Duh? Cowboy butts!" Merilee unwound herself and reached both arms in Cynda's direction, stretching. "But maybe the beach would be better. Yeah. I'll send her to Hilton Head. No, wait. Daytona. It'll be warmer in Florida."

"Florida sounds like a very good idea." Cynda slipped past the bookcase and quietly padded across the library to give Andy a quick check. Still sleeping. Cynda pulled up the sheet and blanket, covering Andy's shoulders.

Definitely Florida. Sun. The beach, the ocean. She needs to clear her head, have a little peace.

After making sure Andy's breathing was still regular, Cynda left the library, walking slowly down the steps, careful not to knock over the books stacked here and there against the wall.

Were all cops messy disasters, or what? They could at

least reshelve the crap they read. By the time she made it to her own hallway, she had stepped over no less than ten piles. Dictionaries, encyclopedias, texts on weather patterns, some treatises on ancient medicine, and, of all things, an elementary Latin learning set. Some of that stuff didn't look like standard fare for reading or studying, and didn't seem like anything Nick would read, or Andy or Merilee, or even Sal Freeman, who often stayed at the townhouse during the week. Cynda mentally filed the book piles under freaky things about HCQ. Maybe the place *was* haunted.

By very nerdy ghosts.

Closer and closer to Nick's room, but she was trying hard not to think about that—in between rehearsing what she might do or say.

Excuse me, but are we getting real here?

Am I just a hot lay, or do you want something more?

Nick, where are we headed?

Each approach sounded more idiotic than the last.

"I'm a fire Sibyl," she said aloud as she wandered down the beautiful Oriental rug leading toward Nick's door. "I'm supposed to be able to communicate, no matter what."

A chill hit her, and she shook all over. She hated the drafts in the townhouse, the sudden pockets of icy air, and the ever-shifting breezes, but she supposed that was the price they paid for such a big space. With every step, her heart beat faster, and she walked a little slower through that endless space.

Stupid hallway was still too dark. It didn't feel warm and personal and cozy yet. She kept having the urge to burn stripes or zigzags into her walls, or hang spotted curtains. Something. Anything to modernize and lighten and make the place more real. Painting her walls had been a compromise, but now she wondered about painting her hallway light lavender, like her room. Maybe with a few well-placed runes and mirrors and a few more sets of wind chimes, the space would seem brighter.

Nick would just looove purple walls outside his door. Her eyes flicked toward his door, and heat started to build in her belly. *He'd probably paint everything black if I gave him half a chance. Including the lightbulbs.*

Her anxiety climbed another notch, and the two sets of wind chimes in the hall started to ring in response. No specific message. Just disquiet. Unease. Excitement. All coming from her. She frowned at the tinkling noises. Maybe no more wind chimes. In fact, maybe she should rip these little metal pipes down, or burn their strings in half.

"Get a grip." She rubbed at the healing bruise under her eye. "It's not like you're a virgin."

"That's nice to know," said a deep, sensual voice directly behind her.

Cynda jumped and whirled around.

Nick stood about a foot away, dressed much as he had been all week, in sexy, faded low-rider jeans and a black shirt, with his coal-dark hair pulled into a ponytail that rested casually against the nape of his tanned neck.

"Don't scare me like that." She shivered. The way he looked at her, she could feel it, everywhere all at once. It made her breasts ache. It made her tingle. It made her *crazy*. "How do you always sneak up on me anyway? I'm a Sibyl, for the sake of the Goddess."

"I wasn't sneaking," he said with a fake-innocent expression. "I was taking my coffee cup to the kitchen."

"Yeah, sure. Do you ever tell anyone the whole truth?"

Nick's face went flat. Cynda counted three seconds, then four, then five, before he said, simply, "No."

Her eyebrows shot up. She couldn't help the reaction. Of all the responses he could have given, Cynda didn't expect *that* one. A tendril of smoke curled up from her bare feet and she got dizzy from smothering a powerful urge to kiss him until he stopped looking so tense.

"Too many years of undercover work, I guess." He gazed at her, and she couldn't look away from his endlessly dark eyes. "Sorry. I'll do better. At least with you."

"Oh. Okay." She wanted to smack herself in the head. *Lame*. Why did her IQ have to start deserting her? Would she ever feel normal and balanced in a conversation with him?

"Cynda," he said quietly, and the husky sound of his voice made every inch of her body smoke. She imagined herself pinned against Nick's door as he tore off her clothes and took her over and over, until neither one of them could stand. She could already feel the heat of his touch, the firm silk of his lips.

Fire danced along her tunic sleeves, and the sleeves started to melt.

Nick strode toward her and Cynda threw herself into his waiting arms. Nick's mouth crushed hers, his hands already moving, stroking her sides, settling on her ass. Cynda moaned and kissed him with what felt like a lifetime of pent-up passion, loving his salty, musky scent, the hint of wintergreen on his lips, the tang of inner fire she tasted on his tongue.

Yes. This was right. This thing between them, whatever it was, wherever it went, it *had* to be.

Nick pressed against her, fierce and possessive, holding her tight, kissing her so hard she could barely get her breath. Flames roared over both of them, tickling and biting, warming without burning, as Nick's golden glow quickly absorbed the fire.

Grinding her belly into his erection, Cynda pulled his head closer, closer, thrusting her tongue across his.

Above her head, wind chimes rang.

And rang.

And rang louder.

Cynda broke away from the kiss, instantly aching for Nick's mouth again.

But the chimes—

A message. A communication from Motherhouse Ireland. She needed to get to the platform in her room, to the mirrors.

A burst of fire slammed against the floor, screaming her frustration for her. The rug smoldered, sending up a distress signal of acrid smoke.

Nick held on to her as she tried to push away. "What's wrong?"

The chimes jangled.

Cynda glared up at them. "It's the Mothers. I have to go."

Louder and louder chimes. More insistent. Absolutely annoyed.

Cynda cupped Nick's cheek and rubbed her palm along the rough stubble of his jaw. "I really have to go."

Nick touched her with his eyes, stroked her arms with his gaze, brushed his mind across her lips and it felt as real and solid as an actual kiss. Cynda's knees went weak, then almost buckled when Nick said, "I'll be waiting right here, firebird. Don't be long."

A piece of her tunic sleeve dropped to the floor, and Cynda stomped the thing to ashes before it burned the rug even worse.

The wind chimes rang so hard she thought they might rip themselves off the ceiling.

With a huge sigh, she forced herself to walk away from Nick, then run, all the way to her door. She grabbed the knob, turned it, and more or less fell into her room.

Her heart skipped and squeezed, and her whole body shook. That man. *That man!* He had to have some kind of power beyond his *other*. He messed up her head. He messed up her mind.

She whirled toward the communications platform, intending to run across the floor and jump to it to see about the message from Motherhouse Ireland—but the message was standing right in front of her on the platform.

It was dressed in bright green robes and leaning on a gnarled bogwood cane, and it did *not* look happy.

"M-Mother Keara," Cynda whispered.

The old woman who had raised Cynda said nothing. Her hair, all gray now, fell in long ropes across her stooped shoulders, and her still-lively green eyes blazed beneath her wrinkled brow. Cynda caught an eye-watering draft of bay and rosemary, rushleek and mint, mixed with strong, fresh smoke. Her belly lurched from the force of it, and she was so worked up and emotional she almost burst into tears.

Home. She smells like the kitchens at Motherhouse Ireland.

After a few disoriented seconds, Cynda sprinted to the table. Mother Keara was no heavier than a bird, but her grip felt like iron clamps as she held Cynda's hands and stepped off the platform. When her feet rested firmly on the polished wood floor, she let go of Cynda, gazed around the room and finally sniffed, which was as much approval as she ever showed.

"Colorful at least," she murmured. "Ample space for the platform and mirrors, plenty of room for your harp. Excellent work with such a bland, dark canvas, *a chroí*."

Cynda smiled at hearing the term of endearment, which meant "heart." Mother Keara had given her that nickname so long ago. What had she been—six years old?

"Are you still playin' the harp at night to soothe yourself to sleep?" Mother Keara looked at her expectantly.

Cynda's smile slacked. Why hadn't she thought of doing that? Not in weeks. Months, even. Because raics and patrols and Nick were ruining her mind. That's all there was to it. She had to force herself not to glance toward her door and imagine Nick standing out in that hallway, waiting.

Mother Keara gestured to the four-poster. "Sit, sit, there on the corner of your bed, where I can see you better. And about that harp, don't be lettin' go of what your heart needs."

But I don't know what my heart needs anymore, Mother. Cynda's lips trembled.

Aloud, she said, "All right."

For a moment, Mother Keara gave no hint of why she had come in person. Cynda risked a glance at the mirrors hung at various intervals on the walls above the platform behind them, but the mirrors were all dark.

So, this was a private call. Cynda's ears only.

What have I done?

She tried not to look nervous, but Mother Keara could read her face even if she put a bag over her head. What was the point?

Gradually, the typical scowl on the old woman's face deepened. "You and I have need of an understandin', Cynda."

Okay, shit. Just, shit. I totally don't need this tonight. The few times Mother Keara had said those words to her in the past, Cynda hadn't liked the bargain or punishments that followed.

Whatever it was, it would likely eat up all of her time with Nick tonight. She didn't want to surrender that to anyone. Her muscles tensed, and the urge to cry came back, followed quickly by an urge to scream. She fought back both of these, but the other sleeve of her tunic burned off and dropped to the floor.

She stomped it out.

Mother Keara didn't comment on her loss of control, but then, she rarely did, unless an important building went up in smoke, or Cynda managed to murder a favorite tree or plant.

"I know you've been grievin' over changes and losses in your life, but you must hear me well." Mother Keara came forward and took Cynda's hands in her own again. "That pain gives you no excuse for rash action."

Cynda wanted to pull her hands away, but she didn't dare. "Excuse me?"

Mother Keara squeezed her fingers firmly. "Don't be pretendin' you don't know what I mean. I raised you. If your stomach cramps at night, I feel it in my own belly. You've been distracted lately, and slow to respond to the chimes. Somethin' has your attention, and it's not your triad, your duties, or even the grief and pain you need to resolve."

Cynda let out a defeated sigh. "You're talking about my feelings for Nick."

"Don't you dare say you have feelings for that creature! And don't be speakin' of him like he's human." Mother Keara let go of Cynda's hands and pointed a gnarled finger directly into her face. "He's no such thing. He's a demon in man-skin, and you best not be forgettin' that."

"I don't forget Nick has a demon-half," Cynda shot back, her temper blazing even if she *was* talking to Mother Keara. "I just don't think it's an issue anymore. When I was worried a few months ago—*I* was the one who came to the Mothers about Nick's twin Creed when Riana wouldn't. Do you remember that?"

"Yes, *a chroí*. Do you?"

The draperies started to smolder, but Mother Keara raised a hand and used her elemental power to snuff the flames. Cynda looked away from the old woman's unflinching stare, blinking back tears.

In moments, the old woman was patting her hands instead of squeezing them to death. "You told us you didn't trust the demon-man, that he might have dual purposes, that we needed to be sure of him. Yes?"

"Yes," Cynda said, hating the tearing sensation in her chest. "But—"

"I say to you the same thing about Nick Lowell. Don't trust the demon-man." She cupped Cynda's chin and turned Cynda's eyes toward her own. "Someone's killin' fire Sibyls. Someone who knows our ways."

"Ooh, no. No, you don't." Cynda twisted her face out of Mother Keara's grip. "You can't possibly think Nick has anything to do with murdering Nori and Maura and the rest."

"We don't know a thing about this being's true motives, about the damage done to him by his years undercover with murderers and maniacs." Mother Keara's voice got louder. She leaned forward, gripping her cane with both hands now. "We don't know the extent of his power. There's energy in this house even we can't read— huge, and dangerous. Nick Lowell can hide himself, even from our keen instincts, which may make him the most dangerous creature we've known to date. Worse yet, his soul seems darker, more twisted, less innocent than his twin's."

"Nick is a good man!" Cynda yelled before she could stop herself.

"He is not, *a chroí*!" Mother Keara thumped her cane hard on the wood flooring. "Nick Lowell isn't a good man, because Nick Lowell isn't a *man* at all." Her eyes seemed unbearably bright. "He's a Curson demon who killed his birth surrogate leavin' the womb. He helped drive his grandmother to an early grave. He killed his own mother in front of your eyes!"

"To save me. To save Riana and Merilee." Cynda had to use all of her emotional reserves not to look away. Her head spun. Her insides heaved. If it were anyone else saying these things, she would already have grabbed her sword and had done with it, but this was Mother Keara. This was the woman she most adored in the universe, the woman she'd die for.

"Nick's more human than demon." She met Mother Keara's flashing eyes, chin up, back straight. "I swear it."

Those wild Irish eyes narrowed to angry slits. "And you know this how?"

Cynda started to answer, then felt suddenly exposed, transparent, as if Mother Keara could read every kiss, every touch, like they were written into her skin. Confusion roiled in her mind until she didn't know what to say at all.

"Fire Sibyls fear no creature, Cynda, but neither do we take untenable risks like those fool Russian sisters of ours." Mother Keara's snort of disgust rang in Cynda's ears. "Motherhouse Ireland does not, and will not ever approve of a union between a Sibyl and a demon. Do you grasp what I'm tellin' you?"

Cynda didn't even try to answer. She didn't know whether to cry or swear or fetch her sword after all.

Mother Keara's eyes widened. Shock and anger spread across her aged features, and her voice turned ice-cold. "I'll make myself more clear, then. If you pursue a relationship with Nick Lowell, you'll be expelled from Motherhouse Ireland, removed from your triad, and cast out from our way of life. Stripped of your talents. Do you understand *that*?"

Darkness flickered at the edges of Cynda's vision. The fire inside her shrank and shrank, until she felt as cold as the Mother's words. Her teeth chattered, and she wrapped her arms around herself to keep from wailing.

Cast out?

Her elemental talent would be burned away. She'd be broken down to nothing but a human shell who could walk and talk and do menial jobs. She'd never see her triad or any of her sisters . . . or Mother . . . again.

Her heart crumpled in on itself. She couldn't imagine speaking or moving. She'd just stand right where she was, until tomorrow, or the next day, or until somebody took away the terrible threat and let her breathe again.

When she saw that Mother Keara was waiting for a response, more or less insisting on an answer with that stern glare, Cynda felt six years old again, homeless, with no one and nothing but the Sibyl family she had just been threatened with losing.

"Yes," she whispered, her words like glass cutting into her mouth and throat. "I understand."

A strange look crossed Mother Keara's face. Was it surprise? It looked disturbingly like disappointment, but Cynda couldn't begin to interpret it. Not now, with her soul and heart ripped in half. As she stared, the look shifted to a bright, loving grin.

For the first time ever, Mother Keara's smile didn't feel worth the capitulation.

"Sibyls and triad first, above all else," the old woman said.

"Sibyls and triad first," Cynda repeated, partly because she believed it, and partly because she knew it was what Mother Keara wanted to hear.

Mother Keara labored forward and rewarded her with a quick kiss on the cheek.

"You've always been closest to my heart, Cynda, and one day, perhaps destined to become a Mother in your own right. Don't go throwin' away all I've given you, or all you've given yourself."

Cynda kissed Mother Keara back, feeling the smooth, soft wrinkles of the old woman's cheek on her lips.

More my mother than the one who birthed me . . .

Mother Keara's eyes glittered again, in a better way, less ferocious, at least. "We have our understanding, then?"

Numb, Cynda forced herself to nod.

Puppetlike, she walked Mother Keara back to the communications platform and helped her to mount it.

The old woman chatted about upcoming equinox festivals and the progress of a few initiates Cynda had known, but Cynda didn't hear more than a few words.

Everything seemed dull and shattered.

By the time she placed Mother Keara in the platform's center and started her dance around the old woman, she just wanted to be alone. Maybe forever.

Cynda raised her arms and concentrated on her steps and patterns, on the elemental fire-force needed to seek out the old channels and grind them open.

I am the pestle of my triad, she thought as she spun in a wide circle around Mother Keara, faster and faster. *I am the connection between mortar and broom. I stand in the fire and speak when no one wants to hear my words. Let the flames burn as I speak when cowards would choose silence. I speak until no smoke obscures the truth.*

Above them, Cynda's image became a blur in the collection of projective mirrors on the wall. The sets of wind chimes in her room rang softly at first, then louder and louder, taking on the rhythm of her dance. Cynda turned loose her inner fire, for once secure in the knowledge that she would burn nothing, harm nothing, as the energy transformed into powerful, pulsing demands on the old channels that riddled the universe. Sparks skittered along the table's lead-lined lip, and little flames shot upward, not too high, just high enough. Heat blazed inside Cynda as the air changed, the light changed. Electricity crackled through the room, and the carved bog-oak mirror leading to Motherhouse Ireland brightened.

Smoke swirled in the glass, then parted to reveal waiting adepts.

The women stepped forward and began their own dance.

Cynda poured her anguish into the chaotic abandon of the dance. She joined with her fire Sibyl sisters with a loud, gut-level cry, spending the full force of her elemental power reaching across time and space, opening the channels, opening the world before her.

Mother Keara's presence and essence flowed past Cynda, into the channels, and the old woman was gone, gone, back across the sea, sweeping back to the secret little valley near Kylemore Abbey faster than any human eye could see.

When Cynda sensed the transfer was complete, she slowed her steps, then carefully completed and closed her patterns, moving her feet in ways she had known since her childhood.

She had been taught well. She had learned well.

In her most prized bog-oak mirror, Mother Keara now stood with the adepts on the communications platform inside Motherhouse Ireland. She blew Cynda a kiss and turned away.

Cynda drew air through her teeth, in and out, in and out, and watched until the mirror went completely dark.

Then she climbed off the platform. Her legs seemed too heavy to move, but she walked to her door.

When she opened it, Nick was standing in the hallway, right where he said he would be.

Cynda searched inside herself for words, explanations, something tangible to give him so he would understand what she had to do.

The look on his handsome face went from avid pleasure to confusion to concern, then to unhappy understanding.

Some things don't require discussion.

Hadn't he said that to her?

"Whatever it is, we can—" he started, but Cynda shook her head.

The hurt in his diamond-black eyes clawed at her insides.

Her throat closed off completely. She choked when she tried to breathe.

Before he could say anything else, she shut the door—but her fingers wouldn't turn the lock. Her arms and legs mutinied, and she couldn't even move.

Minutes dragged by.

Cynda stood there with her hand on the door handle, blood thumping in her temples, terrified Nick would say something she could hear through the thick wood.

Or knock.

Or kick the door down.

But he didn't.

A cry tore its way out of Cynda's locked throat. She leaned forward and pressed her face against the cool, hard wood. Her knees refused to hold her, and she sank slowly to the floor, crying so hard the sobs made her body ache.

Slowly, Cynda curled herself into a ball, her head still against the wood.

She stayed there for an hour. Then hours. Finally, all night. She had no idea what else to do.

(12)

Andy Myles left for a much-needed vacation before sunrise on Saturday morning. Nick put her on the red-eye to Florida himself, way before first light. All through the airport, she'd seemed draggy, tired, almost out of it. Definitely broken, definitely needing time to herself to patch her insides together again. He hoped the sand and sun would restore her. He also wondered if someone would be putting him on a plane for the beach soon. He was so pissed he might fry his brain cells and end up like Andy—permanently.

He seethed as he crouched in a little stand of elms near Strawberry Fields in Central Park.

Whatever the Mothers had done to Cynda two nights ago, she was damn sure going to tell him about it *today*. He had tried to talk to her four different times on Friday, but he couldn't get her away from her triad, and she didn't sleep in her own room last night. He had slept in a chair outside Merilee's library after he made sure that's where Cynda was, just to be sure he was close enough to help if anything went down.

How was he supposed to guard a woman who was avoiding him?

The last thirty-six hours, he could swear they dragged on forever, even at times like this, when he left Cynda with the Sibyls to protect her and went out tracking leads on Max Moses. By God, they would discuss everything, even if he had to throw her over his shoulder, haul her down to the stone basement gym she couldn't burn, and lock her inside.

Well . . . after everyone took care of business—the business he was about to haul back to the townhouse.

Nick flexed his fingers, ignoring the cold, the polished-steel scent of impending snow, ignoring the way the dawn light turned so gray it looked like sheet ice across the sunless sky. Wind whipped through the branches and undergrowth concealing him, sounding like bones rattling in a can. He had been waiting for this moment. He could almost taste the satisfaction of the next twenty minutes.

Max Moses had some explaining to do, if he lived long enough to speak.

He had managed to stay underground since the Sweetbriar house catastrophe, but Nick knew Max had needs that wouldn't let him stay hidden forever. Delilah Moses had been right about a goat being a goat. Max was back on the bottle and the blunt and who knew what else. True to the scuttlebutt Nick had picked up on his travels yesterday, Max was less than ten yards from him, finishing an illicit buy.

Let the bastard have his drugs.

By the time Nick finished with Max, the scum would *need* something for his nerves.

Deep inside Nick's mind, Gideon snarled like a hungry panther. Nick's demon-half surged, rose, outlined his flesh with a golden line of energy. If he wasn't careful, he'd singe his jeans.

Too much frustration.

Too much outright rage. He had to be careful.

Nick narrowed his eyes, waiting for the transaction to proceed.

It took a few seconds, but Max finally finished his purchase.

The mule took Max's money and ran, literally, jogging onto one of Central Park's paved paths. Dressed in his expensive sweats, jacket, and sneakers, the guy would have been hard to pick out as someone who moved drugs for a living.

Max, on the other hand, looked rougher than usual. He wore a pair of grimy jeans and a hooded sweatshirt full of holes and stains, and his face was more fading bruise than pocked skin. Most important, Max didn't have a bit of jewelry Nick could see. Unless his grubby clothes were talismans, or he had some crap hidden in his pockets, he was toast.

As Max gazed into his bag in full view of dozens of joggers and walkers—a no-no for any junkie who hadn't already lost his self-respect—Nick moved

The hood on Max's sweatshirt made for easy pickings. Nick had to exert all of his self-control not to yank the scum into the trees so fast and hard his neck snapped.

No one saw a thing.

No one seemed to hear a thing, either, not even when Max crashed to the ground in the underbrush at Nick's feet.

His bag went flying.

Flailing, whimpering, Max tried to flip onto his belly to make a grab for his dope, but Nick moved too fast for any human to react. He dropped to one knee and held Max on his back with the force of one slightly glowing hand on the man's throat.

Max coughed and sputtered. He grabbed Nick's wrist with both hands, but the effort was futile.

"Thought you knew better than to cross me." Nick let Gideon's near-presence add an echoing resonance to his words.

Max's eyes went wide. He didn't bother whimpering about police brutality, or posturing about how Nick couldn't hurt him. In the circles they traveled, such myths didn't even exist.

"I had to." Max's voice came out in a crooked whisper. "I told you—I *had* to."

"Make me understand." Nick increased the pressure of his grip. "Make me believe you."

This turned Max's expression from pathetic to miserable. His greenish bruises stretched as he grimaced. "Downy's got me mum, like I said. If I don't do what she says, the nut-bitch will kill her. Are you wantin' Delilah dead?"

"Where's Downy keeping her?"

"At the Bronx house I told you about, last I knew. She could'a moved her by now."

Nick shifted his weight and managed not to kill Max in the process. Gideon's closeness made the tang of Max's fear almost palpable. Fear and something else. The sharp undertone of rage. "I need more details, Max."

Max hesitated.

Nick ratcheted the pressure on the man's throat one more notch. "If you want Delilah to live, if *you* want to live, you'll tell me everything you know. *Now.*"

With a slow exhalation of breath, Nick allowed Gideon to step forward another fraction. He knew what would happen, that Max would see Nick's outline shimmer and shift into something alien, something *other*. He bared his teeth to heighten the effect.

"Jesus, Mary, and Joseph! You're like them!" Max squirmed against the ground, then went still save for panting. Nick eased Gideon deeper, and reverted to his human form.

Max gaped at him, then said in a rush, "When I found out Mum had been grabbed, I went to the Bronx house. You know, just to see what I could find out."

Nick nodded and eased up on the man's neck.

"Place looked empty, only when I got close, I got jumped. And they kept me there until *she* came." Max closed his eyes for a moment. "That Downy woman. Mean-faced. Mean-hearted. She had Delilah in cuffs on her wrists and arms. It was right pitiful."

Max shuddered.

Convincing enough, except this was Max, and Max really *knew* how to lie.

"Go on," Nick said. Not encouraging. Ordering.

"The ones holding Mum for Downy, they aren't people, see? They aren't even—well, whatever you are. Or those gold monsters I set on you at City Island. These are all something else. They're . . . all demon. Mostly you can't even see 'em, and they keep tabs on those Sibyl chicks, finding out their schedules and stuff, trying to figure out when they'll be apart and all."

Nick felt his eyebrows lift.

An organized group of Astaroths?

Snow started to fall.

Nick frowned at his captive. "You're a sensitive. What do you sense about these demons?"

Even though Nick had once more eased the pressure on Max's throat, the informant looked ashen and sick. He shivered. "They're evil. Pure evil, like they're made out of hate. They want the fire bitches to die. All of them. 'Cause it's what *she* wants."

"Why?" Nick asked himself more than Max.

"I don't know," the informant said. Then, as Nick once more let Gideon get close, "Jesus! I don't know!"

Gideon eased back, and Nick felt his skin settle into itself. "How many demons are in the Bronx house?"

"A lot. Couple of dozen, maybe more—and that's just the one house." Max twitched. "They've got more houses, and not just in New York. Other cities, too. Downy's collecting demons like crazy people collect cats."

"Give me names, Max. Legion or demon—whatever you've got."

This question drew a bunch of twitches, but Nick didn't even have to up the pressure on the informant's throat to make him say, "Just one. I think he's the head creator, or maybe the boss of all the demons. Guy named Jacob."

Nick turned Max loose so fast the informant didn't realize he was free for a full five seconds. Then he scrambled to his feet, grabbed his bag of dope, and faced Nick, rubbing his throat. Nick's heightened senses picked up the shift from acrid terror to sulfurous anger.

"All of this is boinked, you know that?" The informant glared at him.

"Yeah," Nick replied, mind spinning.

Jake. *Leading* the Bronx house Astaroths?

Helping Downy keep an old woman prisoner?

They're evil. All of them. Pure evil. That was Max's opinion.

Nick's gut burned.

And what's mine?

Downy could be forcing Jake. He could have gotten tired of the penalties for fighting her.

Or he could have been playing me for an idiot all along.

Max shoved his way into the nearby brush, but Nick lunged forward, grabbed him by the collar, pushed him to the ground, yanked his arms behind his back, and cuffed him.

"Max Moses, you're under arrest."

Max squirmed and kicked, then groaned as Nick hauled him to his feet. "For what?"

"Attempted murder of about fifteen cops and a bunch of other people on City Island. Property destruction. We could add conspiracy—I'll keep thinking. Oh, and possession of whatever the hell's in your little bag."

Holding the cuffs with one hand, Nick stooped, collected the bag, and shoved it in Max's sweatshirt pocket.

The bastard actually gave him a little smirk. "You might have me on the weed, but I'd like to see you make City Island and all that other stuff stick to *me*. No judge in his right mind will believe a word you say."

"You won't be seeing any judge here, Max." Nick shoved the scrawny man forward, out of the stand of elms, onto a paved path. When Max staggered, Nick grabbed him and pointed him north, toward the townhouse. "Some special judges in Ireland want a word with you. They're called Mothers."

Max slowed, and Nick gave him another push.

At the edge of the park, he took hold of Max's cuffs with one hand and put his free hand against Max's back. They crossed onto the sidewalk, with traffic whizzing alongside, and Max didn't struggle much, probably scared Nick would shove him in front of a bus.

The long, cold walk back to the townhouse did nothing to settle the fire inside Nick.

All he could think about was an ever-increasing army of Astaroth demons, intent on destroying fire Sibyls.

Cynda.

Not happening.

He'd be damned if they'd get her, or anyone else. He'd behead hundreds of Astaroths all on his own. Even if he had to take Jake down, just like he took down their mother.

I'm going to have to do it after all. Kill my brother. I can feel it in my gut.

Which ripped and tore until he wanted to blow a hole through his own center, just to stop the pain.

Nick's breath curled around him like dragon-flames as Gideon let loose an inner snarl.

My brother Jake.

The leader of the invisible demon horde.

Under Downy's control? Or not?

Nick guided Max in front of him as he crossed against traffic and flipped off the nearest honking driver.

Another family member's blood on my hands.

No.

There's got *to be another way.*

A few minutes later, Nick banged open the townhouse's front door and shed snow and ice on the polished, perfect herringbone hardwood floors as he marched Max toward the conference room.

"This don't look like a real precinct!" Max yelled. "What're you doin'? Help. Hey! Heee-eeelp!"

His racket summoned the troops better than any bell or siren.

Creed, Riana, Merilee, and Sal Freeman came out of the kitchen at a dead run. Riana looked like she had coffee all over her shirt.

More OCU officers poured out of side rooms, along with the North Staten Island Sibyl triad.

The sight of so many cops and the Sibyls in their fighting leathers—with swords and daggers clearly visible—made Max clamp his mouth shut. He gave Nick a look like he might piss his pants.

Cynda came running down the steps, wide-eyed. She was dressed in hip-hugging jeans and a black tunic, and she looked more than fine, even if he had half a mind to cuff *her* once he finished with Max.

Nick couldn't help gazing at Cynda for a few seconds before putting his hand on Max's head and forcing him forward, through the conference room door.

Everyone else came rattling in behind him. Freeman immediately sent the OCU officers out again to attend to whatever they'd been doing, but he let the Sibyls stay.

Nick pushed Max all the way to the front of the room and spun him around.

He waited for his audience to sit down, glaring first at Freeman, then at Creed, then at everyone else, one at a time.

They all eased themselves into desks facing Nick and

Max, Cynda on the far right. Nick didn't want to be so aware of her, but her presence grabbed a part of his mind and wouldn't let go.

"What's going on?" Riana asked, obviously rattled.

Nick shrugged. "I caught up with Max. Thought I'd bring him in."

"You . . . went after him alone?" Cynda looked surprised, then worried.

"That's how I've always done things." Nick couldn't help the Gideon-enhanced sharpness in his tone. He turned his face toward her and held her gaze without blinking. "Sorry I forgot to ask your permission."

"Or mine," Freeman said, his voice as cold as the weather.

Nick chose to give that remark a pass. For now. He and Freeman would have to resolve their differences later, or he *would* hand in his badge and work on his own.

Instead of getting into it with the captain, he shared the information Max had given him in the park. As he spoke, Merilee and the air Sibyl from Staten Island scrambled to get out their pads and pens and keep up.

Max squirmed a few times, but Nick kept him quiet by turning his head toward the increasingly angry armed Sibyls. As he spoke, he didn't hold back on the parts about Jake, even though it made his gut ache worse.

Creed's expression suggested he felt sick, but Nick knew he couldn't help his twin.

What was, was.

They'd just have to deal with it.

After relating all he had to relate about the Downy situation and the Bronx house, Nick said to Cynda, "I hear the Mothers like to do their own interrogations in situations like this. Why don't we go upstairs and get them on the line?"

Cynda's cool, collected expression faltered. She stammered for a moment, then came back with, "I'm not sure that's a good idea, Nick."

He forced his best smile. "I can always buy some plane tickets, and we can do this exchange in person."

Riana, Merilee, and the other Sibyls looked confused, which surprised Nick.

So, whatever happened the night before last, Cynda hasn't even told them.

He didn't know if that made him feel better or worse.

"I thought I was going to Ireland," Max mumbled, obviously confused.

Riana pushed out of her desk and stood. "I think it's a good idea." Her gaze flicked from Nick and Max to Cynda as everyone else got to their feet, and she hesitated. "If you don't want to send him, Jewel can do it." She gestured to the tall, brunette fire Sibyl from North Staten Island.

Cynda's mouth came open, but she didn't say anything.

Merilee stepped in with, "That's probably best." She gave Creed a little nudge, and he came forward to take control of the prisoner. To Cynda, she said, "Why don't you and Nick have a little chat?"

"Also a good idea," Riana agreed immediately.

Cynda wrapped her arms around her middle and looked like she wanted to die.

As Nick surrendered Max to Creed, the informant balked and strained to turn back to Nick. When Creed let him, Max asked, "Will you at least rescue me mum if you can?"

Poor bastard has no idea what's waiting for him in Connemara. Nick pushed the prisoner toward Creed and said, "Yeah."

At the same moment, Cynda said, "I'll save Delilah."

Nick locked eyes with her. Electricity seemed to crackle across the room.

Creed took Max off Nick's hands, and he and Freeman and the other Sibyls started to leave the room.

Cynda glanced after them and chewed on her lip.

Nick realized she was thinking about bolting out the door behind them.

Not happening, firebird.

He waited until Max, Creed, and Freeman cleared the door, then slipped forward while Cynda's attention was still on the procession of Sibyls.

Before she could get away from him again, he grabbed her around the waist, hoisted her, and tossed her over his shoulder.

She yelped with surprise.

Merilee, who was last in line, jumped at the sound, slowed for a second, but didn't turn to check.

At least somebody *in the Sibyl ranks trusts me.* As he finished the thought, he couldn't help putting his free hand on Cynda's firm ass to steady her.

His jeans caught fire.

"Don't do this," Cynda snarled as she pounded on his back with flame-coated fists.

Nick shifted his grip to keep her from kicking a hole in his ribs and said, "You're the one who's always wanting to talk, firebird. So let's talk."

He strode out of the conference room, carrying the swearing, fire-spitting Sibyl toward the basement, and just let his clothes burn.

Blood rushed to Cynda's face as Nick carried her over his shoulder while he dodged teetering stacks of books on his way to the basement. She continued to shout swearwords as his clothing sizzled from the flames on her fists and body. He didn't seem to give a damn that he would end up naked by the time he finally set her down.

If he set her down.

His boot heels sounded like gunfire on the wooden steps, and his maddening, musky ocean scent kept washing over her, threatening to take her fire. His skin was cold from his trip out to capture Max, his shirt still almost icy against her heat.

She tried to wriggle out of his grasp. "Nick! So help me, I can cook parts of you you'll *really* miss!"

He clasped his hand more firmly over her ass. "You keep up that noise, everyone in HCQ will be listening at the door."

She *so* didn't want to deal with him right now, with any of this. It was too hard being so close to him, wanting him with such a fierce rush of desire—and more. Something more.

Something she couldn't face right now.

Cynda squirmed and beat on his back, which was hard as a friggin' rock. Right now she hated him. She hated the Mothers. It didn't matter what she did, what choices she made, she was going to lose. And she was so tired of losing.

Losing her birth family as a child. Losing her home to Creed and Riana. Losing other Sibyls.

And now—the decision between losing the only true family she'd ever known or losing Nick.

What kind of choice was that?

The pain in her chest blossomed and a tear steamed away to nothing on her hot cheeks.

Her fists hurt from beating on his back. He probably didn't even feel her blows, but she kept hitting him until she spent so much energy her spurts of fire started to wane.

When he got her inside the basement, he closed the door behind them and locked it, all the while keeping an iron grip around her body. Then he marched her past restacked weights, new exercise balls, and patched mats, to the center of the room. He slid her off his shoulder, keeping her close, his arms around her waist as her feet found the stone floor.

Cynda fought waves of joy at his touch, and her fire diminished until only smoke drifted from her now-bare shoulders. It felt so good to be close to him, to feel his body against hers.

Joy slipped away, replaced by heart-wrenching pain. *Wrong. Every single thing in the world is wrong right now.*

But she still couldn't tear herself from him.

He was so right.

Why did this have to be so complicated? Why couldn't she have him *and* her family?

Cynda gazed into his black eyes and her tortured thoughts faded a bit. She shoved them to the back of her mind. For now. For just this moment.

The concern in his gaze, the pain—and something more—tore at her like a firestorm. The *something more* in his eyes—it seemed to match what she felt inside.

She wanted to kiss him so badly she felt it like a storm in her belly. Her eyes traveled from his face to his bare chest—his T-shirt had completely burned away. Unable to stop herself, she ran her hands up his thighs and across his tight abs, resting them on his pecs. She loved his firm muscles beneath her palms, the smoothness of his skin.

But she couldn't keep this up. She didn't dare. She'd never be able to stop touching him.

"What changed?" he asked her in quiet, low tones, his face only inches from hers.

Nick's breath felt like heaven on her face. "Nothing," she said, wishing that could be true. Her muscles felt close to giving out from the sudden feelings of defeat. "But everything."

Nick dipped his head and caught her bottom lip in his teeth.

Cynda gasped from the sharp pleasure, and before she knew it, she was kissing him deep and long and slow. The instant her lips touched his, she knew if she didn't stay away from him she'd never have enough of him, never be satisfied.

Rational thought burned away like sparks winking out of existence. He slid his hands under her burned tunic and dug his fingers into her skin. Like electric shocks, everywhere he made contact made her whole body feel alive.

Reason tried to batter its way into Cynda's mind again, but her body begged her to forget the consequences of what she was doing. Clenching his hair in her fists, freeing it from his ponytail, Cynda kept going, heart pounding harder and harder each second she tasted Nick's mouth, his tongue. That burning, minty fire. She could drink it. She could drink *him*.

His arms tightened around her as she trailed her fingernails down his sides, lower, to the waistband of his jeans. To the snap and zipper. His erection shoved against the fabric, pushing into her belly, teasing her, tempting her more than she thought she could stand.

Another second, and she would fall right off the cliff—and land at the bottom of her life, broken into bits.

Instead, she broke the kiss, but she didn't move away from him.

"I need you so much it aches," she whispered against Nick's mouth. "It hurts."

"I can fix that," he said in his deep, sexy voice. Every word felt like a tender nibble on her breasts, between her legs. Cynda throbbed all over. But she shook her head.

No.

Aloud, with less conviction. "No." Then the rest of the truth hit her like a hammer to her chest. "I want to *so much,* but I can't."

Nick refused to turn her loose, and Cynda couldn't stop staring at him, into his hypnotic eyes. She didn't want to let him go. She wanted to feel the safety of his arms, the comfort.

"Tell me why, firebird." He kissed her forehead, then rested her head on his bare shoulder and ran his hand through her hair. "What did the Mothers say to you?"

Cynda pressed her cheek against the hard muscle of his chest, and took a deep breath of him. All man. All hers—

Except she shouldn't even be touching him.

He wasn't hers. Nick couldn't ever be hers.

She didn't want to repeat Mother Keara's threat out loud, because hearing the words again would make them more real, and even more painful. But she had to. She was a fire Sibyl and fire Sibyls communicated and didn't hold back the truth. She owed Nick that much.

The pain tamped the fire within her and its loss made everything worse. "They—they said if I choose to be with you, I'll get pitched out on my ass." She turned her face into his neck. "I'll lose everything," she whispered.

"The only family I've ever had. My home, my life, my fire. Everything."

His hands went still, no longer caressing her. "Why?"

Cynda kissed the skin between his jaw and his ear, and more of her inner heat faded because she hated what she had to say next. "You're a Curson."

His steel-hard muscles tightened to complete stone. "What the fuck?" That low rumble, twice as deep. It gave her fresh shivers. "The Mothers approved of Creed *marrying* Riana. Explain why we can't even date."

Cynda held him as close as she could, because she knew she'd have to let him go soon. "Creed submitted to a ritual—and that was with the Russian Mothers. They're more lenient than the other two orders."

For a few moments, Nick didn't even breathe, his warm skin unmoving beneath her cheek. She squeezed her eyes shut, dreading what he'd say or do next.

If he pushed her to take their relationship further, she didn't know if she could refuse him. She balled her fists on his chest. How could she deny herself something she wanted badly enough to even *consider* taking such a risk?

She opened her eyes as Nick eased himself away from her, and she let her palms slide down his chest until he held her at arm's length. His jaw knotted in the corners, and his face reddened like he was swallowing two tons of swearing and unkind comments about the women Cynda loved and considered to be her true family.

After another few moments of silence, his eyes flashed and she sensed he'd made his decision. She could barely swallow as she locked gazes with him.

Steady, with way too much control, Nick said, "I want to speak to these . . . Mothers. Take me to your room. Call them. However you have to do it, I want to talk to them. *Now.*"

A jolt of unexpected warmth rattled Cynda.

Nick wanted to talk with the Mothers?

He would do that for her?

She kept looking at him, only half believing, but the determination in his face let her know just how serious he was.

Of course, it couldn't happen. Her heart ached again, and she shook her head. "I can't open the channels for you. I've been warned. Once the Mothers make a decision, I've never seen them waver from it."

He audibly sucked in his breath and even more stern resolve hardened his features. "Then find me a fire Sibyl who hasn't been warned." He gave her shoulders a squeeze, and Cynda's heart squeezed harder. She so wanted to agree, but she knew she couldn't do that, either.

"It wouldn't be right." She raised her hands and gripped his arms. "I can't ask another Sibyl to do something I know the Mothers don't want. Not after Mother Keara's visit."

"Mother Keara." Nick's dark eyes got an impossible shade darker. "She's the one who came to your room night before last?"

"That doesn't matter. One Mother speaks for all Mothers." Cynda rubbed Nick's arms as if she could transmit her entire understanding of Sibyl culture through her fingertips. "That's how it works in my world. Mothers might fight amongst themselves, but they never contradict each other's decisions or opinions, once they're set."

"Fine." He let go of her. His hands doubled into fists at his sides, and she could almost feel the heat radiating off his skin. If Nick were a fire Sibyl, every combustible in the room would be blazing. As it was, he let off a golden glow that made Cynda blink. "I'll be on the next plane to Ireland. Can I fly directly into Connemara, or do I have to take a shuttle?"

Cynda wanted to grab hold of Nick all over again, hang around his neck, and kiss him for an hour. A day.

He'd do this for me—for us. He's ready to take a risk that big.

She battled the urge to touch him and kiss him until she soothed away his frustration and hers, too. "You can't do that, either." She shook her head, trying to gather her thoughts. "Maybe after we get this J. C. Downy situation under control. Then we can talk about it."

The fire inside her dwindled some more. "But I don't think it will do any good." Her mouth felt dry as she spoke, and she had trouble with her next words. "You'd be putting yourself in danger, too. Once you're in the hands of the Mothers, there's no telling what they'll do to you."

"Bullshit—"

Nick started to argue but Cynda cut in, "Right now we need you here, Nick. *I* need you here." Her lips trembled when she stopped speaking, and she pressed her fingers against her mouth to get control before she moved them away. "You can't be my bodyguard anymore, but I know you're our best shot at stopping these murders."

His mouth came open. He looked shocked for a second or two, then his expression turned to solid granite. "*No one* else is protecting you. When you're not with your triad, you're with me."

"Nick—"

"No discussion." He folded his arms and glowered at her. "You're my responsibility, and I will *not* let you die." His face softened a fraction, and his voice dropped. "Don't think I'll push you and our relationship. I won't. And I won't let you push me . . . not with what it might cost you. I could never, would never, do that to you, Cynda."

A tremor went through her, and her arms actually hurt from wanting to hug him. His determination to talk to the Mothers, his determination not to jeopardize her relationship with those she loved as her family, touched her in ways she'd never been touched before. And the *something more* she'd been feeling inside rushed to the surface.

Dear, sweet Goddess, I think I'm in love with this man.

The look on Nick's face turned so intense Cynda was scared to death he might love her, too. She breathed shallowly, high in her chest, trying not to panic or cry.

There is no crying in baseball . . . or protecting New York City.

They were professionals. They could work together and avoid an intimate relationship. They could do this.

They had no choice.

Cynda walked past Nick to the other side of the room, to get a little respite from the pain of his nearness. He let her go without grabbing hold of her, which relieved her and disappointed her at the same time.

She sat on an exercise ball, hugged herself and rocked back and forth off the tips of her toes. "Let's leave it be for a while. I need to know what's happening in your head about Jake."

She half expected Nick to grunt or refuse to answer, or even blow up because she asked. That had been his pattern up to now, and she couldn't see that changing.

He surprised her by pulling out an exercise mat and easing himself onto his knees, martial-arts style, facing her. After contemplating for a time, Nick said, "I think Downy's using Jake's talisman to force him to do what she says—and maybe all of the demons she's got under her thumb." His voice lowered, and she heard the anger, frustration, and pain in his voice. "I think Jake can't fight her anymore."

The thought of any creature being tortured into submission flowed all over Cynda like a coat of ice dousing her fire even more. "So, do you have a plan? How do we save him?"

Nick gazed at her steadily. "We don't."

Cynda was dumbfounded by his matter-of-fact tone, not to mention what he just said. She rocked back on the ball, then forward, unable to keep from frowning. "We have to."

"What we have to do is make sure Max's word on the Bronx house is true." Nick's voice sounded steady and eerily calm. "We hit the place, spring Delilah and get her into protection. If Downy's there, we take her out."

"You can't possibly believe I'd let you act like it's that simple." Cynda continued rocking on the ball, wishing she was close enough to smack Nick in the head. "You're out of your mind."

In that same serious, even tone, Nick said, "I'm not blowing you off. This is real, and there's no sugarcoating it." Grief touched his features, pulling at Cynda's insides. "If I didn't have my duty as an officer and a rational man clear in my mind, my mother would have murdered you and your triad last fall."

Cynda didn't have a ready response. Yes, he'd acted on that sense of duty, but at the same time she knew it was hurting him inside. All she could do was watch Nick as he continued.

"I know what the Legion does to people. What they're capable of." He lowered his head. The long hair she had freed fell over his shoulder. He looked up again and shoved the strands away with an obviously frustrated gesture. "If Jake stays out of the way, he'll be fine. If he does their bidding, if he tries to hurt any of us, he'll have to be dealt with."

She leaned forward on the exercise ball, belly burning

at the thought of Nick having to survive the death of another family member—and facing the fact that he might have to be the one to kill Jake.

This one would hurt him worse.

This one, he might not get over—if, indeed, he had gotten over any of the tragedies in his past.

Firm resolve settled within her. Damned if she was going to let him be the one to suffer the pain of doing it all over again. She pointed her finger at him. "If Jake has to be killed, I'm doing it."

Something like surprise, then concern, flickered over his features before vanishing. Still in his martial-arts pose, eyes clear and straightforward, Nick sighed. "Cynda, that's not reasonable."

"No discussion." Tears welled in her eyes, and she couldn't hold them back. "It *is* reasonable. There's no way I'm letting you go through that agony again. If your brother has to die, it'll be by my sword. Got that?"

Nick gazed at her steadily, but didn't respond.

Cynda's breath hitched. Once the tears slid down her cheeks, they didn't want to stop. She choked a sob, and she put her face in her hands to rein in her emotions.

A few seconds later, she felt Nick's warm, strong arm around her shoulders.

She wanted to leap off the exercise ball, hug him, and cry until she didn't have any misery and confusion left. Everything felt twisted and broken. It wasn't right, for her to finally love someone other than her Sibyl family, and be denied. It was way past not right for Nick to be facing Jake's death, to even be in danger of being the one who would have to kill his brother.

When she looked up at him, he used his free hand to brush away her tears. The contact made her tremble all over, but she could tell by his expression that he wouldn't let her compromise herself in any way.

"We'll work all this out, firebird." He gave her shoulders a squeeze. "We'll find some way to survive. It's what we do."

He cupped her cheek and gave her a longing look before he said, "Are you coming up with me, or should I send Riana and Merilee down?"

"I'll come up." Her voice was barely audible in the quiet, still basement. "We need to work on those raid plans."

Nick nodded.

He let her go, eased to his feet, and backed away, waiting for her to get off the exercise ball and leave the gym first.

All the way up the stairs, Cynda was overly aware of his powerful presence behind her. At the top, she stopped and turned. With him one step below her, their heights matched and she could look at him directly.

She kept her tone firm. "If we're going to make it through this, I think we need to agree—no holding back information. Not for any reason. Not anything. I won't keep secrets from you if you don't keep any from me."

"No secrets," Nick repeated without blinking.

Since he once told her he never told the truth, she couldn't tell if he was agreeing with her, or humoring her. Cynda gazed into his eyes, trying to read his genuineness. "Do you *mean* that?"

"I mean it." His lips twitched as he made a V over his nose. "Demon's honor."

(14)

A week after his heart-to-heart with Cynda in the basement, Nick checked his watch as he crept out of one unfamiliar backyard into another. Ten of his men dressed in full SWAT gear, Cynda and her triad in their leathers, and the Jamaica Bay Sibyl rangers followed behind him, moving as quietly as they could.

Less than five minutes now.

Today, my brother Jake might die.

Nick ground his teeth. He didn't have any options. Time to accept that fact.

All these years he had found balance inside, maintained the right mental distance from his work, and carefully controlled his thoughts and actions on the job. It was how he survived so many undercover assignments—like five years in the Legion. Through his whole life, it had never been any other way. He would do what he had to do, even if it tore him up inside.

In a few short months, Jake and Cynda had blown that all to hell.

Now it was work.

Now he had to use every year, month, day, and hour of his training and experience to keep himself in line and on task.

Cold air bit at Nick's arm through his NYPD raid jacket, but with his usual mental discipline when it came to the elements, he barely felt the chill as his half of the assault team eased around houses and past ice-covered bushes, creeping toward the target. It was almost mid-March now. According to dozens of special news reports,

all the rain and flooding had moved south, and gotten
even worse. In the Bronx, no snow, but there was still
plenty of ice. The sharp, clean smell of frost and the bit-
ter chill helped Nick focus even when all manner of shit
was about to explode in his face.

Jake.

*Sorry, buddy. Keep your invisible ass out of my way
today.* Please.

He checked the countdown on his watch again.

Four minutes.

The combined OCU SWAT-Sibyl team continued to
use neighboring houses for cover, moving quietly. No
shouting. No marking or checking as they cut through
another set of small yards, crossed two narrow drives,
and wove between chain-link fences—yards with no
yapping dogs. The route had been carefully planned for
maximum stealth.

Nick's jaw ached from clenching as he glanced over at
Cynda. She was walking about three steps away from
him, flanked by Riana and Merilee, face mask zipped,
goggles in place, hand on the hilt of her broadsword.
The trail of smoke he was used to seeing behind her in
battle situations—that was missing.

Even at some distance, he could smell that hint of
vanilla mixed with cinnamon and sense the absence of
the heat that should be roiling beneath her skin. The
way she looked, the way she moved—he noticed her at
every level, even five minutes from battle. He didn't
bother telling himself not to react. That was impossible.
No question about it, as soon as he snuffed the threat to
the fire Sibyls, he was on the first plane to Ireland.

Three minutes.

At Nick's signal, the team picked up its pace to a rhythmic jog. His blood thumped with the military strike of
boots on grass, gravel, and pavement. The closer they
came to target, the more his gut heaved at the thought of

Jake, somewhere inside, maybe captive, maybe not—but definitely at risk. He couldn't stop checking on Cynda, either. Her presence drew his attention like a magnetic field.

Somehow he'd survived an entire week of wanting this woman he couldn't have until he got his chance at those damned Irish Mothers. He knew Cynda had been just as bothered. She had burned up three different workrooms at the townhouse, having tantrums over just about anything. In between those outbursts, he hadn't seen her burn at all. Not even a spark.

That worried him, but he understood.

Her triad didn't.

Apparently, Cynda wasn't practicing her "Don't hold back information" rule with Riana and Merilee. When Nick asked her about it, she said she didn't want to put her triad sisters in a bad position with the Mothers, or make them feel like they had to police her.

Bullshit.

Cynda needed her triad. Needed their support. She shouldn't be doing this alone.

But that was her call, regardless of whether he thought it was fucked up.

Riana was doing a lot of griping about Cynda's increasingly erratic control over her fire talent, though. Pretty soon, Nick would have to tell his brother's wife to stuff it, and that wouldn't go over well.

Two minutes.

Being around Cynda without touching her had chewed into Nick's patience and self-control, never mind the slow-assed surveillance of the Bronx house they were forming up to raid. Yeah, sure they had to be careful. The Mothers hadn't been able to drag any new information out of Max Moses, so the OCU had to operate on the intel they could gather on their own. Freeman didn't want more people wounded, or permanently out of commission like the officer who got her leg shattered by a wood fragment on City Island.

Nick had no desire to see anyone hurt again—but a week had almost killed him.

His body armor felt like an old friend. The loaded Glock in his hand felt better. As long as he kept Jake to the side of his thoughts, Nick was primed to kick some ass.

Intel suggested the best approach to the two-story fieldstone house was on foot, setting up perimeters in diminishing circles. Officers from the Fiftieth Precinct had cleared the area, manned the outer rings, redirected traffic from the key roads, and allowed OCU and Sibyls to cover strategic inner rings. This time, four Sibyl triads would be going in after Nick, Creed, and twenty OCU SWAT officers.

Standard issue for this raid included goggles and earplugs everyone could employ if they had to kill half demons like Nick. They also had a special four-man "gold team," decked out in EOD bomb disposal suits and armed with tricked-up M4 carbines, that would take the lead if the Cursons decided to put in another appearance.

The goals were simple enough: rescue, capture, clear—and get the hell out with all personnel intact.

Three different watch patrols had made visuals through the back window using telescoping lenses from about forty yards away. The high-tech surveillance had verified that Delilah Moses was on-site, chained in a back bedroom, at times under the guard of an unknown female, estimated age fifty-five years, dark hair, average height, no obvious distinguishing marks, no facial match on any database. At other times, no one at all seemed to be on guard, but Nick, the Sibyls, and the OCU assumed that's when the invisible Astaroth demons were taking care of house business.

As the large fieldstone house came into sight, Nick's blood pumped a little faster. He gave a hand signal, and the final containment ring deployed, leaving him eight regular officers, two gold team members, Cynda's North Manhattan triad, and the Jamaica Bay ranger Sibyls. Creed had the other ten SWAT members with them, as well as two triads from Staten Island.

There would be no "knock and announce" today.

This was a high-risk warrant, with an old woman's life at stake.

They'd just kick down the doors.

Nick's group would make entrance through the kitchen, as per architectural plans pulled from city records and recon photos. They would follow a direct route down the hallway and deploy into the bedroom and fetch Delilah. Meanwhile Creed's team would be blasting through the front with flashbangs and Stingers and as much commotion as possible to draw the fire off the rescue team.

One minute.

Seconds now.

As Nick's team formed up using leafless trees for as much cover as possible, Nick sighted the back door and gestured for SWAT to deploy.

Polycarbonate lenses firmly in place, four SWAT members ran forward. Two carried the battering ram. Nick and the other six SWAT officers fanned out behind them.

Just before he left the cover of the trees, Nick caught Cynda's eye as best he could with those goggles covering half her face.

Be careful, firebird, he mouthed.

Instead of telling him to fuck himself, Cynda nodded.

God, he hated how flat she'd been since the Mothers interfered with her life and choices. The thought made him grind his teeth, but he had no time to dwell on it.

Adrenaline surged through his body, making everything inside him sizzle and pop.

He turned to the officers on his left.

"Move," he commanded, and ran ahead with his team.

Frozen grass, mud, and ice crackled under his boots. Cold air smacked across his nose and cheeks. He sucked in a single chilled breath as he reached the back steps and signaled for the battering ram.

Nick's guys stormed up the back steps and bashed in the back door.

At the same instant, at the front of the house, flash-bangs exploded with ear-jamming concussions. Noise, yelling, and commotion came next.

Muscles tight, Nick followed his team through the ruined door. They streamed into the kitchen as Creed and his team hollered and pounded into the front rooms.

Nick's mind blasted into high gear, along with all his senses. His heart banged with each quick breath he took, and blood roared in his ears. Place smelled like pine. And it was cold. The air felt flat and empty. He didn't hear anything but Creed and SWAT shouting and beating on the walls.

Nick glanced left and right as he charged through the kitchen. No plates. No trash. No crumbs. Damned if this room didn't look just as freaky-clean as the Sweetbriar house.

Unease crept through Nick's insides.

He turned left behind his team. The hallway—he could tell the place had been scrubbed from top to bottom. Nothing on the walls. No dirt, no marks.

No people or demons anywhere. He doubted they would find a single fingerprint, other than their own.

The watch officers hadn't reported any changes across the last twenty-four hours. No comings, no goings. The unknown female should have been in here. Probably with a shitload of demons—and definitely Delilah.

How could the place be empty? Not possible.

Boot heels echoed on hardwood as they trooped into the bedroom where Delilah Moses was supposedly captive, but Nick could see the truth for himself.

Nothing.

Nada.

The roaring sound in his ears ebbed, along with his heart rate.

Not a bed or a chair or a couch or chain in the room. Not even a scratch on the friggin' walls, which looked as if they had been painted yesterday. Smelled a little like it, too.

SWAT yanked open the closet, which was just as empty as everything else.

They stepped back, gave him a questioning look, and waited for his instructions.

"Signal the Sibyls," Nick growled, jamming his Glock back into its holster. "Search every stone, crack, and closet. And check with the watch. I want to know how Downy got the vic out of this place unobserved."

Nick prowled the empty bedroom, finding nothing, then moved through the hallway and kitchen to a chorus of "Clear! Clear!" as each room in the house was searched, with no results.

From a vantage point in the center room—probably a formal dining area in the house's heyday—Nick watched as Sibyls streamed through the entrances, weapons ready. One after another, the women stopped and examined the museum-perfect house. Looking as pissed as Nick felt, they sheathed blades or slung bows over their shoulders.

We waited too long. Frustration bubbled like red-hot ore inside. He kicked against a baseboard. *Or they knew we were coming. Again.*

He scanned the area, searching for Cynda.

There she was, walking slowly through the hallway

from the bedroom, easing her sword back into its scabbard. The sight of her cooled his anger a few degrees, and eased the gnawing worry deep in his chest. Except, to Nick's sharp eye, it didn't look like her blade had ever ignited. The oil was smooth and dark along the metal, unheated, undisturbed. She spotted him and came toward him, unzipping her face mask and propping her goggles on her forehead. As she had at the Sweetbriar house, she seemed distant, busy in her mind, like she was digging for some memory she just couldn't find.

"Familiar, like the last place?" he asked as she entered the room where he stood.

She glanced at the high ceiling, the windows, and folded her arms. "Yes. I'm missing something."

Nick expected smoke to curl up from her shoulders, but nothing happened. Her listlessness punched at his gut.

Could a fire Sibyl's heat go out?

Because it seemed to him that's what was happening, and he couldn't let it stand.

He dug his fingers into his palms. They had to get resolution with Downy fast, so he could get his ass to Ireland and have a word with this Mother Keara.

Cynda's head turned as she inspected the room, and her gaze came to rest on the small closet on the back wall. Nick had left the door open, and he shook his head. "It's empty. I already checked."

But Cynda was focusing on the outside of the doorframe, at an uneven spot on the right.

She walked forward, reached for the spot, and ran her fingers along the side of the molding, coming away with a dark chunk of wood about the size of her pinkie finger.

"This is polished," she murmured. "I think—I think it's bog oak. From Ireland. What's it doing *here*?"

Nick's blood surged. He lunged toward her, wrapped her in his arms, and moved her away from the closet, keeping his body between her and the open space. He could hear his own breathing, harsh and jagged, as he waited for the ambush.

No demons came exploding through the closet's pine paneling.

Nick counted to five.

Still no demons.

He was acutely aware of the fact that Cynda's leathers and skin felt almost as chilly as the room. She was shivering, pale from the cold, but she wasn't drawing any fire to her, or stirring the flames inside as she gripped the little fragment of Irish wood. He wanted to shake her until she warmed up—*woke* up, or shook off this pall over her elemental talents.

He shouldn't have allowed her to come on this raid. She wasn't in top form, but he thought the action might rev her up. Mistake. He'd put her at huge risk.

What had he been thinking?

Nick didn't want to let her go, but he couldn't just stand there in the middle of a potential hot zone, cradling her against his chest.

She gazed up at him, green eyes sad but at least less distant, and pushed gently against his chest.

"Creed!" Nick called as he let Cynda go. "Get in here. We've got weirdness."

Then he yelled for SWAT assistance, and ordered them to examine the closet more closely.

One of the gold team officers in the special bomb removal gear hustled into the small, empty space and tapped around the walls to check for panels or compartments. The remainder of the gold team positioned in front of the closet door, carbines aimed into the space. The other sixteen SWAT members spread into two rings inside the room.

The Sibyls withdrew toward the room's two doors, with the earth Sibyls stepping just outside and the air

Sibyls running a few extra steps to get some distance for their arrows or throwing weapons. The fire Sibyls stayed in front, zipped their masks, pulled their goggles into place, and drew their weapons.

Nick noted that the other three fire Sibyls, all with different types of swords, immediately lit fires along their blades.

Cynda didn't.

She was too far away for him to say something to piss her off and kick-start her flames, so he once more stepped between her and the closet door. Creed stood beside him on the left-hand side, just behind the gold team. Nick saw him glance at Cynda, and knew he was worried, too.

Seconds later, the officer in the closet knocked on a bunch of boards that sounded hollow instead of solid.

"Got it," he said.

"Breach," Nick instructed, gripping his Glock, squinting into the darkness of the closet for any hint of red demon traces.

Everyone went stiff. The gold team raised their weapons higher as the officer in the closet lifted his leg and crashed his booted foot through the false closet panel.

Wood splintered inward, and the officer used his elbow to break out the rest of a four-by-six-foot opening.

Air flowed steadily out of the opening. Fetid, rich, gravelike.

The officer shined his flashlight into the space, then leaned into the gap and looked down. "Goes into the floor, sir."

"It's probably a tunnel," Creed said, staring into the closet, sniffing the air.

Nick knew his twin could detect the same odors as he could, thanks to their *other*-enhanced perceptions. "Yeah," he agreed. "With another opening, judging by the breeze."

He was already remembering Jake's visit to the town-house basement. Jake's clothes had been covered with dirt. All that dust, especially on his hands and nails. Downy had them digging an escape route even then, and he hadn't said a word. Not a hint of caution or warning.

Whose side are you on? How will I figure that out before I have to put a bullet between your eyes?

"Are we going in?" Creed asked.

Nick's muscles tightened. That's exactly what he wanted to do, with everything he was made of, but there was no way he would let SWAT and the Sibyls take that kind of risk, especially after City Island.

Common sense said they should secure the house and the tunnel opening, and send for a tactical surveillance robot. The tunnel could be wired with explosives, stuffed with Astaroths, collapsed in the middle—endless possibilities. The robot would tell them what they needed to know. The chances Delilah or Jake were in that tunnel now were next to nothing anyway. Downy and her demons were long gone.

Nick growled low in his throat, but he said, "We're pulling back until we get a tactical bot down that hole to scope things out."

Creed gave a frustrated grunt, but Nick could tell his twin agreed. A few Sibyls, Cynda included, grumbled, but he heard weapons scraping against leather sheaths.

Merilee said, "Well, this has been one big fat waste of time, hasn't it?"

Once more, Nick's attention pulled to the tunnel opening.

Definitely knew we were coming, didn't you, Jake?

For the first time, Nick understood that he wasn't just fighting J. C. Downy and a bunch of mindless minions. He was matching wits with his own brother—who apparently thought and planned much like Nick and his twin.

And what would he, Nick, do in Jake's shoes?

If I had a bunch of invisible demons at my disposal, I'd line that townhouse with spies, top to bottom, back to front.

Fuck!

Nick narrowed his eyes. *All the Astaroths would have to do is avoid Creed or me, and anyone with goggles— which no one wears inside the townhouse.*

"We need to get to HCQ." Nick jerked his thumb southward, toward Manhattan. "I think our problem starts at home." To the SWAT members, he said, "Secure the house. Gold team, stay with the closet until we get you some relief."

Creed kept his gaze on Nick, but gave orders to get the officers on the move. Sibyls stood aside to let them exit first.

Nick glanced at Cynda on his way by, to be sure she was with her triad. She was handing her wood fragment to Riana, and he heard her say, "This needs to be analyzed. I'm sure it's bog oak. See if we can pin it down to a specific origin point."

Riana tucked the fragment into her jumpsuit pocket as Merilee muttered, "What would a piece of rare Irish wood be doing here? That just seals it. Everyone in Ireland must be as weird as you, Cynda."

He would have loved to hear the crackle of fire in response, but none came. His throat caught as he swallowed. A lot of work to be done in a hurry, because this thing with Cynda and her fire couldn't go on. He didn't know what it meant, but he was damned sure it wasn't healthy for her.

Nick was all the way out of the house with Creed beside him when Gideon started grumbling in his mind. Poking. Digging. The beast let out a loud, angry wail.

Muscles tense in response to the inner nudge, Nick checked over his shoulder to make sure Cynda and her triad stayed close.

Merilee and Riana were deep in conversation a few paces behind, passing the piece of wood back and forth.

Nick stopped and turned. His senses rushed to full, screaming alert. Gideon blasted forward, beating against his skull.

Cynda wasn't with her triad.

Cynda wasn't anywhere in sight.

(15)

Cynda walked behind Riana and Merilee as they headed out of the fieldstone house, leaving the gold team in possession. Her shoulders sagged from the huge sense of letdown at not finding Delilah Moses, and her ribs and chest ached from the frustration of not being able to call her fire when she wanted it.

She felt like she was losing her mind.

As she reached the front door, something clamped its hand over her mouth.

At the same time, it snapped off her sword belt. The blade slapped to the floor, noise muted by its leather sheath.

She tried to scream. The thing kept her mouth covered too tight. No sound at all.

Before she could claw at its hand, it yanked her off her feet, straight up in the air, almost to the top of the raised ceiling. Fear tore through her in a dizzying rush. She reached deep inside, tried to yank out her fire—but it wouldn't come.

It still wouldn't come!

Powerful arms restrained hers, and a leg locked her knees into position so she couldn't kick.

Her mind spun with more fear. *Astaroth*. It had to be one of the invisible winged demons.

With all her strength, she tried to kick, tried to throw an elbow. She even tried to bite the hand covering her mouth, but it managed to keep her lips pinned closed.

Shit, shit, shit!

She was completely trapped in its hold.

Cynda tried again to summon her inner heat, letting her terror fuel her, picturing her body blazing with fire and absolutely frying the creature who had her captive.

Nothing happened.

Tears bit at her eyes. No way her fire had failed her again. No way! But not even a trace of smoke rose from her skin.

A strong, unusual scent washed over her.

She went still.

Spicy. Exotic.

Caribbean.

If she hadn't recognized the creature, if she hadn't been about ten feet off the floor, at eye level with the high ceiling's yellow painted trim, and if she hadn't been having so much trouble igniting her inner fire, she would have kept trying to roast her captor like a big demon marshmallow.

Instead, she hung there, moving slowly up and down as the thing flapped its wings. She was pissed enough to be warm for the first time since her talk with Nick in the basement.

Cynda tried to look down at the officers who should have been below her, but the way the Astaroth held her, she couldn't even dip her head.

Why wasn't the gold team responding?

Couldn't they see her dangling in midair?

Her heart beat in her throat. Slowly, a degree at a time, her insides began to heat in response to the threat.

A little late, thank you.

"You found the bog oak I left," said a low, quiet voice in her ear. "Do you know me?"

Cynda nodded and thought again about trying to bite the fingers covering her mouth.

This was the Astaroth from the alley. The same one she'd thought tried to help her and Nick by dumping paint on their attacker during that first fight with the invisible demons. She remembered the creature's smell more than anything else. And now, he even felt oddly familiar, because she had spent time in his brother's arms.

Jake.

He turned her slowly toward the center room and the entrance to the tunnel. Cynda's eyes widened.

The gold team wasn't responding because the four officers lay sprawled on the floor near the closet, looking like broken aliens in their bomb removal space-suit gear.

That did it.

Fury rocked her, harsh and total.

Cynda broke out in flames.

Hot, welcome fire rushed across every inch of her skin. Her goggles snapped, cracked in half, and fell on the floor. Her leather suit began to smolder and burn in patches. As wonderful, welcome flames charged up and down her legs and arms, she shifted her face just enough to bite down on one of Jake's fingers.

She sank her teeth into him as hard as she could.

Nothing happened.

Jake didn't move his fingers, let her go, or respond in any fashion. Coppery warm blood trickled through her mouth, so she knew she had wounded him, but the demon didn't twitch.

Cynda didn't smell anything burning, not even her own clothes. She took her mouth off Jake's fingers and spit the mouthful of blood against his hand. It trickled to the floor far below.

Her flames waned.

The Astaroth had absorbed her elemental blast completely, with seemingly no effort at all.

I'm dead.

"Please don't do that again," Jake said with no change in his tone. "Speaking is . . . difficult right now. I must conserve my energy." A sigh hissed past her ear, sending unpleasant chills up and down her spine. "If my strength fails, I'll carry out my orders whether I wish to or not."

Cynda regulated her breathing and went very, very still. Whatever he was talking about, she did *not* like the sound of that.

Jake flew slowly toward the closet and her heart thundered. As he passed over the prone forms of the gold team, he murmured, "They aren't dead. I had no command to kill them."

Leaving, of course, the obvious question.

Who *had* he been commanded to kill?

Cynda was pretty sure she knew the answer. Smoke rose from her hands, wrists, and fingers.

Now the friggin' fire comes back, when I can't use it!

She pitched the force of her inner energy into controlling the heat, so none of it escaped onto her skin to burn Jake. Not that it hurt him. Like Nick, he must have absorbed her heat.

From somewhere behind her, Cynda heard Nick shouting her name. Her heart jumped against her ribs, making her breath catch. He had realized she was missing!

In her mind, she saw him thundering toward the house, Glock drawn.

Thank the Goddess. He'll save me.

But she didn't want to see Nick's face as he pulled the gun's trigger and killed Jake—which he would do, she had absolutely no doubt.

Just the thought of it opened a gash in her heart.

Not happening. She wouldn't let him face the pain, the agony of killing another family member.

If Cynda didn't kill Jake herself, he wasn't dying today, end of story.

"Um, hurry," she tried to say against the gag of his fingers, but Jake didn't change his pace.

He carried Cynda into the closet, flying so smoothly

they might have been propelled by well-oiled cables instead of wings. For a second, the Astaroth held them above the opening to the dark tunnel below.

"Don't be afraid," he said in that flat, expressionless voice.

Cynda almost bit him again.

Yeah, right.

Jake tightened his grip on her mouth, arms, and legs.

Wind blasted past her face as she heard the sound of wings snapping together.

The two of them plummeted straight down into pitch-black cold, faster than a wind-assisted arrow fired from Merilee's bow.

Cynda's belly dropped to her toes as they whipped in a giant spiral. She screamed her lungs out against Jake's palm, any sound lost in the rush of their free fall.

Bile roiled in her throat, and she almost puked. She shook violently from the rush of chilled air, striking so deep inside it made her joints hurt even through her protective leathers. Her face mask yanked at the snaps that secured it to her neck. Smells spun by. Grass. Wet sand. The sick-sweet reek of sewage. The rotten-egg stench of chemically treated natural gas.

Jake's wings unfurled with a rippling *whump*. Cynda felt the sting of weblike lace against her arms and cheeks as they touched her, then spread wide.

Immediately, their descent slowed. Slowed more. Jake let go of Cynda's mouth. She coughed and caught her breath as he touched down, settling her on hard, packed earth without so much as a jolt or rattle.

He urged her forward in the absolute darkness, five steps, then six, holding her by her shoulders so she didn't fall.

He turned her loose. Cynda went to her knees on hard earth and hacked. She gasped for a real breath, sucking in the rich aroma of damp dirt. She spit more of the coppery taste of his blood, mingled with the acidic bite in her mouth from almost throwing up.

What were they, a quarter mile down? More? She half expected to hear the bleat of a subway horn and see the blaze of the headlamp just before she got crushed by tons of onrushing steel. But they were probably lower, even, than most subway tunnels.

"Be still," the Astaroth instructed from behind her.

Like that would be a problem.

To see, she'd need to turn her palms into torches. With that natural gas smell hovering somewhere above them, Cynda couldn't conceive of risking so much as a spark.

Where is he taking me? And why? If Downy has his talisman and he's been ordered to kill me, why am I not dead already?

A wave of earthy energy buffeted Cynda.

"Hold your breath," Jake commanded.

Cynda didn't hesitate.

Just as she filled her lungs and clamped her mouth shut, the earth behind her gave a violent shake. She heard the rumble-slam of falling dirt, and knew the demon had caused a partial cave-in.

She was trapped.

Totally.

She was Jake's prisoner for as long as it took Nick and her triad to find a way down the tunnel shaft and dig through however many feet of dirt Jake had just piled between them.

Wonderful.

More fear slammed into anger and she had to bite the inside of her cheek to keep herself from igniting.

A blaze of light made her shut her eyes. She reopened them gingerly, spots dancing in her vision until she adjusted to the glow coming from behind her. Jake. She turned and faced him, realizing his skin was emitting enough light for them to see by.

In the eerie glow rising from his body, Cynda saw him in what she assumed was his basic demon form—alabaster skin, almost delicate upper and lower fangs, sleek pointed claws, and two sets of wide, thin wings, partially extended, close to brushing the well-honed circular walls of the tunnel. Jake's eyes were the same disconcerting shade of gold as Nick's in his *other* form, and Creed's, too.

He gestured for her to stand. "Come with me. If I know my brother, we don't have much time."

With that, Jake strode past her, taking his skin-light with him.

For now, Cynda shoved her fear and anger away. It wasn't going to do anything for her. She had to keep a clear mind and a level head.

And she had to hurry.

She pushed herself to her feet and ran to catch up.

Jake didn't slow down for her, and for a time, he didn't speak as they rushed through the straight, level tunnel.

"I don't strive for mystery," he told her a few steps later. "I say what I can. Do you understand?"

Cynda jogged to keep pace with him, drawing air through her nose and letting it out slowly through her mouth to keep her endurance, in case they had miles to go. After thinking about his statement, she asked, "Has Downy given you orders about what you can and can't discuss?"

Jake's head tilted like he was laboring to work out the perfect answer. "I have been given orders about many things."

Cynda's brain buzzed as she moved a little faster, working to piece together what the demon was saying—and not saying. "Then how are you speaking to me at all?"

"With great effort." His pearl-white nostrils flared.

"Orders can be to some extent . . . interpreted. Or delayed, so long as the purpose remains."

Every time he violates a command, he spends energy. And when he runs out of energy, he kills me. Got that much.

While she ran, Cynda pumped her arms with a twinge of hope—yet worry, too. She thought she understood the game Jake was playing. She had played it enough times herself, with her fellow adepts, when they wanted to get around orders given by the Mothers.

"So, hypothetically, if you've been ordered to kill me, you can show me stuff and talk to me, so long as in the end, you're still planning to take my life." She caught up to Jake and had to keep jogging in order to remain even with him, almost elbow to elbow. "That's not violating your commands."

"And if heroic rescues occur, what can I do about that?" Jake sounded oh-so-innocent as his elbow brushed hers.

Exactly like Nick, when he was yanking her chain.

Heroic rescues. Cynda almost stopped running. *Is he counting on Nick? Of course he is. That's why he went to all that trouble to take* me *instead of another fire Sibyl, or part of the reason. He knows Nick will come after me—and any second now.*

She did her best to think fast and frame the right questions. "Can you tell me who J. C. Downy is, and why she wants all the fire Sibyls dead?"

"No." Jake's answer sounded flat against the tunnel's earth walls.

Cynda tolerated a wave of shivers from the cold and imagined a game-show buzzer blaring *wrong question, wrong question.*

She adjusted her phrasing. "But you do know who she is."

Jake's wings twitched higher, tips toward his shoulders. "Yes, and no. I know something more important."

"Which is?" She glanced directly at his intent expression as they continued moving.

His features wavered, then grew solid again, and she knew this answer was costing him dearly. "I know where she comes from."

Cynda's breath swirled out in a wide fog as she jogged. "Where?"

"No." Jake shook his head once. Sharp. Forceful. "I can't speak the words."

Cynda recognized the significance of Jake's elaborated answer. Not just *no,* but *I can't speak the words.* He couldn't tell her the answer outright—but he could "tell" her in other ways?

She could almost hear the game-show music, this time playing something jumpy and nervous. *Contestant in jeopardy.*

"I cannot reveal the master's plans or actions without great loss of energy, punishment, or death for me or my friends and fellow demons." Jake sounded almost off-hand, as if he was speaking to a wall instead of her. Cynda didn't miss that ploy either. Whatever he was about to say, if she asked the right questions, it was important.

"What *can* you do?" She played along, spending a moment's concentration on keeping her increasing inner fire tamped down to a reasonable level.

"Many things." Jake laughed, and Cynda was surprised by the pleasant sound. "I can write on chalkboards. I can speak to my brother so long as it seems to others that I am leading him into a trap. I can even read books. Very educational. Many of us who are more . . . sympathetic to the Sibyls and OCU can read books."

This time, Cynda did stop moving, so fast she tripped

and staggered against the tunnel wall, barely catching herself with both hands.

Jake quickly circled back, took her arm, and pulled her forward.

Cynda stumbled after him, amazed. All those piles of books on the steps—everywhere.

The townhouse has been crawling with Astaroths trying to tell us where they were.

Right under our noses!

She did her best to imitate Merilee, repeating what Jake said to herself over and over, so she'd remember it in detail later. Nick would have to hear this, every word. They all would.

Providing the "heroic rescue" happened in time, and she was alive to tell it.

No wonder J. C. Downy knew everything the OCU planned.

Downy had eyes in HCQ—some friendly, some not, but all under the duress of orders they had to work to contravene. All those breezes and cold rushes of air . . .

Cynda felt like slapping her forehead. *A total idiot.* If she had ever once worn her demon-hunting goggles inside her own home instead of just out on missions, she would have seen dozens of red sulfur traces.

But who wears stupid goggles in their own house?

The air grew colder and her teeth chattered as the tunnel began to lighten beyond the reach of Jake's glow. Were they coming to the tunnel's other end?

Was that good—or bad?

Anything could be waiting for them.

She could be rushing straight toward her death.

But if Jake truly wanted to follow those orders, he could have killed her ten times over by now instead of playing this freaked-out game of jog, jog, riddle-me-this, riddle-me-that.

"People are often very attached to their belongings."

Another offhand remark, so it probably meant something huge. "They move furniture from place to place in trucks, with movers. I've seen that, and read about it. Done a lot of it, too."

"Downy's belongings were in the fieldstone house," Cynda translated, getting breathless from the long trek. "You moved them through this tunnel."

Jake didn't confirm, contradict, or redirect, so Cynda figured she was on track.

"Sometimes, during a move, small objects get lost or left behind," he said. "They may be of little significance, or of great emotional importance."

This was getting easier. She kept her feet churning as she said, "You've left something in the tunnel I need to see."

Again, no response from Jake, except he glowed brighter, illuminating several yards in front of them and behind them.

His chest rose and fell, rose and fell, and even in the dim light, Cynda saw the lines of his face getting tighter. His expression, harsher, more desperate. His claws made clicking noises as he flicked his fingers against his thumbs. Like he wanted to grab something, or was fighting against it.

Cynda didn't remember feeling those claws when he was holding on to her.

Are they getting longer? How much energy does he have left?

Knots tightened in her stomach.

Clearly, not a lot.

Cynda decided she was through asking Jake questions and just kept jogging at his side.

Whatever she needed to find, she would look for it, find it or not. No more pushing the demon. Pushing the demon was a bad idea.

Abruptly, Jake came to a halt, and Cynda stopped

with him. His glow doubled, making the floor and wall before him almost as bright as day.

At eye level, in a hollowed-out alcove, a space about the size of two shoeboxes, she saw three things—a broken stick, a green bowl, and a small crystal glass. The glass had a golden handle fixed across the top and what looked like a golden pestle propped against the rim.

What . . . ?

From the direction they had just come, Cynda sensed more than heard movement. Earth energy—a little jolt of it caused her to stagger.

Riana, in the tunnel, getting rid of Jake's roadblock dirt.

Beside her, Jake's lengthening claws clicked together, and he let out a low, carnivorous snarl. The sound rubbed at Cynda like sandpaper against the back of her neck, and she looked up at the Astaroth.

He gazed at her, golden eyes glowing, lips parted, fangs flashing in the now-silvery glow of his skin.

"I'm . . . very . . . tired," he said, only his voice echoed now. Less human. More animal. More dangerous. His features grew sharper, more pointed, and distinctly less human.

Cynda's heart rate doubled as she processed his meaning.

Tired demon. Murdered Sibyl.

She clamped her lip in her teeth, thrust her hands into the alcove, snatched the bowl and cup and stick, and held them to her chest.

"Get out of here," she said to whatever might be left of the human aspect of Jake. "Nick will kill you if you chase me. If he doesn't, my triad will."

"Perhaps . . . for . . . the best," Jake rasped, swiping a clawed hand in her direction, but yanking it back.

"It is not for the best!" Cynda stomped her foot,

which started to smoke. "What *is* it with you demons and this death thing?"

Jake narrowed his feral golden eyes. Tiger eyes now, slitted, predatory. His voice dropped another octave. "Stuuupid biiiiiiitch." The utterly inhuman sounds grated against the dirt and air. *"Ruuuuuun!"*

Cynda clutched the items Jake had led her to and backed away from the advancing Astaroth.

The demon let out a blood-stopping roar.

She wheeled around, leaped into the pitch darkness, and ran for her life.

(16)

Nick charged down the tunnel, more *other* than human.

Cold air beat against his face. Dirt from the walls and roof jarred loose and scattered into his eyes.

He didn't slow.

Roars bashed through the darkness. His. Gideon's. They were almost one.

The golden glow from his shifted legs, arms, and chest gave Nick just enough light to see by. His muscles strained and burned, pushing him harder, faster. He sucked air through his clenched teeth and threw himself forward with each lunging step.

He couldn't form a whole thought past Cynda. Getting to her. Finding her, grabbing her right back from whatever demon had snatched her out from under his nose.

How could I lose her?

How could I not notice?

The cracked goggles . . .

The blood on her sword sheath and the floor . . .

If she had so much as a bruise, he'd kill anything still breathing. He'd kill anything that even glanced in her direction.

Three minutes. Maybe four. She hadn't been out of his sight any longer than that, and she had been with her triad. Fuck! If he found her dead, he'd rip off his own head—after he tore down the Bronx, and Manhattan, too.

Nothing would mean anything ever again if he lost her, and he knew that with a sudden, desperate certainty.

It had taken him less than a minute to get back inside

the fieldstone house, find the goggles and the blood spattered inside the front room, and spot the gold team down. While Creed called EMS to summon ambulances for the downed SWAT officers, Nick had shifted almost completely and dropped into the tunnel, taking Merilee with him. Creed and Riana came next. No way the women would have stayed behind, not with Cynda at stake.

That dirt roadblock was a pain in the ass.

Riana had used her earth power to knock it out of the way, swearing the whole time.

Nick's internal clock told him Cynda had been out of contact for less than ten minutes.

Too long!

Wind energy slammed into him from behind, propelling him, shoving him down the tunnel even faster. He heard Merilee's distant shout of frustration and fear. She was giving him all the help she could.

Closer. He sensed it.

His blood coursed faster, screaming through his ears. He was driving himself so hard his body threatened to snap in half, but he didn't give a damn.

Cynda was nearby.

His *other*-enhanced perceptions picked up a touch of vanilla here, a smidgen of cinnamon there. She had been this way.

Not long ago.

Almost there.

Nick pumped his arms as he ran. He wouldn't need the Glock still holstered in the belt he'd jerked off before he shifted and jumped into the tunnel. Riana was carrying it for him just as she was carrying Creed's, but she could keep the thing. He could take down an army with his fists and teeth. He could crush a line of demons to dust between his palms.

Cynda's scent grew stronger. A fresh set of roars

ripped from Nick's clenched jaws. He had to get to her in time. That was the only option, the only outcome he'd allow.

"Nick!"

The sharp cry knifed toward him, slicing into his awareness like exploding fireworks. He bellowed in response, somehow doubling his speed.

Cynda's voice!

Somewhere in front of him.

She's alive.

And scared out of her mind.

"Nick!" Cynda called again.

Something snarled like a hunting cat, something close, and Nick knew it was after Cynda.

His cry of rage dislodged huge chunks of dirt from the walls. Nick crashed through the dust and rocks, gold skin crackling. He would *not* get this close and have her killed just yards away from his protection. He *would* reach her in time. He let go of all but a shred of his human awareness, giving his body over to Gideon's raw elemental power.

That tiny fragment of human awareness smelled smoke.

Saw smoke, curling toward him out of the darkness.

Nick-Gideon slammed his feet into earth and skidded to a stop just in time to keep from crushing Cynda.

She barreled at him screaming, eyes wide, red hair plastered to her head, big holes sizzled through her leathers, and her arms loaded full of . . . dishes?

Nick didn't stop to wonder.

Every cell in his body nearly burst with relief.

He let her run right into his arms, scooped her up, and squeezed her to his chest hard enough to make her squeak.

When he said "Firebird," the word echoed around them, *other*-style.

A tortured, untamed roar split the air before the

sound of Nick's voice died away. The sound boiled out of the darkness beyond them, from the direction Cynda had come.

She shuddered and turned her face into his neck.

Nick bared his teeth and clutched her even closer. He wanted to tear into whatever dared to threaten her, rip the being into little pieces and spit it all over New York City. But he had to get her out of here, out of the tunnel, out of danger *now*.

"Go," she was saying. "Please!"

Whatever was in the darkness, it would die later. Nick would see to that himself when he didn't have his arms full of the woman he loved.

He wheeled around, and took off toward the tunnel entrance, carrying Cynda against him. Her skin gave off layers of smoke, and Nick sensed her inner fire only inches from the surface of her body.

Thank God.

Through the haze of Cynda's smoke, another golden glow approached, and Nick knew it was Creed, leading Cynda's triad.

"Got her," he yelled, Gideon increasing the force of his voice.

He heard incoherent shouts, and understood the blast of complete relief they had just experienced.

She's still with us. She's still ours. For once in my life, I saved my family—because Cynda is my family, as much as my grandmother and my brothers.

Nick pressed his lips into Cynda's hair as he ran, and felt her lean into him, tighter to his chest, like she wanted to be right there, always, forever.

Deal.

Creed-*other* lumbered into view.

Nick caught his twin's eye and knew Creed could understand him, even though his brother was in full *other* form. "Behind me," he growled without slowing down.

Creed banged his fists one against the other, flexed his arms, and jetted off toward whatever had been hunting Cynda.

She struggled against Nick's grip, tried to yell something over Nick's shoulder to Creed about being careful, about leaving it alone—but Nick didn't wait for her to finish. As Riana and Merilee reached him, he picked up his speed again, still more *other* than man, but he made sure to run slow enough that the Sibyls could keep pace. His golden glow lit the way, and Riana and Merilee flanked him, near his elbows.

When he glanced right and left at the women, he saw their solid, determined expressions. Total focus on the task at hand—getting Cynda out of the tunnel. They were as good as cops. Maybe better.

If it weren't for Riana's elemental earth talent and Merilee's skill with wind, Cynda might not have survived, no matter how hard Nick had tried to save her. Nick couldn't imagine the Sibyls leaving a man—well, woman—behind. They would fight as fiercely as any Marine, any parent or sibling, to reclaim one of their own.

In his arms, Cynda gripped whatever it was she had hauled out of the tunnel. She took slow, shallow breaths. Her muscles felt relaxed as he carried her, as if she trusted him completely. That only doubled Nick's determination to keep a closer eye on her, to never let her down again.

He cursed himself a few more times for the lapse of attention that almost cost her life. Triad or not, he'd stay even closer from now on. More alert. This was one fire Sibyl who would survive the current nightmare.

If Nick could save every last one of them, he would.

But Cynda . . . if anything happened to *her* . . .

No fucking way.

A few minutes later, he saw the shaft of light that

spilled from the fieldstone house into the tunnel's entrance.

Finally!

All he wanted to do was get everyone out of this mess.

As they stopped running, Nick strained his senses to be sure nothing was close on their tails. Dirt walls stretched behind them into pitch blackness. He didn't see anything, or sense anything, either. The space around them seemed silent except for the rasp of Nick's breathing and the rapid, even gasps of the Sibyls.

For a split second, Nick imagined he could hear Cynda's heart beating, and he loved the sound. He wanted to put his hand between her breasts and feel the rhythm in his fingertips, just to know for sure. To have proof she was really alive in his arms.

As it was, the tendrils of smoke rising from her elbows had to do.

He carried her forward, to the foot of the entrance, where he turned to Merilee.

"Can you handle both of us, then get you and Riana to the top?" he asked, his voice still *other*-deep and loud.

"Yes." She raised her hands and closed her eyes. "Hold on to your nuts."

Nick felt a swirl of air, a rush of elemental force. Then he heard Merilee's wind, charging out of the darkness, rushing toward him like a barely contained tornado.

As Nick moved them into position, Cynda's arms tightened around the dishes she was holding.

He crouched, bunched his leg muscles and sucked in a huge breath, waiting for Merilee's signal.

Air howled and screeched in the tunnel. Earth and dust and grit swirled in every direction. Riana's hair whipped forward.

A sucking sensation pulled at Nick, tried to yank his golden skin right off his bones, then abruptly turned loose. He caught the stinging smell of frost, cold air, and wet dirt.

"Oh, no," Cynda groaned, squinching in his grasp like an accordion.

"Now!" Merilee yelled.

Nick jumped with all his strength, firing them upward toward the entrance, which seemed impossibly high over his head.

The frigid wind Merilee summoned slammed into Nick's feet first, driving them higher, faster toward the light above. Surfing the blast as best he could, Nick held on to Cynda and aimed for the bright square slightly to his right.

When he thought the position was right, Nick leaned away from the air funnel and lunged into the closet. He took one step, two, and staggered into the center room as Merilee's burst of wind smacked the ceiling, spread out, and dissipated, blowing bits of plaster as it went.

His *other*-enhanced senses registered the deadly soft rustle of sixteen handguns being raised and aimed directly at his head. Gideon gave a mighty twitch in his mind, and Nick had to count backward from twenty to keep the beast settled as he assessed the situation.

The remaining SWAT officers stood in two-ring formation, weapons trained above Cynda, more or less between Nick's eyes. They were flanked by nine Sibyls, face masks and goggles in place. Three sets of daggers and knives were poised to find targets above his neck. Three swords blazed. Two short bows and one longbow had arrows nocked.

They didn't know if he was friend or foe.

And Cynda wasn't processing the situation fast enough to tell them. She still had her eyes shut, shivering from the cold, and swearing to herself over the ride up the tunnel shaft.

Nick counted backward again, repeated two mantras,

and felt Gideon's heat and glow ease to the background. His muscles strained and his joints popped as his body settled back into full human form.

Without clothes, of course.

Female OCU officers turned their heads as they holstered Glocks, SIGs, and Smith & Wesson nine-millimeter automatics.

The Sibyls didn't turn their heads—though they did lower their weapons. A few of them checked him out and grinned.

"Where can I get me one of *those*?" asked the air Sibyl from the Jamaica Bay ranger triad as she slipped her arrow back into its quiver.

Another gout of wind gushed out of the tunnel. After a major thump and rattle and a few choice words, Riana stumbled to a stop beside Nick. Her teeth chattered for a few seconds before she was able to say, "Merilee's waiting for Creed. If things get hairy, she'll bring herself up." She slid Nick's holster from her belt and went to hand it to him. Her eyes swept from Cynda to Nick's bare legs. "Oh, damn."

She lowered the holster, then placed it carefully on the floor at his feet and straightened up again, keeping her eyes averted the whole time.

Nick managed to say, "Thanks."

His throat felt dry, and his face was warmer than usual.

"Let me guess," Cynda muttered, finally opening her green eyes and gazing into his face. "You're naked."

With her looking at him like that, the cold didn't bother Nick at all. He didn't want to put her down, ever. As long as she was in his arms, nothing could snatch her away from him, or do her any harm.

He could tell she was thinking about dropping her dishes and running her hands over his chest. Maybe other places, too. With the adrenaline still pumping through his system, it was all Nick could do not to get an erection in front of their audience.

"I have extra pants in the car," he said in low tones, wishing he could yank Cynda to his mouth and kiss her hard and long and slow. "At least I don't have dishes."

"Nobody thinks my dishes are sexy," Cynda fired back.

Nick felt heat along his thighs and caught a whiff of melting hair. He resisted an urge to cross one leg over the other to give his jewels a little protection. "Uh, could you not do that?"

"I'll think about it," Cynda grumbled, and laid her head on his shoulder.

Riana glanced back toward the tunnel as the SWAT team left formation and once more began to deploy out of the house, leaving behind three officers—male—who would take watch over the tunnel entrance when Nick gave them the word. They stood off by the hallway door, waiting. The Sibyls backed off, too, though a few of them kept finding reasons to give him another look. Nick figured they wouldn't leave the house until Merilee was back in one piece.

"Do you think—" Riana began, her voice trembling.

"Creed's fine." Nick turned Cynda and himself, facing away from all the prying eyes. "He'll be back in a few. Hopefully with a demon head in his teeth."

"That's not funny." Cynda went stiff in his arms and pushed against him with her shoulder so hard she forced him to set her and her dishes down next to him. When her feet were solidly on the floor, he saw that her face had gone pale under her freckles. She was still shivering, but Nick could tell more than the cold was bothering her.

He started to ask her what was going on, but she glanced over her shoulder at the lingering Sibyl triads, then back at him with a not-now expression. Smoke curled off the back of her neck, and out of the holes in her leather jumpsuit.

This has something to do with Jake. Nick folded his arms. Screw the fact he was naked.

As much as he wanted to protect his brother, Jake had stepped too far over the line today. Forced, not forced, talisman or no, Nick wasn't sure he cared anymore. The Astaroth was too dangerous, and Jake had almost taken all the light and life out of Nick's world.

Unless the demon had a damned good reason, or Cynda convinced Nick otherwise—which she would try to do, he was certain—the next time Jake crossed Nick's path, it would be the last.

Wind shrieked up the tunnel shaft.

On reflex, Nick put his hands on Cynda's waist and pulled her back with him.

A flash of gold light and blond hair, and Creed and Merilee emerged from the closet.

Despite his thinking to the contrary, Nick felt a moment's relief that Creed wasn't hauling Jake's dead body with him.

This shit's melting my mind. He held back a frustrated sigh.

Merilee smoothed her blond hair and adjusted her leathers as Creed quickly shifted back to his human form, clothing intact.

How does he do *that?*

Creed gave Riana a kiss and gestured to the tunnel. "Didn't find a thing. We can cancel the bot and get some crime-scene techs, but I'd send structural experts in there first to make sure it's stable after all the earth shaking and tornados."

"How about you take care of it?" Nick asked through his teeth, using his hands to give himself a little cover so Riana and Merilee wouldn't have to keep looking at the ceiling.

Cynda didn't bother to keep her eyes off him, which greatly tested Nick's self-control.

"Oh. Yeah." The corner of Creed's mouth quirked. He started for the front of the house. "I'll get your clothes from the car."

"Why do you have an armload of dishes?" Merilee asked, gazing at Cynda, who let off a new round of smoke.

"We need to get these to HCQ. They're—" Cynda glanced at the other Sibyl triads still within earshot, then her eyes settled on Nick. "They're important, I think. I need time to study them, then we can send them to Ireland and Russia for a closer look."

For a long moment, Nick got lost in the fact Cynda was standing beside him, alive, whole, and talking. The sound of her voice made him absurdly happy, even if half his colleagues and a slew of Sibyls now knew his exact measurements.

Riana and Merilee helped Cynda out, one taking the bowl from her arms, and the other seizing the cup with a gold wand inside it and a gold handle across the top. Cynda kept hold of what looked to be a stick with something silver on one end.

Creed jogged back in, carrying jeans and a T-shirt. He pitched them to Nick, who had to uncover himself to catch them.

Cynda's eyes drifted down, then back to Nick's face. She smiled. "You ready to go home, *big* man?"

He loved seeing the fire dancing in her eyes, her hair, along her hands and arms. That was better. That was Cynda.

Nick took his time putting on his jeans, all the while holding her gaze—and trying to figure a way to get himself Sibyl-mailed to Ireland along with those damned dishes.

(17)

Cynda gave up using her pyrosentience and pulled back her fire-awareness as she scuffed her bare feet against the townhouse's cool gym floor. She tried to ignore the room's vinyl-oil-sweat exercise smell as she stared down at the items Jake had given her in the tunnel. The "dishes," as Nick and Merilee called them, were arranged on an exercise mat directly under one of the lights, so they almost glowed from the brightness.

Merilee and Riana stood to either side of her, staring just as hard. Cynda felt the rush of Merilee's ventsentience as she explored the items. Riana's terrasentience made forceful ripples on the ground, too.

Nobody said a word.

At least Nick had already implemented strategies to make sure they didn't have any unwelcome visitors. Five officers wearing polycarbonate lenses and carrying elementally locked nets had swept the gym and declared it clean. The whole place was demon-free, at least as far as they could tell. Cynda was relieved no Astaroths could spy on her while she failed to understand the message she had almost died to receive.

Even as the Sibyls worked to identify the booty Jake had delivered, OCU was meeting upstairs in the conference room, with Nick and Creed and several Sibyl triads, planning shifts to patrol inside and outside the townhouse. Until the Astaroth issue got resolved—which meant indefinitely—they would need guards with demon-hunting lenses to protect HCQ from intruders. Sibyls were already figuring out how they could install chime alarms in their personal residences, keyed to let them know if invisible demons snuck inside.

I wish Jake could sneak in now, though. I need a word with him.

Cynda shook her head.

She just . . . didn't get what the demon wanted to tell her.

The first item, a bowl, seemed larger and flatter than most salad plates, but too small to be a serving dish. When Cynda had handled it, she'd noticed how smooth and heavy it was, made of distinctive green stone with subtle white streaks. No doubt it was Connemara marble, mined near where she had been born.

"Are you sure you've never seen that bowl before?" Riana asked, arms folded, eyes tracing the outline of the bowl.

"Positive. But I've seen bowls like it . . . somewhere." Cynda smacked her forehead as if that would knock loose the information buried in her skull. "Connemara marble isn't rare. Pieces made of it, they're all over Ireland—and exported frequently. I guess Jake wanted us to know J. C. Downy's Irish by birth? Maybe from County Galway, near Motherhouse Ireland."

"That would make sense, since she's targeting fire Sibyls." Merilee pointed to the crystal cup, which had a golden handle across the top, so it could be carried like a pail. The wand inside had a stem and rounded tip, and the tip was full of holes. "Reminds me of a mortar and pestle, but it isn't. Is that Irish?"

"It doesn't scream 'Ireland,' no." Cynda shook her head. "And it's not a mortar and pestle. Herbs and poultice rubs would get stuck in the wand's holes."

"Maybe it's to stir liquids," Riana suggested. "Some kind of fancy beaker?"

Merilee rolled her eyes at Riana. "Beakers belong in labs like yours, not in tunnels with weird demons. I doubt it's a beaker. I'll do what I can to hunt it down on the Internet, if I can get the computer to turn on tonight."

Cynda dug and dug at her own thoughts, but came up with nothing. "It's a crystal cup with a handle and wand. That's all I know. No, I haven't seen it before. But instinct tells me I *should* know what it is. That Jake thought I would know."

Riana's teeth clicked together at the mention of Jake's name, and the room gave a little shake.

Flexing her knees to keep her balance in the sudden burst of earth energy, Cynda decided to change the subject. She gestured toward what she initially had taken for a broken stick. "That's a crucifix made out of Irish bog oak, snapped into two pieces. Jake left the bottom sliver in the fieldstone house's dining room door to get my attention."

Merilee swiped a shock of blond hair from her eyes. "Have you seen *that* before?"

"Not that I know of, but Ireland's lousy with crucifixes." Cynda studied the lines and details of the religious artifact, but no bells jangled in her head. "They're everywhere—eighty or ninety percent of the population is Catholic. Some people have crucifixes on every wall of their home."

"So it's possible you've run into this one before." Riana knelt and touched the dark, smooth wood below the silver figurine of Jesus dying on the cross.

"Possible, yeah." Cynda scuffed her foot against the stone floor again. "How the hell am I supposed to remember one specific crucifix?"

Jake thought I would. He gambled his life—and mine—on my memory. And I'm blowing it.

Cynda's stomach ached. So many things she couldn't get straight, much less keep straight. And she had let herself get taken hostage. That stung worse than anything.

She had always prided herself on carrying her own weight, especially in a battle—and she was so not the oh-rescue-me type.

"So we've got a weird chick from Connemara who probably owned crosses with little silver Jesuses on top." Merilee didn't move to make a note, and Cynda figured she had decided she could remember that much without writing it down. "I wish Andy were here. Sometimes when I talk things over with her, she gives me the best ideas. It's raining and flooding in Florida anyway. Last time she called, she said she might try to rent a car and drive back."

Riana, who looked way tired from the day's excitement, abandoned her examination of the crucifix. "A bowl, a crucifix, and a cup with a wand."

"Big friggin' help." Cynda wanted to throw something—like the crystal cup—against the stone wall and listen to it shatter. "An Irish Catholic woman with dishes and a crucifix. That narrows it down to what, four million people? What am I missing? How is any of this important?"

"Maybe it's not." Riana's expression darkened. "Maybe Jake's leading us in circles. Just blowing smoke up our asses and using you to do it. Damnit, that *pisses* me off!"

Earth energy rolled in every direction.

Cynda fought not to stumble as mats shook on the townhouse's gym floor. Weights clattered. Exercise balls trembled and knocked against each other, along with the dishes. The air took on a heavy, earthy scent as dust swirled around stone and mortar.

"Give me a good reason why we shouldn't hunt that demon to ground and chop off his dick." Riana folded her arms and glared at Cynda as the earthquake continued. "He scared us witless, snatching you like that—and if something had gone wrong, he could have killed you!"

"Ri, slow it down." Merilee held up one hand and managed to look nonchalant even though her sweatpants and sweatshirt jiggled from the force of their triad leader's temper. "You might be overreacting."

"I don't overreact," Riana snapped.

Merilee gestured to the room around them. "If the floor cracks, we get to disagree."

Cynda walked away from Riana and Merilee toward the back of the room and wished with every last drop of emotion that she could burn something down. She scrubbed her palms against her jeans and blouse and glanced at the ceiling as the rumbling earth subsided.

This has to mean something.

It drove her nuts that she had no idea. Almost like the information lay behind some curtain in her mind, some wall she couldn't kick down.

Failure of any sort didn't sit well with Cynda. She wanted, expected—no, demanded more of herself. If she just tried harder, reached deeper, surely she could get this.

Her triad stood in a triangle now, mortar, pestle, and broom, with Cynda farthest from the door. She cursed her brain's drag-ass functioning, and knew she was completely messed up. No way to deny it now.

The tattoo on her wrist felt lifeless and flat. Her fire was already waning again after that brief burst of energy during the raid, and she didn't know how to explain any of it to her triad sisters. She only knew she had to discuss the situation, because the problem had almost cost her today, big time.

Fire-absorbing or not, Jake never could have snatched her or kept hold of her if she had been in top form. She would have found a way to free herself.

"I'd rather we not hunt Jake, because he's Nick's brother," she said to Riana, opening both arms, pleading. "And he's under Downy's control because of his talisman. He can't do anything about that."

Riana, dressed in a stylish green jogging suit, olive cheeks flushed from her fit, started to pace and interrupted. "Maybe. All right. But that doesn't give him a pass to terrify us. We thought we'd find you dead like Maura, that fast, that brutal. It was awful, Cynda. Those minutes in the tunnel—some of the worst in my whole life."

Cynda sighed. "I know that, and I'm *so* sorry. But Jake did everything he could to keep me safe, to hand over things that might tell us J. C. Downy's identity so we can figure out what she's got against fire Sibyls, and maybe find her. It's me that can't figure out the puzzle."

Riana's cheeks turned deeper red. "Creed went after Jake in the tunnel because the Astaroth was hunting you, for the sake of the Goddess. Like some kind of rabid panther. What the hell were you doing lingering in that tunnel with him? And why didn't you stay closer to us so he couldn't have grabbed you in the first place? Do you have any idea—" Her voice broke, then got louder as she wound up. "I don't care what Downy told that demon to do. I don't care about the talisman. If I'd found Jake, I would have brought the tunnel down on his head."

The ground gave another brief shake.

Cynda realized Riana needed to let go of the horror she must have felt when she found Cynda missing, but she was beginning to hit too close to home with her questions.

"Jake is Nick's brother," Cynda said more slowly, feeling a stubborn twist in her chest—but no fire. Barely even a spark.

Did they notice? She hated feeling so empty and cold.

"You didn't see what it did to Nick to aim a gun at his brother, Ri." Cynda closed her eyes and reached as hard as she could for her inner heat. And found absolutely nothing. Her voice dropped in volume even as she tried to keep it steady. "You don't know how the stuff with his parents still tears him up."

"I'm sorry if I'm being unreasonable, but Jake attacked you." Riana's response was quick and forceful as she kept up her frenetic walking. "That means he attacked us. Merilee and I *do* have a say in whether or not we beat him to death for giving us heart attacks. And you—you've never been anyone's hostage. Did you fight him with all you had? Did you even try to get away?" Tears glistened on her cheeks. "Triad first, above all else."

The mistrust and hurt in Riana's tone wounded Cynda in ways she couldn't explain, much less ignore. "Don't you dare talk to me like I didn't try—like I'm disloyal. I'd die for both of you right now, if that's what it took."

She clamped her teeth together. Smoke should have billowed from her shoulders, but she didn't feel *any* elemental heat inside her. Only pain. Only despair. And unreasonable fear that Riana and Merilee would suddenly realize she was defective and walk out of the basement gym, leaving her alone and wondering if she still had any family at all.

I can't have Nick.

I can't please Mother Keara anymore.

Now I'm letting my triad sisters down, too. I can't think. I can't keep myself safe. I'm losing my fire.

If I can't fight, what good am I to anyone?

Since her family abandoned her, her life had been built around her warrior skills. She didn't know if she could live without the ability to burn, couldn't imagine what she would do if she couldn't get a handle on whatever was happening to her.

Merilee eyed Cynda, gaze moving from her arms and legs to her shoulders and hair, and Cynda wondered if she was catching on. Dread pooled deep in her insides. She kept trying to find the words to blurt out the truth, but every time she got close to opening her mouth about it, she couldn't.

Still, when Riana kept up her glaring and pacing, Cynda's own fear and temper rose, fire or no fire. "This isn't just about Jake and today, is it? You're still mad at me for going to the Mothers over Creed being a demon, back when you first fell in love with him."

Seconds passed then, with nothing but a low whistle of surprise—cheering?—from Merilee.

"That did hurt." Riana stopped pacing and faced Cynda. "The fact you didn't believe in me, in my judgment as the mortar of this triad. How would you feel if I almost broke us apart by going to the Mothers about you falling in love with Nick?"

"I'm not in love with Nick," Cynda argued before she could stop herself. "And *you're* not wanting to trust *my* judgment about Jake, are you? Sometimes it's hard."

Why was she lying about her feelings for Nick?

Why couldn't she just spill out everything inside her, good and bad, bright and dark, and get it all out in the open like she was supposed to?

Because she didn't want to bother the people important to her.

That answer was easy enough.

She didn't want to hurt them in any way.

I don't want to burn down the house, do I? Make so much trouble they haul me off and drop me somewhere far away, and leave without ever looking back.

She was so scared of losing Riana and Merilee, she was being a friggin' coward, and she despised herself for it.

"You're in something with Nick, Cynda." Merilee used her wind energy to breeze away dust left by Riana's tantrum. "Infatuation. Lust. Love. You better decide before it drives you nuts, or gets Ri and me baked like little Sibyl dinner muffins. Except, you're not smoking much, are you?" Her face got deadly serious. "You're not burning at all."

Cynda's jaw ratcheted so tight she couldn't have responded if she wanted to. It took all her strength not to sit right down on the cold stone floor and just . . . give up.

"When you sleep with him, we promise we won't go to the Mothers," Riana said, still moving, oblivious to Cynda's problem and even Merilee's comment.

Enough.

She had to get *something* out. Spill bits and pieces until the whole thing fell out.

If Riana and Merilee lost faith in her, didn't want her as their third, she'd have to find a way to cope with that. It wasn't like she could pretend the truth away.

Cynda's jaw loosened, and tears spilled onto her cheeks. Everything in her tried to balk as she made herself say, "You don't have to go to the Mothers. They already came to me and chewed me a new asshole over Nick."

Riana lowered her hands, clearly shocked. "What?"

At the same time, Merilee said, "Well, no wonder you've been ass-backward and upside down. Why did they stick their noses into this? I thought we worked out the whole Curson-Sibyl issue with Creed and Riana."

"Motherhouse Ireland is stricter than Motherhouse Russia about relationships." Cynda hugged herself and refused to let her teeth chatter as the cold grew inside her. "They're stricter about everything. I guess they have to be. Mother Keara has always kept a tight watch on all of us."

After a moment of breathing and centering, Riana walked away from the gym door, toward Cynda, stopping just a few feet away. "I know Mother Keara means a lot to you, honey, but she can't tell you who to love."

"Yeah, well, she did." *Great. I'm crying like a friggin'*

baby now. "She'll—she said she would pitch me out if I pursue anything with Nick. Burn away my connections to fire. I couldn't be part of this triad. I wouldn't be a Sibyl anymore."

"Sonofabitch." Merilee crossed the gym floor until she, too, stood directly in front of Cynda. "Why didn't you come to us right away?"

"I didn't want—" Cynda began, but Riana cut her off.

"That's not right." Riana rubbed the top of her nose, the way she always did when she was trying to keep her thoughts together. "I won't have it. We won't allow it, Cynda. Your heart belongs to you."

Merilee nodded. "We'll defend that to the death."

Cynda wiped her eyes with the backs of her hands and looked at two of the most important people in the world to her. Their reactions brought a little warmth back to her heart, shored her up a fraction, and reinforced the decision she had made to leave her feelings for Nick alone. "Thanks, but I'm not risking it."

"The night Mother Keara dropped that bomb in your lap"—Merilee rolled her eyes skyward as if to say, *of course*—"that's when your fire started going out, isn't it? That's when you lost your sparks."

"You noticed." Cynda's whole body tensed. She stared at her feet because she couldn't make herself look at her triad sisters when she felt so completely ashamed.

"Jake was able to snatch you because you couldn't call your fire." Riana's sentence came out slow, overpronounced, like she couldn't believe she missed that little detail.

Cynda shrugged, still doing an intense study of her own toes. "I might have caught him by surprise and gotten an advantage. By the time I finally got a blaze going, he absorbed every flame."

"You didn't tell us about your fire." Riana looked angrier than Cynda had ever seen her. "If we had known, we would have watched you closer. We wouldn't have let you go on that raid in the first place!"

The ground started a slow, low rumbling, and shook again once, hard enough to jerk Cynda sideways. Rocks tapped to the floor. An exercise ball rolled past her ankles as she recovered her balance.

When she looked up, Merilee was right in her face, blue eyes blazing and narrow. "I cannot believe you walked into a battle with your fire malfunctioning and put yourself at risk like that."

She smacked Cynda in the shoulder with her fist.

Hard.

"Ow!" Cynda grabbed her arm as pain radiated down to her fingertips. "That's gonna bruise."

She tried on reflex to pop Merilee back with a good-sized fireball, but once again, nothing happened. No fizzle, no sizzle, not even a tiny pop.

More tears streaked down Cynda's face. A scream of frustration welled in her depths, but she bit it back.

"Don't you know you're important to us?" Merilee's voice cracked. She looked away and wiped her eyes, then stepped to the side to give Cynda a little space.

Riana was the one studying her feet now, slowly shaking her head. Her shoulders slumped, as if Cynda had kicked her right in the gut.

"I didn't tell you about the Mothers because I didn't want to worry you or make you feel like you had to watch after me to keep me from doing something stupid." Cynda took Riana by the arms, dying twice inside from the awful look of disappointment on her triad sister's face. "I didn't want you two caught in the middle."

"Bullshit." Riana's dark green eyes got darker with her anger. "That's where we belong, in the middle with you. Didn't you learn anything last fall, when this triad almost fractured? Merilee and I *are* your real family. We will *never* abandon you, especially through something like this."

Cynda let go of Riana, trying to absorb what she'd just said.

Her heart heard it, grabbed on to it, but her mind didn't want to believe, just couldn't quite accept the wonder of that reality.

Merilee's hands gripped Cynda's shoulders and gave her a squeeze as she said, "What Motherhouse Ireland doesn't know won't hurt them. If they find out and try to strip your powers, we'll hide you away, and hide with you—and never regret it. We'll appeal to Russia and Greece." Another squeeze, this time almost painful, but perfect at the same time. "We'll find a way to get through it no matter what, Cynda. Nothing but death will separate the three of us. They absolutely cannot use that threat against you, ever again."

"Triad first, above all else," Riana said, only this time, the words didn't stab Cynda down deep. "That includes Mother Keara and Motherhouse Ireland."

She watched as Riana held out her arm and pushed up her sleeve to reveal the Sibyl's mark. Mortar, pestle, and broom, etched across that dark crescent moon. "That's what this means. We're connected, like these symbols. Always. Forever. It's time you let yourself believe that."

Merilee came around to stand beside Riana, and Cynda glanced from one to the other, absolutely unable to speak.

They were waiting for her to say something, but she didn't have the power to generate a single sound.

Did she believe what Riana just said?

Could she?

And even if she did accept that Riana and Merilee would never turn on her or leave her behind, how could she do anything that would consign her chosen family to a lifetime of running and hiding from other people *they* loved?

Riana stared at her. So did Merilee. Waiting. Patient. Refusing to let her off the hook or leave her alone, or for one instant let her believe that one day, they wouldn't be here, right in her face when she needed them to be.

A distant memory sounded in Cynda's mind. Of all things, Mother Keara's voice, from the night Cynda met her.

Sibyl, Mother Keara had whispered as she squeezed Cynda's fingers and drew her closer to an understanding of her true identity, her true power.

. . . S-i-b-y-l. Say the word, child . . .

"Sibyl," she whispered in the present, remembering that long-ago night, and how she wished her words had been loud enough to echo and scare that mean Sister Julia out of her mind.

As it had that sad, wonderful night, Cynda's skin tingled.

Flames pulsed in her chest and spread down inside her arms to her hands. At the same time, her thighs and legs and feet heated to near boiling—

And it felt absolutely wonderful.

My heat. My fire!

Smoke curled slowly from the back of her neck as the fire inside soothed her, strengthened her, helped her find her words and tell her triad sisters, "I believe you."

Merilee clapped once when she saw the smoke, and smiled at Cynda.

Riana's expression lightened, then grew even more troubled. "I'm afraid it won't last. Not if you're shutting down what you feel for Nick."

"It's obvious he needs you," Merilee said. "You need him, too."

Caught up in the blissful sensations of her fire, Cynda wanted to rage and stomp and say she didn't need Nick, that she'd be just fine without him, without risking outright war with the Mothers. A childish part of her wanted to say she didn't need *anybody,* but she knew that wasn't true. She needed Riana and Merilee, and she needed her Mothers and Sibyl sisters in Ireland.

At least Riana and Merilee would stand by her, because what Merilee said was true. She needed Nick. She could survive with her triad sisters and him, even if she had to forfeit the rest. Without him, there was just nothing inside.

Without him, the fire would snuff right out again, she had no doubt.

"I do need Nick," Cynda admitted, but Riana was already talking, going on about how Nick's mental discipline and self-control was good for Cynda, about how he could help her with control and focus.

"And you can help him get through this whole Jake thing," Merilee added. "Like Ri will help Creed."

"I don't think there's any helping a man get through killing his brother." Cynda hugged herself again at the thought.

Her words hung in the air between the three of them until a deep bass rumbled, "I'll shoot Jake if I have to. I've said that before, and I meant it."

Warm chills broke out across Cynda's skin, followed by aches in her chest and belly. When she turned her gaze toward the gym door, there stood Nick. He had changed into black jeans and a black sleeveless T-shirt, and his hair hung over one shoulder, tied into a loose ponytail.

The agony and challenge in his eyes riveted Cynda.

She wanted—needed—to look away from him, but she couldn't. She wanted to run to him, hold him, kiss him until she banished his pain, and hers, too—but that wasn't possible either, was it?

Riana's and Merilee's words jumbled through Cynda's mind, banging against her own realizations about the emotional source of her fire.

It really wasn't an option to keep ignoring her emotions, or pretending they would go away, was it? She couldn't live her whole life trying not to cause serious trouble, in hopes no one would leave her again.

Cynda glanced from Riana to Merilee, both of whom stared back at her, as if willing her to get the point, and fight for her right to love freely, live freely.

She could have Nick.

She *would* have him, and she'd stay a Sibyl, too.

She'd take on Mother Keara and all of Motherhouse Ireland if she had to, damn them straight to hell.

This man was right for her.

Cynda knew it. The fire in her soul knew it, too.

Riana picked up the "dishes" and walked slowly toward the door to the stairs, making small talk to Nick as she went.

Merilee didn't bother stammering or offering social pleasantries. She just gave Cynda a *Do what's right for you* glare, then whisked past Nick and out of the gym, towing Riana behind her.

Riana had the presence of mind to close the door as they went.

Remnants of smoke drifted slowly around the gym, making everything gray and vague.

The only thing Cynda could hear was her own unsteady breathing. The only thing she could smell was fire and smoke and earth and wind and hints of ocean and musk.

Nick.

The only thing she could see, feel, or sense was Nick.

He stayed where he was, muscled arms folded, gazing at her with his black eyes.

"How much did you hear?" she asked, her voice still shaky, her essence wrung out from everything she had just been through.

"I heard you say you aren't in love with me," he said in a quiet tone.

If I slap myself, he'll think I'm crazy. Cynda's throat went dry. She shut her eyes. Made herself open them. Thought one more time about slapping herself.

She was standing alone in a closed basement, only a few yards from the one man who could cost her everything—and she was ready to pay that price. Now she had to make him understand. Now she had to make him believe it.

After running her fool-stupid mouth.

Couldn't something ever be easy? Please? Just one thing?

Before she could begin to try to clean up the mess she'd made with her own words, Nick pinned her again with his intense gaze. "I also heard your triad sisters say they'd stand behind you. And I *think* I heard you say that you need me." He shrugged. "That's something. I'll take it."

"There's more." Cynda got out the sentence, but Nick clearly wasn't finished rattling her down to bones and marrow.

"Riana and Merilee said that your heart is your own." The force of his gaze reached across the space between them and touched her everywhere at once. "Is that true, Cynda?"

Her muscles felt weak, but her voice was strong when she answered, "Yes."

She couldn't tear her gaze away from the man. Her heart beat so hard and fast she was sure everyone in the townhouse could hear it. Heat flowed up and down her arms, across her shoulders, and dropped low, licking across her taut nipples, and lower, streaming down her belly, and lower, to that aching center between her legs. A hundred little blazes broke out across the gym's stone floor and danced like candle flames.

The pain in Nick's eyes doubled. "I don't want to take anything away from you. I won't see you hurt."

More flames grew at her wrists and fingers. She didn't even try to draw them back into the expanding pool of heat inside her.

"When I said I didn't love you, I was lying—to myself more than anyone, because I was scared." Cynda risked a step toward him, and he didn't back away. "I'm sorry."

Nick looked stunned for a moment, like she had slapped him across both cheeks. The lines of his face softened. "I understand, firebird. I know you can't, we can't act on what we're feeling until I catch that plane and talk to the Mothers."

Smoke streamed away from her body as she worked to sort out his response.

He was so insistent about talking to the Mothers. As

much as he could without ruining her life, he *was* fighting for her.

Did that mean he loved her, too?

All this dancing left, right, around in circles, she couldn't take it anymore.

Screw it. Just screw everything.

She was a fire Sibyl. About friggin' time she acted like one.

Cynda faced Nick directly. "No, you don't understand. I love you. I can't ignore that anymore. I refuse."

Now Nick really looked slapped. Caught off guard. He lowered his arms and gazed at her, obviously trying to figure out what he should say.

Cynda would have smiled if she hadn't been fighting eagle-sized butterflies in her belly.

That's *communication, big man. Can you keep up with me?*

She felt like herself again.

Finally.

Nick tightened his fingers into fists, heightening the definition in his arms. He looked barely restrained, and so handsome she could almost taste him.

"Is . . . this what you want?" His voice came out so low Cynda's neck tingled. "Am I worth the cost to you?"

Now she did smile. She felt the answer like a wave of pure, satiating warmth as she said, "You're worth everything."

His hungry look radiated through her essence, speaking louder than any words, shouting at her to move, to come to him, where she belonged.

Cynda felt wanted. She felt beautiful and right and strong again.

She walked across the floor, straight through the jets of fire her own energy created, until she stood inches from Nick, face-to-face, eye to eye. His presence fed into her like sunlight, like the molten rock at the center of the Earth.

She put her hands under his T-shirt, rubbing across the hard ridges of muscle beneath. "Let's keep this simple from now on. Tell me, yes or no. Do you love me?"

"Yes. I love you." No hesitation. No glimmer of worry in those dark eyes. He gave her the answer without so much as a blink, and Cynda felt twice as warm. Gloriously hot.

She slid her hands higher, to his sensitive nipples, and enjoyed the shudder as she brushed her palms across them. "Do you want me, Nick?"

He started to glow. His eyes flamed like black stars, burning into existence. For her. The man blazed for her.

"Yes," he said, his bass rumble stirring her heart.

She pinched his nipples hard enough to make him pull air through his teeth. "Then what are you waiting for?"

Nick let out a growl and unfastened her jeans.

Cynda stepped out of them and kicked them away as her underwear went up in smoke. Nick grabbed her ass, lifted her off the ground, and pressed her against him.

Cynda wrapped her legs around his waist, holding him tight as she slipped her hands from under his shirt, ran her fingers up his neck, and loosened his hair. When it fell around his shoulders, she grabbed both hands full, pulling his face to hers.

The man's lips were heaven. He tasted perfect. Sharp and tangy and male, exactly like she wanted.

As his tongue found hers, she couldn't believe how hard her heart pounded, how desperately she wanted to be body to body, skin to skin, with Nick deep inside her.

She broke the kiss, breathing in quick jerks. "No more waiting." Her voice scraped in her throat as she pulled back to look into his eyes. "Here. Now. Right now."

Nick swept his mouth down to her shoulder through her shirt, then up again, to her exposed neck. She gasped at his sharp nips, his tender bites, and loved the low, ravenous rumble in his chest as he started to move.

With her legs still wrapped around him, he carried her to one of the exercise mats and laid her down. Her naked ass rubbed the cool foam surface, sending new chills up and down her spine.

As Nick knelt between her thighs, Cynda spread her legs wide to give him all the room he needed.

"I want you naked," he growled.

She reached for her blouse, but he caught her wrists in one of his hands.

Big hands. Huge hands. Strong. He feels so good.

Nick's fierce expression sent waves of molten heat all over Cynda's body.

Keeping firm control of her wrists, he eased her arms over her head and pressed them to the mat. All the while, he rubbed his jean-clad erection against her drenched lower folds, the rough, illicit sensation driving her absolutely into orbit.

No question now.

She had never wanted anything this badly. Ever.

All she could do was groan and push her body into his, tempting, asking. She'd beg if she had to.

With his free hand, Nick shoved upward at her blouse buttons. They gave easily, and her shirt fell open, releasing her aching breasts. Her nipples beaded in the cool air even as Nick's fiery stare heated Cynda in ways she had never experienced.

"You're so beautiful," he murmured before he lowered his head and caught one of her rock-hard nubs in his teeth.

Cynda moaned. She arched into his biting, his sucking, as sparks flew through her body. Nick's skin glowed brighter gold, drawing in the heat she surrendered, making it his own, containing her even as he powered her headlong toward the edge.

Nick kept his attention on her breasts, pulling first one nipple into his mouth, then the other. Just the sensation of his breath on the tender flesh almost yanked Cynda into the abyss. She could barely stand the sensation of his rough jeans scrubbing her bare thighs, the feel of the mat beneath her naked ass. She had never been at any man's mercy—she had never been under any man's control, but she didn't give one damn about handing that control to Nick.

He could have it.

He could take her, any way he wanted to.

Cynda clamped her knees around his waist, locked her ankles behind his back, and rode his jean-clad cock while he kept sucking her nipples, pressing his face into her breasts, holding her to the mat, exactly where he wanted her.

A cry of need escaped her throat. "I can't wait. Don't make me wait. I'll cook us both."

Fire skittered around them in a circle, just off the mat. Nick still didn't release her wrists.

Cynda thrashed beneath him. If he didn't give her relief soon, she'd burn off his clothes. Hell, they were both on fire anyway. It wouldn't take much, would it?

Only Nick kept drawing her fire into him, taking it, handling her completely as he drove her insane.

He turned loose her nipple and moved his mouth to hers again, claiming her lips, crushing her mouth with his.

Her blood had to be turning to steam, she was so hot. Every inch of her felt alive, sensitized, ready.

Nick tore himself from the kiss. When he spoke, the deep, ragged sound of his voice made her ache. "Tell me how you want it."

If Cynda could have gotten her hands free, she would have raked her nails from his shoulders to his ass. "Fast. Hard. Now!"

She arched her back so hard she lifted them both off the mat for a split second.

Nick trailed his hand down her belly, rubbing her throbbing center as he unfastened his jeans. Jolts of electricity shot through her, and more fire leaped into existence. Half the room had to be covered by now.

When his thick erection burst free and pressed into her belly, she coated another section of the stone basement with flames.

Cynda moaned from the size of him, from the musky scent of their arousal. Smoke clouded the air in every direction. Fire hissed and crackled, but she didn't have to worry in this stone room. A few mats and balls—those were easy to fix.

Rock didn't burn.

Even though she knew she couldn't get loose from his masterful grip, Cynda twisted her wrists in Nick's powerful hand, wanting nothing more than to reach down and feel him, stroke him—and put *him* exactly where she wanted him.

Inside her. All the way. Deep.

Five minutes ago . . .

She raised her hips as best she could, opening herself wide.

On one knee, he kept her wrists hostage and teased her wet folds with the firm, soft head of his erection. Tickling. Circling all the spots that ached and pulsed and wanted so much more.

"Hard and fast," he murmured, black eyes fixed on hers. "Are you sure?"

"Now, Nick!" She forced her wrists against his hand. "Now before I hurt you!"

For an endless, agonizing second, Nick gazed at her like he might be storing every detail of how she looked, the fire dancing beyond her hair, the heat radiating off her skin.

Then he slid into her. Forcing her wide, stretching her with his steel-hard girth.

Cynda banged her head on the mat and screamed.

Finally, finally, finally!

Fire shot from her fingertips and toes.

Nick let go of her wrists, and she grabbed the sides of his head and kissed him deep, as they lay still for a moment, sharing each other, joined, connected.

Nick nipped her bottom lip, pulled away, and took hold of Cynda's ankles, moving her legs and feet up, so that her calves rested on his shoulders. He eased himself to his knees, hands to either side of her ass, gripping her firmly, but gently, just the right amount of pressure, as he slid deeper inside her.

She moaned again as he seemed to sink to her very core—and stop.

"You fit me," he said in that low, sexy voice. "I may stay right here forever."

"Not if," she gasped, "you don't. Fucking. Move!"

Her body shook as he moved his cock, slowly at first, then burying himself with each thrust.

"So good," he said, but Cynda barely heard him over the crazed noises she was making.

She couldn't help looking at where they were joined, watching him glide in and out of her, harder with every stroke. He did fit, he did, and was it ever amazing to see, to feel. Already her channel was clenching him, so wet she could hear each movement, which only made her crazier.

"That's it," he encouraged, moving faster, doubling her sensations. "Watch. Don't close your eyes."

Cynda watched and moaned and wondered if she'd ever be able to breathe normally again.

Nick pumped his hips, picking up the pace. He let go of her ass and rested his hands on her breasts, massaging, pinching her nipples.

She cried out, but when she closed her eyes, he pinched her harder.

"Watch," he ordered. "Watch me make you scream."

She opened her eyes. The sight of Nick inside her was almost too much.

Fire caught in Cynda's mind and roared. The fires in the gym roared louder. Everything inside her pulled together, holding him, wanting him deeper, taking him deeper.

"That's it, firebird." His voice shook with the force of his need, matching her own.

"Don't stop." Cynda slammed herself against him as he thrust hard and fast, just like she'd ordered and oh, Goddess, he was making her watch, and she couldn't stand another second.

She screamed as her orgasm swept over both of them, flash fire, out of control, sizzling into Nick's golden skin, brighter and louder with each incredible wave of sensation.

She was still screaming, eyes closed now, telling him to stop, telling him he had to stop, but he didn't, and Cynda knew—positive, no question—she was about to completely explode.

She thrust both breasts into his palms as he drove himself deeper still, moving so hard and fast Cynda's body rocked and jerked from the force.

The wave building inside her was huge. Too big. She'd burn down the townhouse. She'd burn down New York, but still, he didn't quit moving.

"Give it to me, firebird," he commanded, and Cynda's consciousness came loose from its moorings.

She screamed again, shaking from the force of another round of pure pleasure. She dug her nails into Nick's skin, into what felt like raw pulsing energy. Her body moved with its own will and purpose then, driving her, driving him.

When she managed to open her eyes, the joy and desire on Nick's face nearly unraveled her completely.

And the big man wasn't finished yet.

(19)

Sweat coursed down the center of Nick's back.

His muscles burned from restraining himself. All he could do, and not much longer.

Thank God Sibyls had their own methods of birth control, because a condom would have melted ten times over by now. His clothes were long gone, no more than ashes smeared on his skin. The gym blazed with fire—floors, walls, everywhere. Pools of it. Sheets of it.

Exercise balls detonated like grenades. The mats were probably melted into puddles. He'd be surprised if the weights hadn't liquefied, too.

But the hottest thing in the room lay screaming beneath him.

He had never known anything so sweet in his life.

The sensation of her wet depths squeezing into him nearly brought out the howling, mindless beast.

As he drove his cock into Cynda, Nick wished he could use his own energy to brand her so all men would know that she was *his*. His now. His forever.

"I can't take any more!" She pounded his shoulders with her fists, but he knew she could last through another round. He could see it in the wild light of her green eyes, read it in her frenzied bucks, smell it in her sweet, sensual musk.

She had one more explosion in her, and he would get her there. He would make sure he left his mark, one way or another.

Her lids fluttered shut as she bit her pretty lip.

"Open your eyes," he said, the words coming out in a

guttural snarl. "Watch us, firebird. Watch us burn together."

Cynda called him six names without ever saying the same word twice. She beat on him again, smashed herself against him—but she opened her eyes.

The sight of her moaning and sweaty and desperate, staring at that sweet, joined spot where his cock plunged into her sleek body, almost punched his ticket.

He bit the inside of his cheek until he tasted blood.

Using his special connection to Gideon, he brought his *other* forward. Barely. Just enough to change his own size, shape, and temperature.

Cynda's eyes went wide as Nick felt the surge of energy flow into his cock. When he looked down, he glowed gold everywhere, and she had fire in new places, dancing between them like dozens of hot little fingers.

"Oh, damn!" she said, only it was more a sob, barely understandable. "Yes. Goddess. Please, no, shit, yes!"

She trailed into gibberish and hit him some more and absolutely lost control, and that's what Nick was waiting for. He slid his hands to her hips and forced her to match his rhythm, open to him completely. With every bit of controlled force he could muster, he drove them both home with deep, rocking thrusts.

The world left him as he came with a bone-jarring rush, keeping his eyes fixed on Cynda's beautiful face.

Her screams filled his ears. Her heady woman's scent filled his nose.

Fire roared over him and he pulled every bit into his own essence.

Give me all you've got, and then some. I can handle you. You're mine, Cynda Flynn.

Did he say that out loud?

He didn't care.

He'd back up that claim with fists and guns and whatever army he could muster. As he collapsed forward, rolling her to her side and pulling her with him as he flopped to his back, he knew he would do whatever it took to keep her.

Including standing down a bunch of old Irish crones who might just be meaner than Cynda.

As he cradled her in his arms, stroking her hair, kissing her head, all he could say was, "I love you."

All she could say was, "Goddamn, I cooked the gym."

Nick laughed.

Did life get any better than this?

She looked at him, her eyes misty and distant, yet completely with him. "I—I—" Her words choked away, then came back, forceful. "I love you, too."

And he knew she did.

Nothing inside Nick doubted her, or mistrusted her, or second-guessed anything about Cynda.

He knew what a risk it was for a woman who had lost so much to offer her heart. He accepted her gift with a kiss, then another, and another.

She met his lips with hers, absolute softness and warmth, and he wanted to stay beside her, bound by flame, for the rest of his life.

As it was, it took almost half an hour for the fire and smoke and soot to settle.

Nick was happy to lie there with his woman in his arms and let all the popping, cracking, and hissing fade away. He could have done without the stench of burned rubber and melted plastic, but he'd get used to that. Probably eight hours of hard labor ahead plus a shopping trip to rectify the damage, but he'd scrub the gym and buy out the sporting goods store with a smile. Maybe he should just set them up on regular shipments.

Weekly?

Hell, no.

Daily.

I wonder if there's any such thing as a fireproof bed.

When Nick eased to his side to face Cynda, she had the cutest streaks of soot trailing down her cheeks and dotting her freckled chin. Never mind the smeared handprints on both her breasts and the hip he could see.

She ran her fingers through his hair. "I, uh, never did this kind of damage before."

Two emotions punched Nick at the same time—jealousy that she'd had any befores, and feral pride that he fueled her fire better than anyone else in the world. "I'll buy a stone house." He turned his head just enough to kiss her tattooed forearm. "We'll furnish it with granite."

She grinned, a little shy, eyes still half-closed. "You talk big."

"I do a lot of things big." He kissed her ear.

Cynda's cheeks turned red. "I can't believe after you wore me out so completely, you can still make me smoke. You'd think I wouldn't have a spark left anywhere."

Nick waited until the cloud of smoke drifted away from them, then met Cynda's sleepy gaze. "We probably should have had this conversation before, but . . . what happens now? Does some coven of ancient Irish witches ride in here on broomsticks to castrate me?"

Her muscles tightened, and he immediately wanted to rub the stress straight back out of her body. "The Mothers don't know, and they won't know until somebody tells them."

He gave Cynda a few seconds to relax before he asked, "And when they do find out?"

Her warm breath tickled his chin as she sighed. "I'll be expelled. And if they catch me, they'll force me to undergo a ritual to seal me off from my fire."

Nick's gut tightened at that thought. He'd been watching her this last week. He'd seen how she struggled, how vulnerable and off-center she'd been without that spark in her depths. No way that was right, for Cynda or anyone else. And no way he would let that happen to her.

He gazed at her steadily, determination flowing into every muscle and fiber. "If it comes to that, they *won't* catch you."

She smiled, but her expression was sad, almost resigned. "I'd like to believe that, but I can't worry about it now."

He brushed damp red curls off her forehead with his fingertips. "Riana and Merilee are on your side. We'll fight this fight—and we'll win. And after we do, how does a long trip to San Francisco sound—just the two of us? Or L.A.?"

That made her face brighten. She played with his hair again, and the warmth of her wrist heated him inside. "I'd rather do Tibet, or maybe Bali."

"Bali." He imagined wild fire sex on the beach, with the ocean to do his cleanup work. "I could go for Bali."

Once more, Cynda's expression turned serious, almost grim. "You've got to understand, I might have put us both at serious risk. I don't want you in the Mothers' hands any more than I want them to catch me. I have no idea what they'd do to you."

"I'm not worried about that." Nick heard the edge of anger in his response.

He wanted those old biddies to come for him. He wanted to understand what they had against him, and he wanted to tell them just where to put this whole expelling-Cynda idea. As soon as he could, he *would* be speaking with them.

She smacked his shoulder. "That scares me, because you should be worried. When they're riled, the Mothers are more dangerous than a pit of saw-scaled vipers. If they get their hands on you, I might never see you again."

Nick shrugged. "Creed went to Russia and came back in one piece."

"Uh, no." Cynda's green eyes flashed. "Don't even think about submitting yourself to that procedure. That could have killed Creed, and you don't need it. You already have control of your *other*."

"Gideon," Nick said, his voice quiet because he'd never told anyone that before. "That's what I call it—him."

Inside his mind, Gideon made a noise something like a contented lion's purr.

Exactly how Nick felt, save for his wish to stalk and eat a few Irish Mothers.

Cynda's hand trailed from his face to his chest, then lower, to stroke his cock. "Most men name these, not their inner demons."

Nick covered her prowling hand with his. "I'll pass on that. Look, whatever happens, we'll survive, Cynda. We. The two of us. We'll do it together."

She slipped her fingers out from under his and drew back a few inches. When she had enough room, she rolled to her back, scooted her shoulder into his chest, and looked at the ceiling. "I can't believe I'm putting so many people in danger."

He touched her still-damp hair and traced the line of her jaw with his thumb. "I made this choice for myself. So did your triad. You're that important to us."

Her lips trembled. "Even if I cook gyms?"

"*Because* you cook gyms." He brushed away a tear that slipped through the soot on her cheek. "I'll never let you down, firebird."

Another tear, and another. Her chest heaved. "I know."

For a time, Nick gave Cynda space and silence, keeping his body next to hers, stroking her face and arm.

He knew she was terrified of losing her life as a Sibyl,

of being separated from her fire. It touched him, awed him, that she would take a risk like that for him. He had to find a way to protect her, not just from invisible demons and J. C. Downy, but from her own people, too. Whatever it took, he would figure something out. Nothing was ever going to hurt this woman again.

One threat at a time . . .

He dipped his head and kissed the corner of her eye, tasting the salt from her waning tears. "Did you and your triad figure out anything from those dishes?"

Cynda twitched and snorted. "Yeah. Sure. J. C. Downy's an Irish Catholic woman with a bog-oak crucifix and weird cup and wand." She smacked her palm against the exercise mat. "Those dishes reminded me of the last two houses we've raided. Something about the pieces looked familiar, but I couldn't place it. I just can't dig it out of my head. It pisses me off."

Good.

He'd rather see her mad than sad or worried. Mad suited Cynda.

"Must be a long-ago memory." He scooted her close to him and grinned at the smoke curling off her elbows and toes.

"That's just it. I don't have many memories before I went to Motherhouse Ireland. I was too young—not even six years old—and that was all . . . too painful." She kicked a foot in the air, like she might be giving some perp a good head-bash. "Mostly I remember the few weeks before my father took me and left me with Mother Keara, and the last night I saw him."

Nick went still, his mouth against the side of her head. "Your father . . . just dropped you off with a bunch of strangers?"

Cynda didn't answer, but Nick could see on her face that he was right.

Who could do something like that?

He held her to him, understanding her attachment to the Sibyls a little better, and wishing he knew where this "father" of hers lived.

Nick wanted a word with that bastard, too.

"I couldn't stay in the village where I was born." Cynda frowned. "My fire—I was destroying things. Everyone was afraid of me."

Okay. Maybe he needed to speak to Cynda's entire hometown. His list was growing.

"My father took me to Kylemore Abbey, this big convent. Since fire Sibyls are usually born in the United Kingdom, local priests know to direct them to Kylemore, because it's close to Motherhouse Ireland. The nuns at Kylemore know how to summon the Sibyls, but even they were scared of me. This one bitch in a habit called me a devil. I'll never forget her."

Nick was adding the Kylemore nuns to his shit-list when he felt Cynda go absolutely stiff in his grip.

He gazed down at her.

Her eyes had gone wide.

Her mouth was open.

For a moment, she didn't even breathe.

Then she yelled, "Shit!"

Before Nick could react, Cynda shoved his arm off her chest, rolled away from him and jumped to her feet. Smoke washed over her shoulders, curled around her head and legs.

She started walking back and forth, waving her hands. "I'm so stupid. I can't believe this took me so long!"

Nick pushed himself to his feet, still feeling loose and spent from their earlier session together. "Uh, firebird, can you clue me in, here?"

"I have to see the dishes." Cynda waved her hands again. "Only they're not dishes. I am such an idiot. Dishes!"

When he approached her, put his arms around her, she banged her fists against his chest, but out of frustration, not to push him away.

"The convent," she said, eyes flaring even brighter than usual. "That stuff is from Kylemore Abbey."

Nick kept hold of her and wondered if he looked as clueless as he felt.

Cynda shook her head. "These houses we've raided, what's familiar is how they smelled. How they looked. That unnatural *clean* thing. Every time I ever had to go to Kylemore, I hated the place because it was so friggin' spotless and sterile."

Now we're getting somewhere.

He well remembered how ill at ease Cynda had been during the raids, how she had sniffed and searched with her eyes, obviously reaching for something and coming up short. He agreed. Not that he'd ever been to a nunnery, but yeah, those houses had been convent-clean and convent-quiet.

He tried to steady Cynda and keep her focused. "And the dishes?"

"The crucifix." She gripped both of his forearms. "Probably off Kylemore's walls. And that bowl. It's a font. You know, to hold the holy water Catholic parishioners dip their fingers in before they cross themselves." More smoke swirled in the sooty gym. "And the cup, too. It's a pot and sprinkler. The priests use them to bless the congregation."

She twisted away and started walking again, this time toward the gym door, in all her naked, fire-lined glory. "This *isn't* about the Legion. At least not directly. What if Ri and the other triads have already sent that stuff to Russia?"

Nick trailed after her. "If the stuff's from Kylemore, what does that mean?"

She spun to face him, her face bright with heat. "I get it now. Jake's message. I understand!"

She smiled, only it wasn't anywhere near gentle and sweet.

Nick actually took a step back, respecting that furious, carnivorous expression.

"I know exactly who J. C. Downy is," Cynda said. "And I think I know how to find her."

(20)

Cynda ran up the stairs from the basement, kicking over stacks of books she now knew had been left by spying Astaroth demons.

"Uh, Cynda," Nick called from below her. She ignored him. Let him catch up and keep up, if he could. This was too important.

Downy's been at the back of my mind all the time. Her heart punched her ribs as her feet pounded across the tile and wood of the townhouse's downstairs floors. *Right in front of me. How could I have missed something so obvious?*

"Cynda," Nick called again as she started up the steps to her bedroom.

"Come on!" she yelled back.

Her stomach ached like she was starving—and she was hungry like a wild thing, to hunt this murderer and catch her before she killed another fire Sibyl. Cynda was up the steps to her bedroom, after passing at least three OCU officers and Sal Freeman, too, when the cold air hit her, head to foot. Bare breasts, bare ass and all.

I'm stark naked.

She stumbled to a fast stop outside Nick's bedroom door and swore a few more times. The energy cooking through the third-floor hallway told her that Riana, Merilee, and the other visiting Sibyls had to be close by. No doubt they had gone to Cynda's bedroom to use the projective mirrors and communications platform to open channels to the Motherhouses.

How could she charge in there without clothes?

She glanced down at herself.

Without clothes *and* with Nick's sooty handprints all over her body.

SONofa—

"I was trying to get your attention," Nick said as he caught up with her. "Though I'm sure everybody downstairs enjoyed the show. I damn sure did."

She glanced at him, face flushed with heat.

Like her, he still had on nothing but what the Goddess gave him at birth.

"Wait here." He opened the door to his room and went inside. A minute or so later, he came back, wearing fresh jeans and a navy sleeveless T-shirt. For Cynda, he held out an NYU sweatshirt and a pair of cutoff sweatpants.

He apologized with his expression. "Best I can do. I don't have anything smaller."

"These will work, thanks." She grabbed the shirt and wriggled into it. The fabric went to her knees, and the hood felt huge and heavy as it flopped against her shoulder blades—but it covered her up. She accepted the cutoffs, too. Those fit like a tent with holes sliced in the bottom, but the drawstring held them around her waist.

Nick's scent covered her just like the clothes. Cynda rubbed her palms against the NYU logo.

Okay, the Mothers would know these weren't her clothes, but no way they'd know for sure the sweats belonged to Nick.

Right?

Dread fluttered in her belly.

Maybe they would.

Somehow, the Mothers always knew everything.

I can't worry about this right now. I'm fine. The clothes are fine.

"Go downstairs," she told Nick, turning to face him.

"Don't you dare risk coming any closer to my room, you understand me? All three orders might have Mothers in the mirrors, and I don't want them seeing you. I sure don't want them grabbing you."

Storm clouds gathered across Nick's expression. He started to argue with her but she put both hands on the soft fabric of his T-shirt, feeling the ripple of muscles underneath. "Please, for my sake, go. So we can find Downy together and get her off the streets. We'll have time to talk to the Mothers after that, I promise."

Nick's face grew even darker. Tight-lipped, he nodded.

Cynda rose to her toes, kissed his rough cheek, then reluctantly left him standing outside his bedroom door.

Please, Goddess, don't let the Mothers grab me.

She hurried to her own room, turned the door handle, and slipped inside.

The second she crossed her threshold, the energy already humming along Cynda's skin doubled. The air in her room smelled faintly of smoke and spices, swirling and mixed in the low evening light spilling through her room's windows. On the communications platform Harper Ellis, the South Staten Island fire Sibyl, stood holding the font, pot and sprinkler, and crucifix Jake had supplied. Around the table, Riana, Merilee, the North Staten Island triad, and the rest of the South Staten Island triad waited, as if for wisdom or some grand pronouncement.

When Merilee glanced in Cynda's direction, the air Sibyl's blue eyes widened. Riana mimicked Merilee only seconds later.

Soon, all the Sibyls were staring at Cynda.

She tried to say something in greeting, but her brain refused to cooperate. As she took slow, centering breaths, she realized all three Motherhouses were already present. She knew them by their distinctive scents, and by the women in the mirrors—Mother Yana in her brown robes from Russia, Mother Anemone in blue robes from Greece, and Mother Keara wearing Ireland's green.

Mother Keara's gaze shifted to Cynda, magnified by the mirror's crystalline glass.

In that split second, Cynda's pulse raced, and she almost fled the room. Years of training as a warrior held her in place, but she fought an urge to cover herself with her arms, as if Mother Keara could see straight through Nick's clothes to the telltale handprints beneath.

Don't be stupid.

But the old woman already seemed to know something. Her expression hardened to inscrutable as her eyes swept from the NYU logo to Cynda's bare, ash-coated feet. When she once more raised her gaze, the message on her face was more than clear.

You've been up to somethin' . . .

Cynda didn't hear the thought, but she felt it like stinging nettles on the back of her neck. She had heard the statement so many times growing up that her mind supplied the rest.

And I will *figure out what it is.*

For a moment, fear threatened to overwhelm Cynda. A ripping sensation in her belly made her dig her teeth into her bottom lip. In her mind, she saw images of the Mothers in the mirrors locking arms in a tight circle around her. She could almost feel them crushing into her, imagined the staggering flow of their monumental power as they called the elements to tear Cynda's fire from deep within her.

She knew the ritual would cripple her.

Just the thought of how cold she would be at that moment, and forever after, left her shaking and pulling at the sweatshirt as if the heavy cotton was forcing the air from her lungs.

Mother Keara simply kept staring from behind the glass, as did all the Sibyls present in the room. It had only been a few seconds since she came into the room, but it felt like hours to Cynda.

She gulped air, doing her best not to break down like an untrained child. Mother Keara might suspect something, but she didn't know. Not possible. Besides, Cynda had already gotten a taste of that breathless, lifeless cold, hadn't she? When she sealed herself off from her triad, and from Nick.

Her pulse skipped, then abruptly slowed as she shook her head from the force of that memory.

No matter what she chose, she'd have to battle for her fire. She'd have to struggle to stay a Sibyl, a functioning, fighting member of her triad. Anger whispered through her mind at those thoughts, soothing her with a rush of warmth, wrapping her chest in protective heat.

It wasn't right for anyone to back her into a corner like this. It wasn't right for Mother Keara and Motherhouse Ireland to interfere with the affairs of her heart, no matter how carefully they kept a watch on the world's volatile fire elementals. They were sworn to use their gifts and training to save the untrained, weak, and innocent from the supernaturally strong—not to fight each other.

Cynda didn't want to war with the women who raised her, but she wouldn't just give herself and her future over to them, either. Not anymore. She picked Riana and Merilee from the sea of eyes staring at her, and let herself feel the steadying influence of their presence. She had her triad and Nick to consider now, and she didn't plan to let them down—or live without them.

Riana and Merilee studied her for a moment, then visibly relaxed.

As their earth and air energy rushed forward to join her own, Cynda lifted her chin and met Mother Keara's eyes, body jumping inside from sparks she refused to let herself shed. With all of her energy and her triad's support, with fire she could taste but didn't spill, Cynda returned the Mother's stare with a little message of her own.

Go for it.

She walked forward, straight to the edge of the table beside Riana and Merilee.

Aloud, she said, "I got it. I remembered where I've seen these items before."

Mother Keara's angry expression softened to one of keen interest. The other two Mothers leaned forward, and Harper quickly set Jake's gifts on the communications platform.

Cynda pointed at each one and named it. To Mother Keara, she said, "I think these might have been stolen from Kylemore Abbey by one of the nuns present the night my father brought me to you. The one who got dismissed a few months after I arrived, for her cruelty to her students and her intolerance of the Sibyls. Sister Julia. Remember her?"

Now the Mother's face was more than easy to read. Any second now, she'd spit a mouthful of molten nails straight through the mirror.

On the communications platform, Harper shrank back as if she feared the same thing. Riana and Merilee leaned to the side, as did the other Staten Island Sibyls, just in case the glass exploded.

"I'll not be forgettin' that *striapach*," Mother Keara said, too low and too quiet. Fire laced the words as she spoke them. Her mirror shook against the wall. "I advised the Abbess Superior to hang her instead of letting her walk away, but such are not the ways of the Church." Her hands twitched, giving off smoke. "Peace-lovin' fools. They don't understand the Legion has eyes everywhere. They're always watchin', just waitin' for an opportunity to recruit somebody unhappy, somebody ripe with information like Sister Julia, to *their* side."

Cynda felt a rush of joy at the new energy binding the room now. Focused. On target. Powerful—and lethal.

"She's definitely got Legion demons at her command. Can you speak to the Abbess and track where Julia went when she left?" she asked. "And we need to know who she contacted—or who contacted her."

Mother Keara kept right on smoking. "Absolutely."

"If the Church has lost her trail, we can certainly find it," said Mother Anemone from Greece, her smooth, high voice ringing in contrast to Mother Keara's gravelly tenor. "Get us her birth name, and any demographics."

"And any items she might have handled." Mother Yana from Russia gestured to the items on the communications platform. "Give me those, and vatever else can be found. Ve vill compare trace genetic material for confirmation."

Mother Keara snarled, sending fire against the inside of the window glass. "Test and confirm and whatever else you'd like. That way, when we find the treacherous bitch, we'll be stringin' her up with no fits of conscience."

While the Mothers spoke back and forth to each other about the best method to contain Sister Julia a.k.a. J. C. Downy once she was captured, Harper scooted the font, pot and sprinkler, and crucifix to the center of the communications platform. Using steps Cynda had known since childhood, Harper danced until the room vibrated with her crackling, sparking fire energy. Cynda breathed it in, let it flow over her, and added hers to the mix. When the objects at Harper's feet began to move, Cynda felt it in her fingers and toes.

Moments later, Jake's gifts lifted from the communications platform, borne on a solid wave of heat, and vanished into the big, dark mirror leading to Motherhouse

Russia. Moments later, Cynda could see them again, on the stone floor at Mother Yana's feet. The Russian Mother gave a polite bow. As she bent to examine the items she received, her image wavered in the glass, faded to a pinpoint of light, and vanished.

After making certain Mother Keara would be in touch with the needed information later that day, Mother Anemone also made her exit.

Harper Ellis stood politely on the communications platform, waiting for Mother Keara to terminate her image, but the Mother waved the young fire Sibyl away. "Thank you, child, but I must speak to Cynda and her triad in private. Leave us."

The whole South Staten Island group looked shocked. Riana and Merilee looked like they wished they hadn't left their weapons down in the tactical room.

Cynda's fingers brushed her own hip. The feel of her sword hilt would have been nice, even though she knew she'd never draw a blade on Mother Keara. As it was, the soft cotton of Nick's shorts gave her a jolt of resolve.

Here we go, big man. Let's hope I don't blow this all to hell.

Despite her earlier bravado, Cynda had to force herself to exchange places with Harper and take over holding open the channel to Motherhouse Ireland. Her throat went dry, and she found it harder and harder to breathe as the other Sibyls left the bedroom.

Before the door closed, Riana and Merilee had climbed onto the platform. They came to stand on either side of Cynda like silent guards, their arms brushing hers. Little bursts of their energy folded around her shoulders like hugs, and she welcomed their support.

Mother Keara studied each woman in turn. "You are one of our strongest triads. And in these troubled times, one of our most seasoned."

Cynda kept her head high and her back straight. This

wasn't quite the lead-in she expected, but whatever. She could take a little guilt heaped into the mix.

Beside her, Riana and Merilee kept their proud, protective stances. Whatever was about to happen, they'd be facing it together, which meant everything to Cynda.

In the mirror, Mother Keara kept up her heated scrutiny, but she didn't make a move to dance them all through the channel to Ireland. Instead, she said, "My next words won't be leavin' this room, except to reach the ears of those you would choose for the task ahead."

Cynda risked a glance at Merilee and Riana. Both shocked and confused. Good. She wasn't alone.

"We have had reports from triads in the Southern United States of a new force," Mother Keara continued. "A new power's disturbin' the rivers, the lakes, the sea, even the moisture in the clouds."

Riana's brows came together. "You mean, something elemental? But water elementals died out centuries ago when Motherhouse Antilla was destroyed. How could a new one just appear out of nowhere?"

The old woman shrugged one shoulder. "We don't have enough information to answer those questions. For now, we're assemblin' a force to approach this power, explore it, determine its intent—and deal with it in whatever manner seems most appropriate. We can't risk the Legion beatin' us to the punch."

"That would be all we needed," Merilee murmured, her fingers traveling to the spot on her shoulder where her bowstring should be. "Unknown water elementals flooding us out, washing us right into demon mouths."

"We have decided we'll be needin' your level head, Riana, and the force of your wind, Merilee." Mother Keara gestured southward. "Wind is the natural containment, the natural control for water. Motherhouse Greece and Motherhouse Antilla were closely aligned before the disaster that took our water Sibyl sisters away from us. The two of you will travel down the East Coast and meet with the triads we've gathered in Atlanta."

Apprehension tightened Cynda's muscles, and she sensed Merilee and Riana tensing, too. "What about me?"

Mother Keara's gaze wasn't angry or fierce, as Cynda expected. More sorrowful, and perhaps a bit worried. "We never wish to separate a triad, but I have realized that because of today's revelations, you must remain where you are and work with Bela Argos and her South Bronx group to coordinate the assault on Sister Julia. You'll be essential in her recognition and capture, since you are the only one in New York who has seen her face." A line of fire spread down her shoulders to her hands. "You'll be knowin' the foul beast on sight, yes?"

Cynda doubled her fists, the heat inside her answering Mother Keara's challenge. "I'll know her, and I'll burn her to the ground."

The thought of being separated from her triad sisters made her heart ache, and she could tell by the looks on Riana's and Merilee's faces that they felt the same way. Still, Cynda could see the wisdom in the Mothers' decision. They had to find out about this dangerous water power, whatever it was. And she did need to take the lead on Sister Julia's capture.

It could be a ruse to separate her from her supports, from her staunchest defenders, but Cynda didn't think so. Mother Keara might be crafty, but she wasn't a liar. Besides, Cynda didn't sense guile or even anger from Mother Keara. Just concern and a level of distraction from her worry about the new Southern force.

This isn't so bad.

I guess she doesn't know about Nick and me. At least not yet.

As Mother Keara moved to withdraw herself from the

mirror, Cynda stepped in front of Riana and Merilee and raised her arms to close the channel.

A glowing, golden Nick picked that second to charge into the bedroom.

Merilee and Riana grabbed Cynda's waist, but she was too shocked to react.

"The other Sibyls came downstairs and I was worried the Mothers had come after you—" He trailed off as he locked eyes with Mother Keara, who was still very much present.

The room prickled with the rush of her anger.

"You," Nick snarled, a deep *other*-like resonance in his voice. "I want to talk to you."

Mother Keara pushed herself forward, her face filling almost the entire bog-oak mirror frame. Smoke billowed from her hair, her ears, seemingly her eyes, as she snarled right back, "And you will. When *I* deem the time right."

Fire blasted across the inside of the glass.

White heat jerked inside Cynda and knocked her off balance. She spun sideways and went to her knees, barely bracing her fall on the table with both hands.

Mother Keara nearly yanked all the fire energy out of the room as she tore loose from communication and shut down her mirror—the entire channel—with a tooth-jarring *pop*.

Cynda glared at Nick, stomach aching, not believing, not able to believe—and absolutely speechless.

From behind her, Merilee said, "Oh, wow, does your timing *ever* suck."

(21)

Three days later, Nick stood on the townhouse's front porch with Sal Freeman, squinting in the bright afternoon sunlight. Below them, at the curb, Riana, Creed, and Merilee finished loading an SUV and one of the SWAT vans. Any minute now, they were wheels-up for Atlanta to confront this whatever-the-hell-it-was that had been messing with water along the East Coast.

Nick's brother and the Sibyls had selected and outfitted a second gold team of six OCU officers. That brought the New York City team down to only sixteen officers, counting Nick and Freeman, who weren't on injured reserve, or out of the game indefinitely. Nick had tried off and on for the past forty-eight hours to reach Andy on her cell and ask her if she could come back early, but no go. She didn't answer, and her voice mail was full.

Added to those problems was Cynda.

It had taken her a full day to warm back up to Nick after his little run-in with the Irish Mother from hell. Little doubt the old hag knew something was going on now, but she had chosen not to act. He and Cynda were taking it day by day, but Nick was staying alert for hints of trouble. If the Mothers came after his woman, he'd be waiting for them.

For now, Cynda's time had been absorbed by a small army of young women from Motherhouse Ireland, about twenty of them in all. Adepts and advanced initiates, sent to shore up the Sibyl ranks for the big hit on Downy, as soon as she could be located.

Teenagers. Nineteen, twenty years old at most.

In less than forty-eight hours, the young fire Sibyls had burned up twelve sets of curtains, two beds, a rug, three walls, and scared the living shit out of a stray tomcat that got too close to the kitchen door.

They were the reason why Cynda didn't turn up to see off Riana and the troops.

She was downstairs in the gym, putting the young women through their paces.

I know I'd lose it if I had to tell my triad goodbye, she had told Nick the night before. *I don't want the younger ones to see me out of control. It sets a bad example.*

No kidding.

If the Mothers didn't hurry up and find J. C. Downy, Nick couldn't imagine what the place would look like in another few days.

The Atlanta convoy gave a few honks and pulled into traffic.

Just then, smoke and the distinct stench of burning rubber drifted out of the partially open front door.

So much for the gym. Again.

Nick's gut cramped, and he contemplated punching one of the porch columns to let off some steam.

"Like we need any more problems right now," Freeman grumbled, seeming to read Nick's mind as he waved the thick cloud of rubber-stink away from his face. "Any word from the Mothers on Downy's 411?"

"Not yet." Nick flexed his fingers and made himself relax. "You'll be the first to know."

Freeman grunted.

Nick followed the captain back inside, past a group of goggled officers patrolling for Astaroths, and walked with Freeman to the conference room door, where he wished the captain luck. It was Freeman's turn to work with New York City's experienced Sibyls, twenty or so strong, not counting the two ranger triads that pitched in when they could. They were scheduled to discuss strategies for containing massive quantities of Astaroths and Cursons, should the need arise.

After leaving Freeman, Nick checked in with Cynda a few times, ate an early dinner, then borrowed the open end of Merilee's temporarily unoccupied library and meditated. When his mind felt clear and focused, or as clear and focused as it could get in a house full of endless friggin' smoke, he opened the windows and balcony doors for ventilation and worked through a succession of wall-to-wall suicide sprints, several sets of squat jumps, lunges, and a bunch of jump push-ups. Then he showered and went to his slightly burned bed to wait for Cynda, hoping she'd get free from her training and babysitting duties before dawn.

He settled onto the somewhat singed sheets, rolled toward Cynda's side of the bed, ran his palm across the burned spot where she slept, and grinned. All in all, he was getting better at absorbing her fire. Another few weeks, and he'd have the hang of it—if they practiced often enough.

In the hallway, wind chimes jangled.

Nick closed his eyes, keeping his hand on Cynda's singed spot, trying not to grind his teeth.

Since the young Sibyls arrived, the damned pipes had been ringing almost nonstop, all over the townhouse. He couldn't see how those girls would be anything but a liability in a battle, but Cynda kept assuring him he was underestimating their skills.

They were definitely going to discuss that tonight, after a little tandem workout.

Nick's body tensed at the thought of her crawling into bed with him. He loved the soft silk of her warm skin, the way she smiled at him after he kissed her, the way she beat on him when he made her wait. He especially loved the way she smelled. Vanilla, cinnamon—so fresh and clean and female.

Right now, he was smelling something else.

Probably something burning or melting. Great.

The chimes kept ringing.

Deep in Nick's mind, Gideon gave an irritated rumble.

Strong odors assailed him. Something like . . . spaghetti. Was it bay leaves? And rosemary. He knew that one from his grandmother's cooking. Onion, and chewing gum, too. Spearmint, maybe. And lots of smoke.

Gideon's rumbling got a little louder.

Okay, okay. He'd go figure out what had been destroyed.

Cold steel scraped against his throat.

Inside his head, Gideon's roar bashed against his skull.

Nick's eyes popped open. Internally, he snatched hold of his inner demon, shook it, and forced Gideon back a few paces rather than risk his *other* exploding outward.

All his muscles tightened, but he went very, very still, not even breathing as he shifted his gaze downward, to the blade holding him hostage in his own bed.

Goddamn. That's a Da-Dao saber.

"That's right, demon." A woman's voice. Gravelly and low. "Keep yourself still, or I'll be takin' your head and makin' my apologies to your kin at some later date."

Nick recognized the speaker even as pungent smoke drifted across his face, stinging his eyes.

Mother Keara.

Deep in his insides, Gideon made a noise in between a snort and a groan.

How had she snuck up on him—on them?

And how in two hells was such a short, ancient female holding a five-foot Chinese great sword at his throat like it weighed nothing at all?

Maybe he needed to rethink how much of a threat these Mothers posed.

If he lived long enough.

Sweat broke out along the back of his neck as the

woman's heat encroached on the bed. He hoped she didn't burn it up with him in it.

He couldn't see her, but he could imagine her green robes and snow-white hair, frizzy around her wrinkled face. Riana had a habit of referring to her as "Yoda-ette," after a short green character with really big ears from the *Star Wars* movies. That image stuck hard in Nick's mind, especially now.

"You'll speak when I allow it," the old woman instructed. "When I give you room, respond."

The nine-pound sword moved a fraction of an inch.

"I hear you." Nick got the words out fast, but the great sword still stung his throat as Mother Keara moved it back against his flesh.

"You are involved with my Cynda, the child of my own heart. Don't think to be lyin' to me, demon."

Well, fuck her.

No, wait. Somebody else can do that. I'll pass.

He hated to answer that question, but when he felt the sword shift, he said, "I am."

Air hissed from behind him, and flames licked over his shoulders. Automatically, he let Gideon come forward enough to absorb the heat, giving his skin a light golden glow.

"Good trick," Mother Keara said. "I must admit, it would serve you well with a fire Sibyl—but you'll cease dallyin' with Cynda this night. Tell me you grasp my words."

The sword shifted.

Nick said the first thing that popped into his head. "Go to hell, you meddling old bitch."

He waited for the bite of the great sword's blade, but a few seconds later, it simply settled back into place against the center of his throat.

A raspy laugh startled him. The sword gave a slight

twitch, shaving off a bit of his stubble. He swallowed carefully, feeling the sharp steel edge dangerously close.

"I can see why my *a chroí* likes you, Curson. You are fearless. Foolish, but fearless."

Time passed.

Nick wondered if he could shift to his full *other* form and eat the old woman before she got his head. Probably not. Plus, that would piss Cynda off in a major way.

At least he knew the crone wasn't likely to harm Cynda if she showed up.

If Mother Keara intended to act immediately on the threats she made to Cynda, she wouldn't be here with her giant curved sword, punching *his* buttons.

But he did make a mental note to keep Cynda at arm's length from here on out. He'd have to, if he was going to protect her from these nightmarish women.

"Do you love her, then?" Mother Keara asked.

The great sword moved an inch away from his throat.

"Yes." He clenched one fist, but otherwise remained motionless. "I'm not giving her up—and you won't kick her out. You need her too much."

The sword shifted back into place faster than Nick expected. Pain lanced through his neck as warm blood trickled to his chest. He counted backward a few times to keep Gideon calm.

"It is not for you to say what happens to Cynda. She made her choices." The voice behind him turned hot and hard at the same time. Fire jetted against his back. Seconds later, as he absorbed it, the heat eased off, but the Mother wasn't through. He heard her breathing, as if to calm herself. In time, she said, "I would be willin' to strike a deal with you on my *a chroí*'s behalf."

Now we get to it. All right, old woman, let's play poker.

When the steel let up, Nick part-shifted his throat to heal his wound, then answered with, "I'm listening."

Mother Keara didn't immediately return the sword to its menacing position.

So, she had some respect for the strength of the hand he was holding concerning Cynda. That was a start.

When Mother Keara spoke again, her words were more measured, more careful. "If you submit yourself to the Russian Motherhouse and allow them to make you safe—for Cynda's protection, you understand—I would reconsider our stance on her expulsion."

Nick finally got to launch into territory he'd been wanting to cover since he first heard the Mothers had come to Cynda about him. With any luck, he could make the old woman understand. "Creed and I are twins, but we're different. I already have control of my *other*."

"Not when you're fully shifted," she countered.

Nick had to give her that point. "True. But my *other* does our combined will, even then."

The sword came back, not as fast, not as close, but close enough. "Your *other* kills, Curson. I'll not be havin' my *a chroí* die by your cruel golden hand."

He spoke then, sword or no sword, not caring what damage the blade did. "I would never hurt Cynda." Once more, the steel cut him. This time, though, Mother Keara moved it away the second after it did damage. Nick part-shifted, just his throat, and healed himself before finishing his thought. "My *other* would never hurt Cynda. Ever."

He heard a long, wavering sigh. "Will you meet my conditions or not, demon? Will you save this woman you love from a loss that would wound her forever?"

Inside Nick's body, Gideon moved, restless. Concerned. Pulling away from him just enough to set off internal alarms.

Not too many options. Screw himself one way, or screw himself the other.

But it's for Cynda.

And she was worth anything. Nick already knew that.

Still, he couldn't afford to have his *other* worried or half-insane and uncooperative when they went after Downy. So, he compromised. "I'll consider it and give you my answer after we take down the woman who's been killing fire Sibyls."

The sword didn't move back against his skin.

"Fair enough." Now the steel swept to his throat, stopping short of drawing more blood. "But don't be thinkin' you can play with us, Nick Lowell. If you run, we'll chase you. If you hide, we'll find you."

I have no doubt . . . but she used my name. He forced himself to keep his expression flat instead of triumphant just in case the old woman could read his face.

Aloud, with a touch of Gideon's resonance in his voice, he said, "I won't leave Cynda—and I don't run from anything."

Mother Keara laughed. Then she moved her sword an inch away from him again and gave him a number and a name. Nick recognized it immediately as an address in South Ozone Park, down in Queens, near Howard Beach, where all the mobsters used to live.

"Motherhouse Greece has traced Janeen Casey, once Sister Julia, through many East Coast cities to that location." Mother Keara spoke quickly, as if she might be running out of time. "And you should know—the first contact made to her upon her discharge from the Abbey, it was the Legion. They telephoned her at her hotel, before she ever left Connemara. We raided the house where the call originated and confirmed that sad fact."

Nick added up the rest. "They must have been monitoring the Abbey as a suspected Sibyl stronghold. So these Connemara assholes arranged for her to accidentally 'find' her first demon?"

A longer, louder snarl issued from Mother Keara. "And taught her to use that demon to hunt and capture more of its kind. Even the Legion house occupants in Connemara couldn't tell us how many demons she's amassed in her travels. If you truly love my *a chroí,* destroy this threat, and all her demon servants with her. Then you'll have a fraction of my respect."

Before Nick could respond, the Chinese great sword withdrew completely.

A wall of fire slammed into his back.

He let Gideon suck up the flames as he rolled over in the bed, the gold from his skin lighting the whole room.

All he saw was his door swinging shut.

He got to his feet, swearing as chimes jangled in the hallway, and jogged out of his room.

Mother Keara was nowhere in sight.

Cynda was coming down the hall, wearing singed jeans and a half-cooked white blouse. She glanced first at the chimes, obviously puzzled, then at Nick. "What the hell's going on? The chimes sounded like the Mothers might be ringing—but not. I don't get it."

Nick frowned in the direction of Cynda's bedroom. When he turned back to her, he said, "I finally got that chat with Mother Keara."

Cynda's mouth dropped open. "She was here? In *your room*?" Panic claimed her face, and she ran to him. As he caught her in his arms, she grabbed him around his neck, running her hands up and down his back and arms, like she might be checking for holes. "Are you okay? Did she hurt you? What did she say? Nick—"

"Slow it down, firebird." He held her and kissed the top of her head, savoring her fresh, feminine scent. Relieved it was nothing like spaghetti and chewing gum. "I'm fine. She offered me a deal on your behalf."

Cynda listened, squeezing him tighter with each word, as he told her how his conversation with the old hag went. When he got to the part about the deal to undergo the procedure that changed Creed, Cynda pushed back from him, smoking from ten different places at once.

"I told you, no way." She shook her head and pointed her finger in his face. It was smoking, too. "No. You are not undergoing that procedure. You don't need it, and I won't have you taking a risk like that."

He held up both hands to slow her down again. "I know how you feel about it." Gideon thumped around in his mind as he spoke. "Believe me, I—we—feel the same way. But for now, we don't have time to discuss it. She also gave me J. C. Downy's real name and address. She's got Legion contacts and a shitload of demons, and we need to mount a raid on a house in South Ozone Park. Right now. As fast as we can get there."

In an instant, Cynda's expression shifted from angry, frightened woman to solid, furious warrior. The smoke died away from her body and she lowered her hand. "I'll suit up, get the adepts ready, and summon the Sibyls. You gather the OCU. We'll meet you in the conference room."

God, he loved her.

"Done," he said, and gave her a quick kiss before he let her go, headed for her room.

He watched her as she ran down the hall, red curls bouncing against her shoulders.

Yeah, he loved everything about her. Just the sight of her got his blood roaring. And he was ready for this raid. Way past ready.

In a few hours, he'd bring in the psycho who wanted to kill Cynda, if it was the last thing he ever did. Screw what the Mothers wanted.

He was doing this for Cynda and no one else.

Nick turned for the stairs. He had lots of doors to bang on, and lots of phones to ring.

(22)

Cynda crouched in a makeshift doghouse on the opposite side of the street from the target front door, smoking even though she was trying not to. Her heart jumped as pieces of plastic flapped against leathers. The sheet of tin over her head rattled in the frigid March breeze.

It's friggin' freezing in here. Her teeth clattered together. *Poor dog deserves better than this.*

She tried to focus on the scents of baking dough, pepperoni, and Italian spices drifting out of neighborhood pizzerias and delis, but mostly, she smelled dog. Big, slobbering, ugly dog.

From nearby houses, music thumped and bumped and bumped and thumped. She had half a mind to send a blast of fire energy at the nearest sound systems, but that wouldn't help. Too many of the damned things. How anybody lived with that kind of noise, she had no idea. Maybe people got used to it, the way dogs got used to plastic houses with tin roofs.

"Three minutes," Nick rumbled from behind her, just outside the doghouse.

Cynda couldn't see him, but his presence fueled her fire. She worked her jaw, drawing the energy back to her body before she melted the plastic.

A barely known enemy.

An unknown number of demons.

Probable Legion presence.

This raid felt like a huge disaster waiting to happen—but what else could they do?

Waste time, and they might lose Sister Julia again.

No fucking way.

But Delilah . . . and what about Jake?

She blew out a fog-laced breath and ground her teeth. At least she had Nick with her. If she couldn't have her triad, Nick was definitely the man she'd choose to cover her flank. He had on his body armor, his raid jacket, and his battle face. When they took position, Nick had already drawn his Glock.

Cynda glanced to her left and right, visually accounting for the ten adepts she'd brought with her. The less experienced initiates had stayed behind at the townhouse with a squad of OCU officers to protect HCQ. Cynda's trainees, also garbed in battle leathers, were all out of sight in clumps of bushes, or tucked behind walls and corners of the yard, or the house next door. Her goggles registered traces of sulfur left by the adepts' fire. No way the younger women could avoid calling a little of the element to them, not with stress this high. Fire Sibyls, even experienced fighters like Cynda, had never been known for perfect control.

Her tattoo pulsed and throbbed, but she ignored the sensation for the same reason. The mark on her wrist had been vibrating since late last night, when the adepts found out about the raid.

Nick hadn't wanted the initiates to come along on this throw-together, but the fact was, the numbers were too low without them. Even Sal Freeman had loaded up for the operation.

Cynda knew her trainees could perform. She just hated putting them in any danger.

But they're Sibyls.

What am I, going soft?

Heart revving like a car engine, Cynda adjusted her face mask and squinted through her demon-hunting goggles at the squat gray two-story house near Hawtree Creek Road and 130th.

This place looked nothing like the other two spotless, lavish houses owned and used by Sister Julia. It was big all right, but with faux-stone porch columns, battered gray siding, rusted awnings over the three front windows—two down, one up. The Ozone house was a total dump. A decrepit fence pocked with gaps surrounded a bare yard, and an old, rambling shed seemed attached directly to the back door by makeshift planking.

Her hand stayed clamped on her sword hilt, but her fingers itched to call fire. Her body ached to get on with it. Now. Not later.

She wanted J. C. Downy—Janeen Casey. Whatever the hell name Sister Julia chose to hide behind, real or invented. Cynda envisioned the woman's china-doll neck beneath her blade. She planned to be the one who brought the Sibyl-murdering bitch to the justice she so completely deserved. And she planned to do it without killing a certain demon, if there was any way to pull that off.

"Two minutes." Nick's voice cut beneath the neighborhood's constant bass beat.

Cynda's pulse surged. The OCU and almost all of New York City's surviving Sibyls were positioning themselves across a one-mile section of southwest Queens. The 106th Precinct had called in its massive Auxiliary Police Force and cordoned off as much of the target area as manpower allowed. Traffic on the two crossing roads had been shut down. Cynda, Nick, the adepts, and Sibyls ringed the front of the area, while Sal Freeman and the OCU were advancing on the back. Warrants had been obtained. High-risk again, so no "knock and announce."

At the appointed minute, Freeman and his men would storm the shed and the back windows and doors, while

Nick and Cynda's group would blast through the front entrances and the single side window.

Cynda hoped she could locate Jake in that trashy bunch of boards. And she hoped Delilah Moses was still in one piece.

With curtains and shutters drawn, the house was boxed up tighter than a postal package. They hadn't been able to see anything through the windows, and no one had come or gone from the entrances.

Yet Cynda could sense . . . something . . . *wrong*.

Shimmering power flowed from her fire adepts, and from the Sibyls in position all around the neighboring yards. Every rooftop had an air Sibyl, distance weapons ready. Earth Sibyls crept through yards just like Cynda and Nick, and other fully trained fire Sibyls had key positions, poised to take medium-distance combat duties for their triads.

But there was other energy, too.

Cursons? Astaroths?

She couldn't tell, and her goggles gave her no information.

All she knew for sure was the Ozone house wouldn't be empty and spotless inside. Sister Julia was in there, with a boatload of her minions, too. Maybe alerted, maybe preparing, maybe even waiting for the assault.

Or maybe about to be caught completely off guard.

Either way, the good Sister was going down.

"One minute," Nick murmured from behind her.

Cynda made a hand signal to her adepts to ready them.

Seconds ticked by in her mind, each one louder than the last.

It sucked that they hadn't had more time to plan, but sometimes careful strikes were a luxury. Her breath came faster, more shallowly. She dug her gloved fingers into her palms.

"On my mark." Nick slipped his hand under the dog-house's back plastic wall and let his palm rest on her ankle. Heat flooded her body, and fire burst from all ten fingertips. "Five, four, three, two, one, go!"

Cynda burst from the plastic doghouse and drew her sword. She ran forward, jumped the small fence, and charged across the street, feet pounding pavement on her way to Sister Julia's two-story dive.

Cold air slapped against her leathers.

Hard to breathe. Hard not to catch fire all over.

This is it. This is finally *it!*

Maura's face danced in her mind, and Nori's too. All the dead fire Sibyls.

This is it.

Her blade blazed as she and Nick led the adepts and the other Sibyls straight to the front door. The mean little nun's face flared through her consciousness like a marked, glowing target.

Eat my steel.

Shouts erupted from the back of the house—Freeman and the OCU.

Yes. Go!

Glass shattered. The *bang-smash* of the battering ram blocked out the neighborhood's *thump-thump-thump.*

This was a wooden house.

Cynda didn't *need* a friggin' battering ram.

Snarling, pouring smoke from her legs and arms, she raised her sword and her free hand, summoned her fire energy, and blasted a gaping hole in the front door.

At the same moment, five of her adepts shattered the glass of the side window with a massive ball of flames.

Somebody screamed.

Shit! Cynda moved again, this time faster, this time running as hard as she possibly could. *That came from upstairs. Was it Delilah?*

If that maniac nun so much as bruised Delilah's elbow, Cynda would slice off Sister Julia's china-doll head and let the sucker roll.

She stormed through smoke and the door's blazing boards with Nick beside her.

She had to find the stairs. *Now.*

The scream came again.

Not pain. No.

Fury.

Bring it on, Sister. I'm on my way.

Nick edged ahead of Cynda as they pushed their way into the long, wide front room of the gray house. About the size of half a basketball court, doors to the left and back. Grime-smeared brown walls. No furniture, no lights. Oily curtains had been drawn, maybe nailed to the sills—and the floor was littered with food cartons, empty drink bottles, and crushed cases of Hostess cupcakes.

Cynda slowed near the room's center, wary, glancing right and left, looking for stairs.

Nothing.

Was that a red trace? There, and there. And there! Her blood chilled colder than the outside air.

This place is jam-packed full of demons.

Heart beating so fast she could barely breathe, she raised her blade. Her sword lit the musty room as adepts poured through the smashed window, blades drawn, goggles trained on the flashes.

"Don't swing." Cynda gripped her hilt with both hands. "Not yet!"

"Astaroths—on the ground and visible," Nick bellowed as they edged deeper into the room, side by side. "If we see you down, we won't kill you."

When he finished, he barked a three-count.

Before Nick reached *one,* the trash-strewn wooden

floor shimmered and came to life with Astaroths, different shapes, different sizes, dropping to their knees. Eight of them. No, nine now. Ten.

So many!

Some covered their heads. Double sets of wings banged into walls and other demons. Fangs gnashed. Some of the demons took more human form, some didn't. A few moaned, seemingly in terror.

Shock spread across Nick's face.

Cynda felt it deep in her insides, too.

The sight of their frightened golden eyes turned her stomach. She didn't want to kill anything that wasn't fighting of its own will—especially not when the Astaroths seemed so clueless and helpless—but she had to keep going. She had to get to those stairs.

Kicking trash out of her way, she took another few steps toward the left-hand door.

As Cynda had been training them to do, half of the fire adepts directed surrendering demons to the far wall, and escorted them out the destroyed window. Outside, the adepts would cuff the demons and fasten their wings together.

We'll worry about them later.

Yelling and crashing broke out at the back of the house.

"For Chrissake," Captain Freeman yelled. "Don't let anything get to that damned shed!"

Gunshots exploded.

Cynda jerked with each blast. Heart racing, she leaped far enough away from Nick to swing her blade. "Time's up! Take 'em out!"

With a lung-emptying shout, she struck at the nearest flash of color.

Contact. Solid. Sickening.

Her whole essence vibrated with horror. The flat,

musty room wavered as the dying demon flashed into view, then burst into elemental particles.

Dirt and fire and air swirled into her face, then hit the floor near the left-hand door.

She choked back a cry.

Goddess, don't let that be Jake.

One of the adepts screamed. Cynda spun to help, but the adept was too far away. Something had the young woman's hair, yanking her backward, but another adept ran the demon through.

Cynda's stomach ached.

Not Jake. Please.

She made herself face the room's side door and track red flashes with her goggles, but she didn't see any.

Nick fired his Glock. Fired again. Kicked something.

Invisible claws slashed at Cynda and ripped her leathers. Her arm stung. Her shoulder burned. She dodged to the side, letting off a blast of smoke.

Before she could right herself, a fist slammed into her goggles.

Her head snapped back. Pain blasted through her face, her ears, and flames fired from both shoulders.

Now she couldn't see a damned thing! Eyes tearing, nose running, she ripped off the smashed goggles and rammed her sword forward like a stave.

Bits of earth and fire dropped to the floor in front of the doorway, stirred by a gust of wind.

Not Jake, she repeated to herself as she slashed backward, striking another demon and killing it, too. *Not Jake.*

Head pounding and swimming, she pushed ahead, thrusting her sword to clear the way. Another demon fell and reverted to the elements.

A snarl caught in her throat. She jabbed her sword harder.

Not Jake, not Jake, not Jake!

The house shook from unfettered earth energy as Sibyls poured into the big room behind Cynda. Plaster and nails and boards dropped in every direction. Flames roared even though she had warned everyone that Astaroths could absorb fire energy.

"Nobody gets by," Freeman shouted from the back of the house. *"Hold that fucking door!"*

Cynda's tattoo burned. She lunged through the door into a long center hallway, using her sword like a battering ram. Blows bruised her arms, her back.

Where the hell are those stairs?

Nick made it into the hallway but went down with a heavy crunch and thud. He fired into the air above him. Dirt spattered his face.

Not Jake . . .

But Cynda smelled him!

Smoke rose off both hands. Her insides pinched and twisted as she turned a full circle, sword raised, cutting through the cloud she had just created.

That Caribbean spice. Yes. Definitely. But where?

As she faced the far end of the grimy hallway, hands struck Cynda in the back like a one-two knockout punch. Air whooshed from her lungs. She flew forward a few paces, and her chest seemed to crush in on itself. Cynda coughed and gasped and shrieked at the same time, pinwheeling her arms, almost stopping—

Another push.

Damnit!

This time she staggered down the center hallway like a flaming drunk. Every muscle tightened, way past ready to fight. Hands gripped her shoulders, righted her. She swept her sword forward, but pulled up short on her backswing.

Jake!

That's his scent. His grip.

He is alive.

Thank Goddess she hadn't just run him through.

"This way," Jake whispered. He urged Cynda forward at a jog.

Breath shallow in her throat, she went where he directed her, straight past a door on the left, leading to Freeman and the OCU's fight in the kitchen.

At the end of the hall, Jake pushed her through a door on the right.

Stairs!

Cynda slammed to a stop at the foot of a wide landing, barely keeping her balance and her grip on her sword. The smell of pine cleanser and bleach stung her eyes and nose—but in the low light of her wavering blade, she saw what she had come here to find.

Dread mingled with rage, and Cynda's arms started to shake. Her heart slammed against her ribs, and her lips pulled back as she snarled like a wild animal.

Right in front of her a few steps above the lower landing, clinging to a flimsy-looking banister with one pale hand, waited Sister Julia.

Behind Sister Julia, one step up, with her hands shackled but her feet free, stood a bruised, furious Delilah Moses.

23

The ex-nun looked much as Cynda remembered, only without the habit. Sister Julia's brown hair had been bound into a tight bun, directly on top of her head. In her simple black dress, with her stack of talisman necklaces weighing her down, the woman seemed even more petite, with her pale, fragile features and startling red cheeks. Her glassy brown eyes burned with hatred.

"Thank you, Jacob," she said in the crisp, self-righteous tone Cynda had first heard all those years ago at Kylemore Abbey. "Good boy. That's the one." She didn't try to come down those last steps to the landing. Instead, she placed her thin, ringed fingers on her necklaces. "If she touches me, harms me in any way, kill her instantly, and our hostage. If any Sibyl or police officer touches me or harms me, do the same."

Bitch!

Cynda's gut burned. Her skin burned brighter. White-orange flames. Smoke lifted from her elbows as she tested the heft of her sword.

That scrawny, pearl-white neck, only a few feet away. She could strike! But the thick, musty air around her twitched and shivered and Cynda sensed Astaroths at both her elbows, not to mention behind her, above her.

Damnit! Astaroths all over the landing. Probably the stairs, too.

"You cannot allow her to reach the shed," said a strained, quiet whisper very near Cynda's ear. "If you have to die to prevent it, do so."

"She's not going anywhere," Cynda growled, not

caring who heard. She felt like she could eat straight through the landing and kill Sister Julia by spitting splinters, if it wouldn't set the Astaroths on Delilah.

From behind Cynda, Nick roared her name and thundered down the hallway, firing his Glock at demons and shadows as he came.

"Knock it off!" Cynda shouted. "Stop shooting!"

Sweating, swearing repeatedly under her breath, Cynda held her position on the landing between Sister Julia and the kitchen, where Sal Freeman and the OCU defended the entrance to the shed. The tattoo on her wrist crawled with energy.

Sister Julia turned slightly, grabbed Delilah Moses's handcuffs, and forced the old woman into a shielding position on the step in front of the nun.

Cynda bit her lip hard to keep from blasting Sister Julia with a wall of heat. "Leave Delilah alone."

Delilah cursed Sister Julia and spit, but the ex-nun didn't react at all except to gaze into the air beside Delilah and say, "Snap her neck if these people get any closer to me."

Delilah gagged and tried to twist, then went still. Cynda could tell from the color on the old woman's face that a demon had hold of her.

Cynda wanted to kill the winged bastard. She wanted to kill *something*. Her sword seemed to tug against her strength, wanting fire and blood and vengeance. *Now*.

Sister Julia shifted her attention to the empty space beside Cynda. She gestured toward Nick, who had reached the landing, Glock still in hand. "Kill him."

Cynda's heart skipped. Heat surged up her throat. "Jake." She doubled the force of her grip on her sword. "Don't do it. Fight her."

Sibyls crowded toward the stairs, weapons drawn, but Cynda shook her head. "Get everyone out of here. Tell the air Sibyls to stay alert, but hold fire." She tipped her blade toward Sister Julia's necklaces. "If we touch her, the demons have orders to kill the hostage."

"And you, dear." Sister Julia's smile took on a new dimension of hatefulness. "Let's not forget that."

Nick made a sound in his throat, low and menacing. Cynda knew his *other* had come forward, that he was moments from shifting into a furious Curson. She thought about telling him that he could solve Jake's dilemma by getting out of the house, but she knew Nick would never leave her inside.

As instructed, the Sibyls withdrew—but Cynda noted that the fire Sibyls stayed close. Fighting distance. They formed a line between Sister Julia and the evacuation beginning behind them.

Goddess, I love my sisters, every one of them.

With them, with Nick, she wasn't alone. She had a chance here, didn't she?

"Hostage," Nick called toward the kitchen, still gripping his Glock like it was part of his body. "Hold your fire. Hostage present!"

The commotion in the kitchen lessened. A few more shots were fired. Freeman barked orders, but Nick told him not to approach, to keep his officers away from the hallway, landing, and stairs. Freeman acknowledged with a string of four-letter words.

Cynda felt Nick's presence beside her, the heat of his body inches from her own. He took in the scene, added up, assessed. Probably came up with the same answers she did.

Checkmate.

And, *This fucking sucks.*

Her stomach ached twice as hard. Her sword felt heavier and heavier. It would be almost worth what would happen, to kill this bitch.

The demon beside her let out a low, anguished moan.

Jake's doing his best, but it won't last. If I coldcock the Astaroth, will she order Delilah killed for that?

Cynda eyed the stack of necklaces around Sister Julia's neck, and the rings on her fingers. One of those rings controlled Jake. And the rest—shit. If Sister Julia died, would that cancel her commands?

How fast could I get to those talismans and give other orders?

"Did you hear me?" Sister Julia's eyes narrowed at the empty air next to Cynda. "I said kill that man, Jacob. Kill Nick Lowell."

"No." Cynda cocked her sword another inch, arcing it above her head. She wanted to swing the blade so badly the muscles in her shoulders throbbed. "Leave Jake out of this."

Sister Julia's china-doll face cracked into a sick, twisted smile as she studied Cynda. "You fancy this godforsaken demon? That shouldn't surprise me. Very well. I'll release him to your friends. Delilah, too. For a price."

Cynda didn't lower her sword. "I don't make deals with maniacs. You're surrounded and outnumbered." Smoke drifted around Sister Julia as Cynda spoke. "Half your demons surrendered or died in the living room—maybe more. Give it up."

As if she didn't hear a word Cynda said, Sister Julia kept smiling. "You and the other fire . . . Sibyls leave here with me. We walk out the back door together, and I give you the demon and the old woman."

Out the back door. Where the shed is. Does she think we're idiots?

Cynda said nothing in response. Sister Julia was obviously crazy. How the hell would they get her out of here without more people dying?

Beside Cynda, Jake gnashed his fangs and clicked his nails together.

Cynda's skin crawled. She remembered those noises from her time in the Bronx tunnel.

Clock's ticking. He's about to lose it.

Sister Julia seemed to be assessing her situation now, gazing slowly around the large landing, the hall, and through one of the doors leading to the living room. From her vantage point, she could probably see that the back of the house had been secured and was now in the hands of the OCU. Sal Freeman and however many armed officers had survived the fight stood between her and whatever was in that shed. The ex-nun had to realize the front of the house and the grounds outside were filled with Sibyls. She still had her talismans, her controlled demons, and her hostage. Strong bargaining chips, but not strong enough to trade for so many lives.

Sister Julia once more returned her attention to Cynda. "I can be reasonable. I'll surrender the woman, the demon, and . . . half of my talismans, after you—just you—accompany me out of this house."

Jake snarled, from somewhere around Cynda's elbow. Smoke rose from her hands and fingers, and fire burned at her ankles.

Any second now, Jake would act.

Cynda's muscles tightened so hard her joints hurt. She'd kill the demon if she had to. She'd save Nick, but Delilah and who knew how many others would die. Her stomach kept roiling, and she breathed a jet of fire across her own lip. "Release Jake from his command to kill. Right now. Then we'll talk."

The woman's brown eyes narrowed to slits, and that fake smile stayed plastered to her pale face. She gripped the banister beside her so hard her knuckles stood out against her skin. "If you agree to my terms."

"She's not going anywhere with you." Nick lifted his Glock. Lowered it again. His fingers went white against the grip.

Sister Julia glanced from invisible Jake to Cynda to Nick, then back to Cynda. She shifted her gaze to the front of the house, and the kitchen area, and once more to Cynda's face. "Their lives for yours. All of them. That's not such a bad bargain, is it?"

Jake blew out a breath. Cynda had a sense he wanted to agree with Nick, but he couldn't speak against his master.

Cynda glared at the crazy ex-nun and slowly lowered her sword to her side. "Why are you so interested in me?"

"You—you cost me everything." The red in Sister Julia's cheeks crept higher and lower, coloring her forehead and chin. "I received my first formal reprimand the night you arrived at Kylemore. The Abbess Superior believed I should have been kinder to you. A child clearly in the palm of the devil himself." She shifted to a strained, sad expression. Her hand trailed down the banister. "Not long after, I was separated from my order. They gave many reasons, but I always knew the truth, that it was your influence. You, and your filthy, evil kind."

"But the demons," Cynda said as Nick moved closer beside her. "How did you get so many?"

Sister Julia smiled again, and Cynda clamped her mouth shut mid-sentence. "A gift from God, to aid me in my quest. I found the first one before I ever left Ireland, walking about a bog coated in mud, trying to learn to be visible."

She brushed her skeletonlike fingers against her necklaces. "Demons find their own with surprising ease. As we traveled, each fiend helped me find another, and another, and another, and stole their talismans for me, to put them in my service."

Jake panted and snarled, panted and snarled.

Cynda knew the demon was suffering, but she didn't know how to help him. Couldn't, without costing Delilah's life. "Philadelphia, Boston . . ." Cynda recited the places where fire Sibyls had been attacked, hoping to hurry Sister Julia along, to the point she might release Nick if Cynda agreed to leave with her.

"Baltimore, and Washington, D.C." Sister Julia lowered her hand and rubbed her fingertips across her talisman rings. "The organization that originally created my god-sent pets got in touch with me again here, in New York City, and offered to assist me in my efforts." Her eyes shifted toward the kitchen, and a cold wave of dread washed through Cynda.

She was pretty sure she knew what was in that shed now.

Cursons. Courtesy of their old enemies, the Legion.

Yep. Jake was right. She'd die before she let Sister Julia down those steps now. No question.

"In truth, my quarrel is with you more than anyone." Sister Julia's sigh was dramatic, almost overwrought. "Save for Mother Keara herself, but that blight should be scrubbed from this mortal plain any moment now."

Cynda stood straighter and lifted her sword a few inches. "What does that mean?"

Sister Julia positively beamed, realizing she was winning. "Come with me now, and I'll tell you."

Jake came to the point of ragged growls. A slight noise told Cynda the demon had probably gone to his knees on the landing in a last desperate attempt to stop himself from following his instructions.

Nick growled. Voice lower than low, he said, "Don't take a step, Cynda."

My life for all of theirs. Smoke rose from Cynda's feet and arms. Holes gradually appeared in her leathers.

Assuming she can kill me.

If I get her out of here, I think I might have a fighting chance.

She eyed Sister Julia. Yes. Get her out of the house, away from Jake, Nick, Delilah, and everyone else. The thought sent shivers of cold terror through every inch of her—but a tiny part of her mind relished the thought she might get to fight the nun alone.

Wit to wit, hand to hand, sword to neck . . .

Yeah. I could handle that. But what did she mean, about Mother Keara being scrubbed from this mortal plain?

Cynda knew she had to do this. She had to go with Sister Julia, even if Nick blew a gasket.

But how would she ever get past him? He'd do something to stop her. Or try to.

Still, she had to figure a way.

Carefully, making sure Nick couldn't see her, she gave Sister Julia a look, a message with her expression.

You win.

The ex-nun might have been insane, but she read the sag in Cynda's shoulders, the droop of her head. To the space where Jake stood moaning ever louder as he worked not to kill his brother, Sister Julia said, "Do not kill the officer. Disarm the fire bitch instead."

Nick grabbed Cynda around the waist, jerked her across the landing toward him, and yelled, "Don't touch her, Jake! Don't make me shoot you."

Shit! Cynda gripped her sword as hard as she could, and kicked at Nick.

He held fast, but at least both of them blocked the stairs so Sister Julia couldn't flee.

Bastard. "Let me fight!" Cynda hit him in the shoulder with one fist.

Something tugged at Cynda's sword. She swore, leaned toward the pull. Her wrist twisted and throbbed. She fought to keep hold—and failed. The hilt was torn out of her grip.

"Shit!" Heat blasted from both of Cynda's hands, following the blade, coating it in red-hot flames. If she could have drawn the metal back to her, she would have, but powerful wings stirred the air on the landing with a mighty flap, lifting the sword out of her reach.

Nick pulled Cynda forward, this time against the dirty brown wall supporting the stairs, facing Sister Julia.

At the same moment, Delilah struggled to get away from Sister Julia, but the ex-nun backhanded the old woman. Delilah dropped to the step behind Sister Julia and sat still, head down.

From somewhere above, Jake laughed.

Sister Julia laughed, too, but Cynda shivered in Nick's arms.

That demon sounded half-insane.

Didn't Sister Julia notice? Probably too crazy to give a damn.

Cynda's hand ached to have her sword back. Something was about to go down, hard and heavy, and she didn't have her blade *again*. Just her fire, burning in a huge ring around the landing.

Useless against these demons.

Another laugh from Jake, and Nick went totally still. His skin glowed.

Cynda froze in his grasp, heart smashing against her chest and throat. Smoke rippled across the large landing, ringing the fire, coating their feet and curling up, up, to where Sister Julia stood, with Delilah Moses sitting right behind her.

Cynda tasted bile in her throat. *What's Jake going to do?*

He had to be under orders not to hurt Sister Julia. He couldn't override those, could he?

Her eyes traced her sword's journey from the landing to the steps, to Sister Julia, who held out her hand to receive the blade.

The sword lowered itself toward her waiting palm.

Cynda realized she wasn't breathing.

The sword swept over Sister Julia's outstretched hand.

Jake didn't give it to her!

The sword plunged down, hilt first, behind the ex-nun instead—very near Delilah.

Sister Julia stood still, her hand still out and waiting, obviously shocked.

A thrill shot through Cynda. Fire blasted across her shoulders. She pulled out of Nick's grasp and got ready to leap for her blade, but stopped at the sound of a huge thump.

The banister beside Sister Julia shattered. Wood rained onto the landing. Jake and something invisible crashed to the floor nearby. A hard punch—fist on flesh. Bone cracked. He was taking out the demon who had been guarding Delilah.

Behind Sister Julia, Delilah moved sideways.

Silence.

Why hadn't Sister Julia intervened and grabbed Delilah? Given Jake new orders?

Holding her breath, fists doubled and burning, Cynda felt ready for anything.

"Sonofabitch," Nick muttered.

Cynda's hands dropped to her sides. Her mouth came open. The pounding of her heart slowed, replaced by a gnawing, sick sensation in her belly.

Sister Julia was still standing on the step where she had been, not moving at all, except to gaze down at the tip of Cynda's Celtic broadsword.

The blade slowly emerged from the ex-nun's belly.

At a sharp upward angle.

Red billowed beside the silver steel, and the stain spread outward from the mortal gut-cut, darkening Sister Julia's black dress.

Blood trickled from her lips, then coughed outward in a crimson gout. Her eyes went wide and grew still.

Like a felled tree, she pitched forward, stiff and unmoving.

Cynda and Nick jumped aside to let the dead woman crash down the steps and fall to the landing between them. Cynda's sword was still lodged firmly in her back.

Delilah Moses stomped her heel against wood and hooted, yanking Cynda's attention up the steps, to the old woman. Delilah's shackled hands were still raised from thrusting that broadsword straight through Sister Julia's miserable insides.

"You didn't go givin' *me* any commands, did ya?" Delilah laughed loud and long at the bleeding corpse on the landing below, gasping before she said, "Devil's *always* in the details."

Mouth open, stomach slowly churning, smoke puffing in fits and spurts from just about everywhere on her body, Cynda blinked at Delilah.

Sister Julia hadn't put any commands on the demons concerning Delilah doing the killing, had she?

Unbelievable.

The sound of rasping, jerking breath met Cynda's ears, and she realized it was her own.

So it was over?

Just like that?

The Sibyl-mark on her wrist still burned and vibrated, but relief mashed Cynda's muscles into pudding.

Nothing was happening. No reprisals or explosions or Astaroths dropping out of the air to tear people to bits.

Nobody was dying.

It *was* over.

The Sibyl-killing bitch was dead.

Delilah grinned at Cynda. "Folks like her think they're so smart, but they're bound to forget somethin', if those with good ears listen close enough. Thank you again for my blessin', and I'll be wantin' another soon, on account of this service."

Then the old woman cursed the corpse in Irish.

When Nick glanced at Cynda, she translated as best she

could, mind and body swimming with a sense of unreality.
"May a cat eat your bones, and may Satan eat the cat."

"Guess those old bargains *do* come in handy." He
took her hand and squeezed it. "Not bad."

"I think we should take her to Ireland," one of the fire
Sibyls called from the doorway to the front room. "The
Mothers would like Delilah. A lot."

Cynda started to agree, but a Mediterranean breeze
drifted across her senses. Too strong. Too close.

What—

"Sorry," Jake said in her ear.

He shoved her toward the wall, away from Sister Julia's body.

Cynda stumbled. Slid in the blood, then banged into
the wall by the stairs, propelled by the demon's hands.
Pain shot through her chin and shoulders as Jake flat-
tened her face-first against the filthy brown plaster and
held her still, arms behind her back. His body pressed
into hers like a shield.

Fire snapped from every inch of Cynda's body, burning
big holes in her leathers—not that flames mattered
against Jake. She didn't struggle against him for the same
reason. Total waste of energy. Her heartbeat sounded in
her ears, and she did her best to breathe. Fear and exhaustion flowed through her in equal measure. She wished
more than anything she could get off a good kick to Jake's
nuts, because she was getting damned tired of the Astaroth snatching hold of her.

And *this* time, he was doing it of his own free will,
damn his hide.

If he ever touched her again, he'd regret it.

Cynda managed to turn her head away from the stairs.

Nick was down, but he was pushing himself up, already trying to reach for her.

Something knocked him sideways against the wall
beside her.

A stampede of air, footsteps, and mumbling broke out along the stairs, beside Cynda and behind her. Wings flapped, seemingly everywhere at once.

"All right, all right," Delilah said. "I'm movin'."

Cynda regulated her breathing, tried to focus and understand, and thought she did. She stopped pushing against Jake. His grip eased a fraction.

Sibyls cried out, came running—but Cynda heard the footsteps stop.

Nothing happened. Her fellow warriors didn't know what to do.

They were confused. Afraid to act. Not certain of the consequences to her.

Neither was she.

Though she felt certain Jake wouldn't hurt her.

"That's it," Delilah said, sounding delighted. "Take what's yours. Now go on. Get out of here!"

Snapping and cracking echoed through the room. Sister Julia's body twitched and jerked on the floor behind her, flopping into Cynda's ankles.

A single gunshot blasted through the house, followed by thumps and bangs from the kitchen.

"They've freed the shackled demons," called a nearby Sibyl—Harper Ellis. Cynda recognized the voice. "What do we do?"

"Be still," Cynda instructed, praying to the Goddess she was making the correct call. "Just . . . wait."

She thought she knew what was happening. She didn't know if it was a good thing or a bad thing—but deep in her soul, she was certain it was a *right* thing.

Cynda didn't think anyone ought to get in the way.

"Thank you," Jake said, this time loud enough for everyone to hear. "Search Sister Julia's room upstairs. You don't have much time."

The demon let go of her.

Still smoking like an industrial chimney, Cynda stepped

away from the wall, rubbed her wrists, and gazed down at Sister Julia's body through a haze. The dead woman's hand drifted upward. A ring slid off her finger and vanished.

Jake's ring. The other half of his talisman. Gone, like so many of the other talismans the woman had been wearing. The demons might have trampled Cynda and Nick, they were so desperate to get those chains and rings.

Seconds later, energy surged through the room, then seemed to rush away, leaving the house altogether.

"They've gone," Delilah said from her perch at the top of the steps. "Godspeed to them that belongs to God."

Nick grumbled to himself about brothers and demons and kicking ass.

Cynda let out a shaky breath of relief.

Nick's brother Jake was his own man again. Well, his own Astaroth. The people who created him had died the previous fall, so his talisman wouldn't force him to return to any master. He was free now. She hoped the same was true for the other demons, or at least most of them.

As the OCU and Sibyls crowded in, pointing and asking questions, Cynda realized a few pieces of jewelry still remained. The sight of those few gold chains jabbed at her conscience, and a tiny bit of darkness settled inside her at the thought of how many Astaroths might have been innocent, unable to stop their own actions. She knew it would never go away, that little stain inside her, and her heart ached for Nick, and what he must feel over the deaths of his family members.

She wished she could wrap her arms around Nick, hold him, and never have to let him go. With what she was feeling over this small tragedy, she couldn't imagine the hurt burdening his spirit over the major losses in his life.

But she'd work to heal it. Somehow, she'd find a way. His hand brushed her shoulder. When she met his gaze, his dark eyes looked bright and concerned, as if he might know exactly what she was thinking.

"They're gone," she said. "All the captive demons."

He nodded. Seemed relieved.

"How many down?" she asked Harper without looking away from Nick.

"We've got four wounded," the young fire Sibyl answered. "And three dead." She named two of the North Staten Island triad and one of the initiates, and more darkness drifted into Cynda. Tears burned in her eyes. She couldn't let herself start crying now, or she'd never stop.

She so wished Riana and Merilee were here. Maybe they had reached Atlanta by now.

Please bring them home to me, safe and sound and in one piece. Please.

Sal Freeman edged in beside them and gazed down at Sister Julia's body. He rubbed the back of his head. "That shed was full of Curson demons, had to be twenty of them, crammed like sardines, standing like statues— but they're gone now. Took off, all of them. We ... didn't feel right shooting them."

Before Cynda could say anything, he added, "I've called for ambulances and the morgue. Half my people are unconscious from the fight, and I've got four dead."

More darkness.

More death.

Cynda closed her eyes, feeling some of the fire inside her shrink to embers. She had never been so tired in her entire life. She wanted off that landing, out of the Ozone house, and back to the townhouse, to shower and sleep for a month.

But from all the way upstairs, Delilah Moses called, "Here. I think this is what he meant."

Somehow, Cynda found the strength to look at the amazing little woman. Delilah's hands were still shackled, but she stood near the top step, held up her arms, and waved papers tightly clenched between her fisted fingers. Her bare foot tapped impatiently on the wood floor.

Cynda had no idea what Delilah was talking about.

"He said to search her room, didn't he?" Delilah gave her an exasperated frown even as Nick started up the stairs, moving much slower than usual. "That demon who was always so nice to me. Jake. I think he wanted you to find these."

Nick managed to smile at Delilah as he reached her. Cynda heard him thank her for all she did. He took his cuff keys and freed her, then relieved her of the papers she carried.

"Looks like a picture of Connemara, that first one," Delilah said. "The Abbey's marked."

Nick's smile faded as he studied the documents.

Cynda heard a high-pitched noise in her head, as if her thoughts were trying to short out. She started to shake.

What had Sister Julia said about Mother Keara?

That blight should be scrubbed from this mortal plain any moment now.

She thrust out her arm and stared at her pulsing tattoo. Mortar, pestle, and broom joined around the dark crescent moon. Now she focused on it. Now she listened, with every fiber of her being, to the simple message it spoke.

Not "noise" from the adepts being nervous about the raid.

No.

An actual communication, from far away, barely intelligible but carried by a force of need unlike any Cynda had ever known.

Help . . . Help . . . Help . . .

Her heart beat in time with the words.

"These are diagrams like Merilee would make," Nick

said as he came down the stairs faster than he went up, but Cynda barely heard him. "Tacticals. Schematics. And photos, too, some aerial. They're marked with today's date."

Freeman and the OCU limped toward the stairs.

So did the Sibyls who could still move.

Cynda grabbed the papers out of Nick's hand and felt his hand steady her from behind as she shuffled through them.

Connemara.

No . . .

Topical maps. Routes. To the Abbey.

"No, no, no! Fuck! This is Kylemore." She waved a photo and diagram of the Abbey, with big Xs in key spots.

Her skin went past hot. Her entire body smoked and burned. "The tunnels have been marked," she shouted. "No!"

The secret routes through the mountain. The routes that led to Motherhouse Ireland.

The ink on her forearm sizzled deep in her skin, repeating its plea time and again. The Mothers only had a handful of initiates still in residence. The rest were here with Cynda, or deployed to other cities to fill the gaps.

She dropped the papers.

Raw heat, pure fire fueled her legs and arms as she yanked her sword free from the ex-nun's body and sheathed it, blood and all.

Please let us be in time.

Cynda started running, with Nick beside her.

"They're attacking Motherhouse Ireland!" she called to the Sibyls and initiates as she streaked past them, headed toward the nearest communications platform in a triad house about two miles away. *"Move!"*

24

Nick helped Cynda through the front door of the Queens duplex. She was breathing hard from the sprint to the vans and the speeding drive from South Ozone Park, and he could tell by the look on her face she was exhausted.

Fourteen of the surviving New York City Sibyls—the ones who could still move—ran, fell, or hobbled in behind her.

After that came the surviving initiates, covered with grime, splinters, and blood. The nine young women crammed into the space around the older warriors, grim-faced, hands on the hilts of their swords. Delilah Moses brought up the rear, walking better than some of the Sibyls. The old woman absolutely refused to be left at the Ozone house, and nobody had time to fight with her. Besides, as she had reminded them twice already, they owed her.

The whole place stank of gunpowder, copper, and sweat.

Nick had never been here before, but like all Sibyl dwellings, the duplex had a giant table, a bunch of mirrors on the walls, and a ceiling lined with wind chimes. The metal pipes rang as soon as they got the door closed. Rhythmic sounds. Urgent beats. Cynda and the fire Sibyls were sending out the call for help. In minutes, the message would travel all over the world.

Harper Ellis jumped onto the platform and got busy, leathers smoking as she danced. Cynda stood beside Nick, tight-lipped, her green eyes wide and haunted.

Every few seconds, she gave off sparks and little spurts of fire. He didn't think he had ever seen her this upset.

His gut boiled at the sight of her pain. If he could have carried it for her, he would have. And what did it mean, if Motherhouse Ireland bit the big one? Nick wasn't sure, beyond the loss of people Cynda loved, but it felt like a major imbalance in the universe. Like the whole Sibyl network might collapse.

Was that what Sister Julia had wanted?

It was damned sure what the Legion wanted.

But not Jake, or the rest of those poor bastards.

Nick hoped most of the captive demons got away clean, that they were headed someplace peaceful and safe, for a good long time.

As for him and the Sibyls, from what Nick could reason out and piece together, the situation was fucked up beyond comprehension. They had no way of knowing how many demons were in Ireland, how many would keep fighting even though their mistress was dead—or how many of the creatures weren't and never had been under Sister Julia's control.

The Legion was in this now, up to their bloodshot eyeballs.

He had no doubt those crazy bastards were calling the shots.

With his free hand, Nick pulled his cell from his pocket and punched Creed on speed-dial. The damn phone refused to connect. Again. It had been doing that off and on all the way to the duplex.

Sibyl energy.

He tried again. This time, the call went through.

Nick put the phone to his ear and cursed under his breath as his twin's voice mail picked up after one ring.

It was a thirteen-hour drive from New York to Atlanta, if they didn't take too many piss breaks. The caravan should be there by now. Riana and Merilee should be in contact with that water-demon thing.

"We've got major trouble," Nick said into the phone after Creed's voice mail beeped. "Sixteen March, around eleven-hundred hours. Get your ass and all the Sibyls you can find to Motherhouse Ireland. Legion attack. Let me know you got this message."

He punched off and pocketed the phone, leaving the ringer on high.

It was the third message he'd left, and still no callback.

Cynda tensed beside him, and Nick's attention shifted to the platform.

Harper Ellis had her arms in the air. Sweat covered her young face. She was frowning. Her feet slowed down. Stopped. She whirled to Cynda, eyes wide. "I can't get through. That's never happened! I don't know what to do."

"Get off the table," Cynda told her.

The kid jumped straight from where she stood, bumping into a few of the battered Sibyls. They muttered to the girl, but kept her from falling on her ass.

Cynda broke away from Nick, loading more smoke into the room as she went.

He didn't know what to make of her expression. Fury, mingled with fear. And yeah, determination. Before she started dancing, she caught his eye.

"Communications might be down," she said slowly. A little too slowly. Her gaze flicked to the initiates. "I'll have to open both ends of the channel from here. It's tricky."

The older Sibyls in the room straightened. He saw the women lay hands on their weapons as they spread around the table, earth with earth, air with air, fire with fire, and joined hands.

Tears coursed down a few cheeks.

Cynda started to dance. Fire flared from her shoulders, and cropped up along the communications platform's lead-lined lip.

Nick watched, wondering how Sibyl communications could be down. Sibyls used mirrors and chimes to talk, for God's sake. It wasn't like glass and metal pipes couldn't get cell signal.

Was something blocking the ancient channels?

Could that even happen?

Wait. Wait a minute . . . shit.

Maybe the communications area had been breached. Or maybe the Mothers and all the Sibyls at Motherhouse Ireland were already dead.

Cynda had gotten his attention because she was worried about the young fighters, and how they'd react if she yanked open the channels to reveal a stone hall full of corpses—or demons.

To hell with that.

Nick strode forward, pulse pounding in his fists and neck.

No way was Cynda beaming herself into some battle or slaughterhouse without him.

By the time he reached the table, he sensed more tension in the room. That weird energy, that sense of something huge about to break open. He had felt it before, when he'd watched Cynda do her steps back at the townhouse.

Nick ducked under the Sibyls who had locked arms beside the table.

Something buffeted his back. Wind. Earth energy. A lot of heat.

He absorbed what he could, knowing the women had to be supporting Cynda, concentrating their elemental talents on the dance she was doing. He jumped from the floor, vaulting over the table's ring of fire just as the flames jumped higher. His raid jacket smoldered as he landed on the flat, wooden surface a few feet away from Cynda.

Above him, the chimes started a different staccato ring, matching her steps. Pipe to pipe, set to set, the sound flew around the room, turning circles just like Cynda.

Nick was careful to give her plenty of space, but he got as close as he could, and closer when she slowed to dance in front of the center mirror. Arm's length, at her back, right where he belonged.

Nick stared at the black glass, waiting.

Cynda's hands and arms went white-pale from her effort. Her shoulder muscles strained, and her energy fluctuated as she battled to finish what Nick figured was a complex bunch of energy transfers.

I'm right here, firebird. He didn't know how to give her elemental energy, but he sent the force of his feelings and hoped for the best. *Come on. You can do this.*

She kept at it, not giving up. She'd never give up—he knew that for sure.

Seconds later, fog appeared in the mirror.

Nick drew his Glock and kept himself ready.

The fog brightened, as if someone had switched on a lamp at the mirror's center. Then the smoke in the glass swirled.

More energy swept around the duplex. Chimes blasted and rang. For a split second, Nick imagined the pipes were screaming. The sound grated up and down his spine, and he tightened his grip on his weapon.

The scene in the mirror came clear.

Cynda's breath caught.

The stone room Nick was used to seeing at Motherhouse Island—the walls had turned black.

Streaked by fire.

Pieces of mirror frames hung at odd angles. No furniture in sight. Women in charred green robes lay like broken dolls on the floor.

God.

Cynda shook all over.

Nick couldn't see her face, but he could imagine her look of horror. He was about to reach for her when she said, "Harper. Get up here, hold open the channel, and come through last. Everyone else, follow me."

Harper leaped onto the table right behind Nick. Flames licked over his shoulders as energy flowed between the two women.

Cynda stepped toward the glass.

Heat blasted around Nick, holding him back like a burning, shoving wall.

He squinted into the blast and saw Cynda shimmer. A second later, she lifted off the table and vanished.

Shit!

Nick half shifted and powered himself through the thick curtain of elemental force. Driving with all the power in his legs, he ran a step and hurled himself upward, toward the scene in the mirror.

The room went black.

Sound and air sucked out of his ears.

He roared from the pain, roared with Gideon punching at his ribs and spine, but heard nothing at all.

His skin jammed against his bones.

His gut yanked like somebody had tied a string to his middle, fastened the end to a rocket, and hit the go switch.

Nick pumped his legs once and tumbled through what felt like empty space.

(25)

Not even daring to breathe, Cynda landed on the charred wooden platform in the communications chamber at Motherhouse Ireland.

When she took her first breath, the stone room stank of blood and acrid fire and smoldering wood. Black and white smoke drifted around the chamber, and gray light and rain slanted through shattered, barred glass in windows above her head.

Too late. A sob burst from her throat. Fire charged through her belly, but she held back the flames, had to. Had to get down and see what was left.

Goddess, was *anything* left?

Afternoon, her brain automatically calculated. *Five-hour time difference. And it's bad weather. No sounds of battle. No red traces. No demons. This room is clear. But—there on the floor.*

Women in green robes. Obviously Mothers. Obviously dead.

"Noooo," she moaned, as if her soul-deep grief might blaze out of her chest and bring the women back. Her limbs didn't want to follow her commands, but she turned, and saw two nuns from Kylemore kneeling beside an injured Mother.

The right height. The right hair.

Please—

Cynda raced to Mother Keara's stricken form and dropped to her knees, pulling the woman's head into her lap. On either side of Mother Keara, two Kylemore Sisters worked to clean cuts and bandage wounds in Mother

Keara's arms. Mother Keara's green robes lay in burned tatters. Her Chinese great sword had been snapped in half, the pieces rammed into the stone mortar at her feet.

Tears flowing, Cynda stroked Mother Keara's small, frail cheek.

Behind them, Nick came through the mirror and half fell, half jumped off the communications platform into the devastated stone chamber at Motherhouse Ireland. Sibyls poured through the mirror behind him, landing on the table and jumping off, weapons drawn. The mirror shook on the wall. It was cracked at the top, and that crack was spidering out and down with each new arrival. Soon it would shatter the mirror completely.

Cynda didn't want to think about it, couldn't even begin to face that fact right this second. Mother Keara's skin felt too cool beneath her fingertips. Where was the fire? The fight?

Goddess, she's in trouble. I'm going to lose her!

"*A chroí.*" Mother Keara coughed.

Cynda started to tell her not to speak, but Mother Keara blurted, "They caught us at trainin' and chattin' with Russia a few hours ago, but we purged our grounds and closed the tunnels after some sisters came through to help." She managed a cackle. "The demons are outside our walls now, by the Goddess! Chased out and held off by what Sibyls we have, and those what showed up by foot and car."

"Ssssshhh." One of the nuns stroked Mother Keara's weathered hand. "Your *a chroí* has come to defend her Motherhouse, just as you knew she would. You need rest now, like you promised. Let us take you to the infirmary."

"I'll see to my own wounds, damn ya," the old woman growled, but she didn't give off even a puff of smoke. "And I'll not be abandonin' my house in its time of need!"

"Go with the nuns," Cynda urged, wishing she could take Mother Keara's wounds herself and bear them for her. "I *will* take care of the Motherhouse. I'll take care of everyone."

Mother Keara's gaze brightened for a fraction of a second. Cynda thought she looked . . . proud.

Then her eyes fluttered closed.

Pain flared in Cynda's center, as if somebody had torn her soul in half. Fire burned along the outsides of her hands, but she couldn't give her heat to Mother Keara. The old woman simply couldn't take it. She was barely hanging on.

Choking back a round of crippling sobs, Cynda cut her gaze to the nuns. "Take her to the healers. Do whatever you can, please!"

One of the nuns spoke in low, soothing tones to Mother Keara as they worked to lift her, but Cynda couldn't hear what the woman was saying. Something in Irish. It sounded like a blessing.

A mind-scraping crack made Cynda shriek and jump to her feet. She whirled back to the platform, hand on the hilt of her sword.

Delilah Moses was hauling herself down from the table and swiveling her head, taking in her new surroundings. Harper Ellis had just come through the channels. Behind Harper, the mirror cracked again. Wood snapped.

It splintered completely.

The glass crashed to the floor and exploded to sand and fire with a loud *whump*.

The channels behind the destroyed mirror slammed shut with the force of a small grenade, popping against Cynda's eardrums.

She stared at the closed stone wall, at the still-smoldering sand on the floor. No more mirrors. That was it. They were completely cut off from rapid transport now.

Fucking wonderful.

She ran a hand through her hair.

"We'll have to get reinforcements the old-fashioned way," Bela Argos, the earth Sibyl from the South Bronx triad, said, sheathing her daggers. "Plane, train, boat, and automobile. Every projective mirror in a hundred miles probably broke when that mirror's energy turned loose."

"May the Goddess speed the fighters who can reach us," said Harper, who was lining up the initiates beside the table.

"Wait a second." Cynda gestured to the nuns, who bowed their heads and kept a firm grip on the now swearing, spitting Mother Keara. "Delilah, help the Sisters—and don't argue with me, or I'll melt your ass to the rock floor."

The old woman didn't even open her mouth. She just scooted toward the nuns like she had wheels under her feet.

One less problem.

Cynda needed victories where she could get them.

Eyes watering but focusing more easily now, Cynda glanced at Nick.

He had a tight grip on his gun, standing with his arms at his sides. The lines of his handsome face had hardened into a mask.

Fire rose and fell on her shoulders and arms, keeping time with her breathing. She could tell Nick wanted to hold her, protect her—but how could he save her from this?

The other Sibyls and the younger fighters stared at her, waiting for her to lead them.

And she had promised Mother Keara to do just that.

Was it possible? Cynda bit at her lip and tried to manage her fire, pull it inside her to shore up her failing energy.

Could she take charge of this unbelievable mess and make a difference?

"Right beside you," Nick murmured. His expression softened just enough to communicate the full depth of his support.

He's here beside me. He'll do his best to stand in for my triad—and he's a damned good fighter. We're all good fighters.

After another few breaths, Cynda nodded. She steeled herself inside, then faced her troops, such as they were.

"See to the dead," she told the initiates, sliding her sword from its sheath. "Mother Ailis, Mother Quinn, and Mother Murphy need their rites and ceremonies."

To Nick and the Sibyls, she raised her blade. Flames licked along the steel. "East turret. We need to see what the hell's going on."

Fire trailed behind Cynda as she led the way out of the communications chamber and upward, through the underbelly of Motherhouse Ireland. Tears stung her eyes, and she couldn't unlock her jaw. Didn't even try.

My sanctuary.

My first home.

Her raised sword blazed through the arched passages. Her thoughts darkened with each step. Even though her muscles knew the way, she barely recognized the soot-streaked hallways. Everything smelled like smoke and sulfur and blood. Broken torches hung limp in sconces. Bits of furniture, spears, and broken swords littered the stone floor.

And bodies . . . oh, Goddess.

Flames poured from her hands. Cynda gripped her sword with both fists, so hard the hilt dug into her palms, but she couldn't begin to control her fire.

Two green-robed trainees lay sprawled at the foot of the winding stairs that led up to the east battlement.

She littered the air with bursts of heat. Her blade glowed brighter, pulling from her raging inner fire, until the center went stark white.

Thank God Nick was here. Without Riana and Merilee, with Mother Keara down and wounded and half the other Mothers dead, his presence was all that anchored her. She sensed him nearby, drew from him. Her legs felt like so much concrete, but she stepped over the dead girls and kept going.

My home.

My friends.

My family.

"They'll pay," Nick rumbled from behind her.

"Damn straight," somebody answered from farther back. Cynda couldn't place the voice.

Fire spit and hissed and roared from other fire Sibyls and the initiates. Heat radiated from every stone, hung in the air, flowed around Cynda, feeding her energy, feeding her rage.

Body burning inside and out, she hefted her sword and took the stairs two at a time. The big east turret was just ahead.

Motherhouse Ireland was a mimic to Kylemore Abbey, built into the rock face of a small mountain, with two sides facing a stretch of the Dawros River. Only the east wall of the Motherhouse was vulnerable to breach. Otherwise, attackers would need to blast through the center of the mountain, or bash through solid stone pillars with boats.

Or fly.

Images of Astaroths flashed through Cynda's mind as her legs pistoned up the tower steps.

Why hadn't she killed every damned one of those monsters when she had the chance?

She didn't even care about Jake at the moment.

She wanted all the double-winged demons toasted and drowned at the bottom of Connemara's bogs.

Noises drifted toward her. Screaming. Shouting. Dull roars.

Shit.

Her heart punched against her ribs.

The closer she got to the battlement, the louder it got, and the more flames she shed on the stairs around her feet.

Think, damnit. Plan. You've got to keep it together. You promised. This is your fight.

Astaroths could absorb fire, but they couldn't deflect arrows and bullets, right? And she had Nick. She had eight air Sibyls, all of whom wore intact goggles with demon-tracking lenses.

How many warriors got here before we came?

And what kind of army are we facing?

Her chest ached. Her gut burned worse than ever. She wanted to yell her head off and explode into a murdering, sky-sweeping fountain of fire.

Instead, Cynda reached the top of the steps and shoved through the battlement door.

Sword crackling, she stormed directly into hell itself.

Screams battered her ears. Battle cries echoed on stone. Women shouted directions and commands. It was hard to see the big turret. Fire jetted, huge gouts, forming trails of murky black smog. Wind blew the smog sideways, sucking it up and back. The afternoon reeked of copper and smoke and hot steel.

Sulfur, too. Strong. Choking.

Demons.

So much wrong energy.

Everywhere.

Nick reached her, Glock drawn, and brushed her free arm. Together, they jogged forward to let her fellow warriors onto the top of the turret. She squinted through the smoke and saw—only three Sibyls, weapons out and fighting.

Blood stilled in Cynda's chest.

"Where are the rest?" Nick asked.

"Please don't let this be all," Bela Argos said from somewhere behind Cynda.

More fire curtained the air around her. She stopped to avoid it, then had to hit her knees to duck a snarling, diving patch of air with a spear on either side of it.

Astaroth.

Steaming all over, Cynda rolled to her back and barely got off a blast to knock the spears sideways before an adept got hit.

She saw the demon's outline in the thick cloud of smoke.

Rage flowed through her veins, across her skin. She started to leap up and swing at the bastard, but a hand shoved her down to her knees again.

"Stay put!" a dark-headed air Sibyl wearing cracked goggles shouted as she ran past, pitching a slew of throwing knives at the demon as it swept away from the battlement's toothy edge.

Beside Cynda, Nick crouched and aimed his Glock.

The Sibyl missed.

Nick didn't.

The gunshot barely registered against the other noise. He unfolded from his crouch, gun still poised, and searched the smoke-clogged turret for more movement, or the traces of sulfur he could see without special lenses.

"They're pulling back again!" cried the air Sibyl with the throwing knives, shifting to the other side of the circular space. "Stand down! Stand down!" Her accent sounded Scottish. To Cynda, she said, "The threat's passed for a moment. They won't be back for half an hour, if they stay true to pattern." When she caught sight of Nick, she looked surprised, but also grateful. "American?"

"New York," Cynda called, getting to her feet.

"About bloody time," said a young fire Sibyl without

goggles, who hurled a blast of flame at a retreating set of spears. The fire did nothing, but the movement in the smoke revealed the demon's position.

The earth Sibyl on the turret, also without goggles, sent a wave of earth energy forward and slowed the creature. An arrow fired from another turret struck the demon. Wind released in a swirl, and a spew of earth and fire rained to the stone courtyard below.

Cynda sheathed her sword and felt a rush of triumph at the two kills, until she heard Nick say, "Sonofabitch."

"Have a look at 'em," the air Sibyl said. "They'll behave nice now. We've got a moment to breathe."

As walls of flame and smoke parted to show the scene below, Nick came to stand behind Cynda, hand resting against her waist as she lowered her sword. Not because she wanted to. Because the damned thing suddenly felt like it weighed two hundred pounds.

Around the castle, in the defensive structures, she saw precious few Sibyls. Maybe eighteen total, three on each turret and six scattered along the eastern battlement.

Not enough.

Can't be enough.

That truth sank through her belly, through all her muscles. A weakness, almost a hopelessness, but with a quick burst of fire in her chest, Cynda tried to burn it away. And only a handful had goggles to track invisible demons. Cynda figured the lenses had been broken in battle, just like her own.

She didn't need goggles to see the magnitude of their problems, however.

On the east flank of Motherhouse Ireland, grass, trees, and bushes had been burned away, leaving a bare stretch of earth roughly the size of ten football fields.

"Goddess spare us." She folded her arms and fought to control her trembling.

The fields were filled with glowing, roaring Cursons,

separated by blank patches of ground Cynda assumed were jammed with invisible Astaroths. And who knew how many of the monsters were flying around above the place like vultures?

"Shit. Those are Asmodai." Nick jerked a thumb toward the foot of the castle's eastern wall, where a row of tall, gangly demons pounded against the stones. "And there. Coming out of the trees."

Cynda wanted to vomit.

"Legion." She heard the dry, cracked sound of her own voice. The trembling in her limbs shifted inside, stealing her breath. "Asmodai are short-distance weapons. They've got to have Legion masters somewhere close."

"Cranking out more Asmodai." Nick swore and trained his Glock on the basic, simple demons, but didn't fire. "Those things aren't hard to make. A handful of dirt, a lit match, or some air trapped in a jar—and a half-hour ritual."

He was thinking like a seasoned fighter, saving his elementally locked ammo for the Astaroths and Cursons. More complex. Bigger threats. Harder to kill.

Cynda's emotion gradually drained to nothing, giving way to cold logic and planning. She wondered if they had enough bullets, arrows, and knives. Motherhouse Ireland had swords in the armory, but few distance weapons.

Her battered group from New York, which now seemed huge, formed in silent ranks behind her as the triad that had been fighting on the turret came toward them.

"Buggers hit and draw back, hit and draw back," explained the fire Sibyl with the British accent. "We've tried all we can think of, but the best thing is just killing however many we can. They'll wait a bit now like we said, half an hour, and come at us full force again. They've been doing it all morning. You can almost set a watch by 'em."

"Wearing you down." Nick gripped Cynda's waist more firmly.

Below them, at the castle wall, the demons shrank back a few yards, then a few more, and seemed to be huddling in discussion.

Resting?

Planning?

Messing with our heads?

"Yes, well, effective strategy," said a blonde with powerful earth energy. "Precious few of us still able to fight. Some dead, even more wounded."

Drawing in smoky air and coughing it up again, Cynda steadied herself to ask the question she most dreaded. Her words caught a few times, but she finally forced out, "How many of the Mothers are still alive?"

The British fire Sibyl lowered her gaze. "Four, if Mother Keara's holding her own. Kylemore's nuns have two of them in the infirmary with broken bones and the like. Mother Eileen's along the east wall." The girl pointed to a small figure moving up and back, up and back, organizing the fighters and obviously giving orders.

We have one Mother to fight with us. One. Just one and a handful of worn-out fighters against fields of demons—with more demons on the way.

Heat surged up Cynda's throat, but she choked it back, mindful of the adepts behind her.

"We're from the next county," said the blond earth Sibyl, sheathing her daggers at her waist. "Came in through the main gate before Mother Eileen pulled up the drawbridge. Air Sibyls will have to lift in other triads who reach us."

Cynda shivered on reflex. She hated riding Merilee's tornados, but right now, she'd welcome the sight of thirty or forty of the funnels. A hundred.

Nick eyed the demons outside the east wall. "How

long will it take the other two Motherhouses to get Sibyls here?"

"Over land?" Cynda glanced at the smoke-obscured sun, feeling the question drop like a stone in her gut. "I don't know. We've never had a Motherhouse attacked before. I'm sure there aren't any hard-and-fast plans in place for this. I'd say by morning, if we're lucky."

He drew a sharp breath. "Will the nuns at Kylemore help?"

Cynda clenched one fist and banged it against her sword sheath. "No. They don't fight or interfere in Sibyl business or battles. They just attend the wounded." Before he asked, she added, "Ireland doesn't have the equivalent of an OCU. There is no cavalry, Nick. It's up to us to defend the castle until Greece and Russia arrive, or other large groups of Sibyls."

At that, Nick looked away from her, his lack of comment speaking volumes.

She couldn't cry or scream or vomit or anything. The initiates. The Motherhouse. "We've got to hold the line until tomorrow. We have to find a way."

The British fire Sibyl gave her a weak smile. "Because tomorrow's lucky, right?"

The girl sounded so tired and scared, but hopeful in spite of everything.

"Tomorrow," Cynda repeated, confused. Then, "Oh, yeah. St. Patrick's Day."

"Mother Keara told us about you." The British girl's face went slack, but she rallied long enough to add, "She said you'd come to save us—and here you are."

Oh. My. Goddess.

All of Cynda's nerves switched off at once. Numb all over. Reality blew away from her like smoke on the wind. For a long few seconds, she couldn't grab it back, couldn't focus her thoughts past what the girl said.

It really is up to me now. This Motherhouse. All of these people.

If it weren't for Nick's hands on her waist, she might have fallen to her knees under the weight of that realization.

The British fire Sibyl fainted.

The Sibyl's triad sisters leaped and caught her before she struck the stone surface of the turret. The sight stirred Cynda back to life, and she rushed forward to help them steady her and get her weight supported.

"Take her below," Cynda urged as she turned the girl's arm loose. "We'll spell you. Get some rest."

"Yeah," said the blond earth Sibyl as she and the other member of the girl's triad carried her toward the battlement's door. "Every half hour, remember, unless they change their pattern. Gonna be a long night."

Once more, Nick came to stand by Cynda, staying just close enough to lend her his strength. She leaned against his powerful arm, watched the exhausted triad limp out of view, and wondered how long her own adepts would last. They were going on a full day with no sleep, no food, no relief. She glanced around at the smoking turret. And a shitload of turmoil.

Riana.

Merilee.

What she wouldn't give to have her triad sisters fighting beside her.

To the experienced Sibyls she said, "Spread out along the wall, and to the other battlements. Let's give these fighters some relief. Each triad take an adept. The rest of you, head for Mother Eileen. Keep a close eye on your watches, and on the demons. Raise the alarm if they so much as twitch in this direction."

The Sibyls and the adepts fanned out without hesitation, questions, or complaints. Cynda couldn't help but feel pride, and gratitude for every one of them. They might be young and green, but they were warriors, to the last woman.

Cynda checked her watch. Twenty-five minutes until the next attack.

Two minutes before the attack was due, Nick's phone rang.

Cynda felt the shift of his balance as he took the cell from his jeans pocket and punched it on.

"Yeah. Where?" He glanced at his watch. "How many?" Then one more time, "Yeah." He punched off the phone and slid it back into his pocket. "Creed's been trying to call for an hour."

"Sibyl energy." Cynda chewed at her lip as she surveyed the empty turret.

Nick scrubbed a hand across his chin, keeping his gaze fixed on the demons below and his Glock ready in the other hand. "Lots of static, but I think Creed said ETA eight hours, maybe less. They've picked up ten triads."

Thirty Sibyls! First good news in hours.

Hope flared though Cynda's mind. "Are they flying?"

Nick gave her a quick look.

She stared at him. "What?"

"I couldn't hear him that well." He shrugged, still keeping watch on the demons. "But I think he said they were on the water. Maybe they're coming by boat."

"From Atlanta?" So much for hope. She kicked at the stone surface, feeling absolutely sick inside. "*Damnit!* They won't be here for days. You must have heard Creed wrong."

The air on the turret shifted.

Cynda's skin prickled.

Her head snapped up, and her heart raced. Every bit of her frustration and misery and grief converted to heat, and that heat surged through her fingers, arms, and legs. It warmed her blood. It fed her fire.

Her sword seemed to fly into her grip. She didn't remember drawing it.

Flames roared from the blade.

Energy blasted through her entire body as she saw the demons on the ground charge forward and sensed Astaroths filling the air above her.

"That's it." Her voice sounded more like a wolf's snarl than human speech. "Come on. Riiiiiight here."

A fierce, raging hunger gnawed at her belly as she swept her sword above her shoulder and held it, poised and waiting and blazing. The huge problems of the world narrowed to one moment, to now, to the turret atop Motherhouse Ireland.

Time for payback.

Time for demon blood to flow.

It's up to me.

It's up to us.

One step at a time—and this step, she could take, and Nick would help her.

He let out a low growl, then moved a step away from her so she'd have room to swing.

Glock raised, he said, "Heads up, firebird. Here they come."

26

Smoke stung Nick's eyes.

Blood rushed in his ears.

Women shouted. Battle cries rang across the castle.

Nick caught a breath of sulfur and fire and shared his mind with Gideon, sharpening his senses as the first Astaroth plummeted toward them. He saw red streaks and spears, sensed the demon's hatred and resolve.

He knew Cynda wanted these kills, needed them, but he wasn't letting this first asshole anywhere near her if he could help it.

Jaw tight, Nick waited, waited, almost there . . . and he fired. Blew the damned thing out of the sky not five feet from his own head.

Dirt and wind and fire exploded into Nick's face. Gideon snarled. Nick snarled with his *other*. His skin glowed bright gold as they worked together to defend Cynda and her Motherhouse.

But . . . thirty-one rounds left. Got to keep count.

The magazine in his Glock—almost empty. The two in his pocket. One more shot before he reloaded.

Make 'em count.

Two more red flashes streaked through the air above the turret.

Cynda blasted the turret with flames, sending black smoke swirling around the Astaroths.

Nick blew one apart.

Thirty rounds left.

Screaming like a banshee, Cynda separated from him,

tracked the demon's image in her smoke, and plowed into the other demon with a ferocious downswing.

Nick's breath caught hard in his chest, but a burst of elemental energy told him she'd nailed her target.

When she looked at him, her voice echoed through his mind. Things she'd said to him over and over, in that other world, back in New York City.

I'm a warrior. How many times do I have to tell you? Fight with me, or get out of my way . . .

"With you," he yelled out loud.

He had never known a woman—a warrior—like Cynda.

Keeping her in his periphery, he covered her, picking off incoming as she smoked out yet more diving Astaroths and hacked them to pieces. Dirt streaked her face. Her leathers barely covered any part of her body. The sight of her shrieking and smoking and swinging that burning blade made him think of Valkyries and Furies, legends and myths.

She topped them all.

I'd die for her right here. She's worth it. They're all worth it.

Time shifted, moved differently as they danced through the smoke together. Killing in tandem. An accurate, deadly team.

Seconds turned to minutes. Minutes turned to seconds. Elemental energy filled the space around them, expanding reality, contracting it.

Nick had no idea even what day it was. He stopped caring. All that mattered was Cynda and this fight and demons dying.

A part of his mind kept up with images from other turrets and the wall. Swords flashed. Arrows flew. He saw Sibyls fighting and falling, but he couldn't hear anything beyond Cynda's battle cries and his own *other*-joined roars. He couldn't feel anything but the fire in his blood as he fired, and fired, and fired.

The hit-and-run attack shut down as fast as it began.

Calls of "Stand down!" echoed across the battlements.

Half an hour until the next raid. Half an hour to rest. He needed to breathe. He needed to think of something to kill these assholes faster and better.

Nick's pulse hammered in his temples. Cynda was still shrieking, backing up, her blade tip trailing along the turret's stone surface. Then she was laughing, and jamming her dirt-coated sword back in its sheath, and sobbing.

Shit.

He ran forward and caught her in his arms, let her fall against him, beating his shoulders with her fists as fire bit into his skin.

Not much was left of his raid jacket. His jeans were more holes than fabric now, but he didn't care.

He took her heat and held her tight body against his, where she belonged. Then he kissed her damp head and stared over her shoulder, through the smoke, at the demons regrouping and massing along the castle's east wall.

Rage crawled through his insides.

The bastards could do this all day. All night. Forever. The Legion had finally formed and executed a perfect plan, using Sister Julia to get things rolling. Don't go after the few hundred triad-assigned fire Sibyls who really knew how to fight. Go after their future. Destroy the next generation and smash the Motherhouse by letting small groups of Sibyls feed into the castle and picking them off.

Tire them out.

Never let the women amass a full fighting force.

By the time this was over, what would be left of *all* the Sibyls—not just in Ireland, but worldwide?

As air Sibyls cleared the smoke above Motherhouse Ireland, Nick kept his grip on Cynda and counted heads on their side.

Two fewer than when they started. Two more Sibyls down—or dead.

Fuck!

Just in case the demons below changed their strategy, he pulled Cynda against one of the stone walls for cover and held her there, temporarily safe in his arms. She felt so warm, so alive.

How could he keep her that way?

What could he do to help save these women?

Part of his attention stayed on the wall behind him, the noises, the energies, in case the demons got creative. The rest of his attention focused on Cynda.

"How many rounds do you have left?" Her voice was nothing but a whisper against crackles and pops of nearby fire.

He'd been hoping she wouldn't ask that.

But he gave her an honest answer. "Couple of mags. Not enough."

Silence spread between them.

She clung to him, went limp, and cried softly against his neck.

He had nothing left to give but his embrace, his kisses, even as he beat himself up inside for not being able to figure out a new plan.

Cynda let him be her strength for a minute, maybe two, before she pulled back and rested her forehead against his chin. Her red hair tickled his lips, and he closed his eyes, squeezed her shoulders, and kept thinking. Reaching. And finding nothing.

Damn.

"We can't stay behind the walls and let them keep hitting us, Nick." She spoke without moving or smoking or sparking, even once. "We'll never do enough damage.

We won't make it until morning, and those demons will kill the rest of the Mothers and adepts."

This is where I'm supposed to have the heroic idea. Piece together some weapon with spit and string and two tiny wires I jerk out of a lightbulb. Motherfucking sonofabitch.

He stroked her soft hair, not caring about the soot and singed edges, and breathed that hint of vanilla and cinnamon. Even smoke and sweat and battle couldn't dull it completely. "You know this castle like the back of your hand, firebird. How do we get outside that east wall, make a hit, and get back—fast?"

She hesitated. Ran her fingertips along his arms, then sighed. "We don't. With the tunnels sealed, the drawbridge is the only way in or out, unless you count the windows."

Nick opened his eyes and stared straight ahead, at nothing at all. Dug deep through his mind. Deeper. Rifled past fifteen or twenty ideas he rejected himself, then came up with, "What about the earth Sibyls? Can't they tunnel us out?"

Another sigh from Cynda made his heart sink.

"The water table's too high because of the river and bogs." She pressed her head into his cheek. "If we dig that deep into the ground, we'll flood out and drown."

Nick pulled Cynda tighter against him and leaned his shoulders against the rock wall behind him. Her heart beat against his, and just for that moment, he didn't let himself feel anything else, focus on anything else.

For now, they'd have to keep fighting.

And thinking.

If it was the last thing he ever did, he'd keep her alive.

But for how long?

Over the next hours and half a dozen brief attacks, they lost two more Sibyls.

Nick helped Cynda try three or four plans to improve their odds, none more successful than the one before—though the air Sibyls creating treacherous crosswinds over the castle did crash a bunch of winged demons into turrets, teeth-first.

That felt damned good.

For a minute.

By full dark, Nick was down to ten rounds.

With no discernible change in the demon ranks below.

Half an hour to the next attack.

Bright moonlight reflected off the river and bogs, off the smooth castle stones, and Nick let his skin glow a little brighter as he and Cynda rested against the turret wall. They were both breathing hard. Sweating and shivering.

He had completely lost the thread of real time, but he knew it was still hours until help might come—if it did. Too many hours. It might as well be days.

Cynda curled against him, shoulder bleeding from the last attack. Her head pressed against his shoulder as she meditated, healing what she could. Nick held her close, drinking in these minutes of peace, savoring every second he had with her.

She glanced down at her tattoo and rubbed the mark. Then she sat up and pulled out of his embrace. When she looked at him this time, her green eyes shone with tears. "Mother Eileen just sent me a message. She said if we lose another Sibyl, we'll lose the wall. They can't hold it anymore. We're done, Nick. This next attack might be our last."

Nick's chest ached. He felt like something was ripping him right down the center. "No."

She cupped his cheek with her palm. "We could put the surviving adepts in the ancient crypt below the communications room, with Mother Eileen, Mother Keara, and the nuns."

"No," he said again. Nick went stiff, fighting off the misery in his body, his mind. The soft tips of her fingers brought him toward reality, a step at a time.

"The earth Sibyls could bring down the stones around them for extra fortification, and the rest of us could take the battle to the demons. Kill as many as we can." She traced his whole face, her skin warmer, giving off a little smoke as she went. "If fortune favors us, the demons will have to regroup. Maybe we'll break through the lines, find a few of those Legion bastards—and the Mothers and the younger girls will make it until morning, until help comes."

Nick pushed her hand away, then grabbed her by both arms. "No way, firebird. You're not dying. Not tonight."

She gazed at him, so sad, so burdened, like she was carrying a thousand pounds, dead center on her delicate, soft back. Her look said, *I'm a warrior, Nick. How many times do I have to tell you? Fight with me, or get out of my way.*

Everything inside him seemed to catch on fire. He choked. Gripped her too hard, made himself ease off, but she didn't back down.

"I have to do this, Nick." She leaned toward him and kissed the line of his jaw. "I'd rather you defend the Mothers and the youngest. They're our hope. We need to save as many as we can."

Her smoke joined with his golden glow as he forced out, "I'm *not* leaving you."

"Figured you'd say that." She actually smiled at him, then cupped his cheek with her palm again.

"I have to do this," she repeated, and Nick heard the finality in her statement. More than that, he felt it in his own gut.

Half his mind saw the big picture, knew how right she was—but the rest of him kept searching for that miracle plan.

How could he love somebody this much and still fail her?

He had to save her. *Had* to.

But as he stared into the depths of her green eyes, he understood life and death weren't the only issues at play, or the only measure of success and failure.

This situation went way past the two of them.

He had never been afraid of dying, and, he realized at that second, neither had Cynda. That wasn't the point anymore.

Dying for nothing, for shit reasons, would suck. But fighting the right fight, to protect the future of fire Sibyls and maybe the future of all the women warriors—that wouldn't suck. Maybe that was winning, in a way. Maybe that was succeeding.

Keeping his attention on her face, her touch, he stanched the flow of his rage with every bit of strength he possessed.

I'm a warrior, Nick . . .

He knew that now, in ways he never did before, despite his immense respect for her fighting skills.

They *were* the same inside.

They would both do whatever they had to do, whatever it took.

Only this time, they wouldn't survive.

He pulled her into his lap and kissed her, tasting her sweet, soft lips, loving the warm feathering of her breath across his face. She wrapped her arms around his neck and he kissed her again and again, trying to burn each scent and sensation into his mind forever. If there was an afterlife for Cursons, these were the images, the pictures, the feelings he wanted to take with him.

Cynda knotted her fingers in his hair and tugged against it as he pulled his lips from hers. "If you have to do this, firebird, then *we* have to do it. Together."

Some of that terrible burden shifted from Cynda's features, and he knew that he hadn't let her down after all, because he couldn't find the way to save her. Cynda needed a partner, an equal, someone to stand beside her, battle beside her, and he was that man, for however long they could last out on that field of demons. He expected Gideon to wake and get restless, knowing what he had planned, but the beast inside him remained silent and passive. Agreeing.

Deep inside Nick, some of his own darkness faded away.

This was right. Absolutely and completely. Maybe the most right thing he had ever done, other than loving Cynda.

Nick kissed her again, adding another memory to that stash he hoped to have for eternity.

"If I had asked you to marry me, firebird—"

"I would have said yes." No hesitation. No lie in her expression.

He nodded.

That was enough.

The best thing he'd ever heard.

The perfect memory.

He let her go, and they stood together. Smoke drifted across the moon.

Nick didn't spare the demons a glance. "Take care of the adepts and gather the Sibyls." He rubbed his palm across Cynda's shoulders. "I'll get the injured Mothers and the nuns."

Her lips brushed his cheek again. "Meet you in the communications chamber."

Muscles still aching from hauling wounded into the crypt before they sealed it—and from where Mother Keara kicked him about five times while he tried to help her—Nick stood next to Cynda and did a quick count in the stone hallway leading to the drawbridge.

Twenty-five Sibyls, total. Arms bandaged. Faces burned and bruised. Leathers tattered and shredded.

Nine fire Sibyls formed the front rank nearest the drawbridge, swords drawn, while Harper Ellis manned the drawbridge crank to his left. The women had sunglasses to help with flashes from demon explosions.

Eight air Sibyls made up the second line, wearing every last pair of goggles they could find, patch, or tie together. Each of the women would fight with bow and arrow—good—or throwing knives—not so good, but it would have to do.

Seven earth Sibyls, the group Nick and Cynda would join, manned the third wave of attack, farthest from the drawbridge, daggers or staves firmly in hand.

The damp air in the bridge passage soothed his singed face and arms as he squeezed Cynda's hand in his.

They would *definitely* do some damage.

He felt a twinge that he'd never see Creed again, and never know what had become of Jake—if his Astaroth brother had found a way to heal himself after all he'd been through.

But the time for regrets was long gone.

"Stay low," Nick said to the waiting Sibyls, doing his best to push away his thoughts about his blood family. "Don't get distracted from the plan. Fire Sibyls focus on Asmodai and keep them off our asses. Air Sibyls, you're on Astaroths. Cynda and I will work with the earth Sibyls to thin the Curson ranks. If you lose your plugs or goggles, retreat. If you're cornered, kill Cursons first—but don't forget to close your eyes if you don't have sunglasses or goggles."

The small army nodded as one, looking as grim as Nick felt.

Cynda took her turn. "The more Cursons and Astaroths we hit, the more chaos we cause, the more holes we punch, and the better chance we give the Mothers and adepts."

Once more, the army responded, this time with a murmur of determination.

Nick knew they were ready.

Half-joined with Gideon, glowing and focused, he was ready, too. "Plugs in place, now."

The Sibyls jammed bits of cotton, cloth, or wax into their ears. Nick and Cynda did the same, gazing at each other.

The world went quiet, except for the steady pound of blood in his ears.

Then, because it didn't matter anymore who saw, who knew, or who cared, Nick took his woman into his arms and gave her a last, long kiss. Her body seemed to melt into his, shoulder to hip, and her fire flickered along his shoulders.

He let it burn, loving the heat, the press of her leather-clad body against his, and loving her, more than anything.

When he pulled back and let Cynda leave his arms for what might be the last time, he didn't look at the waiting Sibyls again. Instead he and Cynda walked to their spot in the third line.

Nick turned to Harper and raised three fingers.

Two fingers.

One.

None.

The young fighter threw her weight into the lever and rotated the crank.

Nick turned and grasped Cynda's fingers with his. He felt the groan and shudder of the heavy drawbridge in his bones. Seconds later, the big door slammed down so hard it made his teeth clamp together.

The fire Sibyls stormed across the wood, shrieking loud enough to be heard through the thick rubber plugs in Nick's ears. His pulse surged with the incredible sound. Adrenaline pumped into his muscles as their swords crackled out into the night, headed for the rows of Asmodai pounding on the castle's stone supports. As planned, a contingent of three women didn't make the left turn around the castle wall. They swept right instead, toward the nearby woods. With any luck, they'd reach the trees to search out Legion members who might be close and replenishing the golemlike demons for the frontline attack.

Air Sibyls pounded across the bridge next. Before they ever reached the turn, they deployed in lines and clusters, aimed into the air, and started firing on targets.

Our turn.

Nick's energy hit peak. His thoughts sharpened down to the here, the now, this moment. His lips pulled back. He filled his lungs and let out a Gideon-echoing bellow.

Cynda let go of his hand, but he knew she'd stay close.

They had agreed—together, all the way. Together, until they both fell.

With Cynda beside him, her sword burning in the moonlight, Nick charged forward, holding his Glock ready.

His feet pounded into the wood of the drawbridge. He leaped off, hitting the ground at full stride, still sensing Cynda next to him, and the earth Sibyls, too.

They went wide, chewing up ground, giving the air Sibyls room to work.

The corner of the castle loomed.

Nick pushed himself harder. Cool night air flowed into his face, keeping his eyes wide.

They passed the corner at a dead run, and the front ranks of Asmodai, too.

From the corner of his eye, Nick saw the big ugly bastards already crashing to the ground and disintegrating into whatever element made them. Fire raged over the demons' heads. Swords flashed in the silver light, chopping, hacking, hewing.

Dirt and bits of flame and wind smacked against the top of his head, letting him know the Astaroths were taking a beating, too.

Good, Nick thought, but he didn't think anything else.

He just saw, sensed, moved, with Cynda matching him, stride for stride.

The first line of Cursons glowed in front of him. Their roars rattled against his plugs as the demons lumbered to meet their charge, swinging massive fists back and forth.

Nick sighted the nearest Curson and shot the fucker right between its golden eyes.

He got his lids closed before the demon exploded, kicking up a big chunk of dirt and rocks.

Satisfaction and rage powered Nick at the same time. His gut churned with his legs. Now they'd mow down as many as possible before the flashbang shock wore off the other demons—

But the Cursons were still coming.

The demons hadn't been affected by the explosions and immobilized the way they had been back on City Island.

Shit!

Some spell or protection? Maybe they're wearing plugs and squeezing their eyes shut, too.

Didn't matter.

He pulled up hard. Cynda stopped beside him, eyes wide, mouth open. She only hesitated a second before she took her stance, sword raised.

Earth energy bathed Nick, and he knew it had wrapped Cynda, too. Half the earth Sibyls were on protection duty, while the other half would use daggers like Cynda used her sword.

Hearts or heads.

The demons would die, only not as many as they'd hoped.

This was it.

For a split second, Nick let himself glance at Cynda.

Fire ringed her whole body. She absolutely blazed in the darkness.

Beautiful.

And mine.

He gave her a quick salute, then faced the onslaught.

"Make it count," he told himself, even though he knew nobody heard those last words.

A big, fast-swirling cloud drifted across the moon.

Nick aimed his Glock and squeezed the trigger, dropping demons in every direction. One. Two. Another. And four. Muted by the earth energy, the Curson explosions didn't faze him. He didn't even hear the concussions.

He hoped Cynda had hacked a few of the bastards to bits, but he didn't look. Couldn't stand what he might see.

Five shots left, if he hadn't miscounted.

With every nerve and muscle burning, Nick fired his weapon and killed Cursons until the slide locked back, the gun's chamber empty—no bullets left in the magazine.

The demons kept coming. Started to close in on him. He threw his Glock in the first one's face. Then he shifted completely, letting Gideon sweep across his awareness.

We'll get a few more this way, by God.

As Nick's consciousness started to fade to the background, he thought he heard something strange.

Wolves.

Lots of them.

Howling?

Confused, squinting in a golden flare that half blinded him as his earth protections fell away, Nick shifted back to his human form.

He whirled to his right and spotted Cynda.

She was down on her knees, shaking off that last flashbang.

Another cloud covered the moon.

Cursons surged around him, fists raised, blocking his vision—but the demons all stopped moving at the same time as if somebody had pushed a big red *stop* button. Their bellowing and snarling choked off at the same moment.

For a second, everything and everyone at Mother-house Ireland seemed to be listening.

Then the wolves howled again. Nick felt the sound along his neck and arms. Gideon snarled—but not at the wolves. *With* them.

And Nick knew.

The huge, snarling Russian wolves his brother Creed had described to him so many times. Supernaturally huge and strong, allied with the Russian Mothers. As deadly as any Sibyl.

Nick heard them easily despite his plugs.

The Cursons around him started moving again.

They *ran*.

Away from Nick. Back the way they came.

Nick forced his exhausted muscles into action and staggered to Cynda.

Her sword lay in the trampled dirt beside her. She had her arms wrapped around herself, holding her ribs. Blood covered the right side of her face. And she was laughing.

But damnit, she was alive.

She was alive.

Nick grabbed her, yanked her to her feet, and pulled her against him as fur brushed past them on both sides.

A pack of the biggest, meanest-looking gray wolves Nick had ever seen blasted through the field, snarling, a fur-covered wave of pure feral hunt-lust, carrying with them a powerful thrust of earth energy.

The shaggy beasts launched themselves at the fleeing Cursons, ripping off demon heads.

Nick barely got his eyes closed and Cynda's face pressed against his shoulder before the night lit up with death flashes.

He blinked away the glare in time to see wolves hit the ground. They leaped to their feet and hurtled straight back after the demons.

Nick swept Cynda into his arms and got the hell out of the way. Back to the castle. To the corner of the east wall, where exhausted fire, air, and earth Sibyls who had charged out with them collapsed to the ground, laughing and sobbing and pounding their fists into the moonlit dirt.

Nick got Cynda to the relative safety of a jutting stone overhang, then turned to see what was happening behind him.

Out of the woods, sweeping behind the wolves like a silent tide of raw elemental power, came the brown-robed earth Sibyls from Motherhouse Russia.

Daggers flashed.

The ground shook.

Nick raised his hand to shield his eyes and Cynda's from the glare of dying Cursons. Cynda slid her arms around him, pushed her face into his neck, and cried, her whole body shaking from what he knew had to be joy, relief, fatigue—all of it, probably.

A change in the moonlight jerked his attention upward.

Nick's jaw dropped.

Those clouds over the moon . . . they weren't clouds at all.

It's a new type of cavalry.

Visible and way more human-looking. Wearing god-damned jeans and T-shirts, with holes cut out for the wings.

In the sky above the battlefield, Astaroths with talismans engaged the Astaroths with no talismans, all of whom had become visible. No doubt the controlled Astaroths were pouring all their energy into the fight—which they were losing.

Rows of human-looking winged demons swept high, then plummeted down, spears outstretched. Their foes tried to fight, but most of the Astaroths who had been devastating the castle's defenses exploded into air, dirt, and fire, and littered the battlefield below. Some put up their hands and landed. Nick presumed they were surrendering, and as if to confirm his thoughts, a few talisman-wearing demons landed and held them at spear-point.

With a fierce blast of shock, Nick recognized Jake flying past, about a hundred yards away. His brother was leading a flying contingent west, toward the castle's turrets.

For a moment, Nick didn't have a clue what to feel beyond complete amazement. Jake and his line of demons immediately started kicking ass, beating back some of the assholes who had been dive-bombing the battlements above Nick's head.

When he left that house in South Ozone Park, my brother wasn't running.

Jake knew what was happening here. He and his friends had gone to get help.

Nick hugged Cynda closer, and kissed the top of her head for all the times she had defended that damned

Astaroth. He supposed he'd learn to listen to her instincts even more closely over the years, wouldn't he?

And he had a lot to talk about with Jake when this was over. More than a lot.

He shifted Cynda's weight, pulled out his earplugs, and let them fall to the ground.

New roaring sounds tore into the night, this time from the north side of the castle, back toward Kylemore Abbey. Nick recognized the rumble of funnels like the one Merilee created in the tunnel at the Bronx house, to lift him and Cynda to safety.

So the air Sibyls had arrived, too.

They must be coming over the mountain behind Motherhouse Ireland, airlifting themselves onto the turrets and battlements.

A soft rain started to fall, putting out blazes and tamping down the sulfur stench roiling off the battlefield.

He was about to let himself feel actual relief, maybe even sit down and kiss Cynda and rest, when yet another wave of motion and sound drew his gaze south, out over the river.

Only . . . the river was gone. Sucked completely away from its banks, leaving nothing but mud and weeds lying in its wake.

"Oh, shit." Cynda dug her nails into his neck and chest.

All around them, Sibyls cursed and clambered to their feet, edging back toward the battlefield, confused, not knowing where to run.

Nick couldn't move.

He couldn't stop Cynda when she twisted out of his grip, or go with her when she tugged at his arm and tried to get him to run.

His entire body had gone cold.

My nightmare.
The tidal wave.
Here it fucking comes to kill us all.

A wall of water with a big dark shape on top came sucking across the empty riverbed, bearing down on Nick and Cynda and the castle—and every last one of the Sibyls who had made it to Motherhouse Ireland.

27

Every cut, bruise, and fracture in Cynda's body jabbed at her consciousness as all the healing energy she had managed to muster drained straight out of her toes. She dug out her earplugs and threw them at the castle wall.

Rain splattered against her face. The ground beneath her rumbled from the approach of the water.

Blood hammering, she yanked at Nick's bare arm again.

"Come on, come on, move! We're not dead yet."

No response.

Shit!

Her leathers, no more than two singed drapes hanging around her shoulders and hips, flapped against her skin as she tried to drag him away from the damned tidal wave steaming straight at them.

A tidal wave.

On a friggin' river.

With a house on top.

The sight of the house made Cynda let go of Nick.

Sibyl survivors hobbled past them around the corner of the castle, getting out of the way, trying to escape the inevitable flood and devastation.

Cynda couldn't stop staring at that house.

"Okay, whatever." She didn't even have enough energy left to smoke. Instead, she walked in front of Nick, turned her back on the wave, put her hands on his shoulders, and rested her cheek on his bare chest. "Just kill me now and do it quick. I can't take any more."

Nick's hands pressed into her waist. He turned them

sideways, and Cynda watched the approach of the wave, house and all. The rain stopped, but water from the wave sprayed toward them. Salty, yet fresh, too. Cool. Almost cold.

Shit.

In a night full of horror and miracles, when Russian wolves ate exploding demons on the battlefield behind her, earth Sibyls rocked the Connemara bogs, air Sibyls rode tornados into the castle, and winged Astaroths skewered each other by the light, by the light of the silvery moon—that house riding the crest of the freak wave had to be the weirdest thing Cynda had ever seen.

Except it wasn't a house.

She squinted, her breath tickling her cheeks as it bounced off Nick's bulging muscles.

It was a boat on top of that wave. A big boat, like a yacht.

Cynda lifted her head off Nick's chest, faced the water, and squinted harder.

Women dressed in black leather jumpsuits dotted the yacht's deck.

Her eyes opened wide. "It's a yacht full of Sibyls. Riding a tidal wave. In a *fucking river*."

Nick didn't respond at all.

Maybe she actually did die back there on the battlefield, fighting a hopeless battle with Cursons. This had to be the afterlife, and the Goddess's idea of a great big joke.

The wave slowed with a groan and loud swooshing noise, and the roar died completely away.

Water began to splash away from its base, and the swell gradually subsided, lowering the yacht until it rocked and slapped on the river's surface. More sucking sounds followed, as the Dawros River gradually regained its normal shape and depth between its banks.

Cynda heard a bump and realized the boat had beached in the shallows about three hundred yards from where she stood with Nick. It stayed upright and level, held in place by a steady flow of wind.

The Sibyls on board hurried up the deck, jumped to the ground in front of the castle, and ran to their right to join the remnants of the battle. Which, from the sound of things, was nearly finished.

It was the next group of people that caught Cynda's interest.

She studied them as they came toward her. Sparks danced along her skin, slowly at first, then faster and thicker as she got more certain.

An ache bloomed in her chest, but it was a happy ache, an excited ache, and her belly felt warm and suddenly much, much more relaxed.

"Creed. Riana. And Merilee. Andy!" She would have run to her triad sisters and friends if she hadn't been too banged up to move, and if Nick hadn't suddenly come to life, taken hold of her waist, and pulled her backward into him.

His lips pressed into her hair, and she laughed.

"My triad!" she shouted, managing a little blast of flame.

The fire lifted above them all, and showered down in bright orange sparks.

"What in the name of—" Cynda started to say as Creed jogged toward them with the others close behind.

"You okay, bro?" Creed came to a stop a few feet away, looking just like Nick with shorter hair, only clean with fresh jeans and a white T-shirt—and a little damp.

When Nick nodded, Creed said, "Andy can do water. And you're naked again."

"Fuck you" was Nick's astute comeback. He squeezed Cynda's waist. "Bet that was one hell of a ride from Atlanta." His hands moved upward and stroked Cynda's arms, like he was checking to be sure she was in one piece.

Cynda still wasn't sure she hadn't died and gone to some freaky-assed afterlife. "Andy . . . water . . ." She wished her brain would work. Wondered if it would ever function properly again. She pressed into Nick, letting him hug her—and hold her up.

Riana came to stand beside Creed, followed by Merilee, who was leading Andy.

Andy had her wild red hair tamed into a ponytail. And she had on Sibyl battle leathers, with what looked like a wide-barreled dart pistol holstered at her waist.

Definitely too weird for words.

The smell of stiff new leather, barely broken in, competed with lingering smoke and sulfur from the battle ending behind Cynda. In the moonlight, Creed and her triad . . . and Andy . . . looked silvery and powerful. Clear as day, Cynda could see them, yes, but she still couldn't believe they were standing right here with her.

"I'm so glad you're not hurt," Riana said, and then Nick let Cynda go, and her triad and Andy were hugging her, and she was hugging them.

From behind her, Cynda heard Creed say, "Remember that Legion guy Andy and I busted last year? The one who had that minor water talent?"

Cynda envisioned the little scum who had tried to kill them all by sucking the water out of their bodies, and Nick said, "Yeah. Frith Gregory. One of the townhouse servants."

Cynda finally let go of Riana, Merilee, and Andy, and Andy started fiddling with the grip of her bizarre dart gun. "When he attacked me, my body's water, he must have released some power inside me." A little rain started to fall again. Andy rolled her eyes, closed them, took a deep breath—and the rain gradually subsided. "My fluid balance went crazy inside, I was sick all the time, dehydrated or overhydrated—shit. I thought I was losing my mind, but I guess I was just finding my, uh, element."

Nick came to stand beside Cynda again. He leaned forward, almost pushing, but held on to her so she didn't fall. "Is that an HKP-11, Andy? An underwater pistol like the Special Boat Service frogmen carry?"

"It fires fifteen feet—about eight fathoms underwater," she said. "Out of water, it's good for about a hundred and sixty feet."

Nick looked like he wanted to snatch the HKP and start taking it apart.

"Oh, for the sake of the Goddess," Cynda muttered. Andy rolled her eyes, while Riana pinched her nose and Merilee hissed out a gust of wind.

"Have you fired it?" Nick started to reach for the stupid dart gun, but Cynda elbowed him in the breadbasket.

He made a little *ooof* sound and stepped back, turning her loose.

Cynda stood on her own power, pleased she didn't just fall and bust her ass on the castle grounds. Dart guns. Honestly. But she also thought about the plumbing in the townhouse. The exploding water at crime scenes. Even the heavy rains and snows, and the floods in the Southern states after Andy left on vacation.

Andy was the water "force" Cynda's triad had gone to confront.

Andy.

"I'm so glad to see all of you." Cynda heard the catch in her own voice. "I love you all so much. But about the water thing"—she giggled, then gulped air, and managed not to burst into hysterical, exhausted tears as she more or less fell back into Nick's arms—"that is so not something I can process right now."

Nick lifted her and cradled her to his chest, and for once, Cynda didn't fight him at all. It was too much of a relief not to have to support her own weight. Her entire being ached at the same time, especially the toes on her right foot. She gathered her healing energy again, released it through her body as best she could, and said, "Take me inside. Please. I've got to sleep."

Of course, Nick asked something else about that idiotic goddamned underwater gun instead.

Cynda rolled her eyes, closed them, and fell asleep before she even heard the answer.

She woke to the soothing feel of warm water bathing her foot, her ankle, then her leg. Her hair, face, and arms felt damp, and she was naked, lying on a soft, soft pallet, with a cushion under her head.

The smell of mint and healing sage, light but sweet, rose around her. When she opened her eyes, she saw high ceilings and stone walls with carved stone trim. Nearby, a fire crackled in a small, rounded fireplace, and Cynda knew she had to be in one of the infirmary's private rooms. Nothing felt broken save for a few toes. Lots of bruises and healing cuts, and her right ear still throbbed a little bit. All in all, though, she thought she was doing pretty well.

When she swallowed, she tasted the rich malty kick of Irish whiskey, and knew somebody had been feeding her that old-fashioned healing elixir. Probably Mother Eileen. She always did favor the stuff.

Soft pink sunlight splashed through the row of windows located near the ceiling.

"How long have I been out?" she mumbled.

"About twelve hours." Nick's handsome face shifted into view. His black hair was damp and loose like he'd just had a bath, and his dark eyes flickered with concern and affection. "Happy St. Patrick's Day, firebird."

When she tried to sit, she saw he was naked, and heat coursed through every part of her.

Nick pushed her down to her pallet with one finger. "You've got to rest."

He stroked her leg with a warm, wet cloth and a burst of sage filled the room. Nick must have been handling her nursing himself. She wasn't sure she had ever found any gesture so sweet, and her heart gave a little squeeze.

Other than the whole I'll-fight-and-fall-beside-you thing, of course.

She would never forget that, never let his choice to stay beside her while she defended her Sibyl family diminish in her mind.

He really was perfect.

He asked me about marriage before we charged out to die in that battle. And I think I said yes.

Thank the Goddess.

Nick moved the cloth lower and rubbed it gently across her sore toes. "Our reinforcements busted a cell of ten Legion masters in the woods around Kylemore. And the adepts and the surviving Mothers made it through the fight just fine, even if Mother Keara did kick Creed in the balls when he helped get them out of that crypt. I'd have paid money to see that."

Cynda grimaced and smoked as the healing waters seeped into her aching bones, but almost instantly, relief replaced the pain. Nick kept talking in an even, almost hypnotic voice, distracting her as he did his work. "My brother Jake and his buddies are camped with the air Sibyls on the battlefield. The air Sibyls don't like—"

"This castle," Cynda finished for him, trying out her toes, moving them without as much pain. "It's too confining, the way so much of it's closed in by the mountain. I've heard that before from Merilee a thousand times."

He moved the cloth to her other foot and kept up the careful bath. "All those Russian wolves and the earth Sibyls don't seem to give a damn. They've scrubbed the joint top to bottom, repaired a bunch of shit, and they're bunked in with the adepts and trainees. The women, I mean, not the wolves. And, uh, a few Cursons who showed up with Jake and crew to fight on our side."

Cynda smiled. "Jake came through."

"Yeah, yeah. I know I'll be hearing about that for a while." Nick's muscles rippled as gave her ankle a tweak, and his smile melted Cynda at whole new levels.

"No you won't." She stretched her neck to each side, pressing her shoulders into the soft pallet, loosening up. "I'm so glad he's all right, and with us." She sighed. "This ought to be an interesting few months. Astaroths. Cursons. And Andy—and don't say it, you big ass. I know she has a cool gun."

Nick grinned and eased his cloth up Cynda's leg to her knees.

Goddess, that felt good.

"Don't forget Delilah Moses," he said. "She's hanging out with the Mothers and visiting with Max. When the Mothers let him go, he got himself busted over in Connemara. Delilah says he's better off in jail. That way, he's staying out of trouble."

Cynda groaned.

But Nick kept rubbing her knee with that cloth. The sage swirled through her nose, then her mind. Her thoughts gradually left images of jails and battles and problems and tidal waves as Nick worked the cloth back down her calf, changed sides again, and moved from foot to ankle to calf, then thigh. Her thoughts gradually left everything but Nick and the warmth of the fire and the growing, just-right heat of his touch.

Ripples of pleasure coursed over Cynda's skin, followed by small flames that heated the sage water and helped it sink deep to where she needed the healing energy.

Her eyes drifted shut.

How could the man be so big, so strong, yet so absolutely gentle?

Cynda realized she was wet everywhere, even places he hadn't bathed.

When he moved his cloth to her hip, she shuddered. She wanted his hands on her everywhere, and his mouth. She wanted to feel his weight, feel proof that they were alive, that the nightmare had ended for now, and she was safe, finally and truly.

Nick's hand slid around the patch of hair between her legs, brushing the cloth over her belly and chest, trickling warm droplets down her sides.

His tongue followed the rivulets, and Cynda gasped. Her eyes flew open, and she bit her lip.

She held herself motionless, soaking in the water, soaking in Nick's sensual progress as he slipped the rag up and down, back and forth, kissing everywhere he bathed. On her chest now, between her breasts, closer and closer to her waiting nipples. They started to tingle, but he stayed away, just missing with every pass.

"Don't tease me," she whispered, already near to breaking out in flames all over.

"I never tease." His voice sounded as warm as the water he trailed across the pulsing nubs.

Cynda groaned and reached up and touched them herself.

Nick's instant rumble of arousal vibrated from her shoulders to the wet spots his cloth had left on her thighs.

She pinched her nipples to tease *him*, rubbing them back and forth. The tingling doubled, as did the fire in her belly and the moisture between her legs.

"If you do that again, honey . . ."

She glanced at Nick, at his heavy-lidded, hungry expression, his bare muscled chest.

So handsome.

And naked.

How did she get this lucky?

I am Irish. And it is *St. Patrick's Day.*

With a grin, she did that again.

Her whole body trembled as Nick dropped the cloth on the pallet. He pushed her hands to the side, straddled her in one fluid movement, and leaned forward, pressing his erection into her belly.

Heart skipping, she slipped her hands into his hair and pulled him to meet her. When he kissed her, she wanted more, had to have more, *now*.

Her sensitive nipples rubbed his hard chest as he slid his tongue into her mouth, answering her like he read her mind.

Then his lips moved down her jaw to her chin, then to her neck and ear.

Smoke billowed around the tiny room, playing in the sunlight, swirling past them in curls and puffs. Cynda breathed it in, smelling Nick's salty ocean musk, and sage, and the faint touch of whiskey still in her own breath.

Braced on his knees and one powerful arm, he found her breast with his free hand and took up where her own fingers had left off, squeezing and teasing until her center pulsed with raw need.

When his fingers flicked across her hard nipple, she arched her back, moaning. "Don't make me wait, Nick. Not this time. I need you too much."

"Beautiful," he murmured, pinching first one nipple, then the other, sending hot flashes of fire down Cynda's thighs, straight to the spot where she wanted him most. "You mean everything to me."

He kissed her.

Cynda forced her hands down, shoving past his chest, positioning his throbbing cock between her thighs. She ached to feel him inside her, tensing, waiting, wanting it so much she thought she might fry into nothing but sparkles and ash.

"Please now," she said into his mouth, digging her nails across his rock-hard ass as flames danced over the ceiling above them. "Please."

Nick shifted his weight, let go of her breast, and stared at her as he moved himself into position.

The feel of his eyes on her face, her body, the soft touch of his cock at her sensitive center—too much. She shook from the force of her own heat.

"Please," she whispered again.

Nick rocked forward and buried himself inside her.

Hot. Deep.

His dark eyes gazed at her like he wanted nothing else in the universe but this, but her.

Yes.

He stretched her as wide as she could go, filled her, exactly right. Her knees jerked upward and her chin snapped back, stretching her neck as she took him, held him, squeezed her channel around him with all her strength. The sensation of flesh on flesh drove her straight to the total agony of wanting more, and more, and still more.

He found her mouth with his and pumped his cock, keeping his lips firm on hers.

Cynda held him tight. She rocked to meet him and the fire raging through her threatened to burn them both to pieces.

Nick's skin glowed as he sucked in her flames and kept driving himself harder, building speed, just like she wanted.

Her body vibrated with every thrust. The slick, fast sound of their joining seemed to echo off the stone walls, and the fire in the hearth roared along with the blood in her veins.

I'm alive.

He's alive.

Cynda tore her lips from his and bit his ear. She

wrapped her arms around his neck, lifted her knees higher, and held on, whispering, "I love you."

Orange light filled the space. Fire seemed to burst out of both of them. She felt so close to Nick. Consumed by him. And she wanted it that way.

"More." She tugged at his hair. "I can't get enough."

Balanced on his strong arms, he drove into her. The muscles in his neck and shoulders bulged from the force. With each sweeping plunge, Nick seemed even more a part of her.

Tears slipped down her cheeks as she blazed everywhere, throwing fire, swirling it around the room until it wrapped them both in a hot orange haze.

"Cynda." His rough whisper joined with the crackle of flames, sweeter than any music.

She crushed herself against him, letting him inside her soul as her body seemed to split wide open.

Her hips bucked.

She moaned loud and low as sparks danced across the insides of her lids. Sheets of flame washed up and back, up and back as she clamped on Nick's cock, drawing out every second of that perfect ecstasy.

His body tensed, and he let out a growl as he spent himself inside her. She loved the way his eyes closed, the way his jaw locked. *She* gave him that pleasure. He was hers, right now, and always.

"I love you," she said again as she went limp on the pallet, jerking each time he moved inside her, finishing, bringing them both back to earth with a soft, soft landing.

He stayed inside her and she kept him there, never intending to release him.

His lips brushed her chin, her cheeks, her nose and eyes.

The last thing she heard before she fell back into deep, endless sleep was "I love you, too, firebird."

(28)

On the third morning after the battle to save the Sibyls, while Cynda was out working with her triad, the adepts, and the initiates to rebuild the castle, the Irish Mothers came for Nick.

He knew who it was when the knock sounded on the arched door of the small stone room he had been sharing with Cynda.

Instinct. And that surge of elemental power always present when the Mothers were around.

The strange thing was, he had been expecting the Mothers to visit him ever since he kissed Cynda goodbye and sent her on her way this morning.

No sense wasting time.

He got up from his meditations, did a last gut-check with Gideon, walked to his door, and opened it.

Outside, Mother Keara was waiting for him, along with Mother Eileen and the two Nick hadn't met except to carry them to the crypt during the big fight. They had on their green robes, and each woman had her white hair fastened behind her head. Mother Yana from Russia was also present, and Mother Anemone from Greece, wearing the colors of their order.

Elemental power hovered around them, so thick and strong it made the air shimmer. The scent of spice and smoke, ocean and oils, ice and forests, and even wolf musk mingled together, piquing Nick's senses, bringing to mind ancient chants and secret rituals, hidden scrolls and stones carved with runes no one could read. Knowledge older than time. Somehow *outside* of time, separate from it and protected in ways he might never understand.

All six women greeted him with a polite nod, showing respect even as they came to take his freedom.

He appreciated that much, at least.

They stepped aside to let him out, and Nick went quietly, making no protest when they led him deep inside the castle—or when they closed him into an elementally locked stone cell with a stone slab for a bed.

They left him alone without so much as an apology or explanation, but that didn't bother him, either.

He had been expecting that, too.

If Nick had learned nothing else through his love for Cynda, he had grasped the fact that, right or wrong, fire Sibyls never backed down from their chosen course of action.

Now more than ever, with their ranks decimated and their stronghold breached and broken, they needed to protect their own.

In their shoes, he might have made the same choice.

Then again, maybe not.

Nick sat cross-legged on the stone bed and sighed. His heart felt heavy in his chest, and his gut tightened at what he soon would have to do.

In a short time, the women of Motherhouse Ireland had become as much his family as Creed and Jake. He'd still die for them, without any complaints.

He could only hope that in the end, they would feel the same way about him.

Nick also hoped that when it came time to make his choice, Cynda would forgive him.

Fire roared like an orange cyclone around Cynda, blurring her view of the Mothers.

She couldn't believe it. She could *not* believe they wanted to take her to the meditation rooms and lock her away from her triad for a day.

Bullshit.

She stood by the big arched windows at the back of the castle's highest chamber and blew flames directly out of her arms and shoulders. Her clothes were already ash, and she didn't give a single hot damn.

Beside Cynda, Riana raised one hand. The stone floor rattled and shook.

On Cynda's other side, Merilee narrowed her eyes. Wind howled into the mix, throwing dust and clattering stones around the meeting chamber they had just finished clearing and repairing.

The adepts who had been helping Cynda's triad fled, trailing smoke as they went and slamming the big chamber door behind them. To their credit, the youngest initiates had taken off the second the six Mothers had filed into the room.

Smart girls.

Mother Yana approached the triad first, heading directly for Riana, her balance oddly undisturbed by the rattling stone floor. She reached Riana and took her hands.

Through the growl of her fire and the low rumble of Merilee's wind, Cynda heard the oldest Russian Mother's words.

"Ve cannot interfere in this, child. Come. Stand aside. Ve'll stay to support your pestle, but you must let her Mothers do as they see fit."

Riana's look said, *Go to hell*. The chamber rattled again. Several stones on the floor split down the middle with a sound like rifle cracks.

Cynda had no doubt that if Riana had been armed, she would have pulled her daggers, even on the Mother who had raised her.

Her chest tightened with pride, with resolve.

My triad. My family. They will not *separate us, especially not now.*

"Bring Nick here." Riana's tone matched the dark depths of the earth energy boiling off her body in solid, almost tangible waves. She directed her comments to the Irish Mothers. "Bring him now. And don't you dare put a hand on Cynda. There will be no 'cooling-off period' or contemplation time."

Cynda's fire flared in agreement. No friggin' meditation and thinking and calming down.

Let's get this done.

Mother Anemone made an attempt to move toward Merilee, but wind kicked at the statuesque woman so hard the chamber door behind her smashed open against the outer wall, wrenched off its hinges, and slammed to the floor. The windows behind Merilee exploded outward. Bits of glass and wood rained to the stone floor behind the triad.

Blond hair sticking straight up from the force and pressure of her elemental outburst, Merilee kept her cold blue gaze on her eldest Mother, and the Irish Mothers, too. "We're not playing this, ladies. Don't even think it. If you want to have a *cruinniú,* if you want to conclave, then we're doing it right here, right now, today. Cynda's not going anywhere with any of you."

Mother Anemone's blue eyes narrowed in response.

She looked half-furious, half-impressed as she glanced from Merilee to Mother Yana and Riana, and then to the Irish Mothers. She didn't speak.

She also didn't take another step toward Merilee.

Mother Keara moved away from Mother Anemone, and her sharp eyes focused on Cynda.

Blazing green orbs, wide and wild and full of fire and power.

Cynda didn't flinch or surrender even a spark of her protective fire. If they wanted her, let them come and get her. She'd like to see *that* happen. Heat surged through her, barely bridled. When she was a child, Mother Keara's glares had broken through her temper every single time, but this wasn't about temper. It was about truth and choices, and about Cynda's right to decide on the people she loved.

I'm not backing down.

Mother Eileen and the other Irish Mothers shifted into position behind Mother Keara, facing Cynda. One put a hand on Mother Keara's shoulder.

Mother Keara shrugged off the contact and came forward a few steps, braving the edges of Cynda's firestorm.

The old woman's huge power slammed into Cynda, tugging at the cyclone, jerking at the flames, trying to draw off some of the fire. Cynda ground her teeth. Pushed back with her own heat. Shoved.

Hard. Harder.

Sweat broke across her forehead.

Cynda raised both fists and let her fire fly into the roaring cyclone.

She couldn't win this fight, but by God she wouldn't lose, either. Not if she had to give up her last breath to her fire energy and drop dead right where she stood. After charging out on that battlefield with Nick, expecting to lose him and everything else, this felt like child's play.

To Cynda's surprise, Mother Keara blinked first.

She eased out of the cyclone and stopped trying to control it.

Was that a smile? I swear she smiled.

"I'm takin' this to mean, *a chroí,* that you're in agreement with your triad," Mother Keara shouted over the fire's angry snarl. "If we're to have our *cruinniú,* you'd rather it be now instead of tomorrow."

"Yes," Cynda shouted back, still pissed beyond measure. "That's what I want. Now go get Nick."

Another few seconds went by. Then Mother Keara lifted both hands, palm out, and said, "Done. *Cruinniú* now."

Stomach tight, muscles throbbing from the heat spent on her fire, Cynda let go of her elemental energy.

Flames bounced against the ceiling and floor, then drew back into her body.

She shook even after Riana quit rattling the floor and Merilee let the wind die away to a soft breeze.

So this was it.

Her fate would be decided in minutes.

Her service to the Motherhouse, Nick's service, none of that mattered.

Mother Keara still wouldn't approve their union.

She was going to expel Cynda—or try to.

Well, let her.

Because I'm not friggin' going.

Cynda gazed at Mother Keara, aching down in her depths, feeling as if someone was trying to tear out her heart. She hated the old woman for forcing this issue, but loved her, too, the way a child always loves her mother—even when that mother is *wrong.*

Slowly, watching for any sign of sudden moves or bursts of energy, Riana, Cynda, and Merilee locked arms.

The Mothers moved quietly past them to the head of

the chamber, ignoring the broken glass and bits of wood, and turned to face the triad.

To the youngest Mother, Mother Keara said, "Fetch the demon, and I need a chair." She rubbed her lower back. "I'm gettin' too damned old for all this hoo-ha."

About half an hour later, the Mothers were seated in chairs at the far end of the chamber, and the adepts had carried in a scarred, charred wooden table and placed it in front of them. One adept stood behind each Mother, in case the women needed something, or had an errand that needed running.

And to learn, Cynda thought.

To see what happens when a Sibyl goes against her Mothers' choices.

She had dressed herself in jeans and a white tunic after burning off her other clothes, and she stood on the left of the chamber with Riana and Merilee, holding their hands. Every few minutes, tears slid down her cheeks. There was nothing she could do about that, even if it made her mad as hell.

She didn't want to cry about this. She wanted to pull Merilee, Riana, and Nick behind her, back them slowly out of the castle, and blow shit up.

Like that would help anything.

But it would damned sure feel good.

The chamber door opened.

Heart pounding, Cynda let go of her triad sisters and turned, expecting to see Nick.

Instead, it was Andy, hair down, sleepy eyes half-open, dressed in a canary yellow robe. An air adept in blue robes walked with her, doing her best to contain the ever-widening water slick spreading out from Andy's feet.

Andy kept scooting away from the girl, like she had

no idea what the hell was going on. When she drew even with Riana, Merilee, and Cynda, she glared at the three of them and jerked a thumb toward her companion. "This little twit keeps calling me a mother and telling me I have to be at this kri-new. What in the living fuck is a kri-new, and why did I have to get up and put on a Big Bird suit to come to it?"

"It's a conclave." Merilee reached out and straightened the shoulder of Andy's robe. "You're the only water Sibyl, so that makes you the new Antilla Mother—uh, New York Mother, I guess. Water Sibyls always wore yellow robes. You're representing your element."

Andy leaned into Merilee's face. "I'm getting my gun if anybody calls me a mother again. *That's* what I'm doing. Got me?"

Merilee held up both hands and shrugged.

For the first time all morning, Cynda felt a little like laughing. Since she didn't want to drown in a spontaneous waterfall, she refrained.

Riana had to look away to keep herself composed as Andy and her nervous little attendant made their way to the table with the other Mothers.

When Andy got settled at the table's far right end, Cynda glanced over her shoulder—and saw Nick standing on the other side of the room, gazing back at her with those intense black eyes.

Her chest squeezed tight the way it always did when he looked at her like that. Her hands tingled, craving the steel of his chest, the silk of his hair on her fingertips. She wanted to kiss him and hug him and apologize for all the Sibyls, for this entire unfair and ridiculous mess.

But he didn't look angry at all, or even hurt.

He just looked handsome as hell in those jeans and that dark green sleeveless T-shirt, with his long hair loose on his shoulders.

And a little worried.

"Order," called Mother Yana, the oldest Sibyl in the room and the senior Mother.

Cynda tore her eyes from Nick and forced herself to face the great table. Smoke rose from her tunic, and her right sleeve was already history. At least she was barefoot. No boots to melt.

The glare off Andy's yellow robes made her shake her head—that and the fact that Andy's eyes kept drifting shut, popping open only when her attendant nudged her shoulder. Cynda figured for that air Sibyl's sake, it was a good thing Andy didn't have her SIG and cuffs handy.

Mother Yana pushed herself to her feet and met Cynda's gaze.

"Cynda Flynn, Mother Keara has informed us that she varned you of the consequences of pursuing a relationship vith Nick Lowell, a Curson demon who has not submitted to the ritual to make him safe in our presence." The ancient woman's smile wasn't unpleasant. More sympathetic than anything. "Is this true?"

Cynda's heart started a hard, relentless pounding, but she held her head high even as Riana and Merilee squeezed both of her hands until they were damned near numb. "Yes."

Mother Yana sat and lowered her gaze to her fingers.

When Cynda glanced at Nick, his head was high, too, and his shoulders squared. He stood like a soldier at parade rest, giving up nothing with his expression or body language.

That one's mine. Just look at him. Who wouldn't *want that?*

Mother Eileen spoke next, bringing Cynda's attention back to the front of the room. "When faced with the choice between your triad and life as a Sibyl and this man, you chose the relationship."

After carefully reclaiming her hands before she lost circulation, Cynda took a very slow, very warm centering breath. She focused on Mother Keara, and made sure her voice sounded loud and strong when she said, "I chose Nick. *And* my triad. *And* my life as a Sibyl. I love them all, and I won't surrender any of them."

Mother Keara's face went flat. She stared at Cynda with those blazing green eyes, and frowned. "Nick Lowell is this important to you, that you would set aside all that you've ever known? You would surrender everything to love him?"

Once more, Cynda glanced at Nick.

This time, he was looking straight at her, black eyes calm, but waiting.

Her stomach burned hot. Smoke drifted off her shoulders and arms. For a moment she couldn't breathe, but she balled her fists and answered Mother Keara. "Yes. Nick's worth that much to me. But I refuse to give up my triad and my connection to fire." She calmed herself as best she could before the smoke got too thick, and made herself continue. "I don't mean you any disrespect, Mother. I love you very much. But I'm a Sibyl now, and a member of the North Manhattan fighting triad, and that's what I'll be when I die. If you want any part of my identity, you'll have to take it by force. I won't be handing it over."

"She's ours," Riana confirmed, moving in close in case they needed to defend themselves.

Against six Mothers.

Shit!

Merilee pulled in tight with Cynda, too, and a breeze stirred at Cynda's bare ankles. "You can't have her. You'll have to fight us all."

Mother Yana smiled openly this time, at Riana. Cynda saw her wink and clasp her hands together, as if she was fiercely proud of the strength of Riana's triad.

Mother Anemone kept her eyes on the table, but Cynda thought the woman might be smiling, too.

Andy was sound asleep. When she snored, the air Sibyl attendant rolled her eyes and nudged her shoulder again. Lightning fast, Andy grabbed the girl's robe collar, pulled her close, and whispered, "Don't *do* that, okay? Last warning."

Smoke played around Mother Keara's shoulders. She focused on Nick this time. "And you, Curson. Nick Lowell. We do appreciate all you've done for us. Don't be thinkin' we're ungrateful."

Nick stood motionless, arms still folded, gaze forward now, at the table and the Mothers. He didn't say a word.

Excellent choice, Cynda thought, blood heating at the injustice.

She still could not believe any of this was happening. After they got through it in one piece, she'd need to blow up a *bunch* of shit, just to let off enough steam to sleep tonight. After a long, sweaty round or two with Nick.

Nowhere in her mind would she consider the loss of her triad, or her Sibyl identity, or Nick. It wasn't happening. Wouldn't happen. All that fear had left Cynda on the battlefield, and right that second, even staring down a table of women who might try to wreck her life, she felt as strong as any Mother.

Mother Keara wasn't finished with Nick. The old woman's green eyes bored into him with her next question. "Since *a chroí* wishes to stay in her triad, stay a Sibyl, and keep you as well, will you submit yourself to Motherhouse Russia and undergo the ritual to make yourself safe?"

Cynda started to say something in protest, but Riana's grip on her elbow slowed her down.

Nick kept his stance, and he didn't look at her. Her body tensed, waiting for his response, praying he wouldn't agree to that insane, dangerous procedure.

"I will not submit to the ritual," he said.

Relief slammed into Cynda. Fire lifted off her toes and fingers, and she let it go with a rush of breath. The flames dropped to the floor, and Riana's earth energy quickly snuffed them out.

Nick let his arms relax against his sides and faced Cynda. His expression softened, and he let her see that kindness, the love and gentleness they shared each time they touched. "I do plan to marry you, firebird. As soon as you're ready. I'm not going away unless they kill me."

Before Cynda could tell him she was ready right now, Mother Keara shot to her feet and slammed both hands against the table.

Cynda jumped. Yanked a load of fire energy toward herself.

She raised her own hands and gathered the heat, hating the idea of fighting Mother Keara, but ready to do it. Smoke poured from her neck and face. She tasted flames on her tongue, felt them flow into her lungs when she breathed.

Beside her, Riana and Merilee drew their elements toward them.

Nick resumed his at-rest position, tight line, muscles tensed, his skin glowing a light gold.

The man was ready for anything.

At the front of the room, Mother Keara broke out laughing.

The sound echoed against stone walls.

Andy swiveled her head to take in what was happening, obviously confused.

"Good for you," Mother Keara said to Nick. "I knew she made a good choice."

Cynda blinked.

She eased back on the fireball she had been forming, then let it go out altogether. The stone-hard tightness in her chest loosened a fraction, but she had no idea what Mother Keara would do or say next.

"What's going on?" Andy asked, tugging at her wet yellow robe.

Nick seemed too surprised to move.

Cynda felt the same way.

Judging by the quick disappearance of earth and air energy, so did Merilee and Riana.

Mother Keara spent a few moments glaring in Andy's direction, briefly reminding Cynda of all the ancient stories about how water Sibyls and fire Sibyls didn't always get along.

When Mother Keara once more faced the room, she spoke to Cynda. "It's rare for a fire Sibyl to marry, and rarer still for that union to succeed." She gestured to Nick. "If you weren't willin' to risk everything for this man, your relationship wouldn't be lastin' more than a few months—if that."

Cynda lowered her hands and stood between her triad sisters, giving off tiny puffs of smoke. Once more, she was feeling relieved. Maybe. Still confused. A little pissed at Mother Keara, at all the Mothers.

Was this just another lesson, like so many before?

But she didn't think so. Mother Keara would never hurt her casually, or for sport.

No.

This had been an important test, to be certain Cynda was ready for the monumental choice she was making, to love Nick, to have a life with him. She reached inside herself and soothed the heat roiling through her insides, spreading it through her body to take the edge off her tension.

When she turned her attention to Nick, the warmth inside her doubled. He had straightened, come out of his ready posture, and he was studying Mother Keara intently as she spoke again, this time to him.

"Any man willin' to surrender even the smallest piece of himself could never survive life with a fire Sibyl."

Mother Keara smiled. "If I don't miss my guess, you'll do just fine, Nick Lowell, even with a Sibyl as strong as my *a chroí*."

"Thank you," he said, still standing straight and tall, muscled arms flexed.

Simple. Brief. Totally Nick.

Cynda broke away from Riana and Merilee and crossed the room to join him. She couldn't believe the force of the emotion swirling through her body, just as powerful as any fire she had ever touched. She really did love him, with every bit of her being. And it felt damned good.

When he saw her coming, his eyes softened, and he pulled her to him, holding her with one arm around her shoulder as they both faced the big table.

Instead of ending the conclave, Mother Keara reached into her robe pocket and drew out a bell. When she rang it, the chamber door opened, and an adept came in bearing a silver tray with a chalice, a plate of bread, and what looked like two small metal bands about the size of . . . rings. As the adept approached the table, Cynda saw the ornate metalwork on the bands, which had been fashioned out of a series of Celtic knot patterns. The metal itself was steely gray, so bright it looked almost white in the sunlight.

Is that tungsten?

The metal that won't burn?

Mother Keara's tone grew considerably lighter. Lilting. Actually—happy? "In older times, young couples in love often chose handfasting, to declare their love and bind themselves together for a year and a day. At the end of that time, they decided if they wanted to join for another year, for eternity, or go their separate ways."

Oh. My. Goddess.

Cynda's heart started to pound again.

She cut her eyes to Nick.

No smile. No expression at all.

What are you feeling?

Her heart pounded harder.

"Usually, cords of leather or cloth were used, but leather and cloth won't be lastin' long around our kind." Mother Keara held up the bands. "We have these for the ceremony. They're a bit more durable."

Dumbfounded, Cynda stared at Nick.

When he looked at her, he winked. "I'm ready if you are."

Cynda's mouth came open. She just stood there like a huge idiot, gaping at Nick, barely processing when Mother Keara said, "Cynda Flynn, do you come here of your own will and desire, to join with this man?"

Somebody nudged Cynda.

Riana. Or Merilee. They were both behind her now.

"Yes, I do," she choked out, heart beating so hard she was sure she'd explode any second. Smoke billowed off her feet and hands. She needed all her control to slow it down. And she didn't slow it much.

"Who accompanies you, and offers you blessings?" Mother Keara asked, sounding way past happy and pleased with herself, puffing up a little, like a preening bird.

"We do," Riana and Merilee chorused.

Andy raised her hand at the table. Water dripped from her fingertips. "And me."

Cynda's head swam.

Nick faced her and smiled, and stroked her arms with his strong but gentle hands.

There's no one but you, his gaze told her. *You're mine now, and always.*

"Approach me," Mother Keara commanded.

Nick offered Cynda his arm, and she took it. The pounding in her heart gave way to a light, hot sensation, like a ring of perfect flames fueling every beat and breath.

Together, they walked to the table and the Mothers, and stood, arm in arm.

Mother Keara beamed now. Cynda had hardly ever seen the woman look so excited, and that doubled her happiness. "By air, fire, earth ... and water ... may your love be natural and strong, constant and eternal. Let wisdom guide you, let your wills bind you, let love and passion bring you joy."

She picked up the larger of the two bands. "Nick, I don't have the power to bind you. Cynda, this right belongs to you. If it's your wish to join this man to you, speak now, and ask him to place this ring on his finger if he agrees."

Hand shaking, Cynda took the ring and felt its cool strength.

Yes.

Tungsten.

A ring that won't ever burn, no matter how hot things get.

She gazed at Nick.

Just like him.

"I join you to me," she whispered, and held up the ring. "Do you agree?"

Nick slid his finger into the band.

Cynda stared at the beautiful metal circle and tried to breathe.

"Cynda, I don't have the power to bind you," Mother Keara said. "Nick, this right belongs to you. If it's your wish to join this woman to you, speak now, and ask her to place this ring on her finger if she agrees."

Nick picked up the smaller band and held it up. He locked eyes with Cynda, and in a deep, spine-tingling bass, said, "I join you to me, firebird. Do you agree?"

Shaking so badly she almost couldn't hit the target, Cynda slid her finger into the ring. Nick kept her hand in his, resting his band over hers. Joined. By the bands.

By the heart. Cynda still couldn't breathe. The metal felt cool against Cynda's hand, so she warmed it. Nick's hand gave off a soft golden glow in response to her heat. He dipped his head and kissed her fingers before turning her loose.

Dazed, too happy to even begin to think straight, Cynda watched as Nick took the ceremonial drink from the chalice, then offered it to her. She sipped the rich liquid, and almost coughed.

Fire came out of her ears.

Literally.

Goddamn. Irish whiskey.

Mother Eileen gave her a wink.

That cleared her thoughts a little.

Her knees threatened to buckle, but not completely because of the joy of the moment.

Nick ate a bite of bread from the plate, then offered her a bite, which she accepted, kissing his fingers as she swallowed.

Fire broke out along Mother Keara's arms, then ringed her completely as she smiled. "In the name of the Goddess who resides within all of us, and by the fire in my heart and soul, I witness this handfasting, as do we all."

"As do we all," the Mothers proclaimed, with Riana, Merilee, and Andy, too.

"Cynda and Nick, may your love endure." Mother Keara's smile got even broader. "And may we all be back here in a year and a day, to do this again—bigger and better."

Nick pulled Cynda to him and took her lips with his, joining his mouth to hers soft at first, then harder and hotter and more demanding. She didn't even try to control her fire as she pressed herself against him, surrendering everything to his glow, his embrace. The scent of ocean and musk washed over her. Wintergreen stung her tongue as she tasted him.

Mine. Mine forever.

Her body ached for more. Always more, with this man. She knew she'd never have enough. A year and a day, ten years and ten days, forever. Never enough.

From somewhere a million miles away, Mother Keara said, "This conclave is over. Go in peace."

Cynda kept kissing Nick, vaguely aware that her triad was leaving. That Andy and the other Mothers were leaving.

Go in peace.

But she wanted to stay right here with Nick, forever. Or anywhere. Even a shack in the woods would be just fine with her.

Nick pulled back and gazed at her, dark eyes dancing with his own inner fire. "Guess we should go, too, firebird."

Oh, did that ever *sound like a plan. The perfect end to the perfect handfasting.*

"Not you, Nick," Mother Keara said, startling Cynda out of her haze. "You can't go yet."

She came from behind the table and approached Nick, flames dancing at both shoulders. "Tonight marks the spring equinox, one of the four times a year a Sibyl can't control her own reproductive abilities. Sacred nights belong to the Goddess, you understand, so we need to talk."

Nick went stiff in Cynda's arm. "About what?"

Mother Keara's green eyes glittered, and Cynda had a sinking feeling about where this little conversation was headed. So much for an entire day of hot sex—she'd have to wait a few hours.

Damnit.

"We must discuss sex, of course," Mother Keara said to Nick. "Conception. The facts of life as they pertain to fire Sibyls and Cursons."

Nick's neck flushed a deep red.

The color slid slowly to his cheeks, finally claiming his whole face. "Cynda." His voice sounded unnaturally quiet as he let her go. "Help me out, here?"

She rubbed her palms against his T-shirt, enjoying his muscled chest, and brushed his stubbled cheek with her lips.

This man.

I'll love him until the day I die.

But some things, she just couldn't save him from enduring.

Cynda stretched on her toes, pressed her mouth to Nick's ear and murmured, "I'll see you back in our room."

For a second, Nick looked hopeful.

Cynda sighed and gave him a little push. "As for the sex talk with the Irish Mothers . . . sorry, big man. You're on your own."

Acknowledgments

As always, I extend my appreciation to my readers. I hope this story burned you up in all the right ways.

A loud and special thank-you goes out to New York City's Irish Arts Center, and specifically to instructor Alexei Kondratiev, who offered his expertise in correcting the Irish words and phrases used in this book.

Extensive thanks to Cheyenne McCray, who forfeited a vacation to critique this and set me straight. Also, to Tara Donn, for her time, skill, and knowledge. I count on you ladies more than you know. Without you, these stories would never sparkle.

Again, I had the benefit of two editors on this piece. First, my thanks to Charlotte Hersher, who slipped this story in under the wire. Additional thanks to Kate Collins for working on this story. I'm blessed to have such intelligent, insightful women to guide my writing.

To my wonderful agent Nancy Yost, I extend tremendous respect and appreciation. You're still making it fun, and I owe you even more chocolate.

Turn the page to catch a sneak peek at

Bound by Light

the next sizzling novel in the trilogy by
Anna Windsor!

(1)

*April, twenty-five months after the
Battle of Motherhouse Ireland*

There were some situations where violence and sarcasm just weren't appropriate.

For the life of her, Merilee couldn't think of a single one of them, especially not at three in the morning, confronting a naked demon in her bathroom, *after* her leather jumpsuit had been burned off from the waist down.

Thank you, Cynda, my dear, sweet triad sister. I so love night patrol with a psychotic pregnant fire Sibyl.

If it hadn't been for her friend Andy's relatively new elemental control over water, Merilee might have lost the top half of her jumpsuit to Cynda's hormonal outburst, along with everything else. No more patrols for Cynda—not until the fire Sibyl delivered her little spawn of Satan and settled down again. Well, as settled down as fire Sibyls ever got.

Merilee leaned past the door she had just opened and glared at the tall figure partially hidden by billowing mists from the dripping shower. "Hey. Surfer boy. Get away from my tub before I shoot holes in all your wings—and a few things you don't want to talk about."

For a long moment, the demon didn't move, keeping his well-defined back to her. Beads of water formed across his muscled shoulders and slipped down perfect, touchable skin. Merilee caught a delicious, exotic scent, something spicy and unique, almost Caribbean.

Her heart rate increased.

Not familiar.

But then again, she was exhausted, singed, and pissed off, so she couldn't really count on her memory.

Which Astaroth was this? They all looked alike when they deigned to be visible. They all acted alike, too. Arrogant, a little flighty and air-headed, and entitled.

Damn it, whichever demon this was, he knew better than to use her bathroom. The winged surfer boys preferred the fourth floor of the large townhouse on New York's Upper East Side just as she did, because it was brighter and more open, with plenty of windows and terrace doors to access the sky and open air.

Only, Merilee lived here in "Head Case Quarters," the combination OCU headquarters and boardinghouse. These Astaroth visions of perfection just passed through after getting rescued and regaining their talismans, until OCU processed their paperwork and they found housing.

They ought to show a little respect. Which, of course, they never do.

Still keeping his back to her, the demon reached a tanned, sculpted arm to his left and grabbed her favorite fluffy yellow towel off the rack.

Merilee stared at the darkened skin.

What the hell?

Were those faint lines scars?

They were . . . and becoming more visible by the moment.

But Astaroths never had scars. And Astaroths were always pale. They never stayed visible or solid long enough to get tanned. Even when they took solid form, they retained that translucent, pearl-white quality—which this one didn't seem to have. But he had the height and build, and the dead-giveaway blond hair they all seemed to manifest in human form, and he was wear-

ing a thick gold chain around his neck. Not to mention
the fact his presence made her Sibyl tattoo tingle along
the inside of her right forearm, and her instincts shout
demon so intensely the sensation used up what little energy she had left.

Yep.

Tanned and scarred or not, the trespasser was an Astaroth.

And now he was wrapping her towel around his ta-
pered waist, covering powerful thighs and a rock-hard
ass any woman would die to squeeze.

Maybe it was the yummy Caribbean smell or the tan,
or the fact nightmares, pregnant triad sisters, patrols,
and emergencies wrecked her sleep on a regular basis,
but Merilee barely contained an urge to let loose a little
burst of wind. Aimed just right, she could flap the towel
and get a second look at that fine behind.

She actually lifted her hands and stretched her fingers
through the doorway before she caught herself and
rubbed her temples instead. With a sigh, she said, "You're
probably new, and I know you're drawn to the windows
and light, but the library and hall bathroom up here are
mine during night hours. Visiting Astaroth demons stay
on the second or third floor. We've got lots of empty
rooms—with their very own bathrooms."

The Astaroth turned to face her.

Merilee, who had been about to ask him less politely
to get out of her space, clamped her teeth together.

She drank in the sight, from his damp, close-cropped
hair to his slick, unbelievably chiseled chest and the talisman necklace and ring hanging in plain view. More
scars covered his chest—wounds from what, she didn't
know, but she could tell they would have hurt like ever-
loving hell.

Her eyes drifted lower. To the way that towel barely
clung to his waist, tempting her yet again to use her ele-

mental powers to move the cloth. Droplets of water slipped into the trace of blond curls just above the towel's edge, and Merilee couldn't help seeing herself pressing her lips against his tight abs, licking him dry.

Her entire body shuddered with the force of that image.

He folded his arms and studied her with eyes unlike any demon's she had ever seen. Brighter, yet also serious, with traces of something like sadness—and the *color*. A pastel indigo, almost gray, like storm clouds rolling across a bright sky.

Steam flowed around Merilee's face as it escaped from the bathroom.

Thank the goddesses of Olympus, one and all.

Otherwise, the supernaturally handsome Astaroth might have noticed when her cheeks flushed red-hot.

As it was, he surveyed Merilee's burned, crumbling jumpsuit top, the remnants of the pashmina shawl she used to conceal her weapons, her yellow lace panties, and her bare, soot-streaked legs. The demon didn't seem at all concerned about the olivewood reflex bow and quiver full of arrows still slung over her shoulders, visible because the shawl had been so singed and melted.

His gaze held her so deeply, so totally, he might have been appraising her body, her soul, hell, maybe even her DNA.

Her skin tingled everywhere he looked, but he didn't smirk or grin, even though he had to have seen the effect his presence had on her.

After a pause sufficient to allow Merilee's heart to tap-dance along her ribs, the demon said, "Jake Lowell. I took the last name of my brothers."

His deep, sexy voice reminded her of wind rushing through mountains—and sounded familiar enough to make her process what he said.

Jake.

Jake Lowell.

As in, younger brother to Creed Lowell and Nick Lowell. The half-demon cops who just happened to be married to Riana and Cynda, her triad sisters.

As in, Jake Lowell, the Astaroth who had once been ordered to murder Cynda—and who damned near carried out those orders.

Merilee's mouth went dry, and her jaw tightened for entirely new reasons. She had to force her muscles to cooperate long enough to say, "I—I thought you were abroad. Or in school. Or . . . somewhere else." As the steam in the bathroom slowly dissipated, she eyed the talisman around his neck, trepidation edging out the magnetic shock of his presence. Her fingers curled. Primal instincts demanded that she grab her bow and nock an arrow. Maybe shoot him once for good measure. After all, she was the broom of her triad. She glanced at the tattoo on her forearm, focusing on the broom etched into her flesh. Wasn't it her job to sweep up all the messes?

But in the end, Jake hadn't killed Cynda. He had done everything in his power to save her, and now he had his talisman back. Nobody could use that necklace or signet ring to order him to kill.

Unless he loses it again . . .

"I got back to Manhattan this evening." Jake glanced around the bathroom, then down at the yellow towel barely covering his manhood. "Sorry. My brothers told me to shower up here."

Merilee bit back a few choice swearwords for the twins. Nick and Creed knew she had a hair trigger right now, with both her triad sisters out of sorts and now officially out of commission, and so much happening in the city. She could easily imagine the mirror-image bastards sending their younger brother straight into her line of fire, just for kicks.

"They must have thought you'd be out longer," Jake added with a frown.

"I'll just bet they did." Merilee relaxed her arms and felt a flash of pity for Jake, who, all that murdering-Cynda stuff aside, seemed too serious and quiet to be related to either of his jerk-monkey brothers. "Well, no harm done. And I guess we never really met when you were around before. I'm Merilee."

Jake's unnerving eyes shifted back to that stormy gray intensity. The force of his gaze touched Merilee directly in the center of her being, setting off shivers that only doubled when he said, "I know who you are."

Her body vibrated with each rumbling word, and her mind instantly blew through several hundred interpretations of that comment.

Get a grip. He means he saw you when he was around two years ago—and Nick and Creed probably filled in the details.

From seemingly a great distance away, Jake asked, "Any skirmishes with the Legion while you were on patrol?"

"No, it was just Satan tonight." Merilee couldn't quit staring at the man. *Demon. He's a demon who almost murdered my triad sister.* She made herself breathe, then realized what she had just said. "I mean, three satanic cultists. They were trying to summon the Prince of Darkness to help their candidate win the presidential election in November."

The sadness edged out of Jake's expression and his whole body seemed to relax. His eyes never left Merilee's, but now she saw sharp intrigue instead of storm clouds.

Jake gripped her yellow towel with one hand, keeping it firmly in place. "Do you believe the biblical devil exists?"

Merilee's response, like her response to all theoretical or academic questions, came easily and quickly. "Mythic monsters are always part fact, part fear-based storytelling. I've got nine research volumes in my library supporting Mephistopheles, and twice that many disproving all things Beelzebub. Which translates into, we've got no idea, but my triad's not about to take chances and find out."

"Have you read Wray and Mobley's *Birth of Satan*?" Jake kept hold of the towel as he spoke. "I liked the balanced Catholic and Protestant take on our need for a cosmic scapegoat."

Merilee's senses slipped off alert as her brain clicked into full action mode. She almost gave a complex, studious answer before she remembered she was talking to a gorgeous, half-naked, wet Astaroth demon in her bathroom doorway, at three in the morning—while she wasn't wearing pants.

And the Astaroth had just referenced a book she hadn't even finished reading.

A smile tugged at her lips as she looked at Jake's intelligent, interested expression—and tried to keep her eyes away from the muscled arm and hand holding the yellow towel. "You're . . . not a surfer boy, are you?"

Confusion flickered across Jake's handsome features. "I'm a police officer. Just hired by the NYPD."

"What?" Merilee propped a hand on her hip. "Since when does the force allow demon cops—well, ones they know about on the front end, anyway?"

"Since Sal Freeman wrote my letter of recommendation and asked for me." Jake's voice and gaze remained steady, though he looked disappointed, like he really had wanted to debate the existence of Satan. "That's why I got the off-season hire, too."

Merilee let out a breath, barely able to grasp the fact that Jake might not be a transient presence in her life, or

the townhouse, even if he did stop using her bathroom.
That thought unsettled her at bedrock levels, and caused
little jets of air to swirl around her ankles and elbows.

A small gust struck Jake in the chest and face, ruffling
his short, damp hair and rushing the last drops of water
still finding their way to the towel.

His mouth twitched, like he might be about to smile.

Annoyed with herself, Merilee pulled in her wind energy and covered her discomfort as quickly as she could.
"You're a Lowell. Of course you're a cop. What else was
I expecting?" She finally managed to pull her eyes off the
demon-man and studied a spot on the wall somewhere
over his left shoulder. "We need all the manpower we
can get right now, with the Legion going insane and all
the political rallies and protests. Crowds suck in supernatural terrorists like big cosmic magnets."

"The Legion's taking more chances," he said more as
a statement of fact than a question.

"Hell, yes." Merilee figured Jake's brothers had
briefed him on the massive increase in Legion activity
over the past twelve weeks. "They took as big a hit as
we did in the Battle of Motherhouse Ireland, but they're
more in our face than ever, and our numbers suck—
OCU and Sibyls alike. Which you probably know."

Jake's expression turned dark, along with his eyes,
which seemed to reflect every nuance of his mood. "We
have to stop them, numbers or not."

"Really? No kidding. I thought we were just supposed
to pick our noses on night patrol." Merilee gripped the
doorframe with one hand and dug her nails into the
wood.

Jake looked confused all over again, and Merilee realized he didn't completely follow sarcasm.

*Give him time. If he sticks around this place, he'll
learn or die.*

Understanding dawned across Jake's perfect face, faster than Merilee expected. "I'm sorry," he said. "No offense intended."

Merilee relaxed her grip on the door.

Just like that he apologizes?

She narrowed her eyes. "Are you sure you're related to Creed and Nick Lowell?"

Jake shrugged. "Scholars of demon creation could debate that point."

Under the force of his gaze, Merilee's nipples tightened, distracting her beyond measure.

Hecate's torch, she needed a good night's sleep. Without an Astaroth in her bed.

And without nightmares of a man who seemed to be carved out of stone, or the abominable Keres, either. Those black faceless monsters with their creepy feathered wings and long fangs terrified her like she was a little girl hearing horror stories from adepts at the Motherhouse.

More jets of wind slipped from her control.

Jake's yellow towel flapped, and Merilee's entire body flushed hot scarlet in response to her sudden glimpse of paradise.

Jake glanced down at his settling towel, then at Merilee again.

This time the bastard did smile.

He looked on the verge of asking her something, but Merilee panicked before he could say a word. "I really need a shower so I can crash. Can you—uh, shove off now?"

Once more, Jake seemed disappointed, but she didn't see any hint of anger or annoyance as he started toward her. She also didn't see any of the arrogance or cockiness she expected. Overall, Jake Lowell appeared to have more humility and self-control than his brothers, and he was tons harder to read than any Astaroth she had met so far.

His talisman necklace gleamed in the bathroom lights as he drew even with her in the doorway, paused, and gazed down at her with those heart-grabbing eyes. His unusual Caribbean scent washed over her, along with the heat of his nearness.

Her breath jerked and stuttered like the inner wind she was trying to suppress.

She mentally grabbed hold of buzzing emotions and gave herself a forceful inner shake. *If a bad guy takes control of that necklace, you could wake up and find Jake Lowell ready to eat you for breakfast.*

If you wake up at all.

She stepped aside to let Jake pass, heart thumping so hard she was pretty sure he could hear the *pound-pound-pound.*

He kept his eyes on her for a few more agonizing seconds, heating the wind inside Merilee until it became a sirocco.

Then he walked past her without making a sound and without looking back. Seconds later, he vanished from view, heading down the stairs.

Merilee leaned against the bathroom door and tried to gather herself. She had experienced powerful initial physical attractions before—but that—that—

Damn.

That wasn't natural.

Eyes closed, she rubbed the sides of her head, trying to chase off a dull, tired throb and the hazy stupor of Jake's presence.

There had to be an explanation for her over-the-top response to him.

Like, way too long since she'd been to the gym and picked herself up a fine boy toy for a night of recreation.

Or, not enough time for deep yoga and more meditative workouts.

He's a demon, *for the sake of Olympus.*

Hmm. Maybe Astaroths had hidden powers when it came to sexual attraction.

Maybe a person could be allergic to a demon presence, and manifest that allergy with mindless lust.

In this crazy world, anything was possible.

Right?

Merilee opened her eyes and glanced toward the door of her large combination library-bedroom, at the end of the hall on the right. She'd have to drag out all the papers and research info on Astaroths and make sure she hadn't missed anything.

Some of those documents were so dry and boring, they ought to help her fall asleep in a hurry. That would be a plus.

As she closed the bathroom door, Merilee couldn't take her eyes off the spot where she last saw Jake on the townhouse stairs.

"At least I might not have nightmares tonight," she muttered to herself. "I could *definitely* handle a juicy erotic fantasy for a change."